"Chloe Liese's writing is soulf_____ ___-worthy way that made me fal_____ romance novels in the first place! Her work is breathtaking, and I constantly look forward to more from her!"

—Ali Hazelwood, #1 *New York Times* bestselling author of
Love, Theoretically

"Each time I read a book by Chloe Liese, I think there's no way it can top the last one. AND THEN IT DOES. *Better Hate than Never* is no different. It's honest, sweet, and wonderfully spicy! And as someone who lives with chronic migraines, I really appreciated Chloe's sensitive and accurate representation of what life is like for us. It's so good to be seen. Kate and Christopher have a special place in my heart."

—Sarah Adams, *New York Times* bestselling author of
The Rule Book

"*Better Hate than Never* is a fiery slow-burn that blazes into the loveliest, sweetest connection, with characters who learn how to communicate and, by book's end, do so impressively. Chloe Liese consistently writes strong casts brimming with people I want to hang out with in real life, and I'll happily gobble up anything she writes." —Sarah Hogle, author of *Old Flames and New Fortunes*

"One of my favorite things about Chloe's writing is the love she paints each of her characters with. Kate and Christopher are opposites in so many ways, yet Chloe masterfully brings them closer step by incremental step for a love story that is honest, achingly earnest, and deliciously hot. The tension stretches out like honey for a payoff that is wonderfully satisfying. These two will stay with me for a long time." —B.K. Borison, author of *Business Casual*

"*Better Hate than Never* is the boy-next-door hate-to-love romance novel I didn't know I needed! Packed with witty banter, clueless lovers, and meddling family members, it's a perfect Shakespeare reimagining! And no one pairs sweet and steamy quite like Chloe Liese!"   —Alison Cochrun, author of *Here We Go Again*

"[A] sweetly sexy love story that not only includes a paean to the joys of fall flavors, particularly in the form of doughnuts, but also addresses the challenges of living with ADHD with insight and compassion."   —*Booklist* (starred review)

PRAISE FOR
Two Wrongs Make a Right

"Champagne and chocolate in book form. Prepare to be completely swept away."
     —Helen Hoang, *New York Times* bestselling author of
     The Heart Principle

"Absolute romantic perfection! *Two Wrongs Make a Right* is sexy, and smart, and achingly sweet. I absolutely adored every word."
     —Christina Lauren, *New York Times* bestselling authors of
     The Unhoneymooners

"These two wrongs are so very right for each other. Equal parts smart and steamy, with razor-sharp wit and an elegant, playful rhythm that would make Shakespeare proud. There's no warmer hug than a Chloe Liese book."
     —Rachel Lynn Solomon, *New York Times* bestselling author of
     Business or Pleasure

"*Two Wrongs Make a Right* is an excellent addition to any contemporary romance lover's keeper shelf! Trope lovers will swoon as Bea and Jamie journey from annoyances fake dating to unlikely friends who fall in real love! Chloe Liese nails the fast-paced ensemble chemistry of the source material and delivers a sophisticated playfulness of prose that echoes Shakespeare himself."

—Rosie Danan, author of *Do Your Worst*

"*Two Wrongs Make a Right* is a deeply tender romance that plays delightful music upon both the heartstrings and the funny bone. Full of charm, zest, and sensual heat, and with characters who are sure to join the ranks of readers' beloved favorites, it is the perfect book for anyone who loves love."

—India Holton, national bestselling author of *The Ornithologist's Field Guide to Love*

"*Two Wrongs Make a Right* overflows with snappy banter, heartfelt emotion, and delicious swooniness and heat. Bea and Jamie's tenderness and care for one another shine on the page, and Liese's wit and humor undergird the entire story. This book is a true pleasure to read, sure to delight her many current fans even as it earns her many new ones."

—Olivia Dade, national bestselling author of *At First Spite*

"*Two Wrongs Make a Right* is like hot chocolate and a croissant. It's whimsically patterned leggings on an autumn day. It's cozy, soft, sweet, and satisfying—Bea and Jamie are opposites-attract excellence; I loved their banter, and even more than that, how they evolve to become each other's unwavering pillar of support and protection."

—Sarah Hogle, author of *Old Flames and New Fortunes*

"Lush, swoony contemporary take on Shakespeare's *Much Ado About Nothing* ... Liese weaves in aspects of Benedick and Beatrice's love story (and famous dialogue exchanges) in winking, witty ways. It's the perfect acknowledgment of this endlessly intoxicating, sparring, enemies-to-lovers couple." —*Entertainment Weekly*

"*Much Ado About Nothing* gets a sexy contemporary spin in this fake-dating romance about an unlikely pair who attempt to get revenge on their matchmaking friends and family by pretending to fall in love and then dramatically break up." —BuzzFeed

"From a meet-cute that crackles with wit and humor to pages upon pages of scorching tension, Liese has crafted a warm, delightful novel that emphasizes acceptance, communication, and the self-worth we can discover by both daring to love and letting ourselves be loved. ... An effervescent reimagining of the Bard packaged in an opposites-attract romance." —*Kirkus Reviews* (starred review)

"In this lighthearted rom-com riff on Shakespeare's *Much Ado About Nothing* from Liese ... the banter is easy and the heat level is high." —*Publishers Weekly*

"Liese (*Everything for You*) nods to Shakespeare's *Much Ado About Nothing* here, and readers will enjoy the snarky banter and other similarities to the play, along with the enemies-to-lovers plot, solid character development, and a little heat." —*Library Journal*

Once Smitten, Twice Shy

CHLOE LIESE

BERKLEY ROMANCE
NEW YORK

BERKLEY ROMANCE
Published by Berkley
An imprint of Penguin Random House LLC
penguinrandomhouse.com

Copyright © 2025 by Chloe Liese
Readers Guide copyright © 2025 by Chloe Liese
Excerpt from *Only When It's Us* copyright © 2020, 2021, 2023 by Chloe Liese
Penguin Random House values and supports copyright. Copyright fuels creativity,
encourages diverse voices, promotes free speech, and creates a vibrant culture.
Thank you for buying an authorized edition of this book and for complying
with copyright laws by not reproducing, scanning, or distributing any part of
it in any form without permission. You are supporting writers and allowing
Penguin Random House to continue to publish books for every reader. Please note
that no part of this book may be used or reproduced in any manner for the
purpose of training artificial intelligence technologies or systems.

BERKLEY and the BERKLEY & B colophon are registered trademarks of
Penguin Random House LLC.

Book design by Kristin del Rosario

Library of Congress Cataloging-in-Publication Data

Names: Liese, Chloe, author.
Title: Once smitten, twice shy / Chloe Liese.
Description: First edition. | New York: Berkley Romance, 2025. |
Series: The Wilmot Sisters ; 3
Identifiers: LCCN 2024025163 (print) | LCCN 2024025164 (ebook) |
ISBN 9780593441541 (trade paperback) | ISBN 9780593441558 (ebook)
Subjects: LCGFT: Romance fiction. | Novels.
Classification: LCC PS3612.I3357 O53 2025 (print) |
LCC PS3612.I3357 (ebook) | DDC 813/.6—dc23/eng/20240617
LC record available at https://lccn.loc.gov/2024025163
LC ebook record available at https://lccn.loc.gov/2024025164

First Edition: January 2025

Printed in the United States of America
1st Printing

For the tender hearts,
the sensitive souls, the hopeless romantics

I hope you never change
and never forget what you deserve—
love that makes you feel like you never have to.

Love sought is good, but given unsought is better.

—WILLIAM SHAKESPEARE,
Twelfth Night

Dear Reader,

This story features characters with human realities who I believe deserve to be seen more prominently in romance through positive, authentic representation. As a neurodivergent person with often invisible chronic conditions, I am passionate about writing feel-good romances affirming my belief that every one of us is worthy and capable of happily ever after, if that's what our hearts desire.

Specifically, this story explores the realities of being neurodivergent (autism) and living with a chronic condition (mixed connective tissue disease and celiac disease). No two people's experience of any condition or diagnosis will be the same, but through my own lived experience of these realities, as well as the insight of authenticity readers, I have endeavored to create characters who honor the nuances of their identities. Please be aware that this story also touches on the topic of a toxic, emotionally abusive past relationship, but that relationship is not revisited, nor does the past abusive partner make an appearance at any point in the narrative.

If any of these are sensitive topics for you, I hope you feel comforted in knowing that only affirming, compassionate relationships—with oneself and others—are championed in this narrative.

XO,
Chloe

· PLAYLIST ·

Once Smitten, Twice Shy

Juliet

December

The pub is a kaleidoscopic blur as I spin, arms up, whiskey glass in hand. Warm golden light winks off the crowd's sweat-soaked skin. Stained-glass sconces bathe the room in a hazy rainbow glow. The lead singer's shiny red guitar, the drummer's ringing cymbal, flash beneath the lights as the cover band's music pounds through my body.

I hadn't planned on getting myself squished into a throng of dancing, headbanging people. I was just going to pop in for a drink, then slink back to the Scottish cottage I've been hiding in since I flew across the Atlantic last week, desperate for an escape from my blown-up life back home—a reward for finally getting my butt in the shower, dressed in something besides pajamas, and out of the house.

But as soon as I opened the door, the quaint, adorable pub drew me in, and I told myself maybe I'd linger a little, soak up the ambience. Then the cover band kicked off The Proclaimers' iconic "I'm Gonna Be (500 Miles)" right after I threw back my first whiskey and the bartender silently slid another one my way.

A sign from the universe. *Stay, just a little longer.*

That song's still playing, the small crowd's enjoyment of it contagious, everything in the pub dialed up to a ten of color and vitality;

loud, happy music that elbows my heartbreak to the edges of my thoughts. For three and a half glorious minutes, I dance and sing, and for the first time since everything went to hell, I actually believe what my sisters, my friends, my parents, keep telling me—that I'm going to be okay, that one day I will be healed from the hurt of realizing the man I'd been planning to marry was a manipulative abuser.

But then the song ends, its joy draining from me as quickly as the music fades from the room, before something terrible takes its place.

A love song.

Groaning, I knock back the rest of my whiskey. Everyone starts to pair off. Arms curled around waists, draped over shoulders. Soft laughs and long kisses. I turn, trying to find a crack in the crowd, a path to slip through and escape, but I'm locked in. Could this moment get any worse?

Despite trying to block out the words, this new song's lyrics sink into my brain. Aaand there's my answer—this could get worse, because it's not just a love song. It's a *sad* one.

"Dammit," I mutter as I spin around, determined to try my luck at escaping through the couples surrounding me to my other side.

"Oof." I bump into a very hard chest and startle, not just from our collision but from the feel of soft flannel plaid beneath my palms, the faint scent of clean, herby soap.

Slowly, my gaze drifts up, up, still up . . . My mouth falls open.

Standing before me is a *very* tall, *very* striking man. I stare at him, stunned.

The man stares right back. Wide, catlike sage eyes flecked with silver. Long, straight nose, two sharp cheekbones. The rest is a mystery, hidden beneath a thick beard and hair that spills to his shoulders in soft waves.

My brain's all over the place—the wedge of pale, freckled skin at his throat revealed by his open shirt collar; the clean, herby scent clinging to him—but finally it settles on the most important detail: his hair. His gorgeous hair. The color, burnished-penny copper in shadow, golden bronze where it catches the pub lights' candle-like glow.

I curl my hands into fists until my nails press crescents into my palms. He looks like a Highlander romance hero ripped out of the past and wrapped in modern clothes.

Highlander romances are my weakness.

As are redheads.

Slowly, he holds out one hand, an unspoken invitation that I'd swear I hear, crystal clear, in my head. *Dance with me?*

My heart takes off in my chest, nerves coursing through me. A romance novel junkie, a seasoned matchmaker, a veteran flirt, I'm used to cruising through these moments. But since ending my relationship with my ex, recognizing how I'd built him up in my head through those rosy romantic lenses instead of seeing him for who he really was, I've lost my confidence in this. I doubt myself.

Heart thumping, flustered, I take a step toward him. But instead of taking his hand, I give him my whiskey glass. Maybe I'm testing him. Maybe I'm testing myself.

His mouth lifts the tiniest bit at the corner—a whisper of a smile?—as he takes the glass, reaching easily with one long arm around a couple to set it on the bar. Then he simply steps just a little closer, hand outstretched again.

My heart thumps in my chest.

This was not the plan, a nervous voice whispers in the back of my head. *The plan was baby steps. The plan was to stop hiding in the cottage, inhaling shortbread and rewatching* Fleabag. *The plan was to get out, have a few drinks, then go home without incident.*

Dancing with a handsome stranger who makes my heart fly definitely qualifies as an "incident."

I tell my feet to walk away, my body to back off. But I don't move an inch. I just stare up at him, at those wide sage-and-silver eyes holding mine. God, they're lovely, framed by faint crinkles at the corners, like he spends life outside, his gaze narrowed against the sun.

"Would you . . ." His voice snaps me from my trance. My lashes flutter as I blink and sway a bit, the low, rich rumble of his voice a wave rocking me back. He clears his throat. "Would you . . . like to dance?"

As I process his words, I realize the similarity of his vowels to mine. "Wait." I tip my head. "You're American?"

He nods.

Well, there goes my Highlander fantasy. Which is honestly for the best.

His brow furrows as he searches my expression. "Something . . . wrong?"

"I just thought with the red hair and"—I gesture up and down his body, which looks as impressive as it feels, long-limbed, broad, filling out faded jeans and a deep green plaid flannel shirt rolled up to his elbows—"your build, and, well, the location, that there was a good chance you were local. I mean, you know . . . Scottish."

"Ah." He clears his throat and glances down at the ground. "No, I'm just visiting."

"Me, too."

Relief sweeps through me. We're both only here by chance, in passing. What harm could there be in a dance with a handsome stranger I'll never see again? That, I tell myself, hardly qualifies as an "incident."

"Well, then, if your offer still stands," I tell him, smiling wider than I have in weeks, since everything fell apart, "I'd love to dance."

He doesn't say anything in response, but his touch is warm and sure as he wraps his hand around mine, drawing me close. Our bodies connect, and heat races through me, everything that's dimmed and dulled in my sadness the past month flickering awake.

Our chests brush, our hips. His hand curves gently around my waist and draws me close. My hand settles on his hard shoulder.

His gaze sweeps over my face, my hair, my eyes, my mouth, like it's memorizing me.

A blush warms my cheeks.

I force out a slow, steadying breath. There's no need to get romantic about this. In fact, there is every need *not* to get romantic about it, because this is where I get myself into trouble—my romance-novel-loving, pie-eyed optimist, foolishly hopeful heart stubbornly sees things the way I *want* them to be rather than the way they *are*. This is the mistake that cost me so much with my ex. It's a mistake I'm not going to make again.

I need to burst this swoony bubble, shatter the magic of the moment.

"So." I clear my throat.

He stares at my mouth intently. Then says quietly, "So."

I narrow my eyes, playfully glaring up at him. "You're supposed to help me out here, not just repeat what I said."

He's still staring at my mouth. Another wave of warmth floods my body.

"Not a big talker," he admits. Deftly, he spins us, moving me safely out of the path of a dancing couple who've become very enthusiastic about kissing at the expense of their balance.

He peers my way again, his gaze settling first on my mouth, then on my eyes. He looks at me for so long, I feel every hair on my body stand on end.

"You're staring at me," I whisper.

He swallows audibly, his gaze fixed on mine. "Sorry. It's . . . hard not to."

My blush deepens, and I smile wider as I lean in, like a flower drawn toward the sun. I drink him in, his soft, clean scent; every stunning shade of his hair—cinnabar, russet, auburn—like a fire's dancing flames.

"Well, I'll just stare at you, too," I tell him. "So, we're even."

He huffs a laugh that's all air, soft as it gusts out of him. I catch a whiff of smoky whiskey on his breath that matches mine. It oddly comforts me, that we're the same this way—two people alone for now, who've relied on a few whiskeys to get ourselves here.

"Who are you?" he asks, what sounds like wonder tingeing his voice. His fingertips circle the small of my back as he tucks me closer.

A daring thrill runs through me as I stare up at him, this handsome stranger, desire spilling warm and wistful through my veins. I think about how freeing this could be, to live a lie tonight. To be not a heartbroken Juliet but someone else, not even my old self, who I used to be, but someone new, someone better. Is it so bad to want a night indulging in the delectable pleasure of his gaze, his touch, his interest, without worrying about complications or consequences, a night to forget what I've been through?

"Viola," I tell him.

It's not a lie. My full name *is* Viola Juliet Wilmot. I was named for my paternal grandmother, Viola Wilmot, a spitfire of a woman whose presence was so formidable, the notion of my sharing her name as a little girl was laughable. By the time she'd passed away, I'd been Juliet or Jules for so long, it was the only name that felt right.

But tonight, I'm calling on my namesake, channeling my inner spitfire, reaching deep for bravery that, since the breakup, I've been worried I might have lost for good.

He studies me, repeating my name. "*Viola?*"

"That's it," I tell him, tell myself. I am Viola tonight. Bold and brave.

As he peers down at me, a lock of fiery hair falls down his fore-head, into his eyes. Eyes that watch me, curious, kind. It feels so natural, to reach up before he can and brush that hair back from his face. My fingertips hum at the sensation of his warm skin, his cool, silky hair. His eyes slip shut at my touch, like this feels as good for him as it does for me.

"And who are *you*?" I ask quietly.

"Will," he breathes, as I tuck his hair behind his ear and notice an earplug wedged in it. I'm inordinately delighted that it's hot pink.

"Will," I repeat. I find myself smiling as I look at him, putting the name to his face. It suits him.

His eyes slide open as my touch lingers in his hair, curved around his ear. His cheeks turn the same color as his earplugs.

"Does it bother you?" I ask him, tracing the shell of his ear. "The noise here?"

He stares at me for what feels like forever. A swallow works down his throat. Our dancing slows to the faintest sway. "Yes," he finally says.

"I get it," I tell him, smiling. "My sister has similar feelings about sound; well, for her it's more complexity of sound than noise level, but . . ."

My voice dies off as I peer up at him.

Want to go somewhere quieter? I almost ask. But then I pin my lips between my teeth, biting back the words. Because this is all I'm allowing myself. A dance, then done.

"You have a sister?" he asks, snapping me from my thoughts.

I smile. "Two, actually. No brothers. What about you?"

"No brothers, either," he says. "And four sisters."

My smile deepens. "Four, wow! Hmm. I can totally see it. You have strong 'brother of many sisters' energy."

Will's mouth quirks again at the corner, like it did when he held out a hand for a dance and I gave him a whiskey glass instead. "'Brother of many sisters' energy?" he repeats in that low, quiet rumble. "What does that mean?"

I bite my lip. My cheeks are hot. It's impossible to explain what I meant, when I've just met him, only that there's something so comfortingly gentle about him, even in all his imposing, intimidating physicality. He just *feels* like a man who grew up surrounded by women, who's learned how to make them feel seen and safe.

I can't tell him that. That's not what you tell a hot stranger you're just sharing a dance with.

"Forget I said it." I grimace, scrunching my nose, self-conscious. "I talk too much when I drink whiskey!"

"I . . ." His grip tightens faintly on my waist. "I like how much you talk."

My heart's spinning like a top in my chest, butterflies swirling in my stomach. Our eyes hold as the music starts to soften, the refrain slowing. The song drawing to a close. Not so much a sign from the universe, but a reminder—this has to end.

"I should go," I whisper.

I hate the words that just came out of my mouth. I hate that I know they're right. I hate that I know I need to leave before he says another sweet thing, before I let myself get swept away.

I can't stay here anymore, pretending to be someone who doesn't have so much work ahead of her, acting like the woman I'm going to see in the mirror when I get back to my Airbnb cottage isn't a messed-up Juliet who's got a life to put back together, a heart to heal.

Will's grip flexes on my waist, then travels slightly up my back. It's so tender, so sweet. I lean into it, one last indulgence, before I press up on tiptoe and wrap my arms around his neck. A hug goodbye.

"Why?" he asks quietly against my cheek.

I hesitate a beat when his hands wrap around me. For a minute, we just stand there, locked in a lingering hug goodbye. "I'm sorry," I whisper against his cheek.

As I sink down onto my heels, he holds my eyes, his hands' grip softening on my waist.

Ae fond kiss and then we sever, the singer croons.

Our eyes hold as the lyrics hang in the air, a suggestion heavy between us.

My hands, curled around the nape of his neck, pull him closer. Will's eyes hold mine as his hands curve back around my waist again and tuck me in tight. We don't say a word, but I feel like, just how this began, we both know in some silent way what we want, what comes next, what the music's spoken into this moment between us.

Holding his gaze, I press up on tiptoe again. His hands glide up my back, wrapping me close. I drift my hands from the silky tips of his hair, over the sharp curve of his jaw, beneath that thick beard, and cup his face. I press a tender kiss to his cheek, a sliver of smooth, freckled skin at the edge of his beard. "Goodbye," I whisper.

I turn quickly, prepared to have to muscle my way through the crowd, but a path opens among the couples, like it's been paved just for me, reminding me that now is not the time to meet someone, to want someone, to dance in their arms and daydream about staying there.

I slip through the crowd, then yank my coat off the hook and shoulder open the door, sending it banging against the outside wall. A rush of icy December air whips back my hair and cools my flushed face.

As I shrug on my coat, I start down the path, shivering against the wind, the aching pain pulsing through my joints that's bothered me for months. All week, I've noticed the pain has felt harsher. I told myself it must be heartbreak's ache, bleeding through my body.

But now, I'm not so sure.

I walk down the path, and my eyes drift up dreamily to the dark, star-studded sky. I replay those few moments with Will, my handsome stranger. And I smile. Because right now, even though I ache from head to toe, I don't feel heartbroken at all.

ONE

Juliet

July, seven months later

I have never in my life been more drenched than I am right now. Hair plastered to my temples, sundress stuck to my skin, I stumble into the greenhouse behind my childhood home and shove the door shut against the sideways wind that carries sweeping sheets of rain. As I slump against the door, gasping for breath, my reflection greets me in a tall pane of greenhouse glass.

Irises as wide as blue-green china saucers, hair a sopping sable mess, I blink away water and try to catch my breath. There's a tear in my sundress straight up my left thigh from a branch that sank its sharp end into the fabric, then ripped it when I tugged myself free. My pulse is flying after my run from the small woods behind my parents' house toward the nearest shelter (my physical fitness is currently shit). In short: I look like I barely survived a shipwreck rather than a summer evening rainstorm.

I knew I should have stayed inside where I was minding my business in my parents' house, just *New Girl* and a hefty pour of whiskey for company. But no, I had to go and chase the damn cat, who snuck out *again*, and then get myself stuck in a microburst.

Meow. Speaking of the devil, Puck, the ancient family cat, crawls out from under Mom's potting table, his typical fluffy white fur and matching bottlebrush tail waterlogged and dripping. He looks like a mop.

I snort a laugh, wiping water from my forehead before more can drip into my eyes. "Serves you right for running out of the house before the whole damn sky opened up."

Meow, he grumbles, shaking himself to lose some of the water matting down his fur.

"Well, at least you made it to safety, too." Puck twines around my legs, tickling me with his half-wet, once-again-fluffy fur. "Wonder if we can make a break for it yet."

I turn to peer out of the greenhouse as the wind's howl slides up an octave, only to see a wall of rainwater rolling down it.

Looks like we'll be waiting out the storm here, then.

Now that the adrenaline is wearing off and I know I'm not about to be swept away by a storm, my body's usual aches (thanks for nothing, mixed connective tissue disease) make themselves known. My elbows, wrists, hips, knees, and ankles pulse with pain. Sitting isn't going to make it go away, but standing isn't going to make it better, either, so, on a groan, I ease to the floor. A shiver racks me as the backs of my wet legs connect with the tiles. The greenhouse is, as you'd expect, quite warm, but its floor tiles are still cool.

I slump back onto a bag of potting soil and sigh. Per usual, the cat takes my reclined position as an invitation to help himself to my lap.

"Puck"—a grunt leaves me when a paw hits my ovary—"is it too much to ask that you sit on my lap without squishing my internal organs?" His front paw smashes my boob as he crawls up my chest. I wince. "This is all your fault, you cantankerous animal. You just had to make an escape and harsh my fun Saturday night vibes."

The cat plops onto my chest and lazily blinks his mint green eyes, as if to say, *What "fun Saturday night vibes"?*

"Listen here, you," I mutter, scratching behind his wet ears because I'm a sucker for this furball, even when he's a giant pain in my ass, "*New Girl* reruns and whiskey is the definition of a roaring good time."

Meow, he says, swishing his tail.

"You've got a lot of nerve, throwing that in my face. It's a *monthly* horoscope, Puck, and I reserve the right to act on its advice when and how I see fit within the *month* of July."

It's pathetic, that I'm arguing with my cat, since I'm really just arguing with myself, but I've got no one else to verbally process with right now. My parents have been off on one of their post-retirement adventures on the other side of the world for the past few weeks, which is why I'm house- and cat-sitting. Kate, my younger sister, is currently traveling for work, and Bea, my twin, has been holed up in her paint studio the past couple of days thanks to a burst of artistic inspiration. All my friends are busy being full-time employed, happily paired off, hands full with all their commitments—capital-A Adults.

So it's just me and the cat left to muddle over what to do about my life, which has started to feel like an idling engine, running fine but going nowhere. Enter my dauntingly ambitious monthly horoscope:

Time to leave behind the season that left you wrecked and stranded. You aren't helpless or hopeless anymore. Now you prove that to yourself. Now you wade into new waters, not knowing what's on the horizon but trusting the course. Trust yourself to find your way again.

It's not bad advice, especially given how I've felt about my idling-engine life lately. It's just . . . scary. The old Juliet never needed astrological ordinances to kick her butt into gear. But this new Juliet does. And, even desperate to finally feel like my life is moving again, this new Juliet is still frankly afraid to take that first step forward, unsure of what it should be.

Meow, Puck drawls.

I narrow my eyes at him. "You have the audacity to call *me* a scaredy-cat? You were hiding under a potting table because you got a little wet!"

Puck opens his mouth, and while I'm prepared for another sassy *meow*, the last thing I expect is the deep, loud snore that I hear instead.

The cat's eyes and mine widen in tandem. Whereas Puck's survival instincts wisely kick in, sending him leaping off me and under the potting table for cover, I'm frozen, a sopping sitting duck.

Another deep, long snore punctures the quiet inside the greenhouse, snapping me out of my stunned state. Slowly, I ease upright, then onto all fours, crawling only far enough to peer around the edge of the long table that runs down the center of the greenhouse.

There's no one there.

And yet another snore rumbles from the far end of the greenhouse. Even if I can't see them, someone is obviously here, and while I want to tell myself they're probably not a threat, seeing as they're fast asleep, I can't assume they're going to stay asleep or that I'll be safe with them when they wake up. I've learned the hard way that assuming the best of people can epically blow up in your face.

Glancing around, I scour the greenhouse for some kind of tool that I can use for self-defense. There aren't any big shovels or rakes here—those are stored in the nearby shed—not that, with the state of my hands and wrists, I'd even be able to wield one with any particular strength or accuracy. I spot a short-handled shovel leaning against the potting table, which will be perfect. Not too long or heavy, with a small but solid wood handle that leads to a wide, sturdy metal base.

Carefully, I ease up to a squat and awkwardly crouch-walk my way over to the potting table, then grab the shovel. My knees hate this position, so I risk standing until I'm bent at the waist, peering through the tidy rows of flowers on the center table in various stages of growth.

Another snore rumbles through the air.

Quietly, I stand until I'm fully straightened and peek over the flowers. I still don't see anyone, so I start to walk the length of the table, shovel raised in my hands. My heart pounds, faster and faster.

When I finally get to the table's end, another snore rends the quiet, and I come to a dead stop.

First I see brown boots, not like the city guys around here wear, polished and fancy, but scuffed and creased. Next, long legs crossed at the ankle, in roughed-up jeans that are threadbare at the knee, as if they've been bent in and worn countless times. My eyes trail up the weathered denim—long calves and longer, thicker thighs— then land on a sun-bleached olive-green tee, two arms folded across it.

I gulp.

This dude's body is entirely relaxed in sleep and yet his arms are ripped. His muscles have muscles. Veins and ropy tendons weave up his arms. Two bulky biceps peek out from the edge of his shirt's sleeves. All across his skin are freckles.

Swallowing roughly, I clutch the shovel tighter. I'm such a sucker for freckles.

I shake my head to snap out of it. I am *not* eroticizing this in-truder who, for all I know, could be an axe murderer.

Albeit a sleepy axe murderer. So, probably not a very good one. But still.

I tip my head, trying to see his face, but his head is bent, as if his chin is tucked to his chest. I can't see past the ripped brim of his ball cap, which looks like it might have once been white but has faded to dingy oatmeal.

His leg twitches as another snore leaves him. He's either one hell of an actor or he's out cold.

A loud *boom* of thunder shakes the greenhouse and he jolts, as if startling awake. So he was asleep. Maybe he's just some down-on-his-luck guy who crashed here to catch a few winks and ride out the storm before he goes on his way.

We don't do that anymore, Juliet. We don't give people the benefit of the doubt. We don't assume the best of them. That's what got us hurt.

Time to brace for an attack. I lift the shovel higher, standing out of his reach but not so far that I can't swing and hit him with the shovel, if needed.

His ball cap shifts as he sits straighter, then freezes. The ball cap lifts a little, then a little more, as if his gaze is trailing upward. Up me. Finally, his ball cap's brim lifts enough to reveal his face, for his gaze to meet mine. A face that I recognize, a gaze that I've seen before.

Wide, catlike silver-sage eyes fringed by auburn lashes. Long, straight nose. Two sharp cheekbones. That thick, unkempt beard and auburn hair.

It can't be him.

But it could only be him.

"Will?" My voice is hoarse with shock.

What the hell is the hot stranger from the Scottish pub doing in my mom's greenhouse?

So much for his being some innocent sleeping guy. Has this man somehow tracked me from Scotland? Has he been here, biding his time, pretending to be asleep, and now he's going to do—well, who the hell knows what, but it can't be good!

Panicked but determined to defend myself, I lift the shovel over my head and scream as I swing at him.

Will ducks, then rolls away and springs upright in a display of athleticism that has me deeply concerned for my odds against him.

"Wait!" he yells. "Hold on!"

I swing at him again and miss, knocking over a damask rosebush. He lunges and successfully catches the rosebush, which, come to think of it, is odd for an assailant to do, but I'm already swinging at him again as I process that thought. I miss him entirely, losing my balance as the shovel whips out of my hands, then crashes into the table. Thrown off by the momentum of my forceful swing, I stumble back, straight into a potted gardenia that wobbles, then starts to tip off the table's edge behind me.

Will lunges again, catches my hand before I fall, and yanks me toward him, like a swing-dance step that swaps our places, before he somehow also catches the gardenia plant and rights it on the table. I try to yank my hand away as he turns suddenly, which pulls me with him, and, in a chaotic tangle of feet and pinwheeling hands, we crash to the floor, Will on his back, me sprawled on top of him.

In an uncharacteristic feat of agility and speed that I can only attribute to the power of adrenaline, I lunge for a trowel that's resting on the table beside me, then bring it to his throat. I stare down at him, breathing heavily. "What," I gasp, "the *hell* are you doing here?"

He's breathing heavily, too, eyes wide, hands lifted in surrender. "I . . ." He shakes his head. "What are *you* doing here?"

"Nuh-uh, you don't get to ask questions." With my free hand, I shove back the drenched hair that's fallen into my face, trowel still at his throat. "You're in my mom's greenhouse—"

"Your *mom's*?" he croaks.

"—and the last time I saw you, seven months ago, you were in the same Scottish pub as me, so *you're* the one who's going to do the explaining. Now, tell me why you're here."

He swallows. I watch his Adam's apple roll beneath the trowel's tip. His mouth parts, working silently, until finally, he says, "I'm staying next door, with Petruchio. I'm his friend, from college, I swear."

I narrow my eyes at him. Christopher Petruchio is my next-door neighbor, has been my whole life—he's like a brother to me. "I've never heard Christopher talk about a 'Will.'"

"That's because he calls me Orsino," Will says, hands still raised. "Orsino is my last name. Everyone calls me that."

I press the trowel against his throat. "Then why did you tell me to call you Will back in Scotland?"

Says the woman who told him your name was Viola. Maybe he did it for the same reason you did—self-protection.

I push away those sympathetic thoughts. No benefit of the doubt will be given! "How about I just call Christopher," I tell him. "See if he'll vouch for you."

Will hesitates for a beat, then reaches for his phone in his pocket.

I slap my free hand down on his wrist and pin it there. "*I'll* get your phone, thank you."

I tug the phone from his pocket, swipe it to open, then spin it so it uses his facial recognition to unlock. Straight to his contacts, I scroll down and find . . . Christopher's name and his cell phone number.

My jaw drops. The trowel follows, landing with a clatter on the tiles. I was so sure he was lying, but . . . he's not.

The pieces fall into place, as my anxiety clears enough for my memory to work properly. Christopher bustling around the past week, grocery shopping, cooking, stocking up on beer and wine.

He's been prepping for days for what I now remember him saying was a birthday bash for one of his college roommates and also a reunion for his friends from college—friends I've never met because Christopher kept to himself in his college years, while he was in the city, and none of them live here anymore, so they don't see each other often.

The embarrassment that hits me is massive. I just tried to bludgeon Christopher's college friend with a short-handled shovel. Then I held him at trowel point.

Heat floods my face as I stare down at Will pinned beneath me. I am mortified. And I'm even more mortified when I realize that I'm straddling Will's waist. My thighs are pinned against his ribs. My pelvis rests on his, where I feel a solid, thick weight—oh my *God*, I have to get off him.

I scramble off his lap in a very ungainly tumble of limbs, my embarrassment making me clumsy, my stiff joints resisting my sudden movement, and try to arrange myself in a dignified seated position on the floor. I'm not even going to try to stand yet.

Slowly, Will eases up, then scoots back to lean against the table's end, how he was when he was asleep. He draws up his knees and rests his elbows on them as he rubs his hands down his face.

I stare at him, my mind spinning, my perspective rearranging. He's not here with any malicious intent. He's just the sweet guy who asked me to dance in Scotland, and he happens to be my surrogate brother's dear friend. Of all the people I could have bumped into in Scotland last year, what are the chances it was him, a man I had no idea was already tied to someone so important in my life? It's unbelievable.

Some might even call it . . . serendipitous.

I want to wipe that sentence from my brain as soon as I think it.

Those thoughts belong to someone I'm not anymore. Someone who always imagined romantic possibilities—meet-cutes and kismet and love at first sight—who saw the world through rose-colored glasses. I haven't done that since I broke up with my fiancé, quit my PR consultancy work, and hid away in a Scottish cottage, licking my wounds, before I came home and started to get my shit together.

The past seven months, I've dealt with the nagging health issues I'd been ignoring and couldn't afford to ignore anymore. I've taken on less stressful work, built a new routine that has me in a better place: I take care of my body and take my meds; I write freelance on a flexible work schedule; I don't date. In that time, I've pieced my life back together. My connective tissue disease isn't magically cured, but it's better managed. My work doesn't pay what I'd like, but it's enough to get by, which is no small feat, now that I'm the only one left living in and paying rent for the sister apartment we used to share. And I haven't missed romance while I protect my heart, because I get plenty from the novels I've been reading since I found Mom's bodice rippers as a teen in the family library.

Well, I haven't missed romance *too* much.

Except, right now, maybe I miss it just a little. Because this is a moment the old Juliet would have thoroughly enjoyed. The old Juliet would have tossed her hair over her shoulder and said something witty right now, offered this guy a hand up and flirted her way out of the awkward.

What's stopping you? a daring, reckless voice whispers in my head.

I don't know what's stopping me. I don't know what I'm brave enough to do next.

My horoscope's words echo in my head. *Now you wade into new waters, not knowing what's on the horizon but trusting the course.*

Will stands, pulling me from my racing thoughts. I try to stand, too, but between my stiff body and my waterlogged dress, it doesn't go so well. He's there in an instant, gripping my elbow when I teeter sideways, lifting me gently, firmly, until I'm standing upright.

He drops my elbow the second I'm steady and tugs at the brim of his ball cap, lowering it so the shadows over his eyes deepen as he stares down at the ground. "I'm sorry," he says, "for scaring you."

I tip my head, peering up at him, and smile. "I mean, I more than paid you back, with the whole garden-tool attack."

He glances up from beneath his ball cap and catches me smiling at him. His mouth is mostly hidden by the thick beard, but I think it tugs down in a frown. He clears his throat as he shoves his hands in his pockets. "That didn't scare me."

I lift my eyebrows. "Oh, really?"

Now he's definitely frowning. And I'm enjoying it. I have no business enjoying it, but I am. "Nope," he says.

I bite my lip so I won't laugh. "You seemed pretty scared. I mean, understandably so. I was very intimidating . . ." My voice dies off as Will takes a slow, careful step toward me.

He reaches toward my head. "You have a leaf in your hair." Gently, he plucks it from the crown of my head, pinned between two fingers. It catches in the wet strands as he starts to pull away, and he stops, steps a little closer as he peers down at me, brow furrowed in concentration. Tenderly, slowly, he lifts each strand of hair from the leaf so it doesn't tug or snag. And then he brushes each strand back off my temple, his fingertips grazing my skin.

I swallow as my heart takes off in my chest. "Thanks."

He nods.

The rain stops abruptly, leaving us in silence and soft nighttime darkness closing in around the dim lights that brighten the greenhouse. In that silence, I feel the weight of our nearness, standing as close as we stood at the pub, right before we started to dance. I like it as much as I did then. Maybe even more.

On a chirpy *meow* Puck shows himself, twining around not *my* legs, but Will's. Will crouches and scratches Puck's chin. Puck purrs loudly.

Meow. Puck sets his front paws on Will's thigh and reaches for more. Will gently picks him up and holds Puck like they're old friends.

I stare at him, stunned. Puck hates strangers. Especially strange men.

"And who are you?" Will asks my cat.

Puck purrs loudly as Will scratches under his chin.

"That's Puck," I tell him, a waver in my voice. Watching this big, gruff guy cuddle with my cat has butterflies racing in my stomach. "He ran for cover here during the storm," I add.

"You picked a nice spot," Will tells Puck, scratching his cheeks. Puck's eyes drop shut. His purr is as loud as a motorboat.

"What, um—" I clear my throat. "What made *you* come into the greenhouse? Were you waiting out the storm?"

Will glances my way, his gaze fleeting, then dancing over to the flowers. "I stepped out for some quiet, and this place caught my eye. The door was cracked open and it looked . . ." His eyes drift up to mine. "Peaceful and . . . pretty. So I came in."

That's why I come to the greenhouse, too, when I need calm and a bit of beauty—the perfume of my mother's master-gardener magic, rows of pillowy blossoms and stubborn green seedlings wrestling their way up from the dirt into the light, stretching toward possibility, the promise of growing into something better.

"It was warm and quiet," he says after a beat. "Sort of lulled me, I guess. So I sat down, shut my eyes, and then . . ." He shrugs. "You know the rest."

I bite my lip against a smile. "And then you woke up to a woman swinging a short-handled shovel at your head, before she impressively wrestled you to the ground and held you helpless at trowel point."

His mouth quirks at the corner. Damn that beard, I wish it

didn't make it impossible to tell if I just made him smile. "That's how that story goes, huh?"

"I clearly muscled you into submission."

Another mouth quirk beneath that bushy auburn beard. Maybe, just maybe, it's a smile.

A blush hits my cheeks as I stare up at him. "Sorry," I tell him. "You know, for the garden-tool ambush."

He stares at me, unblinking. I fight a shiver that dances down my spine. "It's all right."

I stare at his mouth. And I think he's staring at mine, too.

Suddenly, a phone buzzing pierces the quiet. Will glances at his pocket, then deftly settles Puck against his chest with one arm, freeing a hand that he uses to unearth his phone. He groans as he stares at the screen.

"Christopher and your friends wondering where you are?" I guess.

He nods.

Puck shimmies higher in his grip and plops his chin on Will's shoulder. Will winces when Puck sinks his claws into his shirt and tries to cuddle in even closer.

"Here, I'll take him." I reach for Puck, who grumbles a *meow* as I ease him off Will's shoulder, then step back.

I smile nervously, trying to find my courage. I'm not sure what I'm ready for, what this second chance meeting means, but I want to be brave, to try, even just a little. "We keep bumping into each other," I tell him. "Maybe . . . I'll see you around again. Are you staying long?"

Will's throat works in a rough swallow. He pockets his phone. "Ah, no. Leaving first thing tomorrow morning."

I'll admit it, for a moment, I wait and hope. Maybe he'll follow that up with a *but come have a round with the guys* or *can I walk you back to your house?*

But nothing comes. "Gotcha," I finally muster, forcing my smile to stay intact, praying my face doesn't show how small his crisp put-down has made me feel. "Well . . . bye, then!"

I can't take the embarrassment a second longer. Clutching Puck so tight he lets out a strangled howl of protest, I speed-walk out of the greenhouse.

TWO

Will

I am a begrudging morning person. Growing up on a farm, I've been hardwired to wake up with the sun, but even so, I never wake up happy about it. This morning, I'm even grumpier than usual. Not only am I nursing a headache from all the whiskey I joined in drinking with my friends last night, after I came back inside, just so they'd stop asking why I was so mopey—the hell was I telling them I made an ass of myself with Viola—but I can't get this damn coffee maker to work.

Swearing under my breath, I stab desperately at the buttons on Petruchio's fancy espresso and coffee machine, as I rake my other hand through my shower-wet hair. All I want is a big, hot cup of black coffee in my system before I get on the road and head home. Is that too much to ask?

The machine beeps menacingly, and a shiny nozzle screeches as it starts hissing steam. "Shit." I stab at more buttons, then resort to yanking the plug from the wall. The machine powers off with an ominous fading *whirrrrr* that has me worried I just broke the thing.

Groaning, I scrub my hands over my face. When my hands fall, I glance out the window above Petruchio's sink and freeze.

She stands framed in her kitchen window, too, like a mirror across the yard.

Viola.

Her hair frames her face in soft dark waves that graze her shoulders, the sun catching their frizzy edges in a bronze halo. Even from this distance, I can see how morning light glances off her eyes. It's like looking at the ocean on a perfect day—blue-green irises the color of waves sparkling with sunlight, rimmed by pale gray curls of sea-foam.

I'm mesmerized. I just stand there, staring at her.

Eyes trained on me, she sips her coffee. As she lowers the mug, her eyebrows draw together. She lifts her mug toward me and tips her head.

I'm not great at reading nonverbal cues, particularly from people I don't know. I'm not sure what she's saying.

This time she points to her mug.

I grimace and shake my head a little. I have no idea what she's getting at.

She hesitates for a beat, then steps away from the window. I feel a ridiculous sense of loss, that she's just disappeared. Then again, why am I surprised? She's walked out on me twice before—at the pub, last night—why wouldn't she do it again?

I'm used to being someone people don't find worth hanging around for. And I know it's partly my fault. I don't talk well with strangers. I have zero romantic moves. I've accepted this about myself, told myself it doesn't bother me. Except with her, well, it's been bothering me.

More than I care to admit.

She's back at the window again, and my heart does an absurd flip in my chest. She came back.

And now she's holding up a piece of paper, large letters in black marker spelling out COFFEE MAKER TROUBLES?

She didn't just come back; she's . . . trying to talk to me, still.

And she doesn't seem to mind that it required scribbling a note so I can figure out what she's saying.

My heart's racing, nerves making my hands shaky as I turn and glance frantically around the kitchen for pen and paper. Darting over to the shallow stretch of counter along the far wall, where I see an old-school answering machine and phone set, a jar with pens and markers, I start yanking open drawers. I find a notepad of lined paper that'll do. Quickly, I pluck a Sharpie from the jar, then write CAN'T GET IT TO WORK TO SAVE MY LIFE in big black letters, and tear the paper from the pad before rushing to the window. She's still there, and now she's cradling her mug in her hands.

I lift the paper and watch her eyes narrow as she reads it.

A smile lifts her mouth, then she sets down her mug, bends out of view for a moment, and returns with a new piece of paper that reads I CAN HELP. OK IF I COME OVER?

I swallow thickly, my heart racing faster, nerves darting through me. I could barely handle being around her last night, that creamy white dress plastered to her body, a tear in its fabric revealing a long stretch of curvy thigh. She was rain soaked and stunning, even with a shovel held menacingly in her grip.

Maybe *because* she was holding a shovel menacingly in her grip.

Do I really want her to come over, when I've got no coffee in my system, my brain still barely online because I really do need coffee before I can formulate even the limited number of words willing to leave my mouth on the best of days? Do I actually want to make an ass of myself in front of her again?

A weary sigh leaves me.

I really want that cup of coffee.

And, foolishly, even more than that cup of coffee, I think I want to see *her*, one last time. Even if I will make an ass of myself.

I lift that same piece of paper to the window with my answer:
YES.

———————

She doesn't knock. My only warning that Viola's about to come in is the chirp of the back door's lock code being punched in, before the door swings open.

God, she's beautiful.

She's wearing a pale pink T-shirt, its neckline scooping across the swell of her breasts, and tiny shorts with flowers all over them. Those dark, soft waves that graze her shoulders are now tucked behind her ears, revealing more of her face, the high apples of her deep-dimpled cheeks, as she smiles and shuts the door behind her.

"I keep telling Christopher," she says, breezing past me, "that he needs to get a more user-friendly machine, but he won't listen. It's the least he could do if he's going to sleep through his guests' wake-ups and leave them to fend for themselves."

I turn, mute, tracking her as she frowns in concentration at the machine and pushes a few buttons. "Took me *months* to learn how to work this thing," she says over her shoulder. "What did you want? Coffee? Latte? Espresso? This machine can do it all, so drinker's choice."

She leans over the counter to reach the cord and plugs in the machine again. It puts her wide, round ass in those tiny flower shorts right on display, and oh God, I'm staring. I glance away, my cheeks turning bright red.

"Just, uh . . ." I clear my throat. "Coffee, please. And thanks."

She turns, and her eyes lock with mine, a mesmerizing swirl of ocean blue-green rimmed with stormy gray, thick, dark lashes blinking slowly. Her smile is wide and warm. "Sure thing. Got a mug?"

"Uh. Yes." I spin, searching for the mug I pulled out of the cupboard when I first tried to make a cup for myself. I spot the black ceramic mug on the counter behind me and hand it to her.

She plucks it from my grip, smiling up at me. "Eight or twelve ounces?"

Her scent wafts my way, and Christ almighty, she smells so good, like fresh air and wildflowers. It's taking superhuman strength not to suck in a deep breath just to hold on to that scent. My throat works in a swallow. My stomach tightens as heat rushes through me, low and swift. I'm short-circuiting.

I've never slept over after being with a woman—too many sensory issues like scratchy sheets, mattresses that don't feel right, unfamiliar noises in their place that would keep me awake. I've never seen a woman I'm attracted to rumpled and soft from sleep. I had no idea it would be so damn hot.

"Will?" she presses, her smile faltering.

Shit, I've been staring, probably weirding her out. I clear my throat. "Sorry. I . . . um, twelve ounces. Please. And thank you."

Her smile returns. "Twelve, it is."

I watch her as she deftly operates the machine, trying and failing to think of what to say. It isn't that I don't have things to say, questions to ask—I just never know where to begin, what's the right first move. *Overwhelmed* doesn't begin to cover it.

"Here we are," she says, turning with my mug and hers, which is now also full and steaming. "Just going to help myself to a little creamer." She walks past me to the fridge, drags open the door, and holds it with her elbow.

I take a step and reach for the door to hold it for her.

She blinks up at me, clutching the creamer. "Oh." A smile lifts her mouth. "Thanks."

"Mm-hmm," I manage.

Mm-hmm? That's the best you can do?

I shut my eyes and grimace as she pours a hefty glug of some kind of flavored cream into her mug.

Anxiety seeps through me as I stand there, holding the door, tongue-tied. She's helped me, and now she's going to leave, because why wouldn't she when I'm just standing here, silent and still as a statue?

Say something, you ass. Just talk to her already!

She slides the creamer back into the fridge. I let the door drop but it doesn't close all the way. She shuts it with a nudge of her hip and peers up at me, her mouth opening, like she's about to speak.

This is it. This is when she tells me she's leaving. When I fumble it again.

Just. Talk.

"Thank you," I blurt. "For the coffee. I would have asked Petruchio for help—I'm not, you know, above accepting help, obviously, since you're here helping me—but he's still asleep . . ." I swallow nervously. "All the guys are. Not that any of them could work that thing, either."

Her smile brightens her face, turning those dimples so deep there are shadows in her cheeks. "Happy to help, especially when all the night owls are sleeping the morning away. We early birds have to stick together! At least, I'm assuming you're a morning person, unless you just got up to get on the road. You did say you had to leave first thing tomorrow—well, today."

Something warm and fizzy spills through me. I talked. She talked back. I didn't blow it.

Don't mess this up.

I take a deep breath. "I'm not exactly a morning person, but I do get up early every day. And I had planned to get on the road . . ." I push past my nerves, determined not to mess this up like I did last night. "But I've got some time. I could, um . . ." I lift my mug. "Drink this. With. You?"

I want to slap myself. Why am I so terrible at this?

Her smile turns sparkling, wide and warm. "How about we head outside, enjoy the sunshine?"

I swallow thickly. *Yes*, my brain thinks, but my heart is pounding; my throat is tight. My hands are getting clammy.

She doesn't seem to mind the silence that stretches out, just smiles softly, her eyes holding mine as she sips her coffee. "If you're worried about going outside with me," she says, "because you're concerned I've got more garden-tool weapons waiting out there, they're all locked up in the shed. You're safe. Promise."

Her playfulness, her patience, they flip a switch in me. Finding my voice, I tell her, "Outside sounds . . . nice."

My voice catches before I can continue. I swallow, wetting my throat, then reach for the door, which puts me close to Viola, bathes me in her sweet, soft scent.

I open the door, and a warm morning breeze rushes in, whipping back her hair, making it dance around her gorgeous face. I stare down at her, my heart thudding hard, and tell her, "Ladies first."

THREE

Juliet

My stomach's doing somersaults. Will holds the heavy back door open for me with just his fingertips, and it makes his arm muscles do obscene things. I swallow thickly and force my smile wider, then spin and rush out onto Christopher's back porch before my horny thoughts are projected on my face.

Will's steps are steady behind mine as I cross the small back porch. There's no furniture back here, and I think about where we could sit and talk. We could park it on the steps, but as I glance out across the yard, dappled in buttery morning light, a warm July breeze swaying the trees above us, I know where we should go.

I head down the steps to the backyard as the wind picks up, swaying the swings hanging from the elaborate playground structure that Christopher's and my parents went in on together decades ago, built so it straddles our two yards. It's solid wood and sturdy, in surprisingly good condition for how old it is, though I do know it's been given a little love the past few years, since my mother started dropping casual comments about its future use for whenever we "see fit to give her grandbabies (no pressure, of course)."

Kate, who's two years younger than me and skeptical she'll ever want kids, snort-laughs every time Mom talks about grandkids. Bea, my twin, just grins up at her fiancé, Jamie, who never fails to blush when he smiles right back.

For months, after I broke up with my awful fiancé, every time I caught a glimpse of the playground, my stomach twisted. Because *I'd* been planning to give my mom those grandbabies, and soon. With him.

I smile to myself now, feeling no twist in my stomach, no pang of sadness. Just peace. Tiny moments like this, when I recognize how far I've come, how much I've healed, they are small but sweet victories.

The wind sways the swings again, and my smile deepens.

Glancing over my shoulder at Will, I ask him, "How's a morning swing sound? I mean, I know we've got full cups of coffee, so nothing wild. Just to sit on and . . . have a chat?"

He eyes up the swing set branching off the main playground structure, skepticism written all over his face. "Pretty sure," he says, "I exceed that thing's weight limits."

Taking a sip of coffee, I allow my gaze to travel him. He might be onto something. Good grief, he really is big. And beautifully built. Tall and, while not bulky, definitely muscly. Muscle is heavy, so he might be pushing the weight limit. But Dad's done maintenance, ensuring its structural integrity so Mom's future grandbabies won't get hurt when having fun at Grandma's. Plus, Christopher, who's similar in size to Will, maybe an inch or two shorter, a smidge stockier, sometimes sits on the swings with me and my sisters when we wander out here after Sunday family dinners, nightcaps in hand, talking, gazing up at the stars. Nothing's ever happened.

"I think you'll be fine," I tell him, taking a few more steps, then turning and easing onto a swing. "Christopher sits on these and hasn't broken anything. But if you don't feel comfortable here, we can sit on the back steps, or head around to the front porch."

Will scratches at his neck. "Nah. That's okay."

I watch him walk toward the swing beside me, closing the distance between us as I curl my arms around the swing's rubber-wrapped chains. Planting my feet on the ground, I rock just barely on the swing, then take a sip of coffee from my mug.

Will lowers onto the swing beside me gingerly, his shoulders dropping with relief when it doesn't fall out from under him. Boots planted on the ground, he rocks back, too, sipping his coffee carefully. He glances my way as he rocks forward.

I take him in, a smile lifting my mouth. I'm not sure what I'm doing, what he's doing, either. I just know that while I was so sure he was shutting me down last night, when I spotted him this morning, standing in Christopher's kitchen, I had this gut feeling that whatever happened last night was more complicated than my wounded pride wanted to believe.

Not a big talker, I remember him saying that night in the pub last December. Maybe he has social anxiety. Maybe he's shy. Maybe he needs time to find the words he wants.

While trusting my gut has been hard since that gut instinct led me into such a horrible person's arms not so long ago, this morning, trusting that gut instinct to give Will another chance, to offer help, felt . . . well, it felt easier. Except now here we are and it doesn't feel so easy anymore.

But maybe that's okay. Maybe this is just what it is, to be rusty since I went through a breakup that made me question my romantic outlook, since I've completely avoided any kind of romantic . . . well, anything, for more than half a year.

The wind swirls around us, rustling the trees overhead. I let myself simply gaze at Will, who's peering at me intensely, the same way he was when we danced at the pub in Scotland, when he plucked that leaf from my hair last night. It makes warmth bloom inside me, desire curl like vines through my veins.

"So," I say quietly. "Tell me about yourself, Will—" I hesitate, remembering what he said when I had him at trowel point yesterday. "Or, um, do you prefer to go by Orsino?"

His brow furrows, then it smooths. "Will is just fine, Viola."

My stomach drops. Oh God. Of course, he still thinks that's my name. I didn't clear it up last night. I ran off before I could.

"Actually . . ." A nervous laugh teeters out of me. "About that. Well, truth is, I go by Juliet."

His eyebrows lift. "So . . . Viola's not your name?"

"Oh, no, it is."

He frowns.

Lord, I'm rusty on more than flirting with a hot guy. I'm not even communicating well. I take a gulp of coffee, then spin my swing so that I'm facing him fully, the rubber-wrapped chains crossing over my head. "Viola is my first name. But I don't go by my first name. I go by my middle name, Juliet, actually Jules, most often."

His expression clears. "Ah. I see."

"Sorry about that," I say sheepishly. "I wasn't trying to hold out on you this morning. I would have said something right when I came over to Christopher's, but honestly, I'd forgotten all about it. I was too focused on getting your coffee situation sorted out."

He's quiet for a beat, as he sips from his mug, then spins back so he's facing forward again. "What's next?" he says, pushing back in his swing, then drifting forward. "The cat's real name isn't Puck, either?"

A belly laugh bursts out of me. I'm delightfully surprised by his deadpan playfulness. "I'm sorry, okay!"

"You don't need to be sorry." He peers my way. "I probably weirded you out, back in Scotland, when I walked up to you out of nowhere and nonverbally asked for a dance. I'd give me a not-real name, too."

I swing back, then drift forward, a bit bolder in my swinging now that I've drained half my coffee. "You didn't weird me out."

"But it was awkward." He glances my way, his brow drawn tight. "*I* was awkward."

"I mean, it was a smidge awkward, yes. All first meetings are, at least a little. And sure, you could have thrown a few more words my way at first, but . . ." My stomach swoops as I remember him stepping closer to me, his touch warm and gentle, his gorgeous, intense gaze dancing over me as we swayed to the music. How tenderly he held me, how he told me when I was rambling that he *liked* how much I talk.

Will might have been awkward that night, but he didn't let that keep him from trying, from coming up to me, asking me to dance in his own sweet way. Back at that pub, he was something I wasn't ready to be.

He was brave.

And now, finally, I'm ready to be brave, too.

Inside me, something like a door that's been locked swings open, and out rushes what at first I think is a sliver of the old Juliet. But no, it's not that simple. It's not who I used to be, showing up again. It's who I've been *becoming*, finally showing her face. Someone who's been hurt and who's healed. Someone who still wants to hope, even knowing it could get her hurt again. Someone who can go through hard shit and survive it, maybe a little roughed up, a bit battered and scarred, but also braver and stronger.

And that's when I see it. *This* is that first move I've been waiting for, the first grinding shift into a new gear for my idling-engine life: once again wrapping my arms around the part of myself that desires and delights in others and has no qualms about telling them how much, that has fun flirting and savors time spent with someone she's attracted to. I'm not ready for romantic love, to hand someone my heart again, but I am ready for this. And that's okay. This is enough, this first step.

"You weren't the reason I told you my name was Viola and then left the pub so abruptly. I did it because I was in a bad place and I was being self-protective. You were painfully cute, and I was attracted to you, and I knew I wasn't in any place to handle that. Any other season of my adult life, you bet your butt I would have thrown myself at you."

He falters on the swing and barely avoids slopping coffee all over his jeans, holding it away from him. Dark liquid sloshes over the edge of his mug onto the grass. He looks like I've stunned him. "What?"

I roll my eyes as I sip my coffee. "Please, don't act like you don't know you're hot. You've got the strong and silent, gentle giant thing going for you, and I'd bet my right leg—which is my better one—that you're more than aware of it."

Will blinks at me, looking genuinely shocked. "I . . ." He shakes his head. "I'm sorry, you think the fact that I—how I acted, I mean . . ." He clears his throat. "You didn't think I was . . . weird?"

I smile at him, tipping my head as I take him in. It's ridiculously cute, him sidestepping entirely the question of how aware he is that he's a hottie. Which means he knows he's a hottie, and he's too humble to admit it. Swoon.

"I didn't say that," I tell him. "You were definitely weird. I said you didn't weird me out."

He groans, hanging his head. "I knew it."

I reach my toe out and poke his hip. "I *like* weird. The world needs more weirdos."

Will stares down at his coffee. A gust of air leaves him, an empty laugh. "Not in my world, it doesn't."

"What world is that?"

"It's . . ." He's silent for a beat, his eyes still fixed on his coffee mug. He sighs heavily. His throat works in a swallow.

I let my swing twirl so that I'm facing forward. Maybe it'll help if he doesn't feel like I'm staring him down, waiting for him to talk.

Tipping back my mug, I drain the last of my coffee and set it beside me in the grass. Then I push back on the swing in earnest.

Will's gaze tracks me as I sway forward on the swing, then drift backward, the wind whipping my hair. He lifts his mug to his mouth and tips it back, his eyes holding me as he does.

I watch him rest his mug beside him in the grass, like I did, settle straight on the swing, then push off.

"My world is . . ." he starts, but the swing set groans as he sways forward, cutting him off. Will glances up, frowning. "I'm gonna bust this thing."

"No way," I tell him. "That's the sound it always makes when we use it."

Will's got his swings in time with mine already, his ankles crossed as he sways forward, then rushes back. He's still staring up worriedly at the beam overhead. "If you say so."

I smile his way. "I promise. It's fine!"

And that's when Will's swing snaps from the beam overhead and drops to the ground.

FOUR

Will

"Oh my God." Juliet tumbles off her swing and rushes over to me where I'm sprawled on the ground. I'm gaping like a fish, the wind knocked clean out of me.

I knew that swing set was too flimsy for me. If anyone else had asked me to swing with them on something built for people half my size, I would have flatly said, *Hell no*.

But there's something about this woman every time I'm around her that makes me want to say *yes*.

So I did. And now here I am, knocked on my ass because of it.

"Will, are you hurt?" Her hands dance across my chest, up my neck to my face. "I mean, obviously, you're hurt, but like, seriously injured hurt? Should I call an ambulance? I'm calling an ambulance—"

"Juliet," I croak, clasping her hand as her fingers press into my neck, like they're checking for a pulse. Saying her name required air I don't have yet. I try again to suck in a breath.

She bites her lip, her face drawn tight with worry as I try to get my bearings. But it's damn near impossible when sunshine spills from the sky behind her. It casts another bronze halo around her head, just like it did when I first saw her this morning, like she's an angel the light can't help but love.

"Will," she whispers, her eyes darting between mine frantically. "Are you okay?"

Her hand's trembling. I clasp it tighter and finally find myself able to draw in a big lungful of air. "Juliet." I squeeze her hand as her fingers dance along my pulse. "Baby, it's okay. I have a heartbeat. I'm okay."

Her fingers ease up on my throat; her eyebrows lift. *"Baby?"*

I have no idea where that came from, why the word rolled right off my tongue, when almost nothing does. Stroking my thumb along the inside of her palm, I stare up at her and pray I can, for once in my life, talk my way out of something. "Hit my head. Might be concussed. Can't be held responsible for what I say."

A smile lifts her mouth for a moment, but then it falls, concern returning. "You're not going to die on me, are you?"

I squeeze her hand again gently. "Nah."

But if I was, I think, *this would be a damn fine way to go.*

She doesn't look convinced, so to show her, I plant both palms on the grass and sit up. My head aches as I get myself upright. I reach for where it feels tender, finding a small bump already.

Juliet claps her hands over her mouth. "Oh no. My swing set *did* concuss you."

"I'm not concussed." Groaning, I stand slowly, rolling my shoulders to work out the knot in my back from landing on it hard. "It's just a little bump."

"But it's my fault." She groans, too, as she stands, clasping the side of the swing set and easing herself up. "I'm the one who said we should sit on the swings."

I peer down at her, in her tiny flower shorts and soft pink top, clinging to all those beautiful curves. I want to throw her over my shoulder and toss her onto my bed, crawl up her body, push her thighs wide, and—

I shake my head to snap myself out of those depraved thoughts. This is Juliet, the woman who's like a sister to Petruchio. I have no business thinking about her this way. Since seeing her in what she told me was her family's greenhouse, putting two and two to-gether, I've been telling myself that even if I wasn't hopeless at ro-mance, there'd still be no way I could pursue her.

The Wilmots are a surrogate family to Petruchio; they took him under their wing after his parents died in his teens. Their daughters are like sisters to him, with the exception of the youn-gest daughter, Kate, the only one whose name I could remember because of how often I used to hear Petruchio gripe about her. Turns out he was actually in love with her, and now they're happily dating and living together, at least when Kate's not traveling for work.

The point is, I've got no chance with Juliet. She is both off-limits and entirely out of my league. Rationally, I understand this. But my body, as I peer down at her, at the line of worry etched in her brow that I feel this ache to smooth out with my thumb, is struggling to get the memo.

"You're being really quiet, Will." She steps close, clasping my shoulders.

"I'm always quiet," I grumble.

She rolls her eyes. "Yes, I've gotten that. I meant, more than it seems you normally are. Are you really okay?" Her eyes search mine, that furrow in her brow deepening. "How do you *know* you aren't concussed?"

"Juliet." I gently grasp each of her hands and bring them from my shoulders. I pin them inside my palms. "I'm all right. I promise, I just got the wind knocked out of me, and, well . . . I get tongue-tied sometimes, but especially when I'm around very beautiful women."

Especially you.

Her cheeks turn pink. "You think . . . I'm beautiful?"

My cheeks turn even pinker. "I, uh . . ." I clear my throat as I release her hands and step back. "I shouldn't have said that. I mean, yes, I do—think you're beautiful, that is—but that was a thinking thought. Shouldn't have become a talking thought."

Her face brightens with a smile. "Why shouldn't you have said that? I told you you're hot. You can tell me I'm beautiful."

"Because you're basically Petruchio's sister. He'd have my nuts if he knew—" I manage to stop myself from admitting exactly what I've been thinking about Juliet.

"Let's get something straight." She drags her hands from mine and plants them on her hips, scowling up at me. Hell, even her scowl is cute. It makes her nose wrinkle and turns her wide, pretty eyes adorably squinty. "Yes, Christopher is like a brother to me, but I am not his property whose virtue needs to be protected."

I scrub at my neck, my cheeks turning even hotter. "I know that. I just . . . I just mean you're important to him, and it's a code between friends, we keep an eye out for the people who matter to each other. We don't . . . flirt with them. Or at least try to. Very badly."

Her scowl dissolves. "You've been flirting with me?"

"Like I said, very badly."

She smiles again, and she's so damn pretty, it makes my stomach flip. "I wouldn't say you were doing it *very badly*."

I give her a look.

A soft laugh jumps out of her. "I mean it! I'd just say it wasn't very . . . obvious. But, then again, I'm out of practice myself. Maybe I just didn't pick up on it. It's been a while since I . . ." Her voice dies off. She clears her throat. "I've been taking a break from romance—not that, you know, you're feeling romantic toward me, I just mean . . ." She wrinkles her nose and groans. "I'm not saying this well. See? I'm rusty, too."

"I'm not rusty," I tell her flatly. "'Rusty' implies I was once a well-oiled machine. I'm terrible at it."

"At what?"

"Romance. Flirting. All of that. Always have been."

Juliet tips her head, peering up at me. "I find that hard to believe."

"Well, believe it." I shove my hands in my pockets and nudge a pebble in the grass with my boot. "It's just how it is."

She's quiet for a minute as she stares at me. "Does that . . . upset you?"

I give the pebble more undue attention, scooching it across the grass. "Who likes being terrible at something?"

"Everyone is terrible at plenty of things—we can't be great at everything we do. Being terrible at something only bothers us when that something *matters* to us." She hesitates for a beat, then says, "*Does* romance matter to you? Do you want it?"

I frown down at the pebble, grinding it into the grass.

I've never considered it that way, never asked myself if I was "bad" at romance because I actually didn't *want* it. But, thinking back to when my insecurities started as a teen, when my sensory issues, my social anxiety, morphed from me being a quiet, particular kid to a painfully awkward and shy adolescent, when we figured out I was neurodivergent, I can admit that romantic connection *is* something I wanted. I wanted someone to walk around the farm with hand in hand; who'd trust me with their feelings and hopes and fears and listen to me when I wanted to trust them with those things, too; whom I'd feel so close to that the hunger and want burning through my body would have a place with them, would have *meaning* with them.

But my intense shyness, my need for earplugs in noisy spaces, my tongue-tied quietness, my anxiety when trying to socialize, made it hard to connect that way with girls in high school, then in college. The rare times I managed to click with someone, it only got as far as a couple of dates before I'd get some version of *I don't feel a romantic connection. I think we should just be friends.* So I stopped trying to have romance, when time and again people told me that they weren't experiencing it with me, that they didn't want it with me. I moved on, let myself have what they *did* want from me—a good time in bed and nothing more. Since then, I haven't let myself get so far as even considering what I wanted again.

Until recently—now that I'm faced with the fact that I need to marry, which, at thirty-four, has gone from a far-off problem for future Will to a pressing problem for present Will. I'm already functionally running my family's distillery and farm, but there are giant gaps in the business that I do *not* handle—all the in-person work of maintaining a business's connections, expanding its reach, networking, and wining and dining. That's where I need a partner, someone who'll happily take on the social aspect of running this business, who'll help me step fully into being the next generation leading Orsino Distillery and Farm. No consultant or manager is going to cut it. I need someone with those skills having my family name, being at the heart of our brand as a family-run business. I need a wife, and I intend to find one. I'm just not sure, based on my experience, if she's someone I can reasonably expect to love me romantically and feel me romantically loving her back.

"I guess . . . I'd like to be better at flirting," I finally tell Juliet. "At . . . romance. I've got to settle down at some point. Soon, actually."

"You *have* to?" Juliet wrinkles her nose. "That sounds awfully obligatory."

"It is," I admit, shifting on my feet. "My family business, I'm getting ready to take it over so my parents can retire. And running that business requires . . . well, a lot of socializing and networking, things that are not my strong suit or my interest. Hoping to find someone who's passionate about the business, who wants to get married to join me in that work."

"So . . . like, a mutually beneficial business arrangement?" she says.

I nod.

She tips her head. "And that's the reason you want to be better at romance? To find someone who'll be willing to partner with you. Not to find someone who could fall in love with you?"

I scrub at the back of my neck. "Past experience . . . it hasn't made me think that'll happen. Suppose I just want to find someone I could make happy—make her feel appreciated, listened to, cared for. I'd be faithful to her. I'd . . . you know, hope we could meet each other's, uh"—I blush fiercely—"needs. We'd share a life, a business, maybe a couple kids, if she was up for it. But can't say I'd expect her and I to be . . . in love."

"Why?" she asks.

Because I've tried before, Juliet, and every time I did, I was told I'd failed.

I can't tell her that. It's too damn humiliating.

"Because . . ." A sigh leaves me. I shrug. "Hell, I don't know. It just seems romance isn't for me."

Juliet bites her lip against a smile that still wins out.

"What?" I ask her. "What're you smiling about?"

Her smile widens. "You're giving me major duke-in-a-historical-romance-who-thinks-he-needs-a-marriage-of-convenience-to-carry-on-the-family-line vibes right now."

"I . . . remind you of a duke?"

She waves her hand. "Forget it. I'm being silly."

"No." I take a step closer to her. "I'm not saying it's silly. I just . . . don't understand."

Juliet seems to hesitate, then says, "It's just that in those romance novels, the character who's driven by what they *say* is duty to the people counting on them, rather than the pursuit of love, well, their acting on that sense of 'duty' *is* love. What we're meant to see when they act out of a sense of duty is that they have the capacity for love, even though they don't see it in themselves. That's where romantic love comes in, like a mirror, showing them what they really can have, if they're brave enough to go after it. And yes, romance novels are fictions, happy, hopeful stories. But I think they often capture very realistic human fears and hopes, and how the former often stop us from going after the latter, how love can make us feel safe and brave enough to change that."

I stand there, absorbing what she's said, sifting through it. I'll admit I've never read a romance novel. My mom loves them, historical romances in particular. Every surface of the family home has a precarious stack of well-loved mass-market paperbacks. But I've never thought about what those books might inspire, what Juliet's laid at my feet, maybe without even realizing it: a flicker of hope.

"So . . ." I clear my throat, folding my arms across my chest. "You're saying, if I'm like . . . one of your dukes, who . . . well, things work out for him. Maybe, if I got a bit better at this flirting and romancing, maybe . . . they'd work out for me, too."

Slowly, she reaches for my wrist and clasps it. Her touch is warm and firm and so impossibly soft. "I absolutely think that things could work out spectacularly for you, Will, yes."

Searching her eyes, I ask, "Why . . ." I clear my throat, which has suddenly gotten thick. "Why do you believe in me?"

A smile breaks across her face. "Because I believe we all deserve the kind of happily ever after that we want. If we're brave enough to put our true selves out there, we can find someone who wants us for all of that, who wants that same kind of happily ever after, too."

My heart feels like it's made of sunlight, like it's spilling, hot and hopeful, through every corner of me. "That's a hell of an optimistic outlook."

Juliet's smile tightens. "I'm trying."

"Trying?"

She draws her hand away, crossing her arms against her chest, and glances up at the clouds, frowning thoughtfully. "I've always been an optimist. I don't think I ever stopped being an optimist for others. But I sort of stopped being optimistic for myself."

"Why's that?"

She peers down and meets my eyes, a shrug lifting her shoulders. "Last year, I stayed on that optimism train a little too long, ignored the red flags all around me, and didn't get off before I'd landed in Toxic Relationshipville. Since then, I guess I've been doubting myself. That's why I've been on romance hiatus. I *want* to believe that one day I can love someone again and this time, it'll be a real, healthy happily ever after . . ." She squints a little, her nose wrinkling. "I've been waiting to feel confident about that again, before I put myself out there romantically, but I'm starting to think I'll never feel as confident as I used to. I think I'm just going to have to try again, and hope the confidence follows."

"Do you *want* to try again?" I ask, searching her eyes.

She tips her head to one side, then the other. "Yes. And no. Being romantic, I think maybe it's like riding a bike. You can stay away from the thing for years and then yes, you can allegedly get right back on and start riding again. But even with muscle memory pulling its weight, you're real wobbly at first; you might fall and get a few scrapes. When I think about how great it would feel to fly down the road again, yes, I want to. But when I think about all those wobbles, those bumps and bruises I might get along the way, I don't want to at all.

"I guess, when I think about getting back on the bike, I want somewhere gentle to start, so when I take those tumbles, it won't hurt *too* bad. That's the hard part—figuring out what that gentle place looks like. I'm not sure it even exists."

"Maybe . . ." My voice catches as nerves tighten my throat.

"Maybe it doesn't exist. Maybe instead of looking for a soft place to fall, you just need some . . . training wheels."

It made sense in my head, but I feel like a schmuck the moment I've said it.

Except a smile brightens Juliet's face, and all my self-consciousness evaporates. "My training wheels," she says. "I love that. Though who would want to do that for me?"

I stare at her, my heart pounding. *I would.*

I'll never get to have her, not fully—she's off-limits, out of reach. But I'd take this. I'd take every crumb she'd give me.

Her gaze snaps up to mine. "What did you just say?"

I blink at her. I couldn't have said that out loud. *Oh God. Did I say that out loud?*

Juliet steps closer. "Did you just say, *I would*?"

My cheeks heat. "If I did . . . that was another one of those thinking thoughts that shouldn't have become a talking thought."

"Will, you are a genius."

"I am?"

"Hear me out." She clasps my arms. "I want to get comfortable with romance again. You want to get better at romance. What if we helped each other?"

My heart's pounding, my mind racing, as I process what she's saying. "You think we could be each other's . . . training wheels?"

Her smile brightens. "Yes! I know we barely know each other, but . . . look at us, bumping into each other twice in the same year, in two distinct corners of the world, our lives connected by someone so important to us. Doesn't it feel . . . like something's putting us on each other's path? What if this is why?"

"To help each other out?" I venture.

"Exactly! To help each other. We could be like workout buddies, but for romance. You'd get to find and flex those romance muscles. I'd start to use mine again, get them back in shape. It would put me back on the bike and you . . ."

She doesn't say it, probably because she's too sweet to say something that might prick my pride, so I say it for her: "I'd be *learning* to ride."

Silence hangs between us. Then she steps forward and squeezes my hand. "I'd be wobbling right beside you."

I stare down at her, my insides knotting. It'll be so embarrassing for her to see up close how awkward I am, especially when I'm so attracted to her. But the look of hope in her eyes, how much I hate the thought of taking that away, loosens every thread of my resistance. I couldn't say no to this woman if I tried.

"Then let's do it," I tell her.

She claps her hands together and squeals. "Let's do it!"

"On one condition."

She freezes mid-clap. "What condition?"

"You swear you'll tell me if I'm ever . . . if you don't want to do it anymore. Just don't walk out on me, okay? I need to know you'll tell me to my face if it's not working."

Juliet's expression turns serious. Her hands fall to her sides. "Will, of course. I . . ." She sighs. "I know I've bolted on you—"

"Twice."

She grimaces. "I swear it had nothing to do with you. That was my stuff. The stuff I need to work on. I promise"—she juts her pinkie up into the air—"if we do this, any part of it that isn't working for me, I'll tell you. And same goes for you. We'll talk it out, be truthful but kind in our honesty. That's what friends do."

"So we're friends now, huh?"

She juts her pinkie closer, eyes narrowed. "We better be. We're going to be romance workout warriors, flirty biking buddies. We're going to be thick as thieves."

A smile tugs at the corner of my mouth. I like the idea of being friends with Juliet. Gently, I hook my pinkie with hers. "Deal."

Juliet squeals again, smiling wide. "I can't wait. Oh gosh, I feel like I've been on the Whole30 diet and someone just handed me a plate of brownies. I'm going to gorge myself. When can you start? How do you want to plan it? Wait." Her face falls. "You don't live around here, do you? How are we going to do this if you're . . . well, wherever you are?"

I scrub at my neck. She's got a point. "I'm not too far, couple hours' drive upstate. I could . . . come down on weekends? Take a few weekdays off here and there, too, if we needed them, if that worked for your work schedule."

"I work from home right now," she says. "Freelance business writing. I'm flexible. We can plan it around your work." She peers up at me, her head tipped in curiosity. "What *is* your work?"

My phone starts going off in my pocket, and I recognize its sound as the one I have programmed for my right-hand man, our operations manager at the distillery and farm, Fest.

"Speaking of work. Sorry," I mutter, drawing my phone out of my pocket and frowning down at his text, relieved to see it's nothing urgent; in fact, far from it. Fest has too much time on his hands and an obsession with videos of people falling on their asses. The man laughs so hard at those damn videos, he cries. I only ever feel secondhand embarrassment and sympathy for those poor bastards.

I tap back on the video with a thumbs down, like I always do when he sends this shit, and pocket my phone. "That was my operations manager. Just had to make sure nothing's on fire. My family owns a whiskey distillery and a small farm upstate. My work, my part of it . . . the easiest way to explain what I do is, I make sure none of it goes to hell. Fest, my operations manager, keeps things running smoothly for me and keeps me in the loop when I'm gone."

"So he's like . . . your steward?" she asks.

I frown. "I guess . . . that's accurate?"

She sighs, a smile wide on her face. "You really are right out of a historical romance."

My frown deepens as she loops her arm through mine. "Because I run a farm and distillery?"

She pats my arm. "Don't worry, once you read one, it'll make sense. I mean, only *if* you want to read one."

"You think I should?"

"I think if you're trying to learn about romance, reading about it would be helpful. If learning romance is a workout, romance novels are your protein bar, the kind that taste so darn good, you want to eat them for breakfast, lunch, and dinner." She stops at the bottom of the steps, turning to look up at me. "Would you be okay with that? Reading romance novels?"

"If you think it'll help, I'll take all the help I can get. My mom's got lots of historical romances. I can pick one up while I'm home."

"Great." She beams up at me. "I could pull some contemporaries from my library and have them ready for you when you're free to meet up?"

"Works for me."

"Perfect," she says brightly. "Well, let me give you my number, then you can text me when you have a sense of your schedule and we can get some plans nailed down."

I freeze as it hits me like a truck, what this plan we've hatched is going to involve. I'm going to have her phone number. I'll be texting with Juliet, spending time with her. *Romantic* time with her. Even if it is just for practice.

Juliet tips her head. "Will? What's wrong?"

"How do we explain this to Petruchio?"

She frowns. "What's to explain?"

"Friend code," I remind her.

A sigh leaves her. "That applies? When it's just for practice?"

"If he sees me with you, acting, uh . . ." I blush, my cheeks hot. I hate how damn easily I blush. "Romantic, I'm going to have some explaining to do."

"Hmm." Juliet taps her chin. "I could come to you upstate, and we could keep it between ourselves?"

I shake my head. "All my family is too close by, and I live in a tiny town of busybody gossips. We'd be the only thing anyone was talking about, no matter how much we tried to fly under the radar. I'll have to come here. And I don't . . . I don't want to lie to Petruchio. I know what we're doing is our business, but he's my friend, and if I'm in town, spending time with you, I don't want to be sneaking around behind his back."

"That's fair," she says thoughtfully. "I don't want to lie to him, either. I guess . . . I also don't feel like we need to share *everything* about what we're doing. Like you said, it's our business. I propose a compromise: we tell Christopher we struck up a friendship this morning, because"—she winks up at me—"we did. It's pinkie-promise official. When you come into town, if we happen to bump into or even intentionally spend time with him, my sisters, our friends, we don't practice, just save that for when it's only the two of us."

Dragging a hand along my jaw, I think it over. "That seems reasonable."

"I think so, too," she says. "Besides, it's not like we'll *actually* be romantic and hide it. It will all just be for practice."

I nod. "I'm not actually going to flirt with you. I'll just be . . . practicing . . . flirting with you."

"Right," she says. "Like two actors doing a hot make-out scene on a movie set. I mean, yes, they're making out, but they're not *making out*, you know?"

I barely hold back an audible gulp. I don't think making out with Juliet, whether for practice or not, would feel anything except very much like making out. And I think I'd thoroughly enjoy it.

Will that be part of practicing? *Are* we going to make out?

Juliet grimaces. "Okay, that was an intense example, but dammit, if Emily Blunt and John Krasinski can make it work, so can we! And if Christopher finds out what we're up to, well, he's just going to have to deal with that."

I frown. "Who is Petruchio in this?"

"Well . . ." She taps her chin. "I don't know, the metaphor sort of broke down on me, but what I mean is, they're two hot people who've been together for a long time and kiss other hot people very convincingly for pretend, and their marriage is still going strong."

"Right." I nod. "Got it."

I really don't, but she seems so sure that we can make this work, and I want to be sure, too. Because this is the first time I've had hope for this part of my life in so long, and God, does it feel good.

My phone rings again. This time, the sound tells me it's my mom.

"Aren't you Mr. Popular," Juliet says, releasing my arm.

I silence my phone in my pocket. "It's just my mom, most likely wondering why I haven't told her I'm on the road yet."

Juliet bites her lip. "You let your mom know when you're on the road?"

I shrug. "For longer drives, yes. She's the worrying type."

"I think a lot of moms are the worrying type," Juliet says. "My mom certainly is."

My phone starts to ring again. I yank it out and silence it, then send Mom a quick text that I haven't left yet. "Sorry I keep texting while we're talking. If I don't do this, she'll just keep calling."

Juliet smiles. "That's okay."

"I hate these damn things," I mutter as I start to pocket my phone.

She grins. "You're the emailing type, aren't you?"

"I don't see why more people aren't, frankly."

"Wait." Juliet clasps my hand. "My number. You'll need it so we can make plans. Unless you plan for us to correspond like it's 2003. I *can* give you my Gmail. While I'm at it, would you like my AIM username?"

"Oh, real cute," I grumble.

She plucks my phone from my palm, head bent as she types quickly, then hands it back.

"Being serious, we can talk however you like," Juliet says, smiling up at me. "I'm going to head inside now, let you get on the road." She takes a step back. "See you soon?"

I nod, lifting a hand. "See you soon."

She spins and walks across the grass, up the steps to her own back porch. When she stops one last time and turns, waving brightly goodbye, I feel my heart thud in my chest.

As soon as she shuts the door behind her, I look at my phone, at her contact info. A quiet laugh rumbles in my throat. She did give me her Gmail. And next to her name, there are two tiny blue bikes.

FIVE

Juliet

Most people who've come back from weeks of globe-trotting crash in their beds for at least a day, then gently ease back into their typical routine.

My parents are not most people.

They got home early this morning, talked my ear off over coffee, unpacked all their bags, started their laundry, and then began prep for our usual Sunday family dinner.

I, on the other hand, managed to write a five-hundred-word blog post on the benefits of flexible work schedules that's due tomorrow for one of my freelance clients and decided I'd earned a nap. I somehow slept the entire afternoon away.

Taking the stairs to the first floor, I don't exactly spring my way down how I used to. Ever since connective tissue disease took over my body, I hold on to the railing tightly and pray my shaky left knee behaves itself. It's been frustrating, encountering these new limitations to my body after three decades of operating like a little Energizer Bunny (yes, I got it from my parents), but I'm trying to weather this season of adapting and adjusting with poise and a positive attitude.

Which does feel a little harder when our ancient cat, Puck, who is truly defying death by still existing, beats me down the stairs. He lands at the bottom with a spry jingle of his bell and a little satisfied feline chirp.

"Really, Puck?" I ease my way down the last few steps. "You just had to rub it in?"

"JuJu!" My youngest sister, Kate, nearly collides with me as she darts out of the kitchen into the foyer. "I was just coming to wake you up."

"KitKat." I smile. "Here I am."

"Here you are." She threads her arm through mine. "Enjoy your granny nap?"

"Hey." I poke her ticklish side, making her squeak. "Leave me and my granny naps alone."

Kate smiles down at me, a coy splash of freckles on her nose, that feisty glint in those blue-gray-green eyes Mom gave all of us, her hair dark like mine and my twin sister Bea's, except it's tinged auburn, twisted up in a messy bun on her head. "Warning, Mom tried to make gluten-free dinner rolls again. Dad almost cracked a tooth on one."

I snort. "Oh no."

"Oh yes. But the vegetarian gluten-free potpie turned out pretty well. For being vegetarian. And gluten-free."

"Which means you didn't try to make it this time."

"Hey!" Kate pokes my side. "Rude."

"Katerina!" Mom calls from the kitchen. "You're not harassing your sister while she's walking down the stairs, are you?"

"No, Mom!" Kate rolls her eyes and mutters, "Still treating you like a porcelain doll."

I smile up at my baby sister, who has the nerve to be four inches taller than me. "Guess someone has to, since you and Bea certainly don't."

"Damn right we don't," Bea says, popping her head out of the kitchen. My twin looks a little like me but is so beautifully distinct, with her blond-tipped dark hair and colorful tattoos all over her body. She gives me a wide smile. "Heyyy. Nice dress, JuJu."

I glance between our outfits and groan. "Well, thanks, BeeBee. That's a pretty cute dress you've got on, too."

Bea and I are wearing the same swingy tank top dress, albeit in different colors—hers, sunshine yellow; mine, rose pink. Totally by accident. It doesn't happen often, but when it does, my mom insists on making us take a picture like old times, which she does the second she glances over her shoulder and sees us. Wedging us together, Mom is gentle with my body. These days, she's convinced a strong breeze will make me collapse.

While Mom bickers with Kate (who's a photographer) about how to use portrait mode on her iPhone, I smile. Bea wraps her arm around my waist and makes me laugh as she jokes about Mom and Kate's endless squabbles since Kate moved back home after years of endless traveling for photojournalism work.

We pull apart and walk into the kitchen. I feel my smile slip when I look around for something to do but come up short.

Soft overhead light warms the space, cutting through the hazy steam of vegetarian potpie (for Kate) with a gluten-free crust (for me). Dad stands at the counter, one hand sprinkling the finishing garnishes on his salad, the other resting affectionately low on Mom's waist while she opens a bottle of wine. Kate sidles up to Christopher, whispering something in his ear that makes him smile as he builds a dessert plate of dense dark chocolate brownies and glossy tartlets piled high with fresh summer fruit. Bea and Jamie stand hip to hip at the cabinets, pulling out dinner, salad, and bread plates, stealing loving glances at each other.

They're all so happy.

And God, am I happy for them.

But as I stand in the middle of the kitchen, empty-handed, no one by *my* side, I can't help but feel a teensy bit . . . *un*happy to be the only who's alone.

Rain pelts against the windows, another storm that came through shortly after I said goodbye to Will yesterday and hasn't let up since. I ease onto a stool at the kitchen island and swallow a groan. Another fun development since getting sick—rainy weather makes my achy joints ache that much more.

Mom clocks me wincing as I settle onto a stool and spins out of Dad's arms toward me. "Hurting?" she asks. "Need one of your pain pills?"

I exhale slowly, fighting the frustration that's been building the past seven months. I know Mom wants to take care of me, but the constant fussing over me only makes me feel worse. "Just a little stiff from my nap. I'm okay, Mom. Thanks, though."

I could definitely use an eight-hundred-milligram naproxen sodium for the pain I'm feeling, but not on an empty stomach. It would wreck my insides. I'll take one after dinner, with food in my belly and when Mom isn't looking, so she won't worry even more that I'm hurting enough to need one.

Planting a kiss on my temple, Mom gently rubs my back, like she always did when I was sick as a kid. "You sure?"

"I'm sure!" I pat her hand and try to subtly ease out of the lingering back rub.

To be fair to my mom and her concern for me, I was pretty badly off when my health hit rock bottom at the end of last year, and initially, it was scary. But I've come a ways since I woke up on Boxing Day, my joints so stiff I'd have sworn they'd turned to cement, the weird rashes I'd blown off before reappearing; the fevers and flu-like aches that had wracked my muscles in Scotland, that I'd chalked up to something viral; a vicious spate of digestive issues. It was an avalanche of bizarre symptoms that landed me in the care of a rheumatologist who promised me we'd get my overactive immune system under control.

I've tried to do my part to take care of myself, while my doctor takes care of me, too. But even so, I'm not all better. I might never be, which I'm starting to make peace with, some days more easily than others. I wish my mom could follow my example and start making peace with it, too. I wish she could understand that this new "normal" of mine can be just that—normal.

"How can I help?" I ask, trying to move past the Poor Invalid Juliet bit for the evening.

Mom smiles, patting my cheek. "Just sit there and be your lovely self."

I let out a miserable sigh as she leaves me to my perch at the island, glancing around the kitchen at everyone else, who has some helpful task they're undertaking. Which is when I realize every single one of these fools is canoodling. Dad kissing Mom discreetly behind the curtain of her hair as he tosses the salad. Kate sneaking a bite of brownie with one hand and squeezing Christopher's butt with the other. Bea nuzzling Jamie's neck as he gathers up the plates for dinner.

This is my existence these days—the perennial seventh wheel.

Just as I'm about to settle in for a nice little mope, my phone buzzes in my dress pocket. My stomach flips. I have a message from an unknown number, but I know right away who it is.

> Hi, Juliet. Sorry I'm just texting. Had to get caught up on everything around here, but I finally have a moment to myself. These are all the dates for the next month that I'm free. I can come down for all of those days or just some of them, whatever you want.
>
> This is Will by the way.

A smile lifts my mouth as I scan the dates that he's sent. He's made himself free to come down every weekend for the next month.

> JULIET: That's an awful lot of driving, Duke Orsino. You sure you're up for coming down every weekend?

> WILL: Anything for the Lady Juliet.

I barely muffle a squeal, kicking my feet under the table. Good grief, he's adorable.

> WILL: That was weird, wasn't it? Calling you Lady Juliet. I was trying to riff off the duke thing, but now I'm second guessing myself.

I bite my lip against my smile as I type back.

> JULIET: I thought the "Lady Juliet" was pretty darn cute, but the real winner is you told a gal you'd do anything for her. That right there, 10 out of 10, no notes.

> JULIET: Also, I'm free all of those dates during the daytime. Just a couple evenings I've got friend group plans, but we can practice during the daytime (& you could join the friend fun in the evening!).

> WILL: Well, that was easy.

> JULIET: Well, I'm an easy girl.

I groan, realizing what I just said, and start to type as fast as my stiff fingers will let me.

JULIET: I meant in the convenience sense of easy, not the sexual sense.

JULIET: Now I've said "sexual" & it's totally worse.

WILL: Here I was, thinking your make out example yesterday was intense . . .

I grimace, embarrassed all over again.

JULIET: I TOLD YOU I'M RUSTY. I haven't flirtatiously bantered in over half a year. Cut me some slack!

WILL: I haven't flirtatiously bantered in ever, so you're better off than me.

JULIET: Well, I'm glad you're free next weekend, so we can both start leveling up.

WILL: I'm glad you're free, too. Want to meet for coffee somewhere Saturday morning? Any time after 10am will work. You name the place.

JULIET: Sure! How's 10:30 at Boulangerie?

I send him a pin with the location of one of my favorite coffee and pastry spots.

WILL: Got it. I'll be there, prepared to offer my best (terrible) attempts at flirtation.

A smile tugs at my mouth so wide, it makes my cheeks ache.

JULIET: I'll come prepared to swoon.

"What's that beaming smile for?" Mom asks. Dad turns and glances my way, followed by my sisters, then Christopher and Jamie, all their faces painted with curiosity.

I pocket my phone, still smiling, feeling a lot less like the sad little seventh wheel than when I first sat down.

"Just got the details on my next project," I tell them, sliding off the stool as I scoop up the tray of napkins and silverware for dinner. "And it's finally one I'm excited about."

SIX

Will

Any family dinner at my parents' is rowdy. Add on a birthday celebration, and it's mayhem.

I sit at the long pine table that dominates my childhood home's dining room, crammed between my sisters, their partners, my niece and nephew, and my parents. Wildflowers and rainbow glitter, unicorn cutouts and dishes of my niece Eleanor's favorite foods—birthday tradition, whoever's birthday it is gets to pick the meal—now reduced to abandoned last bites, crisp edges, and crumbs littering the table. Napkins land beside plates. Chairs creak as we sit back. Whiskey and wine are passed and poured.

I'm lost in thought, my gaze drifting toward the window, where, right outside it, the warm summer breeze sways the damask roses Dad and Mom planted on their wedding day, which have grown and thrived for thirty-five years.

Thanks to my earplugs (without earplugs, it's sensory hell), I can actually hear myself think, and I'm hung up on what I've been hung up on for nearly a week now—what I'm going to tell my parents about this plan of mine, without telling them *too* much. Or, more specifically, what I'm going to tell my mom. My dad's a laid-back, quiet guy. He's told me he trusts I'll figure out my future. My mother, however, is and always has been very much up in my business—and she is very in my business on the eventual marriage front.

So far, I've told my parents I'm going to give Imogen, my third-youngest sister, a break from relationship upkeep at the bars and restaurants in the city that stock our whiskey. Immy's a big-time extrovert who's never complained about being the one to periodically pop into the city with her partner, Leo, schmoozing, dropping into our clients' establishments for a bite, leaving them with a fancy thirty-year bottle, a sample case of a new batch we'll be selling soon. She's been doing that happily for years. But Immy just told us two weeks ago that she's pregnant with her first, and with morning sickness having hit hard, the first trimester is taking it out of her. When I told her I'd handle the city runs, she threw her arms around me and burst into happy, relieved tears.

That's what my parents know so far, and it's a solid cover story, not to mention an actual reason it'll work out for me to be in the city on the weekends for the next month. I could get away with that explanation and keep the rest to myself.

But I think I *need* to tell my mom I'm finally kicking off marriage plans, if only to get her off my back. Lately, she's been nearly insufferable in her Help Will Find a Wife campaign, and the tiniest crumb I give is enough for her to picture an entire feast of possibility. For example, I mentioned once, offhandedly a few weeks ago, that it would be helpful if I married someone who didn't hate phones and actually understood social media, and she's been sending me female influencer profiles ever since.

I need her to know I've got it in hand so she lets up a little. I just have to be wise about how much I divulge. If I'm not careful, Juliet and I might find ourselves sharing our cup of coffee tomorrow with a very enthusiastic Isla Orsino wedged between us.

I've got everything in place for me to leave tomorrow. Fest knows how to handle things with the farm and the production side of the distillery. Our tours and tastings run over the weekends like clockwork, thanks to the second oldest of my younger sisters, Celia, who runs them. Logistically, I know everything will be fine.

I just don't know how to tell my mother what I'm going to be up to without inspiring her to even more obsessed levels of interest in my efforts to settle down.

A bottle of open whiskey crosses in front of me, and I pass it along to Demi, wife to Helena, the oldest of my younger sisters, on my right. Demi smiles my way and mouths, *Thanks!*

Just as I turn back, Miranda, my baby sister, sitting to my left, elbows me.

I brace myself for the onslaught of sound and pull out the earplug in my left ear. "What, Mimi?"

She juts her chin toward the kitchen. "Ma wants to talk to you. Says she texted you."

I check my phone and frown in confusion. I didn't feel it vibrate with a text, but there it is: In the kitchen, please.

Sighing, I stand and traipse into the kitchen. Soon as I'm there, I take out the other earplug, then tuck it safely in the small case attached to my keys. I slip it all back in my pocket. "Hi, Ma."

"Hi, Will." Mom's bent over Eleanor's cake, which is covered in fondant, decorating it with tiny edible sugar unicorns and shooting stars. My mother's rheumatoid arthritis isn't going away, but her symptoms get quiet sometimes, and when they do, when her hands are nearly as nimble as they used to be, she goes all out.

After a final shooting star is placed just so, she brushes off her hands. "I have someone I want you to meet."

My stomach sinks. "Ma, no."

"Will, yes." Mom straightens and faces me, nudging away with the back of her wrist a loose wisp of auburn hair threaded with white. "It isn't a lady or gentleman, or, you know, person, I'm trying to fix you up with." She spins the cake stand, inspecting her work. "It's someone even better. It's a *matchmaker.*"

"Jesus Christ."

"William Orsino, you watch your language in my kitchen."

I groan, scrubbing at my neck. "Sorry, Ma. But no match-maker. I don't need a matchmaker—"

"You told me yourself you don't know how you're going to find your someone. This is how! Your father and I met through a matchmaker—"

"A mutual friend at a party is *not* a matchmaker."

Mom sets her hands on her hips. "Fee was only a business friend at the time, and it was a regional networking event. She introduced your father and I because of our mutually compatible interests."

That "business friend" is one of her best gal pals. She and Fee talk on the phone every day.

"This 'networking event,'" I remind her, "involved a lot of whiskey and weed, as I remember the story going."

Mom lets out a prim *hmph* and turns back to Eleanor's cake, adjusting a unicorn. "That's how it went in the seventies when you put a bunch of crunchy people together who were excited about sustainable land cultivation." She spins around. "We're getting off topic."

I fold my arms across my chest, eyebrows arched. "Are we?"

"Oooh." She stomps her foot. "Don't be difficult."

"I'm not trying to be. I'm just trying to tell you I don't want a matchmaker." I sigh, scrubbing my face. "Listen, I know you're worried about me—"

She clasps my hand, a firm, steady squeeze. "I *am* worried about you. I've accepted what you say you want in a partnership from marriage, that you don't expect it to involve love. I respect that. I'd be hypocritical not to—you know that's how your dad and I started out, too. As friends who had a mutually beneficial business interest and mutual interest in the bedroom, too—"

"Ma, please!" I grimace.

She rolls her eyes. "My point is, I'm not trying to push you into something you don't want, Will. I'm trying to push you toward what you keep telling me you want but you don't seem willing to reach for."

"That's because I'm here all the time, working!"

"So take a break and get out of here!" she half yells.

"I am!" I half yell back.

We stare at each other, our faces both flushed, chests rising and falling.

She tips her head. "You are?"

Well, it seems it wasn't so much a matter of finding the right moment to tell her as the right moment finding me. Here goes.

A sigh leaves me. I rake my hands through my hair. "You know how I'm going to start making weekend runs to the city tomorrow?"

Mom's eyes go wide. Her face lights up with hope. "Mm-hmm?"

"I found someone—"

"Ack!" she yelps.

"Not *the* someone."

Mom deflates like a balloon. "Oh."

Eleanor, my niece, bounds in from the dining room, rainbow dress swaying around her, wild strawberry-blond hair topped with a glittery paper crown. "'Scuse me, Nana. Is my cake ready?"

"Yes, sweetheart," Mom says, smoothing my niece's hair out of her face. "Uncle Will is going to bring it in right now. Then we'll put the candles in it and sing!"

Ellie bounds out on a scream of excitement that makes me wince.

As soon as she leaves, Mom rounds on me. "So, who's this person, then? What's the plan? Tell me everything!"

"Ma." I sigh. "It's my business, okay? I just . . . wanted you to know what I was up to, so you can stop your worrying."

"Just a *little* bit of details?" Mom clasps her hands together and gives me big, sad puppy eyes.

I groan. "Ma, don't—"

"Pleeeease, Will? Don't leave your poor old ma in the dark."

"Christ," I mutter.

She swats me on the arm. "Language!" Then she goes back to the big, sad puppy act, hands clasped tight.

I cave. I always cave with my mother. "Fine, but I'm only telling you this, and then no more questions. Promise?"

Mom crosses her heart. "Promise."

"I've found someone who's going to . . . help me . . . find my person." It's the truth, even if it's incomplete. "That's all I'm saying."

Mom's quiet for a few seconds, and then she smiles, wide and pleased as the barn cats after Miranda sneaks them bowls of cream. "Well," she says, gathering up the candles and matches, smiling my way. "I like this plan of yours. It sounds *very* smart."

I frown as I pick up the cake. "Yeah?"

"'Course," she says, patting my cheek. "Finding someone to help you find *your* someone? I had the very same idea."

An exasperated sigh leaves me as I follow her out of the kitchen.

The following morning, I'm frowning at my reflection in my bathroom mirror, inspecting it as I brush my teeth. Celia might be right—I think the beard's gone from semi-neglected to survivalist guy living in a bunker.

I peer down, where Hector, my rescue blue nose pit bull, lies at my feet, head resting on his paws. "Whaddayoufink?" I ask around the toothpaste foam.

Hector lifts his head, tipping it sideways. Then he *harrumph*s and drops his head back to his paws.

"Yeah." I lean over the sink and spit—I've got a sensory thing about having too much toothpaste foam in my mouth—then go back to brushing. "You're right. I'll trim it a bit."

The door to my house bangs open, and I startle so badly, I nearly take out a tonsil with my toothbrush. I glare down at Hector. "Some guard dog you are."

He rolls onto his back and stretches.

"Lazy ass," I mutter.

"Unca Will!" Eleanor shoves the door shut behind her, then skips her way through my home's open concept living, dining, and kitchen area, heading toward the bathroom. "Where ya going?"

"Ellie, do Mum and Mommy know you came here?"

While I was having my coffee and walking through my garden this morning, casually inspecting my veggies, pulling stray weeds, I noticed Helena and Demi's car in the clearing beside my parents' house.

My childhood home is just a couple of hundred feet from my place, which is a former carriage house that I fixed up and made my own when I moved back after college. Helena and Demi stay over at Mom and Dad's when they hang around late and have a couple of drinks and driving back to their place in town above their boutique skin-care and soap shop wouldn't be safe. I'm not worried that Eleanor's still here on the property, just that she left the house and has a tendency to wander off without telling people where she's wandering off to.

My niece is walking my home's floorboards, lost in concentration, her small feet carefully avoiding the cracks. After one more step, Eleanor hops into my bathroom and smiles up at me. Then she crouches, scratching Hector's stomach. He groans happily and wiggles on his back.

"Ellie," I say again. "Do Mum and Mommy know you're here?"

Finally she peers up at me, face scrunched in thought. "Nooo, but they were sleeping. So I couldn't tell them."

I give her a look. "You're not supposed to leave your house without telling someone where you're going."

"It's not my house," she counters.

I sigh. "The house you're staying in, I meant."

"I told Nana," she says, starting to climb the narrow threshold of my bathroom, hands and bare feet pressed against both sides of the doorframe.

"So Nana's awake," I say.

"'Course she is." Ellie gives up on climbing, scrambles onto the toilet, and stands behind me. She reaches for my hair, quickly starting to braid a chunk in the back. "I woke her up. Then we got Hal because he was woke up, too."

Hal, my nephew, is Ellie's two-year-old little brother.

"Nana already make you pancakes?"

"Yep! With rainbow sprinkles. But don't tell Mum or Mommy. Nana says it's our sugar secret."

I mime a zipper dragged across my mouth. "My lips are sealed."

"So." Eleanor tugs my hair, and I wince. "Where you goin'?"

I peer at her in the mirror, her tongue stuck out in concentration as she braids, or more accurately, tangles my hair together. "Ellie, did Nana send you here to ask me that?"

Eleanor makes a wide-eyed *busted* face she doesn't realize I can see in the mirror, her gaze still stuck on my hair. "Ummmm. No!"

I gently reach for her hands, stopping them. "That's a nice braid you did. But I need to get going, so no more braids today."

She leaps onto my back, clinging like a koala. "Mm-kay. So. Where ya goin'?"

"Down to the city. And that's all the details you *and* Nana are getting."

She slides off my back and skips over to my open duffel, which sits on the dining table, ready for me to add my toiletry bag. Poking around its contents, she wrinkles her nose. "Where's the shirt I gave you? You didn't pack it?"

I hesitate, trying to figure out how to get myself out of this.

Eleanor loves giving gifts. Especially on days when *she* gets gifts—at Christmas, on her birthday. Yesterday, after opening her birthday presents, she passed around *her* presents for everyone and very enthusiastically gifted me an eye-singeing burnt-orange button-up.

I'm not an orange-shirt guy. I'm not an orange-clothes *anything*. I'm a ginger. I've got enough orange going on as it is.

"Well, uh . . ." I scratch at my jaw. "Actually . . ." I clear my throat. "I didn't pack it because . . . I was going to . . . wear it today?"

Her gray-green eyes, the same shade as mine, as Dad's and Helena's and my baby sister Miranda's, go saucer-wide. "You are!?" She shrieks in excitement, hopping up and down.

And that's how, thirty minutes later, I find myself, wearing a brand-new burnt-orange button-up, driving down the road.

SEVEN

Juliet

I might be late to meet Will, and it's all my clothes' fault. Nothing looked right, fit right, felt right. I tried on twelve outfits before I settled on a soft, flowy lavender sundress that's comfy and pairs well with my pink and purple flower-print sneakers—a new wardrobe staple to give my joints as much support as possible when I traipse around. But even now, I'm not sure it was the right pick. I'm paler than I like to be when I wear pastel purple, thanks to one of my medications, which has increased my skin's photosensitivity, and the neckline's low and boobier than I remember it being. Not that I'm ashamed to show off the girls; I'm just not sure if it's the vibe I want for my first date—*practice* date!—with Will.

I might be spiraling a little.

I don't know why I'm a ball of nerves, why I woke up jittery, overthinking everything from how much creamer I wanted in my coffee to how to wear my hair. It's just a practice date. It's just Will.

Will, the very hot, very endearing cutie I'm going to spend the next four weekends practicing romance with.

Will, whom I honestly want to do very filthy things with but won't, because we're going to keep this romance practice regimen strictly G-rated.

Or maybe PG. I mean, maybe a handsy kiss and hug goodbye

here and there wouldn't be the worst. Come to think of it, that might be essential material to cover.

I shake my head and blow out a deep breath as I cross the street. I don't need to get hung up on those hypotheticals. Right now, I need to get to the coffee shop, to Will. We'll figure out the rest together. And while we do that, I'll keep reminding myself why I'm going to be just fine practicing romance with a man I am very, very attracted to: Will Orsino's got his eyes set on marrying not for love but for family duty; he's near and dear to Christopher; in other words, he's completely off-limits.

I'm not going to fall for someone who's not looking for love. I might not be ready for love yet, but one day, I hope I'll find it again, with someone who wants love, too. And I'm not going to fall for another one of Christopher's friends. While I know not every friend of Christopher's is my ex—Will thus far has proved to be his antithesis—my ex and Christopher were close, professionally at least, then personally, when he and I started dating, and when everything between us blew up, it hurt not just me but Christopher, too. I've sworn to myself I'll never again get tangled up romantically with someone close to the important people in my life. The potential fallout is too messy, the risk of collateral damage too high.

Considering all that, Will is the safest person I could have chosen as my practice romance pal. With Will, I'm safe—from the risk of falling in love, of heartbreak—and my romance reawakening can finally begin.

So why, even with that reassurance front and center in my thoughts, am I so damn nervous?

As I walk down the sidewalk, I set a hand on my stomach, where butterflies are whipping around wilder than Puck when he gets the zoomies and tears through the house.

And suddenly, it hits me—this kind of nervousness is good.

I'm *supposed* to have butterflies in my stomach. These are exactly the kinds of feelings I want to get comfortable with again.

All morning, I told myself I was getting ready to go practice. I should have realized the moment I woke up that practice was already here.

Breathing deeply again, I open the door to the coffee shop and instantly spot Will, head bent over what looks like a piece of paper, holding a pencil that he moves haltingly across it. A crossword, maybe? He's seated in a cozy corner, the one farthest from the coffee bar, and he's wearing a burnt-orange shirt, its color honestly the last one I would have picked for a man with hair like his, but somehow it works. It *really* works. He looks . . . striking, everything else fading around him, like a fire's flames against a dark night.

Slowly, I weave my way toward him through the tables, those butterflies swirling through me.

It's good, Juliet, a quiet voice says in my head. *It's good.*

I smile. Because, for the first time in so many months, I believe that voice.

When I get to his table, I stop. Will's head is still bent, his pencil moving over what I now see is a sudoku puzzle.

My smile widens. I set my purse on the table and tell him, "I was so sure you were doing the crossword."

He jerks upright, like I've startled him, and blinks up at me. His gaze dances down my body. He swallows thickly, totally silent. And then he shoots out of his seat.

"Hi." He offers me his hand.

I blink, taken off guard. Will immediately yanks it back and shoves his hands in his pockets. "I just flubbed that so bad," he mutters miserably. "A *handshake*? What the hell is wrong with me?"

"Will—"

"Can I have a do-over?" He presses his hands together, holding my eyes. "Please."

ONCE SMITTEN, TWICE SHY · 75

I'm torn. I want to reassure him, tell a little white lie that he didn't flub it to make him feel better.

But I shouldn't lie to him, not when he wants to get better at this. Will and I owe each other the chance to actually get better, and that means we have to make space for not just our successes but also our struggles.

I don't tell him he flubbed it, but I don't disagree, either. I just say, "Rewind time."

Then I reach for my purse and slide it onto my shoulder. I take a quick glance behind me, making sure the path is clear, before I start walking backward. I walk backward through the whole coffee shop, to the door, whose handle I fumble with a little bit as I reach behind me to open it. I whip open the door, step outside, and let it fall shut.

Through the glass door, I see Will standing in his cozy corner, this bewildered expression on his face that's tinged with . . . I'm not sure what, but I think it just might be amusement.

I smile at him, then wave my hand, gesturing that he should sit.

He does. My smile widens. Then I whip open the door to walk in. Take two.

More confident than last time, a lot less shaky, I stroll through the restaurant. This time, Will watches me the whole way, his eyes holding mine.

When I get to the table, he stands, smoother than last time, calmer.

"Juliet," he says, his gaze dancing over me. "Hi."

I smile. "Hi, Will."

He clears his throat. "I'm not going to offer you a handshake this time."

I bite my lip. "Okay."

"But . . ." He clears his throat again. "I'm not exactly sure what I *should* offer you."

"What feels right?" I ask. "What's your gut instinct?"

He scrubs at the back of his neck. "We're not total strangers, but if we were, my gut instinct would be to stand, pull out a chair for you to sit, then push it in."

"Gentlemanly," I tell him. "I like it."

"But we're not strangers," he says, his eyes holding mine. "We've talked enough, we're comfortable enough with each other that . . . well, a hug hello, that's my instinct. I'd ask first, of course."

My smile deepens. This man. "Go on and ask me, then."

He blows out a breath. "Juliet, can I hug you hello?"

"Yes, please." I step around my corner of the table and right into his arms.

Will wraps himself gently around me in a brief, sweet hug. Perfect for a first-date greeting.

I lightly rest my arms around his broad back and breathe him in. He smells so darn good, and there go those butterflies again. I smile to myself, my cheek brushing his soft cotton shirt, and sigh. He lets go, and I make myself pull away. "That was delightful," I tell him.

"Yeah?"

"Yeah." I spy an eyelash I left on the pocket of his shirt and swipe it off with my fingers.

He glances down, frowning.

"Just cleaning up after myself," I tell him. "An eyelash." I blow it off my fingertip, for good luck. "I like the shirt. It's really handsome on you."

His cheeks turn bright pink. Gah, what is it about a man who blushes?

"Don't flatter me," he says, pulling out my chair. "I look like a pumpkin."

I laugh as I sit and he pushes in my chair. "You do not! I wouldn't lie to you. We promised to be honest with each other, and I'm sticking to my word. I really do think it suits you."

Will sits across from me and gives me a skeptical look. "We can agree to disagree, then. I feel like a gourd in this thing."

"Then why are you wearing it?"

"My niece," he says, pushing the sudoku aside.

"Your niece?"

He nods. "She gave it to me yesterday. And then she was around this morning when I was packing up, getting ready to leave . . . I didn't really have a choice."

My heart does a somersault. "You mean she wanted you to wear it, and you're too big of a softie to say no."

He grumbles under his breath, turning the pencil for his sudoku between his fingers.

"Will, that's a compliment." I lean in over the table, lowering my voice. "That's the stuff you tell the lady you're trying to romance. It's very attractive."

Will's head snaps up. "How?"

I sit back in my chair. "You put your ego aside to do something kind for a little person who loves you. That's a major green flag."

A milk steamer screeches on the other side of the table as a throng of people jostles past us, quickly filling up the large round table nearby. They're a rowdy bunch, teens basking in their summertime freedom, talking loud and laughing. The volume in the place instantly doubles.

Will slips a hand beneath his hair and seems to fiddle around his ear.

That's when I remember the earplugs he was wearing when we met at the pub. His sensitivity to noise.

Dammit, I should have thought of that when I suggested where we meet up for coffee. Somewhere with a quiet back patio and outdoor seating would have been much better.

Will forces what I think is meant to be a smile but can only be construed as a grimace. He's trying to muscle his way through it. But he shouldn't have to.

I clasp my purse and slide it back onto my shoulder. "What do you say we get our coffees to go?"

————

Something happens between leaving the table and making our way toward the counter. My nerves are back, and not the swoony butterfly ones—these feel like a swarm of bees stinging my insides, making my hands tingle, my heart race.

Where has my capacity for small talk gone? Why does my smile feel like a rictus on my face? And I thought I was spiraling *before* I got here.

"What is it?" Will asks quietly.

I peer up to see him frowning down at me, concern etched in his expression.

"I, um . . ." I force a swallow down my throat. "I don't exactly know. I think I'm just . . . feeling pretty rusty, right now."

Will slows his walk, his eyes holding mine. "What can I do?"

My heart pinches at his kindness. "Not sure there's really anything to be done," I admit. "Just . . . maybe reassure me I'm not alone?"

"Well, I'd like to reassure you I'm feeling rusty, too," he says. "But remember, I've got nothing to rust."

I nudge him with my shoulder. "Stop it."

He gently nudges me back, peering down at me. "I might not be rusty like you, Juliet, but I am feeling pretty wobbly, even with those training wheels we just put on."

"Yeah," I say quietly. "*Wobbly* is a good word for it."

He dips his head a little, leaning in, and whether he meant to or not, the backs of his knuckles brush against mine. "Some wise woman told me we'd wobble together."

Another swallow rolls down my throat, but this one feels easier. A full, deep breath fills my lungs. I hook my pinkie with his. "She does sound wise. But she also might sometimes find it easier to preach something than to practice it."

He squeezes my pinkie gently, then lets go. "Well, I'll be happy to remind her sometimes, that she's not the only one wobbling. If that helps."

I nod. "I think that would help a lot."

"Can I help the next person?" a voice behind the counter yells.

Will and I both glance forward and in silent agreement move up a few feet to get in line.

I set a hand on my stomach as it grumbles, and I realize the swarm of bees is gone, the only sensation left a sharp hunger, after having skipped breakfast, thanks to my nervous tummy. I scour the display case of baked goods, exploring my options. Thankfully, Boulangerie has a case of gluten-free pastries that are always well stocked.

The line moves up, and the person in front of us orders a drip coffee. I reach in my purse for my phone, so I'm ready to tap and pay after ordering. As I tug it out, my hand catches on the flap of my romance novel, yanking that out, too, and sending it tumbling to the floor.

Will ducks and scoops it up before I've even begun to crouch, then stands just as the person in front of us moves aside. I'm about to thank him, but the words die on my tongue when he sets a hand on my back and gently guides me forward.

A bolt of pleasure zips down my spine.

"You first," he says, eyes narrowed on the menu.

I order an iced oat milk vanilla latte and a gluten-free lemon bar. Will orders a blueberry muffin and a cold brew. I step aside to wait first, making sure to pick the side of the coffee bar farthest from the screeching milk steamers, near the front door.

Will's still holding my romance novel, and I offer my hand to take it. "Thanks for grabbing that for me."

He glances down at the book, then up at me. "Oh, sure."

I take the historical romance, slip it back into my purse, and smile. "Can't go anywhere without a trusty romance."

"What made you start reading them?" he asks. "The romance novels?"

I'm relieved to hear curiosity and none of the condescension I often get when asked about reading this genre, one lots of people disparage as trivial and unliterary. Not that I expected him to be dismissive of romance, given he seemed on board with reading it back when we formed our plan last week. Still, there's a difference between indulging someone and engaging them. It's nice to know he's doing the latter.

"Because they make me happy," I tell him. "I've only realized it recently, but I've struggled with anxiety for a long time; even before I understood what I was dealing with, I think I gravitated toward romance novels because they never made me anxious, because I could always count on a happily ever after. Even when things get rough in the story, it always worked out. That reliability is really comforting. And . . . I love love. Friend love. Family love. Romantic love. Romance novels celebrate all of that."

He nods. "What do you read more of? Historical or contemporary?"

"Historical," I tell him. "But I'd be up for buddy-reading a contemporary with you, if you're still interested."

A couple with a baby stroller is coming right toward me, cutting the corner around the coffee bar awfully close. I'm just glancing around to figure out where I can move so I won't get mowed over, when Will steps close and plants himself right beside me, his hand hovering at my back, so they have to go around us.

Those butterflies are back, swirling in my stomach. So many butterflies.

"You think that's a better choice?" he asks.

I blink, snapped out of my swoon. "Contemporary romance? Definitely. At least, for the purpose of exploring how modern-day flirting and romance can play out." I grin up at him. "Unless you plan on wooing your future wife by waltzing in ballrooms and taking her on courtly carriage rides through the countryside."

Will peers down at me, his eyes crinkling. I can't tell if there's a smile beneath that thick beard, but it feels like a win all the same.

The barista shouts our names, breaking the moment. In two long strides, Will steps into the throng of people waiting for their orders, grabbing both our drinks and pastry bags with one smooth swipe of his big hands. I manage to slip my way through the crowd, Will close behind me, until we're finally outside, greeted by birdsong and the hum of Saturday morning traffic.

"There are some café tables across the street in the park," I tell him. "Want to head over there?"

Will frowns down at the pigeons starting to hop around us. He doesn't answer me.

"Will?"

"I'll eat wherever," he says, still watching the pigeons. "As long as these flying rats aren't nearby."

"Flying rats!" I gasp. "They are not *flying rats*. Pigeons are adorable."

"Adorable," he grumbles, shimmying past me as a pigeon waddles toward him.

"Will, are you . . . *afraid* of pigeons?"

"No," he barks, before hopping back as another pigeon waddles toward him.

"Shoo!" I say to the pigeons, waving them away. They flutter up into the air and land farther down the sidewalk. "See? All taken care of."

Will gives me a narrow-eyed look. "I had it in hand."

"Sure you did." I step closer to him, smiling wide as I loop my arm through his. "Now, let's go claim that empty table across the street. I promise, I'll keep the pigeons at bay."

EIGHT

Will

I've never done this before, outside of business at least—sat across the table from a woman besides my sisters and mother and talked with her, one-on-one.

I've had my share of experience with women over the years, women who *weren't* looking for romance, who wanted physicality and nothing else. But this is different. I'm physically attracted to Juliet, and that is familiar, but . . . the longer I sit here, the more I feel this attraction snowballing as it rolls down the hill of minutes passing while we talk. This is how I've experienced attraction, and yet it isn't *just* that. It's more.

I find myself breathing in not just Juliet's faint floral scent but the sound of her laugh, mingling with the warm July wind; counting every point of contact between our bodies, knees bumping under the table, her hand brushing mine as she picks up the pencil and tries her hand at my sudoku, yet the number that stands out is how many times she's smiled since we sat down.

Six times. Each of them bigger and brighter.

"That has to be eight!" she yells, jabbing at the paper.

"You're rushing," I tell her. "It *could* be eight. You've got to rule out all the other numbers that could be in that box, too. You only know eight goes there when you've figured out nothing else does. It's process of elimination. Takes patience."

She chucks the pencil on the table and harrumphs. "Patience is not my strong suit."

I set a hand over my mouth so I won't laugh. She's too damn cute. "Sudoku is not an ideal first-date game. Noted."

A pigeon hops toward us, and Juliet leans off her chair, shooing it away. "At least not with me."

Another pigeon waddles toward us, on her other side. Juliet turns and shoos that one away, too.

I grimace. "They're surrounding us."

Juliet turns back to me and sighs. "Yeah, they kind of are. Want to move on? Take a walk?"

I shoot out of my seat, slipping the pencil in my shirt pocket, folding the sudoku in half and stuffing it in my jeans. "Ready when you are."

Juliet stands, a small groan leaving her as she does. I frown, a pinch of worry in my chest. Is she sore? Hurting?

"So." She curls her hand around my biceps as we start to walk. "How do you want to do this?"

I peer down at her. "How do I want to do what?"

"Practice," she says. "How meta do you want it to be? Do you want to just ... do it?"

My cheeks heat. "Um ... what is ... *it*?"

Juliet's eyes widen. She slaps a hand to her forehead. "Rusty moment. I didn't mean to sound like I meant that we should, you know, *do it*. I meant *just do it* as in, just go on dates and do our thing. Or, instead, do you want to *talk* about it as we go?"

My cheeks are still hot. I clear my throat. "Right, gotcha." I think about the last time we talked about what we were doing, when she walked in and I choked and offered her a handshake hello. How she made it easier for me to weather that embarrassment by being a goofball herself, rewinding across the coffee shop, giving me a second chance.

Her playfulness helped me not get hung up on it, but the fact that I flubbed it and we both talked about it, well, it stung my pride, I can admit that. All of this stings my pride a bit. I don't like doing things I'm bad at. It's always been easier to tell myself that if I think I'm bad at something, I don't want it, that it's not something I care about.

But it's not that simple. That's why I'm here, practicing with her right now.

It's going to take getting used to, talking it through with her, revealing these parts of myself that I usually keep tucked away tight. It feels like that time I was going through airport security and my luggage was randomly selected for an in-depth search. I had nothing to be ashamed of or incriminating, but it still felt uncomfortable and raw as I watched my suitcase being flung open, my private contents dragged out for all to see.

I'm not used to that feeling, especially with a woman I'm attracted to. But that doesn't mean it's bad. It just means it's . . . hard.

She squeezes my arm. "Where'd you go?"

"Sorry. I'm . . . thinking through my answer."

"Take your time," she says. "I'm not going anywhere."

Juliet tips her head back to glance above us. I glance up, too, just briefly. The last thing I want is to trip on the sidewalk when I've got Juliet hanging on my arm.

The trees overhead sway in the breeze, lime-green leaves, mud-brown branches, dancing against the sky. I have a vivid memory of walking this stretch of the city when I first moved here for college, peering up and watching the leaves wave in the wind, a gemstone tapestry of peridot tipped with gold, bronze, and ruby. Just the beginning of autumn that would never quite match the grandeur of fall upstate but was lovely in its own way.

My gaze slips down to Juliet, her eyes still set on the sky. She looks so peaceful, so reflective. I want to know what she's thinking, feeling, wondering. I want to know so much.

The only way I'll learn any of that is if we talk, if I'm brave and I put myself out there, the way she is. And she *is* brave. I've been harboring an adolescent grudge that made me write off romance my entire adult life. Based on what she told me, she went through hell with the person she loved just last year, and here she is, already trying to come around to romance again.

Juliet's being brave, and dammit, I'm going to be, too.

"I think we should do a little of both," I finally tell her.

She glances my way, her eyes fixed on me as she listens.

"I think the default," I tell her, "should be we both just . . . go for it. But when I'm struggling—"

"When *either* of us is struggling," she says.

"I'm the one learning to ride the bike," I remind her.

She lifts her eyebrows. "And I'm the one who's going to fall off it."

I nod, conceding that. "When *either* of us is struggling, we get meta, we talk about it. How's that sound?"

Juliet smiles. "I think that sounds perfect."

I stare at her as she glances back at the sky, drawn by the sound of two birds arcing and weaving toward the clouds. The wind snaps her hair around her face. I want to run my hands through it, feel it cool and soft across my fingers.

She catches me staring at her and tips her head. "What is it?"

I stare at her, the sun sparkling in her eyes, dark hair whipping in the wind, those soft dimples always waiting in her cheeks. "You just look . . . real lovely."

Her cheeks turn a faint rosy pink. She turns and stares ahead, watching where she's walking. "Yeesh, that got me good. Excellent practice flirtation."

I don't tell her I didn't even mean to say it, that my brain was thinking it and my mouth just said it.

I don't tell her I wasn't trying to practice at all.

———

"What's your favorite season?" I ask.

We're walking toward her place, after I started to feel her slowing down on our stroll around the park. I offered to drive her home, but Juliet said the day is too beautiful to spend in a car. So instead, I'm walking her home—she doesn't live far from the coffee shop where we met.

She peers up at me. "My favorite season? Spring."

"Why?"

She smiles my way as we turn the corner onto the next block, passing a stretch of hedges that stand like sentinels protecting towering brownstones. "It's the season of hope and new beginnings," she says. "The promise of life turning lighter and lovelier. Green grass and fresh flowers everywhere and lush gardens. I'm a sucker for flowers and gardens, though all I can swing at the apartment is a few window boxes and some houseplants. What about you?"

An image jumps into my head—Juliet walking through the wildflower field back home, past the cultivated gardens, up the path to my house. Standing beneath the rose and wisteria trellis that flanks the pavers leading to my front door. I swallow thickly. "Spring," I tell her quietly. "Spring's my favorite, too."

She smiles. "Spring supremacy. Thank you!"

The door of the next house—on second glance, building—down swings open, drawing Juliet's attention, and the smile drops from her face.

And that's when Juliet yanks me into the hedges.

NINE

Juliet

I'm not thinking. I'm reacting. Out of sheer panic.

Will and I tumble through the hedges, their prickly branches grazing my skin.

I yank him down with me because while I can manage to hide by crouching a little, he's so tall, his head pokes out above the hedges. I had to pick a giant to practice romance with.

"Juliet, what are you—"

"That's my sister," I hiss at him. "And *Christopher*."

Will spits a leaf out of his mouth. "I thought we agreed there'd be no sneaking around."

"Well," I whisper, "I didn't exactly expect them to come waltzing out of my apartment right when we were headed toward it!"

"Your apartment?" He frowns. "Why were they in your apartment?"

"Who knows," I mutter while trying to peek through the hedges. I can't see a damn thing. "They've got keys to the place; maybe they needed something I had while they were in the city that would be a pain to catch the train back to Christopher's house to get? That's not the point, though."

"What *is* the point?" he asks. Unlike me, he is *not* whispering.

"Shh," I hiss. "Talk softer. They'll hear you!"

Will sighs heavily.

I listen for footsteps, the sound of Kate's and Christopher's voices. No footsteps, their voices getting no louder. They must be stopped in front of the apartment. I don't know why. What I do know is it's darn inconvenient. My knees ache so badly when I crouch like this.

Will plops fully onto the ground and tucks his legs in, criss-cross applesauce. It puts him very much in my space. "Come on. Sit," he whispers, nodding down at his lap. "If we're going to hide here like bandits, might as well be comfortable."

I eye his lap, my knees throbbing. The thought of sitting sounds so much better, but I vividly remember from our little tussle in the greenhouse last week what kind of heat that man's packing between his thighs, how great it felt, just for a split second.

Sitting on his lap is a bad idea.

"I'm fine," I whisper.

He gives me a stern look. "You're sore," he says quietly. "I saw you groan when you got up from the café table. You were limping a little on the walk home."

Humiliation whines out from my pricked-pride balloon. He noticed.

"Will it feel better to sit?" he asks. "Tell the truth." Will leans in a little, his voice even softer. "We're being honest with each other, remember? You *pinkie promised*."

Dammit. On a huff, I plop down on his lap.

"There," I whisper sourly. "Happy now?"

He shrugs. "Hiding like we're criminals aside, yes."

I cross my arms over my chest, sulking, annoyed that he picked up on my aches and pains, that Will has now become another person who fusses over me. "I feel like a kid in her dad's lap at story time."

"I mean, I think it's a *little* soon for you to be calling me *Daddy*, but . . ."

I gape in shock and glance over my shoulder.

Will's got a hand over his mouth, and his cheeks have turned bright red. He drops his hand just long enough to whisper hoarsely, "Thinking thought. Shouldn't have been a talking thought."

I bite my lip, trying so hard not to laugh. I have to stay quiet. I clap a hand over my mouth, too, as a laugh threatens to squeak out.

We manage to stay silent for a few seconds as I listen for Kate's and Christopher's voices again. They're no louder, no quieter. They're *still* standing outside my apartment.

Suddenly, Will's phone starts to ring. Thankfully its sound is muffled by my butt, but it's still too loud.

"Will!" I whisper-shout, glancing at him again over my shoulder. "Silence it!"

He gives me wide, panicked eyes. "I can't!" he hisses. "You're on my lap!"

"Oh, whose brilliant idea was that?" I hiss back.

He blows out a frustrated breath. "Reach in my left pocket, would you? Just hit the button on the side to silence it."

I hesitate. His pocket is way too close to the very generous part of him I'm trying not to think about, wedged snugly against my butt. "Can't you?"

He gives me an annoyed look as he whispers, "And risk groping you in the process? No, thanks. Even *I* know that's not first-date material."

I press myself harder against his phone as it rings again, trying to smother it with my butt cheeks. "We're not practicing anything right now! Just silence it!"

"Absolutely not," he whispers.

"Christ almighty!" I lean on my right butt cheek so I can reach his pocket and shove my hand behind me, feeling around. My fingers connect with something big and thick, but definitely not rectangular-shaped. I freeze. "That's not your phone, is it?"

Will swallows audibly. "It is not."

I yank my hand back like it's been burned, but Will clasps my wrist, guiding it much farther left, until my fingertips brush the edge of a pocket. "There," he says. "Right there."

Trying my best not to hear how that sounds very much like a command he'd give me in a much more pleasurable setting, I shove my hand inside the pocket, find his phone, and frantically jab at the buttons on the side until it's silent.

Two seconds later, it starts to buzz.

"Take it out," he says, his voice hoarse and urgent. "Please."

That double entendre, I can't get past. I choke on a snort, trying my best to swallow the sound. "But an ass grope is too far for a first date?"

"Juliet," Will growls soft and low in his throat. "I meant the *phone*."

Sensing he just might be at the end of his rope and knowing this whole ridiculous situation is my doing, I reach back into his pocket and pull out his phone, which is lighting up with another call. At least this time, it's only buzzing.

I tap the button on the side to silence it, and my gaze catches on the screen—an up-close portrait of a woman who looks to be in her fifties, maybe sixties, her upswept strawberry-blond hair streaked with white, big amber eyes crinkled with deep laugh lines as she smiles at the camera. *Ma* it says across the top.

"Your mom's so pretty," I whisper.

Will sighs. "She's pretty, all right. Pretty damn persistent."

Suddenly Kate's and Christopher's voices turn louder. I hear the familiar stomp of Kate's Doc Martens, Christopher's long, heavy strides landing beside hers.

I set a finger to my mouth and stare up pleadingly at Will. He doesn't respond, just gazes down at me wearily.

Finally, their voices pass us; the sound of their footsteps fades.

I blow out a breath I didn't realize I was holding and scramble upright clumsily. I'm too desperate to put distance between us to care that I look as unsteady as I feel.

Will jumps up gracefully after me, just how he did at the greenhouse last week, like a big jungle cat, smooth and powerful. The total opposite of my ungainly effort. I'd be irritated if I didn't find it so hot.

We stare at each other for a beat, breathing a little heavily. I flash him a smile that I hope turns that frown upside down.

It doesn't.

"That was an adventure," I tell him.

Will straightens to his full height and glances over the hedges. "They're gone."

"Thank goodness." I shove through the hedges, brushing leaves and dirt off my dress. "Sorry about that. I know it was less than ideal."

Will tugs a leaf out of his beard, eyebrows arched high. "Less than ideal?"

"Okay, it was a shit show," I admit. "I'm sorry, I panicked. I didn't want them to see us when the only explanation for us being together is something we both agreed we're going to keep to ourselves."

Crossing his arms over his chest, Will peers down at me and lets out a heavy sigh. "I understand."

My anxiety drains fifty percent. "You do?"

"I didn't like that we had to hide, but I understand." He drops his arms. "We've got to figure out how to be honest without telling the whole truth. Then, if this happens again, we'll be prepared."

I nod. "You're right."

Will squints up at the sky, brow furrowed, as he slides his hands into his pockets. "I told Petruchio I'll be coming into town on weekends this month, dropping in on bars and restaurants that stock our whiskey to drop off samples and pitch a new fifteen-year we're rolling out. So I have an explanation for being here."

My eyes widen. "Wow, that's a good explanation."

"It's also the truth," he says.

"Even better." I smile. "Do you normally do that?"

"Nah. I do best staying put at home, keeping things running there." He swats away a bee that's started circling his head. "My sister Immy, it's her gig, but she's as sick as a dog right now. First pregnancy, first trimester. She needed a break. I figured I could take a turn and handle it for a while, even if I'm shit at it compared to her."

My heart pirouettes in my chest as I stare at him. First his niece and the orange shirt. Now this. He talks about these choices he makes out of care and love for his family so matter-of-factly, like it's that simple, like doing for others, even when it's outside his comfort zone, is just what's done.

Will catches me staring at him.

I clutch my forearm and wave that arm's hand.

He frowns, clearly confused.

"Another green flag moment," I explain.

"Ah." He scrubs at his neck. "Well, anyway. That's my explanation for why I'm here. So we're set on that front. What we have to figure out is how we'll explain *us* spending time together."

An idea creeps up in my head as I stand nearly toe-to-toe with Will:

Friendship between us, not just in the context of our romance practice, which we're keeping to ourselves, but friendship that *everyone* could see. It would be the perfect explanation for us spending time together, if we bumped into any more friends and family around the city.

The sun jumps out between the clouds, hot and bright. I need to get inside soon, so I won't burn, but for a moment, I let myself enjoy that illuminating warmth, the sense that it's some kind of approving sign from the universe, a reassurance that I'm doing this right.

"Will," I finally say, hand held over my eyes like a visor as I peer up at him. "I think I have our solution."

———————

Seated on my apartment's stoop, beneath the maple tree shading us, Will and I talk through my idea. As we talk, he drags his fingers along his beard, gaze trained somewhere in the distance.

With him staring straight ahead, I have an unadulterated view of his profile. I let my gaze travel his nose, long and straight but for a slight bump on the bridge that lends a rough edge to a face that, were it not half-obscured by his beard, I have a hunch is so good-looking the only word that comes to mind is *beautiful*. Light bounces off his sharp cheekbones, which are dappled with freckles.

Those damn freckles.

"So, what you're saying is . . ." His voice startles me out of my stare, which I hope he didn't notice. If he did, Will doesn't let on. "If I spend time with you around your and Petruchio's mutual friends, and your sisters, no one will think anything of us hanging out one-on-one."

"Exactly."

He nods, fingers still combing through his beard. "And we would shelve the romance stuff when we're with them, right?"

"Right. That way they just perceive us as friends. Which, of course, is all we are!" I add brightly.

Will's gaze slides my way. His mouth lifts faintly at the corner. "Of course."

We're sitting shoulder to shoulder, and somewhere along the way, I started leaning into him. My body is wiped from an active morning, from the heat, which is intense even though we're in the shade. I'm too exhausted to care, to make myself push off of him and straighten up. I trust Will to give me some cue if he's uncomfortable with me slumping into him. We promised to be honest with each other, after all.

I notice him watching me, a little notch of what might be concern in his brow, and flash him a smile that I hope makes me look perkier than I feel. "So, how does that plan sound to you?" I ask. "I'm all ears if you want to go at it from a different angle."

The wind picks up, and it's glorious, cutting through my dress, cooling everywhere it clings to my sweaty skin. I shut my eyes for a second and bask in it.

My eyes snap open when I feel Will's touch at the corner of my mouth, his finger brushing my lip as he drags away a strand of hair that the wind stuck it to.

"That plan suits me fine," he says.

I swallow as I stare up at him, my body hot and achy. And not because I'm sitting on a concrete step at noon in July. But because I love when he touches me. I want him to touch me so much more.

Off. Limits, that wise voice reminds me.

I nod to that wisdom, to Will's agreement with my plan. "Good. Great."

"Only thing is," he says, "for that to work, I'd need to start socializing with them—"

"As soon as possible."

He nods.

"I was thinking that, too. How do you feel about game nights? I'm hosting one tomorrow. We'd need to figure out how we get you there without me being the one to invite you, but I'm sure we'll think of something. Shouldn't make for a late drive home for you either; we wrap up by nine when we have them on Sundays. Everyone's got to get up for work the next day."

Will's eyes are on my mouth as he nods. "Mm-hmm."

My gaze slips to his mouth, too. A mouth I have maybe possibly thought about kissing today. A lot. A cyclist whizzes by on the street, startling us both. Our eyes snap up and meet each other's.

"Let's get you inside," Will says. His voice is rough at the edges.

I blink, confused. "Why?"

"Because you're hot and tired." He eases upright and offers me his hand. "And because I think we've done plenty for our first day."

"I'm not tired," I pout, slapping my hand into his.

He arches an eyebrow. "Pinkie promise?"

I scrunch my face up at him as I stand. Well, more like twenty-five percent is me standing, seventy-five percent is his gentle tug that gets me upright. "I might be slightly fatigued," I say loftily.

His mouth quirks up at the corner. "I'd say you've earned yourself a nap. I know I've earned mine, after that hiding-in-the-hedge ordeal you put me through."

I shove his arm playfully. "I told you I was sorry!"

My knee gives out when it always does—when I least expect it to. I'm dropping fast, bracing to hit the ground, but Will's faster, freakishly fast for such a big guy. In a blur of orange button-up and sun-bleached blue jeans, he's swept me into his arms like a bride.

With our height discrepancy, I've never been this close to his face. So close, I can see every silvery fleck in his pale green eyes, every spiky auburn eyelash, how the tips fade to bronze and then gold.

I swallow so hard, the sound echoes in my head. "I'm okay," I whisper.

Relief and raw embarrassment flood me in tandem. This isn't the first time this has happened. But it's the first time it's happened in front of someone who doesn't know me, and worse, whom I'm attracted to.

Will's eyes bounce between mine. He's breathing heavily. "You sure?"

I force a smile. "Yep."

"Juliet, you just collapsed," he presses.

"Yes, Will, I'm aware." I sound snippy, and it's because I'm feeling snippy. I don't like being babied or fussed over. I'm the oldest sister. *I'm* the one who babies and fusses over others. "I'm steady now," I tell him. "You can put me down."

He narrows his eyes. He does not put me down. "You swear?"

"Yes."

He doesn't push back, doesn't doubt me, smoothly lowering me so I can stand. But he might have been right to. Because my knee wobbles again.

He starts to bend again. "I'm carrying you."

"No, wait!" I clutch his arm. If he sweeps me up in his arms again, I'm going to swoon so hard I might *actually* collapse. "Just . . . let me hold your arm, and you can walk me inside, okay? It's not like I'm going to faint. It's just my knee. It gets wobbly sometimes."

Will frowns down at me and sighs. "All right."

I hook my arm in his and grip tight, then turn toward the front door, Will right there with me. Holding on to his arm, I unearth my keys from my purse and slide my key into the lock. Will reaches for the door and tugs it open as soon as I pull out my key.

We take the stairs slowly, Will following my lead on our pace.

"Where are you staying?" I ask.

"A little studio apartment not too far from here. A family friend's," he says. "She used to live there, above her business, but now she's got a house. It's usually an Airbnb, but she said it's mine as long as I need it."

"That's great." I glance up.

When we get to my door, I slide my key into the lock, then turn his way and force a smile. "Well, thank you, again."

"Thank *you*," he says. "This was . . . I think it was a pretty strong first day."

My smile morphs into something genuine. "I think so, too. You know, besides the hedgerow ordeal and my damsel-in-distress bit just now. A little off the beaten path for a practice first date, but then again, that just means we'll be all the more prepared for the curveballs that'll come when we're putting ourselves out there and doing the real thing, doesn't it?"

Will's quiet for a second, his expression almost somber. "Definitely," he finally says. "Do you, um, live alone?"

I tip my head, caught off guard by the question. "I do. Kate and Bea used to live with me, but . . . well, they live with their lovebugs now. It's just me here these days. Why?"

He scrubs at the back of his neck. "Mind just . . . checking in later, letting me know you're okay?"

Something softens inside me. "Will. You don't have to worry about me, I promise. I fell because I've got joint issues, so my knee gives out sometimes. It's not anything serious. I don't faint or lose consciousness."

His shoulders drop with relief. "Well . . ." He clears his throat. "That's good at least. I mean, not that your joints give you trouble, just that I'm not going to spend the rest of the day wondering if you're out cold on the floor with a head wound."

I bite my lip against a smile. "You still want me to check in, don't you?"

"Yeah," he breathes. "I do."

"Fine." I let out an exaggerated sigh. "I guess I'll just have to text you later on. Ooh, you know what, why don't you get your bang for your buck and practice flirt texting with me while you're at it?"

He grimaces. "I'm not a good text flirter. I don't really text, if I can help it."

I roll my eyes. "You're such a grandpa."

"I'm taking that as a compliment."

A laugh jumps out of me. "Okay, gramps."

Will's eyes crinkle, the only way I know I've made him smile. He takes a step back. "What time does game night start tomorrow?"

"Oh shoot." I frown. "Speaking of game night. We still haven't figured out how we get you invited."

"I'll let Petruchio know I'm in town. He'll invite me. He has before."

My mouth drops open. "You stinker! Why didn't you ever come?"

Will looks sheepish, scratching behind his ear. "Because I'm a shy, awkward introvert?"

"Well, I've got news for you, Will Orsino. You can still be a shy, awkward introvert and have a great time with these people. We're all a bunch of weirdos. *Fun* weirdos. I think you'll have a good time."

Will's mouth lifts at the corner, just the slightest. "I think I will, too."

"Good. It starts at six thirty. When they're on Saturdays, we start at five and do dinner, but Sundays, we start later. My mom's real intense about attendance at Sunday family dinner, so I'm going to take the train to my parents', eat dinner, then head back in and host game night."

"That works. I'm going to spend the daytime stopping by a couple clients. That'll probably take me right up to game-night time. You okay with us not meeting for practice tomorrow?"

"Fine by me. Like you said, we got a good first day in under our belts. We have plenty of time."

He nods, then takes another step back. "All right, then. See you tomorrow."

"Bye!" I call as he flies down the stairs, taking them two at a time, graceful as a goddamn antelope. If that man weren't such a sweetie, I'd be livid about watching his freakish athleticism, when I can barely walk up a flight of stairs. "Text you later!" I yell. "Make sure you text back! Very flirtatiously!"

"Not a chance!" he calls over his shoulder before he bounds out of my building.

I sigh as I shut my door and slump against it. "Stubborn man. He really is lucky he's cute."

· TEN ·

Will

My hands are clammy. My heart's racing. I take a deep breath, then hit the buzzer for Juliet's apartment.

"Hey!" Her voice is as warm and bright as sunshine. "Come on up!"

I yank open the door when I hear the lock disengage, then take the steps up to the second floor two at a time. If I move any slower, I'll lose my courage and turn right around.

I can do this. I'm not *too* wiped from peopling, after making the rounds at two bars that stock our whiskey, but that's only luck—they're two of our oldest customers and I've known the owners since I was in grade school, so they're always easy to talk to. If it had been a newer client, I'd be fried. Still, my social battery isn't at full capacity, and I have to hope that what's left is going to be enough.

On my drive over, I talked myself through my anxiety about it. This is just game night with a handful of Petruchio and Juliet's friends and family. They're people those two like being with, which means they're good people. They'll meet me where I'm at.

Taking a deep breath, I cross the landing to the door and remind myself what Juliet said:

We're all a bunch of weirdos. Fun weirdos. I think you'll have a good time.

"I hope she's right," I mutter to myself. Then I knock on the door.

The door almost immediately swings open, revealing Juliet smiling wide. "Hey, you!"

I feel like I did the time Ma's miserly old donkey, Iago, kicked me right in the chest. Breathless, shock slamming through my body.

Christ, she's beautiful.

Juliet stands on the threshold of her apartment, dark hair piled on top of her head, a few soft tendrils caressing her collarbones. She's wearing a rose-pink crochet sweater, a white tank top visible beneath it. The sweater lists to one side, clinging to the edge of her shoulder. My gaze dances down. She's got on a pair of cut-off jean shorts that hug her wide hips, their fringe kissing her thighs. Bare feet, toenails painted the same pink as her sweater.

I snap my gaze up as fast as I can and swallow roughly. "Hi."

Stepping back, she opens the door wider. "Come on in."

I do as she says, stepping across the threshold. "Petruchio here yet?"

"Yep," she says quietly as she shuts the door. "When he told me you were coming, I said that was great, then I casually dropped that I'd met you in the backyard the morning after the party, said we had a cup of coffee and talked a little."

"Good." I hand her the bottle of Orsino whiskey that I brought. "Here."

She takes the bottle, inspecting it, and lets out a long whistle. "Wowee, thirty years? This is so generous, Will, thank you!" Smiling up at me, she says, her voice softer, "How you doing? Got the earplugs ready to go?"

I pat my pocket, where my earplugs case is stashed, attached to my keys. "I came prepared."

"Great. We can get loud, for game time, at least."

"I'll be fine."

Juliet's smile deepens. Our gazes hold.

I want to kiss her. Badly. I want to cup her face and take her mouth with mine, make her melt into my touch. I want to show her that I might not be the smoothest talker or the most capable romancer or the life of the party, but I'm plenty capable in other ways. Ways that could make her feel so damn good.

But that's not what friends do, and friends is all we are. Especially tonight, around these people.

The sweater slips farther, revealing the slope of her shoulder, a stretch of satin-smooth skin.

Heat roars through me.

She catches her sweater and shrugs it back up. It helps nothing. That sliver of her skin, the dip of her neck, the curve of her shoulder, are imprinted in my brain.

"Here we go," she whispers.

I take a deep breath and follow her toward the crowd.

———————

Beer in hand, I glance around her place. Warm candlelit white walls. Gleaming dark wood floors softened by a large rainbow-striped rug. At least a dozen matching jewel-tone throw pillows on the sofa and on the nearby club chair. Framed abstract art on the walls, surrounded by countless photos. Smaller frames with more photos and art crammed cheerfully across the mantel beside dried flowers that plume from vases decorated with colorful velvet ribbons. It's welcoming and warm and lovely.

Just like Juliet.

"It's a nice place, isn't it?" Petruchio says.

I nod. "Real nice."

He grins, gaze traveling the apartment, landing on a door down the hallway. "I have some good memories here."

I'm not often great at reading subtext, but from the heated, wistful look on his face, it's not hard to see that he's thinking back to a very specific kind of "good memory," one that I'm assuming involved Kate when she lived here.

The exact door he was staring at swings open, and out walks a man, just about my height, but that's about where our similarities end. He's lean like a long-distance runner, clean-shaven, tidy dark blond waves, tortoiseshell glasses, in a button-up shirt whose sleeves are rolled crisply to his elbows and dress slacks.

"Jamie!" Petruchio calls. "There you are."

The man smiles our way and offers his hand, which I'm startled to realize is damp. "Sorry," he says. "I came straight here from the clinic. Just washed them."

Which means Jamie came from the bathroom, where Petruchio was just gazing fondly, reminiscing. I glance at him, confused. He has fond memories of a bathroom?

"No worries," I tell Jamie. "Good to meet you."

"Likewise," Jamie says.

"Jamie," Petruchio says, "this is my good friend, Will Orsino."

"From college days," Jamie says, smiling warmly. "I've heard some good stories about that chapter. Glad to finally put a face to a name." He drops his voice. "I've also heard you're a fellow introvert."

I'm taken aback at first, but my brain catches up a second later. *Fellow* introvert, he said, which means he's in my boat. "You heard right," I tell him.

Jamie nods and offers a wry smile. "From one introvert to another, while I love game night, it can be a lot. I've found the balcony off the office is a good place to go for a bit of fresh air and quiet. Should you ever need it."

I nod, feeling my shoulders drop a little. It's nice to know I'm not the only one here who likes being with people but also gets overwhelmed by them. "I appreciate that, man. Thank you."

Jamie nods. "'Course."

"Need a drink?" Petruchio asks Jamie.

"I do indeed."

"Orsino's brought his family's whiskey with him. A real nice bottle."

Jamie's eyebrows lift as he directs himself at me. "Really?"

"Really." I nod toward the kitchen. "Opened and ready to be enjoyed. You're a whiskey drinker?"

"Love it," he says. "In fact, I'm going to be honest and admit I'm fanboying big-time, just been trying to play it cool so far, but now the cat's out of the bag, I'll level with you: when Christopher mentioned you and your family owned a distillery, I ordered an Orsino fifteen-year the next time I was at the pub just out of curiosity, and"—he slaps a hand over his heart—"I fell in love. It's my favorite now. I've got every one of your whiskies in my liquor cabinet."

I grin. "Seriously?"

"Seriously," he says. "If I had known you'd be here ahead of time, I would have absolutely brought my twenty-year bottle for you to sign."

Petruchio smiles into his drink.

This guy is a damn delight. "Well, there's always next time. I'll be here next weekend. Happy to do it then."

Jamie lights up. "So soon? What's bringing you back? You live upstate, isn't that right?"

"I do, but I'll be down in the city on the weekends the rest of this month."

I tell Jamie about the work I'm taking over for Imogen, and before I know it, I'm answering his questions about our aging and distillation process, debating with him which age is best, Christopher excusing himself with a wry grin and leaving us to our conversation.

"Now, here's a question for you," Jamie says, nodding to my

beer. "Spending all this time with it, do you find yourself ever getting sick of whiskey?"

"Nah." I tip my beer a little, inspecting the bottle. "I just like a cold beer in the hot summer, especially one from a local brewery, one town over from mine. I love whiskey, always will."

"Look at you two," Juliet says, sidling up to us. "Is this a bromance in the making?"

"I'm smitten," Jamie tells her. "We talked whiskey; he answered all my esoteric questions. I've learned *so* much about their aging process. Of course, I fell hard and fast. Will, however, might need to take things slower."

"You kidding? Talking whiskey is my love language. I'm a goner."

Juliet smiles up at us. "Well, that's adorable."

Juliet's twin sister Bea, whom Juliet introduced me to when I walked in, darts past us and opens the apartment door.

"Thanks, BeeBee!" Juliet calls.

When I saw Bea at first, it was a bit shocking to meet someone who looked so much like Juliet. But then I saw all the differences, and not just the obvious ones like her thick bangs, the blond tips of her hair, the many tattoos covering her body. I glance at Juliet, cataloging those differences I noticed, her heart-shaped face as opposed to Bea's oval, her wider mouth and deeper dimples.

Juliet gives me a smile but her eyes are big with warning. I get the hint. I've been staring, and I might give us away. Then again, even if we *were* new friends, I'd be staring at her. I've got eyeballs in my head and she's beautiful.

"Hi!" The shorter of the two women who just walked in, with tight dark curls and a bright smile, yanks me in for a hug. "I'm Margo. You're Will! I'm so glad to finally meet you!"

I blink down at her, taken aback. I had no idea Petruchio talked about me this much. "Uh. Hi. Good to meet you, too, Margo."

"Nice to meet you, Will," the taller woman says, giving Margo a dryly amused look. She's got buzzed hair dyed hot pink and a feisty smile on her face. She offers me a firm handshake, which I take. "I'm Sula."

"Good to meet you, Sula."

"Okay," Margo says, looping her arm through mine, walking me toward the kitchen. "I've been so excited to meet you, because you're *the* Orsino whiskey guy, and I'm a mixologist." She pulls back just enough to look at me. "I'm going to make you my famous custom cocktail that uses your spirits! That is, if you don't mind."

Sula rolls her eyes. "Yeah, you've made it real easy for him to say no, dear."

Margo waves her away. "He'll tell me no if he wants. He's a big boy." Her gaze travels up me. "A *real* big boy. My goodness. And oh so cute. You single?"

I turn bright pink.

"Not for me," she says, jerking her head back toward Sula. "I'm hitched to that one."

"Oh. I'm, uh . . ." I glance at Juliet, and I know I shouldn't, but I can't help it, turning to her for guidance. She's smiling still, though it seems a little tight as she gives me an encouraging nod. I glance back down at Margo. "I'm single, yes."

"Not local, though, right?" Margo presses.

"Upstate," I tell her.

"God, I love it up there," Sula says, walking past us to the kitchen. She cracks open a can of beer and takes a sip. "It's so gorgeous, so idyllic. I want a little house in the middle of nowhere upstate someday. That's my retirement dream. A house in the middle of nowhere."

"Well, until then," Jamie says, "you're always welcome at the cottage. Bea and I barely get up there these days."

I turn toward him. "You own a place there?"

He nods. "My aunt left it to me. Been in the family for a long time. I have good memories there."

"Where at, exactly?" I ask.

"It's in Illyria."

I grin. "That's where I am."

"Oooh," Margo squeals. She claps her hands together. "I just love a good small-world connection."

Conversation carries easily through the topic of life upstate, more questions about the distillery, the farm, and then it moves on to Petruchio telling some of our tamer college stories. It gets a bit loud, but not to the point that I want my earplugs. Juliet was right: they are fun people. Talking with them doesn't feel so hard.

Margo's custom drink is a spritzer riffing on the classic penicillin cocktail—she added ginger beer, lots of ice, a splash of Cointreau, a twist of lemon and orange—and it is *incredible*. I sip it slowly, savoring the drink almost as much as I'm savoring Juliet and her sisters animatedly telling us the story of when Petruchio got his top half stuck under his house's crawl space during a rainstorm in an effort to save Puck—that animal really does seem to have a mischievous streak—and how it took all five Wilmots to yank him out. Just as they've finished, Jamie jogs past us toward the door and opens it for two new people who step in, one with a tight dark beard and short hair, the other with dark hair tugged into a ponytail at the nape of their neck.

"Hamza!" Juliet smiles. "Toni! You made it!"

"Game time!" Bea hollers.

Everyone starts to disperse, but I let myself hang back for the moment. This is a new part of the evening whose choreography I don't know. I bring Margo's custom drink to my lips and take a sip just as a soft hand settles low on my back. I startle so badly, I nearly slop half my drink out of the glass. I catch it at the last minute, righting the glass in my hand as its waves settle.

"Sorry!" Juliet whispers.

I peer down at her, my heart hammering. "That's okay."

She slips her hand from my back and slides it into her shorts pocket. "How's the drink?"

Wordlessly, I offer it to her. "Damn delicious."

Wrapping her hand around my fingers as she cups the glass, Juliet brings it to her mouth. Her bottom lip brushes my thumb as she sips, and heat bolts down my body, tight in my groin.

She darts her tongue out and wets her lip, smiling up at me. "That's phenomenal." Juliet tips the glass toward her mouth again and steals another sip. "Game time's going to start now, and it can get rowdy in here. If you need a little peace and quiet, there's—"

"The balcony off the office," I tell her. "Jamie mentioned it. Gave me the introvert's guide to surviving game night."

She smiles. "Of course he did."

I nod, my gaze fixed on her. God, I've got it bad. I keep watching her walk around, that sweater slipping off her shoulder, the tight fit of her little shorts on her round ass. I want her, and I can't have her. Not now. Not ever. I need to get that through my head.

"JuJu!" Bea calls. "Which game first? Guess Who or Chronology?"

"Chronology!" she yells back. Her smile fades as her gaze travels my face. "You doing okay?"

I tip back my drink instead of answering her and take a deep swig. I promised not to lie to her, and I won't now. "Let's do this."

———

Since game time started, I've met Toni, Juliet's friend through Bea, and Toni's husband, Hamza, plus two late arrivals, Bianca, Juliet's cousin, and her boyfriend, Nick, a friend of Petruchio's from work.

But I'm not focused on any of these people right now, even though they're all settling in around the table, tucked in close. All I see is Juliet.

"Excuse me, excuse me." She squeezes between Kate and Hamza, easing onto her seat, a fresh drink in hand. "I've got this guy's butt to kick."

"Juliet." I shake my head, my expression pitying. "You are in for a devastating loss. Do you know how many games of Guess Who I've played since becoming an uncle? I'm an expert."

"Last time I checked, I beat half these people at the same game to get myself to this championship round," she says. "*And* I just so happen to be undefeated at Guess Who myself, so I suppose we'll see who the true expert is, won't we, Orsino?"

I drain my glass and set it on the table. "Bring it on, Wilmot. Bring it on."

Everyone gathers in close at the table like we're the last two players in a high-stakes poker match, a breath away from ruin or riches. The game starts simply enough. I'm relaxed as we ask our first few questions.

Juliet stares at her Guess Who board, frowning. "Does your person . . . have brown eyes?"

I don't glance at my board as I tell her, "No."

A groan of unease from those behind her. Juliet gives them a scathing look.

"Does your person," I ask, "show their teeth with their smile?"

Juliet sighs. "Yes."

I flip down half my doors, covering faces that don't apply.

"Goddamn," Toni whispers. "You're good."

The buzzer goes off, making everyone startle. "Okay," Bea says, slapping off the buzzer. "Subjective prompts begin *now*!"

The buzzer made me jump, but I'm mentally prepared for this. I've played five different people at this wacky blend of traditional Guess Who and a goofy-ass way that kicks in halfway through the ten-minute window they set for a match. It involves asking each other ridiculously subjective personality-based questions that are somehow supposed to make it clear whom we've picked.

"Does your person," Juliet says, "when they get a little tipsy, lecture people on the validity of a long-term investment in cryptocurrency?"

"Definitely not," I tell her.

Petruchio's friend Nick sighs. "Will I ever live that down?"

Juliet smacks down two doors. "Shit."

"Oooh," her side of the table says.

"Does your person," I ask her, "make themselves poached eggs for breakfast every morning?"

Petruchio gives me the middle finger from where he stands behind Juliet. Junior year, when Petruchio, our other roommate, Grumi, and I finally had a place with our own kitchen, I woke up the first day after moving in to Petruchio in his boxers, poaching himself eggs. He did it every single morning after that, no matter how late he was running or how hungover he was. Always poached eggs. Grumi and I gave him shit about it nonstop.

Juliet snorts. "Hell no."

I sigh, only shutting two more doors.

"Does *your* person," Juliet says, "tell unsuspecting strangers about the digestive benefits of regularly drinking kombucha?"

I frown, thinking. "Yes."

"That was *one* time!" Toni yells from the kitchen as he tops off his drink.

Hamza snorts a laugh. "One time *they* saw you do it, hon."

"Excellent," Juliet quips. Without breaking our stare-off, she flips down a door.

I sit back, examining my options. "Does your person . . . teach at a small liberal arts college?"

Juliet sighs bleakly. "Dammit."

"I need a yes or no, Wilmot."

She gives me a glare. "Yes, okay? Yes!"

I knock down one more door triumphantly. I have two people left who give me vibes of academics with wide smiles who don't bother with an involved breakfast. I can risk guessing, but if I'm wrong, she wins by default.

I sit back and let Juliet take her turn.

"Does your person . . ." Juliet bites her lip and smiles up at me. "Look like someone who is . . . petrified of pigeons?"

I stare down at my chosen character, Daniel, with his burly shoulders, his reddish hair and beard. He barely looks like me, but he's the closest resemblance she's going to find for me on this board. My shoulders start to shake. I bury my face in my hands, wheezing, I laugh so hard. "Yes," I croak hoarsely.

Juliet cackles, snaps down her final two doors, and yells, "I win!"

To a roomful of applause, including mine, she pushes up from the table and starts humming a tune I don't recognize right away. Now she's jogging her way around the table, arms raised in triumph.

"JuJu," Bea says, "are you humming *Chariots of Fire*'s theme song?"

"You bet I am!" she yells.

I snort a laugh as she jogs by me and finishes her lap around the table. Everyone starts to disperse from the table, but I linger, reaching for the box of games Guess Who was stashed in.

Juliet stops across from me, smile wide, eyes bright, and offers me her hand from across the table. "Well played, Will."

Her smile widens as I take her hand and shake it. "Same to you, Juliet."

Our gazes hold for a moment before we let go. Juliet tries to wedge her Guess Who board in the box, but it's not fitting, the other games having fallen in a haphazard heap in the box after we took out Guess Who. I circle the table so I'm beside her, able to help. Lifting out some games, I start to stack them neatly. Juliet reaches for my Guess Who board, latching it onto hers with the little clips that hold the two boards together. I steady the games in their stacked tower within the box, so there's room, and just as Juliet's about to set Guess Who into the space I've created, she freezes.

I frown, confused, and follow her gaze, which is pinned at the bottom of the box.

At first I think it's just a speck of dirt on the cardboard.

But then it moves.

That's when we both scream, "Spider!"

Guess Who clatters to the table as Juliet leaps back, inadvertently knocking the game box sideways onto the floor. I wrench backward, crashing into the wall behind us.

An inhumanly high shriek leaves Juliet as she spots the spider crawling across the floor from the box. She leaps onto the table, dragging me with her. I stumble onto the chair, crouched low, frantically searching for the spider so I can track its path. In sheer panic, our arms wrap around each other, Juliet's around my neck, mine around her waist. Our eyes dart around wildly, searching the floor.

"Where did it go?" Juliet whispers.

"I don't know," I hiss back.

"Right there," Kate says, stepping our way.

As she points toward the floor, I see it—we both do—a burst of small, dark movement scuttling toward us. Juliet and I scream again.

I used to have a soft spot for spiders. They were a reality on the farm that made them feel safe and familiar; I'd read and loved *Charlotte's Web*. I felt spiders were misunderstood creatures. But then I got a brown recluse bite. They've been on my shit list ever since.

I'm trying to summon up the courage to move past my fear of them, to stop this spider in its tracks, when Kate drops a plastic container right over the spider and crouches, slipping a paper beneath it.

"It's just a harmless little spider." Kate stands with the container and its makeshift paper lid.

Juliet and I rear back, clutching each other tight.

"Harmless," Juliet mutters, turning toward me as I turn toward her. Suddenly, we're nearly nose to nose, our mouths a scant inch apart. We spring away from each other, Juliet landing with a plop of her butt on the table, me tumbling back onto the floor.

I brush myself off, trying to recover my dignity. Juliet seems to be doing the same, easing slowly off the table and standing beside me. Both our eyes are fixed on the container as Kate walks with it.

"Kill it!" Juliet yells.

Kate glances over her shoulder and rolls her eyes. "Absolutely not. This is a good spider."

"The only good spider," Juliet mutters darkly, "is a *dead* spider."

I snort a laugh and offer her a high five, which she meets with a resolute *smack*.

"It's harmless—not killing it!" Kate calls over her shoulder. She opens the small window in the kitchen, lifts the screen, then dumps the spider from the container into the window box of flowers. "Off you go, little guy."

Kate shuts the screen and dusts off her hands.

"I'm never opening that window again," Juliet whispers.

"I support that decision."

"You guys going to make it?" Petruchio asks from where he and everyone else has been standing a few feet away, clearly entertained by this, judging by how every one of them is trying and failing not to laugh.

I glare at him.

Bea steps beside Juliet and pats her sister's back. "At least now you're not the only one freaked out by spiders. Strength in numbers, and all."

"No one else here hates spiders?" I ask the room.

Everyone shrugs, nonplussed.

"Fools, every one of them." Juliet blows out a breath and peers up at me. "I need a drink after that. You?"

"Hell yes."

"Margo!" Juliet calls. "Can we get an emotional support drink, please?"

Margo salutes us as she walks toward the kitchen, barely holding in a laugh. "Two emotional support cocktails, coming right up!"

ELEVEN

Juliet

"Good night!" I call out the door. Toni and Hamza, the last to leave besides Bea and Jamie, wave as they start down the stairs.

Bea pulls me in for a hug and whispers in my ear, "He's really cute!"

"Don't know who you're talking about!" I whisper back. I try to pull out of the hug, but she keeps me pinned to her.

"Will," she hisses in my ear again. "I can tell he *likes* you, you goofalloo."

"Banana," I hiss, our old code word from childhood when we wanted the other sister to cease and desist whatever they were doing, and "stop" meant nothing.

Bea lets me go, but she's grumbly about it.

Jamie offers Will a handshake. "Your first game night in the books. What do you think?"

"I think you guys know how to have fun," Will tells him. "It was great."

"Glad to hear it." Jamie grins. "Hope we'll see you around for another one soon?"

Will nods. "I hope so, too."

Bea's been watching the interaction with a smile on her face, but now she turns to me and says, "You sure we can't stay to help clean up?"

"Nope." I nudge her across the threshold. "I've got this. Thanks, though!"

"I'll stay and help clean up," Will says.

Bea's eyebrows lift. She turns to me and smiles, then smiles up at Will. "That's nice of you."

Will shrugs. "Happy to."

Bea gives me a meaningful look that says *We're not done talking about this guy!* I telepathically beam back an *I said "banana."* She turns again to Will. "Great to meet you. See you around!"

"Night!" Jamie calls, before they head down the stairs, hand in hand.

I watch them until they're out of the vestibule before I shut the apartment door. Then I round on Will. "Bea's picked up on it."

"Picked up on what?" he asks.

I walk past him, my stomach knotting with anxiety. I start gathering up snack bowls because when I'm stressed, tidying helps me feel in control. "On . . . us."

Will follows me and starts to pick up bowls, too. "I don't know what that means. We didn't do anything."

I walk past him into the kitchen and nearly drop the bowls in the sink, despite trying to set them down carefully. I'm all shook up, like a bottle of soda whose bubbles are screaming for the lid to crack so they can be let out.

I bite my cheek as I start to run water over the bowls, trying to hold back the words, to keep them inside me, but I'm tired and anxious and something about Will makes me want to pour it all out, to confess that I feel a tug between us that's impossible to ignore.

"From where I'm standing, at least," I tell him quietly, eyes down on the water. "We don't *have* to do anything; some people just have that spark, that chemistry—it just . . ."

Slowly, Will walks toward me, setting the bowls on the counter. "It just *is*," he says.

I stare up at him. "So you . . . do you feel it, too? If I'm reading this wrong, tell me, and I'll drop it for good, I swear—"

"Juliet." An empty laugh, a huff of air, gusts out of him. "Of course I feel it. I've felt it since the first moment I saw you."

Heat rushes through me. I curl my hands around the edge of the sink. "Me, too."

He takes a step closer, his hand sliding along the counter. "I am wildly attracted to you."

"I, um . . ." I list toward him as he reaches past me and turns off the water, which was about to flood the sink. "I am very, very attracted to you, too."

"I know," he says quietly.

I narrow my eyes up at him. "Very sure of ourselves, are we?"

His gaze holds mine. "When talking doesn't come easily with women, you learn to read other signs. Physical signs. That's all."

I sigh miserably, rubbing a hand over my forehead. "What do we do?"

"Well," he says quietly, his gaze on my mouth. "There's what I *think* we should do. Then there's what I *want* us to do."

My heart's flying as I peer back up at him. "Care to elaborate?" My voice comes out breathy and faint.

He hesitates for a beat, then says, "I think we should keep our hands to ourselves. And our mouths." He swallows thickly. "But I really don't *want* to do that."

I nod, then shake my head, a bundle of raw nerves and aching want. "Me, neither."

His hand comes to my face and cups it. "Our plan is to help each other," he says quietly, his thumb grazing my cheek. "I don't want to do anything to jeopardize that."

My eyes fall shut at the pleasure of his touch, the weight of his words. He's right, I know he is. "I don't, either."

"We haven't talked about it, though, if this is something you need," he says quietly. "Practicing this way, too. We can. If you want that."

I shake my head. For me, getting emotionally comfortable and at ease in romance again will lead right into comfort and ease with romantic physical intimacy. But as I stare at him, I'm realizing, even if I *did* want to directly practice the physical aspect, I wouldn't want practice to be the reason for his touch. I would want it to happen because he wanted me and I wanted him and nothing else. And that is exactly what I can't admit or act on, because it would jeopardize all of this, lead me down the path I've told myself I will not go.

Finally, I whisper, "I don't want to practice this way, no."

It's quiet for a beat, and I keep my eyes shut, let myself draw out this moment in which Will is close, touching me tenderly, the fact of our desire heavy in the air between us.

His hand slips gently from my face. "Then let's do some dishes."

There's a lot to be said for a guy who knows how to clean up from a party, and Will is one of them. Another green flag added to the tally.

We've worked in quiet for the past half hour, which, given we just admitted our mutual attraction to each other and established a clear boundary that it's not going to be a part of our romance practice, is pretty comfortable. After I turn on the dishwasher, I glance up and watch Will as he finishes wiping down the table with one last spritz of cleaner and two swift circles of the cloth in his hand.

"Thanks," I tell him, readjusting the claw clip I put in my hair when I started the dishes. "For helping with all this. It made a big difference."

He peers up, his mouth lifting at the corner. "Of course."

I smile. "I'm glad you had fun at game night. Spider trauma aside."

"Spider trauma aside, it was a good time." He gathers up the rag in one hand, spray cleaner in the other, and walks back my way, into the kitchen. "You were right. Your friends are weird. In the best way."

"Yeah." I take the rag from him and drape it over the sink's edge. "They're great."

Will leans a hip against the counter. "Very competitive, though. I thought when I beat Sula at Guess Who, she was gonna throw her game board."

I grimace. "Yeah. Sula doesn't like to lose. She's pretty intense."

"*Sula* is intense?" he asks, folding his arms across his chest. "Says the most competitive woman in the room."

I gape. "What?"

"You did a *victory lap* around the table when you beat me."

"It was a tight match," I say primly, turning back to the sink. I turn on the water, press the water nozzle's button to make it a power-washing spray, and start rinsing out the sink basin. "Can you blame me for celebrating my win?"

"A win," he says, leaning in, "that you clinched because you referenced my fear of pigeons."

"That was a fair play!"

He shrugs. "If you say so."

"Sore loser!" Impulsively, I lift the spray nozzle and nail him in the chest.

Will's mouth drops open. His eyes are wide.

As soon as I realize what I've done, my face does the same thing. "Oh, Will. I'm sorry. I shouldn't have—"

Will yanks the nozzle from me and nails me in the same spot.

I gasp. "Will Orsino!"

He laughs—laughs!—and it's glorious, rich and deep, right from his belly. "Take that!" he crows.

I rip the nozzle back out of his hand and spray him in the face.

"Ack!" He wipes his eyes, then lunges for the nozzle.

Knowing I'm done for, I dart away as fast as my body can move, rounding the island. Will's too fast, though. He leans over the counter and beans me, water spraying into my hair and down my neck.

"You turd!" I holler.

"Says the turd who started it!" he yells back.

I reach for the nozzle, but this time Will holds tight. My grip is weaker than it used to be, but even in my heyday, I would have been no match for him. Grunting with effort, I still try, attempting to pry his fingers from the nozzle. Will doesn't budge, but he's grunting, too. At least I'm making him work for it.

"Woman," he yells, his voice breaking with a laugh. "Stop it! No more!"

The absurdity of the moment hits me, and I double over in laughter.

Will drops the nozzle as another belly laugh leaves him, too. I clasp his arm as I laugh harder, bent over and gasping for breath. "I'm sorry," I wheeze. "I shouldn't have done that."

He snorts, wiping more water from his face with his free hand. "Ah, no harm. I got you back."

I stand, finally able to breathe, my laughter dying. I stare down at myself. "Blech." I shake my hands, sending water droplets flying. "I'm so wet. I need to change."

"Funny," Will says. "I find myself in a similar predicament. Except I have nothing dry to change into."

"Not true," I tell him, starting down the hall toward the bedrooms. "Come on. I've got you covered."

Will doesn't immediately follow me, but a few seconds later, I hear his footfall not too far behind. I open the door to the room that used to be Bea's, which I've now converted to an office. Bea's old dresser is still here. She didn't need it when she and Jamie moved into their place together—they bought a new one that fit all of their clothes.

Bending over, I drag open a drawer and riffle around for one of Christopher's T-shirts. I find a soft white undershirt, then shove the drawer shut. When I stand and try to hand it to Will, he doesn't take it. He just stands there, his brow furrowed.

"What?" I ask.

He clears his throat. His face looks tense. "You have . . . men's clothes here?"

I tip my head, curious. "Yes. Christopher's."

The tension leaves him. Slowly, he takes the shirt from my hands. "Ah. Gotcha."

I lean a hip on the edge of the dresser. "Christopher keeps some stuff here, has for years. Casual clothes mostly, for when he comes over after a day in the office and wants to dress down. He also plays in a pickup basketball league at the court right behind the apartment on Sunday mornings. Then he'll come up to the apartment afterward, shower off, and change."

"Got it." Will nods. "Makes sense."

I stare up at Will, smiling, though I'm trying not to. I've got a little suspicion, and it makes me inordinately happy when I shouldn't be. "Did the sight of another man's clothes in my apartment make you jealous, Will?"

He shakes his head.

"Pinkie promise," I remind him. "Be honest."

Will clasps the shirt tight in his hands. "It wasn't my finest moment. We're . . . we're just friends. What we're doing, it's only practice. I have no grounds to ask about whose clothes you keep at your place."

I search his eyes. "That's true." Pushing off the dresser, I walk past him, toward the door. "For the record, romantically speaking, I don't think a little jealousy is the worst thing. So long as you don't get toxic about it."

"Wasn't jealous," he calls.

I shut the door behind me, smiling to myself, and cross the hall to my room.

Walking around my bedroom, I start to tug my crochet sweater over my head, and my tank top, all in one, up as far as my elbows, before I feel the sweater resist my efforts to take it over my head. I feel around awkwardly, trying to figure out what's caught, and deduce that it's snagged on my claw clip. Sighing, I try to lower the sweater down on my head, hoping it disentangles it from the claw clip. But when I do, the sweater sticks even more. Now I can't even get it back down.

I swear under my breath and plop onto my bed. Maybe if I'm sitting, this will be easier.

It is not easier. I wrestle some more with the sweater, trying unsuccessfully, with my arms pinned up in the sweater, to reach for the claw clip.

"Argghhh!" I yell, kicking my legs in frustration.

"Juliet?" Will's voice is right outside my door. "You okay?"

"No!" I yell. "I'm having a wet wardrobe crisis."

There's a beat of silence, then he says, "Do you, uh . . . need some help?"

I moan in frustration. "Yes. But fair warning, you're going to see my bra."

Another beat of silence. "Uh, okay."

"Come on in, then."

The door swings open. Will walks in, both hands held like a visor over his bent head. He walks in, shuffling carefully, but he still manages to knock his hip into my dresser and catch his foot on my slipper lying in the middle of the floor.

"Will, you can lose the blinders. You're going to have to look eventually. This is a two-eyes, two-hands problem."

Hesitantly, Will lowers his hands. His gaze immediately snaps to my chest and widens. He peers up at the ceiling. His cheeks are bright red. "Sorry. I—" He swallows roughly. "Really sorry."

I'm too sore, too uncomfortable, to care that he just got an eyeful. "Just get me out of this, please."

"Right." Will steps closer, reaching over me. I shut my eyes, wincing as he reaches inside my sweater, his hands working quickly. I feel the claw clip loosen in my hair, the sweater slip back down my body. My arms drop and I shake them out, relieved not to have to hold them up anymore.

I tug my tank top back down and drag off the sweater, flinging it in the corner. "Thank God."

"Will's fine," he says.

A laugh jumps out of me, so hard I wheeze. It's the last thing I expected him to say. "Will Orsino, what am I going to do with you?"

Our eyes meet. Will's expression is intense, unblinking.

I feel myself blush, self-conscious under his scrutinizing stare. "What is it?"

"You just . . ." His gaze dances over my face. "You gave the best damn laugh."

My heart jolts and clatters, like it missed a step and went tumbling down the stairs. "I've been told it's loud."

"Oh, it's loud all right. But it's . . . right, how it should be. Like . . . fireworks. When you're staring up at the sky, watching them light up the night, all sparkle and glitter, there's nothing else that should follow that beauty but an epic *boom*. That's . . . what your laugh feels like, like it should be—as loud as it is pretty."

"Oh boy." A shaky exhale leaves me. "That was a great compliment. Ten out of ten, no notes."

"I wasn't . . ." He swallows thickly. "I wasn't practicing compliments, there."

"I know," I whisper. "But if I tell myself you were, then . . . then I won't want to kiss you so much."

Will's gaze darkens. He takes a step closer to me. I grip the hem of his shirt, anchoring myself, trying hopelessly to pin myself to reality.

"What if *I* want to kiss *you*, too?" he whispers.

I lick my lips, my body listing toward his. "We agreed we shouldn't."

"We did." He brushes back wet hair from my temple.

"Because it wouldn't be for practice," I tell him. "And practicing is the only reason we're ever supposed to act romantic."

"True," he says quietly.

"Then again . . ." I stare at his mouth. "Friends kiss sometimes. We're friends."

A low *hmmm* rumbles in his throat.

I'm full of shit, and we both know it. We wouldn't kiss like friends. We'd kiss like people who want to tear each other's clothes off.

I should pull away. He should, too. But we don't. We stare at each other, chests rising and falling as we breathe.

And then Will's hand slips into my hair, fingers sinking deep. His gaze searches mine, then he whispers, "Fuck it," and wrenches me against him.

I whimper in relief, throwing my arms around him, clumsy, desperate.

Our foreheads meet, breath sawing out of our lungs. Our noses brush. I cup his neck, my fingers sinking into his hair, too.

And then finally, *finally*, his mouth brushes mine, faint for just a moment, then more, pressing deeper, longer. Warm, soft, so impossibly good. Air rushes out of Will as I open my mouth, as his tongue strokes mine. Another whimper leaks out of me, fire racing through my veins, pooling deep in my belly, as he sinks his hand deep into my hair while the other cradles my face. I lick into his mouth and he groans, then deepens our kiss, so deep it feels like sex, the kind that makes you feel taken, consumed, shattered, and put back together.

I whine as he draws back, tenderly kissing the corners of my mouth, my cupid's bow, my bottom lip, which he tugs gently between his teeth. Clutching at his shirt, I draw him closer, desperate not to lose him, to lose this. I never want it to end.

I'm practically scaling him like a tree, pressing up on tiptoes, yanking him toward me. I need more—more of his body against mine, his weight and heat and strength.

Will wraps me in his arms, crushing me to his chest, and my knees nearly give out. The moment our mouths meet, our tongues flick and dance, building to a slow, sensual rhythm—hot, deep strokes that grow hotter, wetter, faster, until each breath is a gasp against each other's mouth. Will's hands are warm and strong, the faintest tremor running through them as he glides them up and down my arms, along my throat, into my hair, cradling my face again, then down my body until they're wrapping around my back again to draw me into him.

I arch up as he presses me closer, my breasts brushing his chest, his fingertips grazing my ribs. "Will," I gasp against our kiss. I cup his cheeks and take his mouth with mine.

"Juliet," he whispers.

Slowly, we break our kiss. I think it's because we both know that if we keep kissing, it's not going to stop there.

And it has to. Because this is *not* what friends do—at least, not friends who are helping each other find their way to a path of happiness that doesn't end with each other.

Our foreheads meet, chests heaving. We stand in silence for a few breaths, heads pressed together.

Until gently, Will draws back. His eyes meet mine. His face is flushed, his pupils blown wide. He looks wildly turned on and mildly panicked. That makes two of us.

My smile is wobbly, but I manage it, even though I'm still flushed, still winded from what we did. I search his eyes, relieved that I don't see regret but still worried. I don't want to lose what we've just begun to build—this space we share that's kind and safe and playful.

I swallow to wet my throat. I'm still not sure of my voice, but I force the words anyway. "You kiss all your friends like that, Will Orsino?"

He stares down at me and shakes his head. "Absolutely not."

I clasp his hand, stroking his palm softly. "Lucky me, then," I whisper.

"Juliet," he mutters, shaking his head again. "That was . . ."

I nod. "Yeah, it was."

His eyes search mine. "We did what we said we wouldn't."

I nod again. "Yeah, we did." I squeeze his hand, trying to reassure him. "But . . . maybe that's what we needed. To, you know, get it out of our system. Now the air is cleared."

The air is not cleared. The air is thick with unslaked lust and raw longing. Will's body is still half-pressed to mine, and I feel him, thick in his jeans, his pulse pounding in his wrist that I hold. I feel how wet I am between my thighs, how my heart thunders in my chest. This did nothing to get it out of our system.

But that's just going to have to be okay.

Because we're not quitting on this. I feel his resolve and mine in our locked gaze, in some unspoken understanding as we pull apart.

Will rakes a hand through his hair, a bewildered expression on his face as he makes a quarter turn toward the door. "I should get on the road." He turns back, searching my face. "Are you . . . are you okay?"

I nod, smiling. I know what we did was a logistical disaster. But God, did it feel good. "I'm okay," I tell him, and I mean it. "Are you?"

He blinks rapidly. "I mean, I'm a little light-headed, but I'll get there."

A soft laugh jumps out of me. I thread my arm through his and walk him toward the hallway. "Can't have you driving home light-headed. Come on, big guy. I'll get you a juice box for the road."

TWELVE

Will

I've been taut as a wire for days now. Everyone at work and home is giving me a wide berth since no one knows what to do with me—I'm as far from my usual self as possible. I've been surly when I'm usually silent, cranky when I'm generally calm. I'm a fucking wreck.

From a *kiss*. Kis*es*.

The best damn kisses of my life. Kisses that make me want so much more from a woman I can't have.

I'm scrubbing viciously at my lunch plate, staring out my kitchen window at my veggie garden, when a knock at my door makes me glance back.

Hector perks up from his corner of my couch and starts to whine.

A sigh leaves me. He only does that for one person.

Miranda, my baby sister, walks in, strawberry-blond hair piled high on her head in a messy bun. There's a charcoal pencil stuck in it, which is typical. Mimi's always walking the land, sketching nature. She's working on her portfolio to apply to art school.

"Hey, Dubs," she says, plopping onto my couch.

I rinse my plate and set it on the drying rack, then turn off the water. "Hey, Mimi."

My sister is quiet, scratching at Hector's ears. I can hear his tail thumping on the couch from here. "Sooo," she finally says, the word stretched out. "What's up your butt?"

I sigh, my head hanging. "Would you believe me if I said nothing?"

She snorts. "Nope. And neither would the entire town of Illyria. People are *talking*."

"Shit." I scrub my face. "Do I want to know what they're saying?"

"The theories are wide, varied, and some, downright disturbing." Miranda plants a kiss on Hector's head before she scratches his ears and tells my dog, "I'm telling you what, there are people in this place who need to get out more. They're losing it. I think my favorite rumor I heard is—"

"Nope, never mind, don't want to know." I scoop up my ball cap and storm toward the front door.

"Where are you going?" Miranda says.

"Back to work!" I call over my shoulder.

Not a minute after I've walked out of my house, I hear her jogging behind me, her long legs quickly catching up.

"You lock the door behind you?" I ask.

Hector will go wandering around the farm looking for me if I don't make sure to lock up. I'm not worried that he'll do anything he shouldn't if he gets loose—he really will just sniff his way around until he finds me—I'm worried about other people. My family loves Hector, and so do our full-time employees and core staff on the farm and at the distillery, but we also have seasonal workers and other random people on the property all the time who don't know him, and with pit bulls' bad rap (a deeply unfair and unfounded bad rap, I'll add), I'm protective of him. I don't want him bumping into people who'd see him as a threat.

"Of course I locked up," Miranda says, falling into step beside me. "Hector was already snoring when I left."

I grunt in acknowledgment. "Thanks."

Miranda tries a grunt of her own, but it comes out more like a pig snuffle, then she gruffs, "You're welcome," her best version of grumpy me.

I narrow my eyes down at her and try to glare, but it doesn't stick. I've always had a soft spot for my baby sister, twelve years younger than me, someone I kept a close eye on and took care of lots when she was little. "C'mere, you pain in my ass," I tell her, hooking an arm around her neck and drawing her close.

"Ew, you stinky man! Get off!"

I tug her closer, making her squeal with laughter and plant her hands against my ribs. "Stop body-odor-shaming me," I tell her. "That's the smell of a hard morning's work. Also, the AC is broken in my office."

"I don't care what's making you sweat; I just want some serious distance from your armpits." She shoves at me. "Let go!"

I give her bun a good tweak, then finally release her. "Why'd you come by, besides to tell me everyone's gossiping about why I'm grumpy?"

She grabs a piece of tall grass and snaps it off, eyes down as she drags the blade through her fingers. "Just wanted to make sure you're okay."

I'm quiet for a minute, weighing what I want to say. I don't like keeping secrets from my family, but I also need . . . well, I need my privacy. I need to figure out this part of my life on my own, and if I tell Miranda, I might as well stand on the table at our next family dinner and shout it, because it will not stay with her. That's just how things work among my sisters.

A sigh leaves me as I lift up my ball cap, scrape a hand through my hair, then tug my ball cap back down. "I'm just . . . struggling a bit with . . . some aspects of work."

Miranda's quiet as she peers up at me, listening. "Is the distillery okay? The farm?"

"Yeah, business is fine. It's just . . . me." I wrack my brain for how to explain myself without giving too much away, but all I can come up with is, "It's complicated."

It's complicated, all right. *I've* complicated it. I wasn't supposed to take things where I did with Juliet. And goddammit, she wasn't supposed to be right there with me. We were just going to help each other out, be a couple of friends in each other's corner. We had—we *have*—no future beyond that. She's looking for the kind of love that I stopped hoping for a long time ago, that I'm still not sure I hold out hope for in my future. And even in those moments when hope sneaks in, Juliet is the last person I should hold that hope for, when she's turned to me to be someone safe, someone who'll help her get ready to find someone who'll love her the way she deserves and wants to be loved. She told me herself she's been hurt badly by someone who clearly didn't love her the way she deserved. If I did act on my attraction, if I did pursue her, what if I did the same thing? What if I hurt her? I'd never forgive myself.

And neither would Petruchio. I wouldn't blame him.

I have very sensible reasons for why we'd never work, and I could have sworn they would be enough to keep me from turning to putty every time she touched me, to stop me from acting on my desire.

But those kisses after game night are all the evidence I need that I was very, *very* wrong. And now I'm torn. Because all I want is to see her again, to spend more time with her. But the more time I spend with her, the harder it's going to become to resist her. And I have to.

"What . . . makes it complicated?" my sister asks.

Blowing out a breath, I rip up a blade of grass, too. "Maybe *complicated* isn't the right word. It's . . . frustrating. Because sometimes you do everything you can, you try so hard to make things go right, and they still go sideways. It pisses me off when that happens." I whip the grass through the air. "Sorry, I'm rambling."

Miranda pokes me with the tall grass in her hand. "You're not rambling. You said like three sentences." She's quiet as we take our next few steps, then says, "I'm sorry that it's hard, that it's frustrating."

I glance her way. "Thanks, Mimi."

"For what it's worth," she adds, "I know you can get through it, whatever it is. You're the strongest person I know, Will. And I don't just mean these guns." She pokes my arm with her tall grass.

I peer down at her and emotion hits me, a lump settling in my throat as I remember so many days of little Mimi, with her sunset hair like mine, freckles on her nose, jogging to keep up with me as I walked across a field just like this. Half my height, talking and talking, always talking to me, because I was the one who was quiet, who listened.

Now, here we are, our roles reversed.

I swallow past that lump and tell her, "Love ya, kid—"

"Love you, too—" Mimi shrieks as I tug her back inside the crook of my arm and hug her. "You smell!"

THIRTEEN

Juliet

Will and I haven't texted all week—not that we texted much the week prior, just enough to shore up our plans for the weekend. And while I do think at some point that man's going to have to come to terms with practicing a flirty text here and there, I'm relieved he didn't try it this week.

Because I am struggling mightily. Every night, since he kissed the hell out of me on Sunday and I watched him drive off in his shiny dark green truck, I've woken up throbbing with release, sweat beading my skin, a white-hot sex dream featuring Will doing unspeakably filthy things to me fresh in my head.

I've tried to reassure myself that it's just because I haven't had sex with someone since my breakup, and my libido got a kick start back into gear because I kissed someone last Sunday night like we were two horny teenagers about to tear off each other's clothes. But it's more than that, and I know it. It's Will.

I sigh miserably, trying to refocus on this article on the gig economy that I have to turn in today. This is the pits. I have a crush on my romance workout buddy.

My phone dings just as I'm getting back in my writing flow. I wrap up the sentence I was working on, then glance down at the screen. When I see the text is from Will, my stomach flips. I groan in frustration with myself. Damn these butterflies!

WILL: Morning, Juliet. Sorry I've been quiet this week. Work was obnoxiously busy.

JULIET: Morning 😌. No sorry needed. I've had a busy week, too.

I have not had a busy week. I've written a dozen easy-peasy articles, did a massive clothes purge, rearranged my library alphabetically, then within each letter of the alphabet, by rainbow scheme, and read more Highlander romances than I have in a *long* time.

Come to think of it, maybe I need to pump the brakes on the horny Highlanders. I'm pretty sure Dream Will last night was in a kilt, and when I was lying beneath him, begging for it, he rucked up that plaid draped against his tree-trunk thighs, took me by the hips, and—

I shake my head and blink rapidly. My cheeks are on fire. Tonight, I'm going to bed with a thriller that doesn't have a whiff of a romantic subplot.

My phone dings again. I peer down to read Will's text.

WILL: I have a couple meetings with clients lined up today, so I was thinking we could meet for a drink and dinner. Would that be good for your schedule?

JULIET: Perfect! I have to wrap up some work myself today, so that'll be good timing.

WILL: Great. Does a pub setting work for you? I know of one that has lots of gluten-free options.

My stomach does a backflip. I press my hand against it. I can't handle these intestinal gymnastics he's putting me through.

JULIET: I really appreciate you thinking about that. How did you know I need to eat GF?

WILL: At Boulangerie, you got a GF lemon bar. Figured it was a dietary restriction. In my experience, nobody willingly eats GF unless they have to.

JULIET: No slander for my GF goodies!

WILL: Slander unintended, promise. Thinking we could meet, 6pm at Fiona's. How's that sound?

I smile. Fiona's is an adorable Irish pub that my sisters, friends, and I frequent, owned by one of my mom's oldest friends, Fiona, or Fee, as everyone calls her. When Fee found out I had to start eating gluten-free, she went so far as to set up a dedicated gluten-free fryer in the pub and tweaked a handful of my favorite dishes to make them safe. It meant the world to me, and the fact that, of all the Irish pubs in the city, Will picked Fee's . . . well, it feels just a bit magical.

Serendipitous.

Dammit, I have to stop thinking like that. I wave my hand in the air, like the word is a gnat I can brush off. I wish it was.

Forcing myself to move on, I type my response to Will and try to ignore the butterflies racing in my stomach.

JULIET: Sounds perfect. See you then.

FOURTEEN

Will

Juliet has somehow beaten me to the bar, even though it's only 5:55 and my journey to our destination involved coming down a flight of stairs. I'm staying in Fee's old studio above the pub, which is cozy and surprisingly quiet for having a rowdy pub beneath it. I pocket the key I used to let myself into the pub from the studio's first-floor landing and walk toward Juliet, trying to slow my heart rate.

Ripped light-wash jeans, another pair of flower sneakers like the ones she wore to our coffee shop date—*practice* date—except these are covered in tiny blue flowers with green leaves. Another one of those crochet tops, like her sweater last week, but a tank top, its midnight-blue color striking against her pale skin. She looks incredible.

Worse, I'm not just knocked sideways by how beautiful she is. I realize, as this awful ache settles in my chest . . . I missed her. I missed her arm hooked around mine, missed her wide, sunny smile, missed the way she wrinkles her nose when she's thinking hard.

Off-limits, off-limits, off-limits! my brain chants.

My heart thrashes against my ribs in protest. My body's tight and hot, drawn like a magnet toward her.

I am so fucked.

I weave through the crowd, going slow to buy myself time, to try to cool off. I mentally run through the bullet points from meeting with our tax consultant lady this week, hoping that'll help.

It doesn't help.

Juliet leans her elbows farther on the bar, laughing as Fee says something to her. I watch the two of them interacting. It seems like . . . they know each other.

Carefully, I ease onto the stool beside Juliet. "This seat taken?"

Juliet spins toward me, wide-eyed, spine straight, looking like I've startled her. When she sees me, her expression brightens, and a smile lifts her lush mouth. "Saved it just for you."

I told myself I wouldn't hug her, that I would keep our touches to an absolute minimum. But that resolution goes right out the window when she sets her hand on my knee and squeezes. "Hey," she says quietly. "Good to see you."

I stretch an arm across the back of her chair and pull her against me, her shoulder to my chest, my chin resting on her head. "Good to see you, too."

I feel her melt into me, her cheek nuzzle my button-up. God, it feels good.

We pull away and she smiles up at me, but her gaze is searching. "Is this . . . Are we okay?"

I've always found reading people hard, discerning the subtext of vague statements, sarcasm, difficult, at least until I get to know people well. Then I learn their pattern, their nuances, of how they communicate. I learn to read them.

It does something to me, to feel like I've learned Juliet at lightning speed, that I can already read between the lines of what she means. At least, I think so. I think she isn't just asking if this moment is okay right now. She's asking about all of this, all of what we're doing.

I brush a strand of hair back from her face and nod. "*I* am. Are you?"

She smiles faintly. "Yeah. I am."

"Now, *this* is precious," Fee says.

Juliet and I snap apart, facing her. Fee's leaning on the bar, her gray hair held back by her usual red bandana. Her brown eyes twinkle as she looks at us.

Juliet clears her throat. "Um, Fee, this is my friend Will. Will, this is—"

A wheezing laugh jumps out of Fee. She slaps her hands on the bar. "Sweetheart, I know who this is. I've known him since he was in diapers. No, even earlier. In fact, I'd say I'm responsible for his existence." She smiles smugly. "I matched up his parents. It's a bit of a skill of mine."

Juliet's eyes widen. She swivels on her barstool toward me. "Seriously?"

I shrug. "It's true." Glancing between Fee and Juliet, I ask, "So . . . how do you two know each other?" I turn to Juliet, "Are you a regular here or something?"

Fee laughs again.

Juliet's still got a stunned look on her face. "Fee's known *me* since I was in diapers. She matched up *my* parents."

Fee leans in and says, "Indeed I did, and you're welcome." She straightens, dragging a couple of empties off the bar beside me. "In the same summer, no less. Trying to think. I hadn't yet introduced your parents to each other at my pub, Juliet. That came later on. August, I want to say? Your mother and I were still roommates, living over the pub, single as could be. When I told her I was headed upstate for a networking event—really, it was more of a giant party of like-minded folks, but it was organized by a bunch of hippies in the area wanting to commit to sustainable land cultivation, so hardly surprising—she decided to tag along, enjoy a weekend out of the city.

"I was planning to poke around at the event, see if I could form some connections with local farmers to source the pub, and I was going to meet up with a friend from college—Will's mother, Isla—who had just moved there after inheriting a pretty piece of land she had dreams of using for sustainable farming. Her land was right up against a distillery, owned by the man *I* introduced her to at the event, Grant Orsino."

Juliet glances my way, then back to Fee. "So our moms met, then?"

She nods. "Maureen and I stayed with Isla in the place she was renting in town—there wasn't a property to stay at on her land." She sighs wistfully. "We had a hell of a weekend, the three of us."

"Isla." Juliet frowns, thinking. "I don't think Mom's ever mentioned her. Why is that?"

"They got on great," Fee says, "but then Maureen came back to the city and met your dad shortly after, fell into her whirlwind romance with him; Isla and Grant were upstate, busy putting their lands and lives together." She shrugs. "Wasn't really a reason for your mothers to stay in touch outside of spending time with me. They're both my friends, primarily. But I've rounded them up every once in a while over the years, when I want to get together with my gal pals. They still get on great. The three of us met up in Ireland, just a few months ago, actually."

Juliet's mouth drops open. "Wait, when Mom went on her girls' trip, Will's mom was with you?"

"She was." Fee grins. "So, you see, it's quite a delightfully small-world moment, seeing you two here. Now, let's have an Orsino whiskey to celebrate this serendipity, shall we?" She winks. "On the house, of course."

Juliet sits back in her seat and smiles. "My belly is a happy place."

I make a noise of agreement into my glass of ice water. I keep chugging it, hoping it'll cool me down. Fee's refilled my glass so many times, she told me after the last round to just grab the damn water gun and handle it myself.

The ice water isn't working. I'm burning up. And not because it's warm in the pub. My body's been on fire the whole meal, while I've been listening to Juliet's sweet little noises of pleasure in the back of her throat between bites, the breathy sigh of satisfaction after she sips my family's whiskey, my favorite batch our distillery's ever made.

I set down my water glass and catch her watching me. "What is it?"

She shrugs, a soft smile on her face as she twists her whiskey glass on its coaster, back and forth. "I just can't get over this. Our moms knew each other. Our parents met the same summer, all because of this battle-axe—"

"I heard that!" Fee calls.

Juliet ducks her head, grinning sheepishly. "A term of endearment!" she calls back.

She swivels her barstool chair back toward me. I turn mine to face her, too. Our knees brush. Her ankle nudges mine. I'm half-hard already in my jeans, and these incidental touches are not helping, but I'm too greedy for how good they feel to be sensible.

"And then," she says, "you and I meet on the other side of the world, then again in my backyard. Right at a moment when we both . . ."

"Needed to," I say quietly.

She nods, shaking her head. "Isn't it just . . . incredible? It's incredible, right?"

I nod slowly. "Yeah. It is."

She smiles up at me and shrugs again, a happy little jump of her shoulders, then drags the menu toward us and flips it open. "I think I want dessert. I need something sweet in my mouth."

"Me, too." It comes out rough and suggestive.

Juliet does a double take, eyes wide.

I shut my eyes and groan. "That was a—"

"Thinking thought," she says, snapping the menu shut. "That became a talking thought."

I hazard opening one eye. My cheeks are beet red. "Sorry 'bout that."

"I'll allow the occasional innuendo," she says, sitting back in her seat. "*If* you try to flirt with me, too."

Nerves tighten my stomach. "Must I?"

She raises her eyebrows. "Come on, workout buddy, this is me adding . . ." She frowns. "One of those disc thingies on your bar to make it heavier."

I grin. "A weight plate."

"Right. This is me adding a weight plate. Well, hold on. You need one on each side, don't you, so you're balanced? In that case, we need *two* things. So . . . I want you to try flirting . . . and compliments." She mimes picking up a heavy weight plate, sliding it onto one end of an imaginary bar, before she strains with an imaginary second plate and barely slides that one on the other end. "Phew. Okay." She wipes her forehead and mimes flicking away sweat. "Now you're all set to go. Flirting. Compliments." She slugs me playfully on the shoulder. "Time to level up."

Her whole act, it's so fucking cute, a laugh rumbles in my chest. My mouth lifts in a smile so wide, it makes my face ache.

Juliet leans close, her eyes sparkling. "Finally." She slaps her hands on my knees and squeezes them. "I *finally* made you smile."

"*Finally?* Juliet, all you've got to do is walk into a room, and I'm grinning like a fool."

Her cheeks pink. "Well." She clears her throat, fidgeting with the tiny gold stud in her right ear. "That was good. Kind of a two for one—a compliment *and* flirtation."

That wasn't practice, I think. *That was just the simple truth.*

But thankfully, I keep that thinking thought where it belongs, inside my head. And I lean in to her, because I'm warming up to seeing how my words impact Juliet, how they make her cheeks flush and her eyes glitter.

"What else have you got?" she asks, leaning in toward me, too.

I set my arm on her chair, bringing us closer, not so close that I'm invading her space, but close enough that I can smell her soft, flowery perfume mingling with the warmth of her skin, see her chest rising and falling faster than it was a moment ago. "If you were a veggie," I tell her, "you'd be a cute-cumber."

Juliet rolls her eyes and groans, "Willlllll."

I grin, fighting the heat that roars through me at hearing her groan my name like that. I know she's exasperated, but damn, it still does it for me.

"Come onnnn," she whines, landing a halfhearted punch to my thigh. "A *good* one. The one that'll sweep your future wifey right off her feet. Let's hear it."

"Okay, okay." I take a moment as the words gather in my thoughts, and graze my fingers along her shoulder. My heart pounds as I meet her eyes. "When I spend time with you, I forget everything else that ever made me happy—the perfect night of games and food and laughter with my family, the unbeatable line in my favorite song, the most breathtaking sunset, the best whiskey I've ever made. And when I'm not with you, when everything else that brings me happiness is all that's left, the only thing I can think is just how much I want to share that with you, how much I want you to share with me what makes you happy, too."

Juliet stares up at me, eyes wide, her mouth softly parted. Then she reaches for her whiskey and drains it. "That . . . will most certainly do."

"Yeah?"

She blows out a slow breath. "Oh yeah." Tipping her head, she peers at me, her gaze dancing over my face. "Now my turn."

My hand clamps down on the back of her chair. "Here?"

Her brow furrows. "Where else? We're practicing, right?"

Practicing. Right.

I groan and scrub at my neck. "Yeah, it's just that . . . I'm going to blush. I always blush at compliments. They feel weird."

Juliet bites her lip against a smile. "I think it's cute when you blush."

My heart jumps in my chest. And dammit, a blush heats my cheeks. "So much for you being rusty."

"I wasn't practicing yet!" She leans in, her expression earnest. "And I *am* rusty, okay? Maybe I don't seem like it to you, but I feel it."

I peer down at her and nod. "Okay. I'm sorry . . . I didn't mean to be dismissive."

"I know." She gently squeezes my knee, her gaze fixed on mine. "*Now* I'm going to practice."

"Okay." I focus on my breathing, trying to cool my body, but her hand's weight and warmth seep through my jeans, my skin, and it feels like it's a match that's caught tinder, a fire racing through my veins. Her soft, flowery perfume drifts toward me. Her hair slips forward, its dark ends sweeping along the edge of her cleavage. I scrunch my eyes shut.

Her touch moves from my knee to my hand, her fingers tracing up my wrist. "So many freckles—"

"Gee, thanks."

She squeezes my wrist. "Give me a second."

I feel a pinch of regret. She said she feels rusty, and I probably just made her feel rustier, responding that way. "Sorry," I mutter.

"No, that's on me," she says softly. "I didn't lead with what I meant to." She pauses, then says, her fingers tracing up my arm now, "I *love* these freckles. I love how many there are."

My eyes snap open and narrow on her. "You're joking."

Her eyes narrow, too. She leans in. "I'm *practicing*. Do you mind?"

I'm skeptical, but I keep quiet.

Juliet peers at my arm, watching her fingers trace a meandering line from freckle to freckle. "I could spend an entire day doing this, tracing your freckles, finding constellations, hidden stories." Her eyes meet mine. "Connecting the dots."

A rough swallow works down my throat. "An entire day?"

"At least," she says quietly, heat in her gaze.

"As you noticed, I have a lot of freckles. Might take longer than that."

A loud belly laugh jumps out of her. "Will, you are the funniest person I know."

"Come on," I tell her flatly.

She slugs my thigh with her fist. "Dammit, Orsino! Stop it!"

"Stop what?" I frown, rubbing at my thigh.

"Stop crushing my compliments. Stop fighting my flirting." She sets both hands on my knees and leans in, pressing our faces so close, she's almost a blur. "I promised you I'd be honest, remember? I'm *not* joking or bullshitting you. I'm not flattering you. I'm flirting with you." Her gaze dips down to my mouth. "I'm complimenting you. And I damn well mean what I say."

My racing heart is tight and aching, like my sides are when I push myself on a run to the point that I can barely breathe, when I'm reaching for a new depth of speed, endurance, capability.

Maybe my heart feels like this because it's doing that same thing—digging deeper, stretching toward a capacity it hasn't had before.

"I know I haven't known you very long," she says quietly, "but you really are the funniest person I know." Her eyes dart up to mine again. "Because when you share your humor, it's always unexpected, and I love the element of surprise; because I can tell you're being genuine and what you say is never at someone else's expense, when most people's humor comes with that cost."

I stare down at her. My throat feels thick. "Thank you."

She beams up at me. "You're welcome." After a beat, she says, "So . . . how did I do? I mean, I know I had my false start there, but once I got going?"

I cock an eyebrow. "Let's just say, if this is you being rusty, I don't know if I can take what you're capable of with the romantic equivalent of WD-40."

"I bet you could take it just fine," she says, leaning close. "Lube *does* serve that purpose."

I turn bright red. "I walked right into that, didn't I?"

Juliet's cheeks are pink, her eyes bright. "You did, and I appreciate the opportunity to practice a bit of innuendo myself." A soft laugh leaves her as she smiles up at me. "That blush." Her hands come to my face as she holds my eyes. "Is a dazzling, dangerous thing."

Oh hell. I'm going to kiss her again.

I *can't* kiss her again.

I swallow roughly as I stare down at her. And I let myself hover on that glorious, torturous edge of desire and acting on it. I won't cross that line again, I've promised myself. But I will toe that line and savor every minute of it.

I bring my hands gently to hers and draw them down from my face, my thumbs sweeping over her skin. All I want is to keep touching her, for her to keep touching me, but if we keep this up, I'm not going to be able to toe that line well at all.

I don't want the night to end just because it's hard for me to resist her, to not act on this wildly intense attraction. I want to give Juliet what she needs, in practicing romance—time to get comfortable with it again, a safe space to flirt and compliment and find her footing.

Nodding toward the dartboard in the corner of the pub, I ask her, "What do you say I kick your ass at darts?"

Her gaze follows mine and she laughs, loud and long, music to my ears. "Oh, Will. Challenge accepted."

FIFTEEN

Juliet

Will's truck is very high-tech—totally electric, he explained (an environmentally conscious man! another green flag!)—and very comfortable. As he drives me back to my apartment, I slouch against the window, sliding my palms along the soft upholstery.

I'm warm from my whiskey, from the pleasure of a night of flirty words and flirtier touches. Even if my heart's aching just a little, remembering that beautiful compliment he paid me.

Because it wasn't for me. That's for the woman I'm helping him on his way toward finding.

I push the ache aside and focus on the joy, on the win that was tonight. That's the datiest date I've been on in eight months. And I had the best time. After Fee slid a slice of flourless chocolate cake my way, I took dessert with me and we left our barstools to play darts (which I'm damn good at), then pool (which I'm not). Will, of course, demonstrated he was great at both, but at least at darts, I was just a *little* better.

I won at darts, and that was thoroughly satisfying, but that wasn't my biggest win of the night. Not once tonight did I feel the tug of panic that I used to when I thought about getting on dating apps, telling my sisters and friends I was considering putting myself back out there. Tonight, I felt safe. That was the best victory.

Will brings his truck to a stop in front of my apartment, then hits the blinkers. He's out and around his car before I've even managed to open my door.

"Lady Juliet." He offers his hand.

I smile and take it. "Duke Orsino. Such chivalry."

He grins at me as I step down from the truck, then shuts the door behind me. The truck chirps twice when he locks it.

I pull my hand away, now that I'm safely on the ground, steeling myself for a well-behaved goodbye. Even though I want to kiss him so much, it's all I can think about, like a movie playing in my mind's eye.

"I'll walk you up," he says.

I stop outside my building's door and turn to face him. "You don't have to. No knee wobbles tonight. Even after my acrobatic attempt at a behind-the-back pool shot."

His grin deepens. "That *was* impressive."

"Right? The only shot I made! Go figure."

I stare up at him, and silence falls between us.

I'm head-to-toe need, terrified that I'm going to act on it again. We haven't talked about the fact that we kissed since it happened last Sunday, but we don't have to. We both know kissing like that is dangerous territory.

The warm night wind picks up, swirling around us, rustling the trees in their tidy dirt squares staggered down the block. "Well," I say, fiddling with my keys, "we did it. Another excellent practice date in the books."

He's still staring down at me, but now his grin is nowhere to be seen. "Any feedback for me? You asked me at the pub, but I forgot to ask you." He rolls his shoulders and his spine, like he's steeling himself. "Be honest. I can take it."

You were perfect, I want to tell him. *And even when you weren't, that was perfect, too.*

Instead, I peer up in thought, tapping my chin. "A solid performance, overall. Flirting and compliments were strong, 'cute-cumber'
line notwithstanding." I wink so he knows I'm teasing.

He shrugs. "I'm a farmer. A veggie-pun pickup line was too
hard to resist."

"I'd like to point out that we're talking about a cucumber and
I'm not *touching* that innuendo."

His mouth quirks, but still no grin. "You aren't *touching* it?"

I fight a laugh. "You couldn't resist your veggie pun. I couldn't
resist a little innuendo about not indulging in innuendo. We're all
works in progress."

Will nods slowly. "What about when we played darts and pool?
What did you think of that?"

"I think that went pretty well. Though maybe let a gal win a
game of pool—she's got a fragile ego."

That grin finally returns. "And here I thought she'd hate it if
she knew I was holding back."

I would, I think. *I loved that you didn't hide your strength because it wasn't one of mine.*

I'm staring up at him, and I shouldn't be, but it's so hard, to end
this night when I don't want to. To be on my best behavior and ignore the raging heat burning through me as our gazes hold.

The wind shifts suddenly, turning the air cool, and cuts through
my ripped-up jeans, a shock to my warm skin. I shiver reflexively.

"Let's get you inside," Will says.

I hesitate for a beat, then force a smile. "Okay." Turning, I unlock the door. Will pulls it open for me and follows me into the
vestibule, erasing the distance between us as he opens the inside
door for me, too. "Thanks," I tell him, "Good night—"

"Juliet."

I freeze, then turn to face him, praying I'm not broadcasting in my expression how badly I want to climb him like a tree right now and drag him up to my apartment. "Yes, Will."

He clears his throat. "For the purposes of this being our second practice date . . . just for the record, hypothetically, I'd want to kiss you goodbye."

Heat bolts through me. I clutch the edge of the door he's holding open, caged inside his big arm draped over me, his broad chest so close to mine. "I think . . . that would be appropriate. Hypothetically."

He dips his head, his voice softer. "I'd ask of course."

"Mm-hmm," I manage. I shut my eyes, because I can't handle looking at him, because if I do, I'll grab him by the collar and crush my mouth to his. My heart pounds; I'm mindless with want.

"But," he says, his breath warm against my temple, he's so close. "For reasons that I know are obvious to both of us since last Sunday, I won't. Just know . . . if I did . . . I'd kiss you good night so damn thoroughly, you'd see stars."

"Okay," I breathe. My knees wobble. I clutch the door's edge harder and lock my noodle limbs, determined to be strong. Will's showing me he can resist this. If Will can resist this, I can, too.

In fact, I want to show him I can do even better than not kiss him good night. I can platonically hug him and walk away just fine.

"How about a hug, then?" I offer, opening my eyes, forcing a nice bright smile.

Will peers down at me, silent. Then he steps closer, so the door falls onto his back. "I can do that."

"Great. Me, too." I throw my arms around his neck and, in an effort to keep my libido in check, think about some of my least-favorite things—Gorgonzola cheese, mansplainers, dropped ceilings, spiders.

It doesn't work. His mouth grazes my temple as his nose brushes my hair. I hear him breathe in deep, like he can't get enough. I turn my head and let myself breathe him in, too, that clean, herby scent mingled with his warm skin. My fingers curl into his hair.

Will draws me tight against him, his hands wandering lower on my back. I tuck my hips up into his and feel what he's denying himself, how much he wants me. A groan rumbles in his throat, just as a whimper leaves me.

"I'm going to go now," he says against my hair.

"Me, too," I mutter against his neck. "I'm going upstairs. Right this second."

"I'm walking away." He sinks his fingers into my hair as our hips rock together. "I'm getting in my truck."

I clutch his shoulders as our eyes meet. Our noses brush. "I'm in my apartment," I whisper. "Heading right to bed."

Bed. The word lands like dynamite between us. We wrench ourselves apart.

Will rakes a hand through his hair. His cheeks are red, his chest moving in big, slow breaths, like he's trying to settle himself down.

I can relate.

We stare at each other, flushed, breathing heavily. Finally, I make myself take a step back into the hallway.

"Good night, Will," I say faintly, a smile tugging at my mouth.

He's grinning, too, looking turned-on and exasperated. He huffs out a breath that's half laugh, half groan. "Good night, Juliet."

I turn and rush up the stairs as fast as I can, clutching the railing, and let myself into my apartment.

Falling against the door, I shut my eyes and blow out a slow, thin breath.

I'm so keyed up, I can barely see straight.

Even though we didn't kiss, not even a peck on the cheek. Even though I didn't throw myself at him and he didn't carry me up the stairs and take me to bed.

I push off the door, headed straight for my library. I have never needed a bleak, brutal thriller more in my life.

I take as tepid a shower as my sore body can tolerate. I wear my unsexiest pajamas. I curl up in bed with my sad, creepy book, determined to overcome this.

But when I fall asleep, even with all that effort, Will Orsino still makes a fantastically filthy appearance.

SIXTEEN

Will

"Orsino." Petruchio throws me a chest pass from the other side of the basketball court where we're shooting around, waiting for the rest of the guys to show for pickup. I catch the ball and shoot a three-pointer that falls through the net with a satisfying *thwack*.

He whistles. "Someone's been working on their game."

"Fuck off," I tell him. "I've always been money on three-pointers."

He laughs as he grabs the ball, which has bounced toward him.

Jamie walks onto the court, dropping his duffel bag at his feet and throwing us a friendly wave. We both wave back.

Petruchio dribbles, then shoots a baseline jump shot. "Nothing but net!" he yells.

"Someone's humble as ever!" I call.

He flips me the bird.

The sound of what seems like women's voices comes from somewhere to my left. Before I can stop myself, I glance up, right to Juliet's apartment balcony. It's the first time I've let myself look, and I'm both annoyed with myself that I already caved—we've been here all of ten minutes—and disappointed she's not there.

I knew what I was getting into when I accepted Petruchio's invitation to join his pickup game, remembering Juliet said this is where he plays, right behind her building. I told myself I could handle it, feeling her close by, knowing that, according to Petruchio, she and her sisters often watch their game from her apartment's little balcony, and there was a good chance they'd be watching today.

But that was before last night—a practice date I told myself was going to go off without a hitch, because I was going to simply ignore and not repeat everything that happened with Juliet on Sunday night.

Obviously, that did not happen.

At least we didn't kiss again. That was a win.

But you sure as hell thought about it, a voice whispers in my head.

The ball hits me in the stomach, punching the air out of me.

"Shit," Petruchio calls. "Sorry, man! I thought you saw it coming."

"All good," I wheeze, scooping up the ball, dribbling it, then taking a shot at the top of the key. It bounces off the rim. "Dammit."

Jamie catches the rebound and pulls back, nailing a tidy jump shot. Another guy I met at game night but didn't talk to as much, Hamza, walks onto the court next, throwing us a smile and a chin nod.

I nod back.

Another sound—this time I'd swear it's women's voices—comes from the same place I heard last time. I glance at the balcony—empty again—and mentally kick myself.

Petruchio jogs up to me. "You good?"

I wrench my gaze away from the balcony. "Yeah. Why?"

He shrugs, taking a drink from his water bottle. "You just seem . . . a little tightly wound?"

A little tightly wound. Understatement of the century. If I were wound any tighter, I'd snap. "I'm fine. Just some stress with work."

It's not exactly a lie. This learn-romance-so-I-can-woo-a-wife plan is directly related to work, and it's definitely stressing me out. I've spent a grand total of three days on it with Juliet, and I'm about to burst at the seams with how bad I want her. I don't know how the hell I'm supposed to survive two more weekends of this.

"Want to talk about it?" he asks.

"Nah." I shake my head. "It'll pass."

God, I hope I'm right. That I can wrestle this gnawing ache for her into submission and get my shit together.

Petruchio claps me on the back. "If you change your mind, I'm here for you."

"Thanks," I tell him.

This time, when I hear those soft female voices, I'm proud to say I don't glance up, not immediately. But once Petruchio does, I let myself, too.

Kate stands on the balcony, some kind of thermos in hand, and catcalls him. "Hiya, hot stuff. You, uh"—she wiggles her eyebrows as she leans into the railing—"come here often?"

Petruchio laughs, the sound echoing off the brick building. "For a view like the one you're giving me, honey, I'd come here every day."

My eyes find Juliet, smiling down at me. I don't even notice what she's wearing, how beautiful I'm sure she looks. I'm locked on that smile; on the way she drags her sunglasses from her hair, sets them on the bridge of her nose, and playfully makes them shimmy up and down; the moment she throws me a little thumbs-up and mouths, *Good luck!*

Heat coils through my body.

It'll pass, I tell myself.

It has to.

SEVENTEEN

Juliet

"Gluten-free cupcakes and a cuddly hedgie have arrived!" The rapid stomp of Bea's boots down the hallway punctuates every word she says. She steps into the room with a jazz hand, the pastry box keeping her from doing it with the other. "They haven't started yet, have they?"

"Nope!" I step inside from the balcony, trying to erase the image of Will Orsino in a heather gray T-shirt stretched tight across his chest and blue gym shorts clinging to those tree-trunk thighs. Christ on a cracker, it's hot out here.

"Cornelius!" Kate croons. She takes the fanny pack–style carrier bearing Bea's pet hedgehog.

"Thanks, BeeBee." I take the box of cupcakes from my twin, setting them on the little café table I've placed behind our chairs for easy access. It might be ten in the morning, but I woke up craving the hell out of cupcakes. Who says they can't be a brunch staple? "You're an angel."

"'Course." Bea kicks off her boots. "So. How's the view today?"

Kate glances over her shoulder, down at the court. "All shirts still on."

I peel the paper off my cupcake and shove half the thing in my mouth so I don't have to be a part of this conversation. In the past, I haven't minded jokingly objectifying these guys when their shirts come off, when it's been my friends and my sisters' partners (whom I've obviously not been ogling) and some random dudes I don't know (whom I have, purely as a woman with eyeballs who enjoys ogling sweaty half-naked men shooting hoops). But it's different now. Now Will is in the mix, and the thought of seeing his shirt come off makes me feel like I'm going to burst into flames.

"That's fine," Bea says, settling into her lawn chair wedged onto the balcony, "I can wait."

Still chewing my massive bite of pumpkin spice cupcake with what tastes like a bourbon vanilla frosting, I busy myself with closing back up the cupcake box.

Kate swats my hand away and yanks it open again, poking around. She scowls. "You took the pumpkin one."

Bea leans back in her chair and points. "I got *two* pumpkin ones and"—she reaches farther back on her chair and plucks out a chocolate-frosted chocolate cupcake—"two death by chocolates for me."

"I didn't know it was pumpkin," I tell Kate. There's frosting on my thumb. I lick it off with a pop. "I thought it was carrot cake."

"Gross." Kate makes a face.

I poke her wrinkled nose. "Don't yuck my yum."

"Carrot cake is there." Bea points to the cupcake in the corner that I'd mistaken for vanilla, based on the heap of creamy white frosting on top.

"Darn." I scoop it up from the box. "Guess I'll have to eat that one, too."

"More pumpkin for me!" Kate takes the remaining half of my pumpkin cupcake from my other hand and pops it in her mouth. Her eyes slip shut as she groans, then says around her mouthful, "Holy shit, that's good."

Bea snorts. "Keep your orgasm sounds to yourself, please."

Kate's still chewing as she peels off the next pumpkin cupcake's paper. "I hate everything right now except heating pads and re-fined sugar. Let me have my joy." She bites into the new cupcake, then explains, "Just got my period."

"Ugh, me too," says Bea.

"I just finished mine last week," I say miserably, before biting my cupcake, right into a mound of frosting. "So now I'm ovulating and horny as hell."

Kate pats my back in sympathy. Bea clasps my hand and squeezes. They both know I've been abstinent since my breakup, that I've needed to be. And they both know I'm a cranky hornball for the second week of my cycle.

A little wave of relief crests through me as I put it together. Maybe *that's* why I'm so hung up on Will, at least in the physical sense. Maybe this will get better soon, and every time I see or think about him won't be lusty torture.

I drop onto the middle seat and Bea wraps an arm around me. "I know it's not a cure-all," she says, "but at least there are sweaty soon-to-be-shirtless men and cupcakes. Even if they are gluten-free."

———

When the guys start peeling off their shirts (understandable; it's hot as hell outside), I make a beeline for the bathroom under the pretense of "really needing to pee."

I can only hide for so long, though, so eventually I make myself head back toward the studio. At the sight of my sisters in their lawn chairs on the balcony, I stop on the threshold and smile to myself. It's a bittersweet image.

When she lived here, this room was Bea's studio, where she painted. The small back room is barer now, and you can actually walk through it—no rolls of canvas littering the ground, or tables of paints, or long, thin strips of wood waiting to be assembled into frames. There are still the bookshelves, filled with my romance novels, but now Kate's backup cameras and equipment, which she stored here when she always worked abroad, Bea's thick books about famous artists, are gone. It's just a room of half-empty shelves, a gold armchair, and an old floor lamp Mom and Dad gave us with a Tiffany-style glass lampshade.

I hardly come in here anymore. I just feel lonely when I do.

But it's moments like these, when my sisters camp out on the balcony, when they're here and happy in this apartment that at one point or another has been a haven for all of us, that I don't feel sad about what's not anymore. I feel grateful for what is.

"You okay?" Kate glances over her shoulder. "Get the runs or something?"

Bea whacks her shoulder. "You know she's self-conscious about when she has tummy troubles."

I used to be, when out of nowhere, eating a food I'd had no issue with before had me sprinting to the bathroom. Now that I eat gluten-free, that's mercifully not a problem anymore.

"I'm good," I tell them, squeezing back into my chair.

Bea offers me our shared mimosa in its thermos champagne glass. I take a swig and let out a satisfied *ahhh*. "What'd I miss?"

I tug down my sunglasses from my hair and keep my gaze lifted, hopefully passing myself off as being interested in the pigeons hopping along the balcony a floor up. I'm not ready to risk a glance at the court yet.

"Everyone's half-naked," Kate says delightedly. "Except Will."

My head snaps down. I peer out at the court, where the game is in full swing. I'm not as relieved as I'd hoped to be.

He's got his shirt on, all right, but he's still a sweaty, sexy sight to behold. His gray T-shirt is soaked, plastered to his body, as he dribbles toward the net and throws his shoulder into Christopher, who's defending him. Will spins, then sends the ball up through the air, just over the net. Jamie catches it and dunks it.

"Alley-oop!" Bea crows.

"No need to gloat," Kate says grumpily.

Christopher's got the ball now, dribbling down toward the other end of the court. One of the regular guys I don't know is defending him well, but Christopher still manages to dribble in, pull up, and sink a jump shot that hits the hoop on a cheery *ding* before it rattles in.

"Woo!" Kate screams.

Bea lowers her sunglasses and says, "No need to gloat, huh?"

Kate smiles sheepishly. "I got swept up in the moment."

While their verbal volley continues bouncing across me, I watch Will lift his shirt by the collar, dragging it over his face to wipe the sweat from his eyes. Thank God we don't own binoculars, because I'm not sure I'd have the strength not to use them.

Even without binoculars, I can see the general impression of a hard stomach, a line of hair arrowing beneath his waistband that glows copper in the sun.

A whimper leaks out of me. I try to cover it with a cough. Kate whacks me on the back. "Mimosa down the wrong pipe?"

"Yep," I squeak.

Kate keeps distractedly whacking my back, her eyes on Christopher. I pluck her hand away and set it on the arm of her chair.

"You good there, KitKat?" Bea asks.

"Very." Kate makes a noise that puts her orgasmic cupcake appreciation sound to shame. "God*damn*, my boyfriend's hot."

Bea and I shudder. Christopher's like a brother to us. We don't want to hear that.

"So." Bea sips from the champagne thermos and sets it on her thigh. "I feel like I have done a very good job all week of *not* asking you about Will Orsino—"

Kate's head snaps our way as she shouts, "Wait, what?!"

"Shh!" I smack her shoulder. "You're screaming."

"What," Kate asks, leaning in, her voice not nearly quiet enough for my taste, given the subject matter, "is going on with you and *Will*?"

"Nothing!" I tell her. I turn and glare at Bea, then say for emphasis, "*Nothing.*"

Bea shrugs, sipping more mimosa. "He stayed after game night last Sunday to help JuJu clean up."

Kate lets out a whistle. "Voluntarily? He definitely wants in your pants."

"Oh my gosh, you two." I throw up my hands, exasperated. "We just hit it off as friends. We're enjoying a single mingle. That's it."

"Hmm." Bea glances back down at the court and glides a hand over her pet hedgehog, tucked into her cross-body carrier, his little nose peeking over the edge as he sniffs the air. "I know, Cornelius, I noticed that, too."

"What?" I ask.

Bea says, "He's a strawberry-blond hunk. You have a thing for redheads."

"So, just because he's a redhead, I must want in his pants?"

Bea turns and gives me a look. "You're telling me you don't want a thing to do with that tall, hot drink of spiced apple cider out there?"

I groan in frustration. I hate lying to my sisters, but I don't want to tell them the truth, either. I know they wouldn't judge me, that they'd support what I'm doing with Will. But our plan, what I'm trying to do with his help, it feels . . . tender. This work to finally move myself forward, to get ready to put myself out there romantically again, it feels like something that's just supposed to be mine and Will's.

Bea misreads my silence and gives me a campy grin. "Come on. You can't tell me that wasn't funny. 'Tall, cool, drink of water'? Tall, hot drink of spiced apple cider?"

I give her a nonplussed stare.

Bea mutters to Cornelius, "Tough crowd."

Kate says, "Let's workshop it." She taps her pursed lips. "Ooh, I've got it. How about, a 'tall, hot shot of Fireball.'"

Kate and Bea cackle in tandem.

I give them a death glare that shuts them up promptly. They both school their expressions as they glance back out at the court. I'm relieved to see the guys shaking hands, slapping backs. The game's over. I made it through without spontaneously combusting. I feel like I ran a marathon.

"Well," Kate says, slapping her hands onto the arms of her chair and standing up, "that's a wrap. I'm gonna go check on the egg casserole."

Bea stands, too. "Right behind you."

I start to get up, but Bea gently presses me down at my shoulder.

"Just relax," she says. "You prepped all the food for brunch. Let us do this little bit and set it out at least."

I peer up at her. "You sure?"

"I'm sure." She lifts her carrier for Cornelius off her shoulders and gently slides it over mine. "Sorry for grilling you about Will, JuJu. I just . . . want you to be happy. If he doesn't interest you beyond friendship, if you're happy as is, I respect that."

I peer down at tiny Cornelius, who yawns adorably, guilt twinging inside me. I don't tell her she's wrong, and I don't confess that she's right, either. "Thanks, BeeBee."

She sets the thermos in my hand and smiles. "You and Cornelius enjoy some R and R. I'll let you know when brunch is up."

Men's voices echo down the hall. I glance over my shoulder and see Christopher walk in, then Jamie, followed by Will. I snap my head back, staring out at the court. My heart's flying.

I hear Kate squawk, imagining that Christopher's pulled her in for a sweaty hug, then Bea's laughter. Jamie's deep voice, his words too hard to parse, then Will's just a little deeper, his crystal clear. "You sure?" he asks, then after a beat says, "Thanks, man."

I swallow, nervous. Should I get up and say hello? Am I being weird or rude, staying put? I'm still debating what to do when I hear a soft knock on the doorframe of the studio. I glance over my shoulder, and my stomach flips.

Will's red-faced and sweaty, smiling ear to ear. "Hey."

"Hey, you." I smile at him, because I can't help it. Because when I see Will, that's all I want to do—smile at his damn cute face and his kind eyes and his sweet gentle giant presence.

He nods out toward the court. "Enjoy the game?"

"Thoroughly. You?"

He nods again, still smiling wide.

My smile grows as wide as his. "You're high as kite on adrenaline, aren't you?"

"Nature's best drug," he says, double tapping the threshold. "I'm gonna grab a shower now, but I'll be quick. That egg casserole you made smells incredible, and I'm starving."

Then he turns and strolls back down the hallway, probably clueless that he's just wrecked me by planting in my mind's eye the image of him showering, lathering my body wash across his skin, that soap drifting down those big, hard pecs I saw his shirt plastered to, those thick arms I've curled my hand around, between his thighs, stroking down—

"Gahh!" I shake my head. "Stop it, Juliet!"

Cornelius pops his head up from his carrier, his dark, curious eyes glancing around, probably wondering what all that noise was.

"Sorry if I scared you, bud." I reach for the tiny hedgie inside his carrier and carefully draw him out. His tiny feet tickle my palm as he settles inside my cupped hands. "Cornelius, I can do this, right?"

He lifts his head up and down. I'm pretty sure he's just sniffing the air, having gotten a whiff of the egg casserole that's come out of the oven, but I'll take his little nod as the reassurance I need.

"Yeah," I tell him, stroking softly down his quills. "I hope so, too."

EIGHTEEN

Will

Juliet called it: I was high on adrenaline earlier. But now, hours later, after a damn good brunch and visit with Jules, her sisters, Petruchio, Jamie, and Hamza, then Toni, who came in toward the end, dejected that he'd had to miss the game ("especially the shirtless part!"), I can't give the adrenaline credit anymore for how good I feel.

In my gut I know what's responsible—*who's* responsible: the woman smiling up at me.

Juliet lifts her eyebrows as I hold open the door to the conservatory, the spot I picked for our next practice date.

"Thank you," she says, stepping past me.

I let the door drift shut behind me, then fall into step beside her, setting my hand on her back. She nearly jumps out of her skin.

I draw my hand away. "Sorry, I—"

"No." She waves her hands, shaking her head. "That was all me. *I'm* sorry." She takes my hand, then awkwardly tries to set it on her lower back again. "Please proceed."

"I don't have to, Juliet." My good mood's evaporated, and the familiar sting of getting it wrong echoes through me. "I shouldn't have assumed. I was just . . . It was instinct."

"Exactly," she says. "And that's what you're supposed to be listening to."

"And *you're* only supposed to be receiving the kind of romance you're comfortable with," I remind her.

She sighs, her shoulders falling. "I am comfortable with it, I promise. I was just zoned out and it caught me off guard."

I narrow my eyes at her. "Pinkie promise?"

She smiles up at me, pinkie outstretched. "I swear."

I hook her pinkie gently, then let my hand fall.

Juliet's smile deepens. "Now, get that hand on my back, Orsino. And let's go look at some flowers."

Gently, tentatively, I set my hand on her back again, like she's asked. I brace myself for her to pull away again, still reeling from that reflex. But she doesn't. In fact, she does the opposite. She leans *into* my touch, just the littlest bit, but I feel it—the press of the curve of her spine into my palm, the warmth of her body. I get a whiff of something faint and floral that I already know has nothing to do with the flowers we're about to be surrounded by. It's her. She smells so fucking good.

"So many flowers, so little time." She smiles up at me and rubs her hands together in excitement. "Where do we even begin?"

––––––––––

We've been walking the place for an hour and a half, seen nearly all of it, and at some point Juliet's hand found its familiar place curled around my arm. The past ten minutes, I've felt her weight more as she leans on me. It makes me feel so good that she does that—that she leans on me. But it also makes me worry that she's hurting, that walking's wearing on her and she's not telling me.

I decide not to bring it up. I've learned, since my mom's diagnosis, not to push, not to act like I know better than someone else what's best for their body. Instead, I point to a bench tucked into the corner of the native plants room. I've saved the best for last.

"Mind if we sit for a little?" I ask.

"Sure." She sounds distracted as I start to walk us toward the bench, but I think she's just taking it all in, peering around, a soft smile on her face. "Any reason in particular?" she asks.

"Because I'd like to take some time in here. This is my favorite room."

She glances my way, her expression curious as we lower onto the bench together. "Why is this room your favorite?"

I ease back and stretch my arm along the bench behind her. Juliet nestles in close against me and sighs. It feels exactly right.

"When I first came to college," I tell her quietly, "I was homesick. My first weekend after move-in, it was so bad, I nearly packed up everything and took the train home. But I knew I'd be miserable if I went home, too. That I'd feel like I'd failed myself and my parents, who were so proud of me for pushing myself out of my comfort zone, throwing myself into city life and a new social circle. So I did what I always do when I'm worked up. I went for a walk."

Juliet settles in closer against me, like she's getting cozy, ready to listen.

I take another deep breath and blow it out. "My student ID gave me free access to the conservatory. I'd seen the place mentioned in my orientation materials, so I walked in, went from room to room, then I ended up . . . here." My gaze wanders the space, drinks in the blossoms, shrubs, grasses, and trees surrounding us. All native to the state, tethered to the land and its seasons. "I walked into this room that was filled with every kind of plant that had been the background of my childhood, and I just . . . felt like I could breathe again, like my heart was beating right, like I wasn't about to crawl out of my skin anymore. I felt like I was . . . home."

Juliet's quiet, but I feel her eyes on me, like the press of a hot summer sunrise burning through the curtains, warming my face. Finally, I peer down at her.

Her smile is still soft, her eyes fixed on mine. "If it's anything like this, home must be pretty beautiful."

I nod. "It is."

Our gazes hold. Softly, I curl my hand around her shoulder. Juliet lets out a faint, content hum.

"So." I drag my fingertips over her skin.

She sucks in a breath, eyes still locked with mine. "So."

"I've got a bit of a hang-up with third dates," I tell her.

She tips her head, confusion written on her face. "Why?"

"Never gotten past one. Been friend-zoned every time. Always the same thing—*It doesn't feel romantic. I think we should just be friends*. Some variation on that."

Her eyes narrow. "What kind of nincompoops were you going on dates with?"

An empty laugh leaves me.

"I'm serious," she says fiercely. "I want names. I want to key their cars."

I snort a laugh. "No keying cars. Their names don't matter, anyway. What matters is that I let them get in my head."

"Will." She searches my eyes. "Is that why . . . you feel the way you do? About romance?"

I hold her eyes as I swallow my pride and tell her the truth. "I just couldn't keep doing something that kept ending in people telling me I was failing at it. So I just . . . stopped trying, stopped hoping for it."

Her hand finds mine and squeezes. But she stays quiet, listening.

I hesitate for a beat, then say, "When I was thirteen, I was diagnosed as neurodivergent—autism, specifically. I've got sensory issues, like with sound, as you know, but other things, too. Sometimes, when I'm trying to express myself, I get this traffic jam between my brain and my mouth. I struggle to read people, to parse subtext. I get exhausted socially quickly and when I'm around people I don't know, my social anxiety is sky-high. I can't relax, can't just roll with it, because I'm too busy trying to keep up with a language that it feels like I only half understand." I swallow, wetting my throat. "I'm not . . . wired like most people."

Her thumb swirls gently across my palm. *I'm listening*, her touch says. *Go on.*

"I know that doesn't disqualify me from loving and being loved romantically," I tell her. "But I also know that I've never encountered someone who made me feel like it didn't. And . . . I don't want to see myself that way. I don't want the person who I share my life with to see me that way, either. So that's why I figured, maybe if I just asked for less from the person I'm going to marry one day, if she expected less in return, I'd protect myself from that."

"I understand that," Juliet says, her voice quiet, "wanting to protect yourself."

I nod. "But . . . since you and I started this, Juliet, I've been thinking, maybe I don't need to protect myself . . . so much as find someone who makes me feel safe enough to try again."

Juliet squeezes my hand hard, her eyes shining. "Exactly."

"I mean, I got over that fear of opening up, putting myself out there socially, after being diagnosed. It took a while, but eventually, I realized, yes, I'm weird, but I generally like my weirdness . . . that's what makes me *me*. Because it's not all hard parts, having a brain like mine. It makes me incredibly capable at diving deep into the things I love and learning every corner of them. My mind's freedom from preconceived *should*s and *can't*s leads me to think outside the box with the business back home, to see solutions in spaces, possibilities in people, that most might not because they don't fit the 'typical' mold; to identify and leverage those skills and strengths. My system is highly sensitive, but that also means it's highly observant, that I notice details, pick up on things, that most people overlook, and that makes me damn good at my work, makes my life feel rich and vibrant. In lots of ways, my brain is incredible. And in the same way I overcame my fear of being misunderstood and put myself out there, found people I felt safe to be my whole weird self with, maybe I can find someone safe in romantic love, too."

A smile lifts the corner of her mouth. "Damn right. The woman worthy of you, Will, she's going to love the hell out of your 'weird' and feel loved right in the heart of it."

"I know," I tell her quietly. "You've been helping me figure that out."

She smiles, bright and dazzling. "Good." Her hand squeezes mine. "Thanks for telling me about this, for opening up. I know it's not easy."

"You do?"

Juliet nods. "Bea, she's neurodivergent, too. So is Kate. I've seen how it goes for them, that it's scary to share that truth when people aren't always kind toward it, to brace for someone to see that part of you as something to put up with, as an *in spite of* part of you to tolerate instead of simply another part of you to know and love."

Love. The word echoes in the air between us. I swallow roughly, my hand that's not held in hers grazing along her shoulder. "Thank you, Juliet."

She squeezes my hand again. "It's something I've been struggling with, actually. Putting myself out there that way." She hesitates for a second, like she's searching for words, then says, "Last year, right after I met you in Scotland, actually, when I got home . . .

I got sick. Well, I'd been sick, but I'd managed to ignore it up to that point. I don't know if it was the level of stress I was under or some switch in my system that finally tripped, but it became debilitating. I had bloodwork, exams, X-rays. I started working with a great rheumatologist, got a diagnosis of celiac disease and mixed connective tissue disease, a new diet to follow, meds to help, but there's no cure, for any of it. It's just . . . there. It's always going to be there. And I have so little control over when it gets worse or when my symptoms get quieter. Whenever I get back to dating, I'm scared I'm going to tell someone about that and they won't want to sign up for that uncertainty." She sighs heavily, forcing a smile. "And while I know, if they don't want all of me, they're not worthy of me, it won't make possibly getting that reaction any easier, not at first, at least."

I stare down at her, my heart aching. I want to reach inside her and wipe out every single thing that hurts her. I hate that pain is a part of her life and there's so little she feels she can do to control that from day to day.

But I do understand it, as a bystander at least, as someone who loves someone who deals with something similar.

I swallow past the lump in my throat, my hand squeezing her shoulder gently, and tell her, "My mom, she's got rheumatoid arthritis. I see what it takes out of her, the battles she fights on the hard days. I know that it's probably not the same, that it's unique from person to person. But just know, Juliet, I think you're a fucking badass. I catch you muscling through it, dragging yourself forward because you want to even though your body doesn't. I wish I could take it from Ma, from you. But I know I can't. And while I wish you never had to hurt, I'll never wish you different than exactly as you are."

Her eyes shine, wet with tears threatening to spill over. I

squeeze her shoulder again, pulling her close. "I'm in your corner just as much as you're in mine, okay? On the hard days, I'll be the arm to hold on to, the pair of hands to do what you can't, the feet that carry you when yours won't take another step. And on the gentle days, the feel-good days, I'll be there, too, grateful that I get to be your friend and see you shine." I hold her eyes, needing her to hear this, to feel this, right down to her bones. "The man, woman, person, whoever they are that earns your heart . . . they damn well better do that, too, Juliet. Or I will do *much* worse than key their car."

Juliet sniffles, bringing a hand to her nose and wiping it. "Dammit, Will."

"Don't cuss me out, woman. I'm being sincere right now."

"I am, too," she says brokenly, fishing around in her flowy pants pocket, pulling out a tissue. She blows her nose hard, and it's *loud*, an adorably goose-like honk. When she pockets her tissue, she peers up at me. "Thank you."

I stroke her arm, my fingertips tracing a shape against her skin I don't let myself analyze, don't allow to monopolize my thoughts. "Thank *you*."

She clears her throat, glancing out at the flowers. "Also, thanks for the way you talked about my future partner. I'm bisexual, and it means a lot that you didn't assume I was straight."

I nod. "'Course, Jules."

Shaking her head as she gazes at the purple coneflower near us, she sighs. "You're such a green flag man."

A soft chuckle leaves me. "I thought that was a good thing."

She nods, still not meeting my eyes. "It is."

"Hey." I squeeze her shoulder.

She peers up at me. "Hmm?"

"We just talked about a lot of hard shit, and it went pretty well, I think."

A smile brightens her face. "I think so, too." She lifts her hand for a high five. "We kicked this third date's ass!"

I meet her high five. "What do you say we celebrate? You an ice cream gal?"

Her eyes light up. "You bet I am. But I've got family dinner in two hours. Should I sneak ice cream before dinner?"

"I'd say you've earned it."

She beams. "Yeah. You're right. I have."

"Come on." I stand, offering her my hand. "I know a place not too far from here that has gluten-free waffle cones."

Groaning, she slaps her hand into mine and lets me tug her up. "Of course you do."

As we turn, Juliet threads her arm in mine. And then she freezes, her eyes wide. I frown down at her. "What is it?"

"My parents," she whispers, "are walking into this room right now."

My head snaps up as I try to follow the line of her gaze. I narrow my eyes, squinting at the middle-aged-looking couple who walk in, the woman's hand curled around the man's arm. There is no doubt that the woman walking in is Juliet's mother. She's her double, fast-forward thirty years.

A fierce, terrible ache slices through me. I won't know Juliet like that. Won't see lines deepen at her eyes, threads of silver start to streak her lovely dark hair. I'm so caught up in these unexpected, unsettling thoughts, it takes me a minute to register that Juliet's tugging at my arm *hard*.

"Come on," she hisses. "We've gotta get out of here!" She glances around frantically, realizing what I already know—we're cornered, no exit but the one her parents have just walked through, no path but the one they're walking down as we speak. Her eyes dart around. She tugs me with her one way, then the other.

"Jules," I say, calm and quiet. "There's nowhere to go."

"Oh, I'll find somewhere," she says.

"Swear to God, Juliet, if you shove me into another shrub, I'll—"

"Jules!"

We both freeze. And then we turn slowly, facing the woman who just called her name, the man beside her, holding her hand.

Mr. and Mrs. Wilmot.

NINETEEN

Juliet

Mom wraps me in a gentle hug, always gentle these days. The sting of that gentleness fades when she says, "Hi, birdie," a nickname she and Dad use for me and my sisters that always makes me feel loved.

I melt into her hug. "Hi, Mom."

Her gaze darts past me to Will as she pulls back. "And who is this?"

"Mom, this is my friend Will Orsino. Will, my mom, Maureen Wilmo—"

"Orsino!" Mom claps her hands on her cheeks. "Oh my goodness, you're Isla's son, aren't you?"

"Uh, yes," Will says, smiling nervously. "It's nice to meet you."

I was expecting Mom to put the pieces together, especially considering Orsino is a rare last name. I imagine Will was, too. But I'm still not prepared, and I don't think Will is either, for the moment she launches herself at him and wraps him in a hug.

"My goodness, let me look at you," she says as she pulls back. "Isla's gorgeous red hair." Her hands land on his face, framing it. "Her incredible cheekbones, well, I think so at least, you've got an awfully thick beard, don't you?"

"Mom." I swat her gently. "Down, girl."

Mom swats me back. "Oh, let me admire him. This is so nostalgic. So special. To see Isla and Grant's kid, the product of that incredible summer—"

Dad clears his throat and smiles. Mom waves her hand. "It's just the best surprise," she says.

Dad offers his hand, and Will takes it. "Good to meet you, Will."

"Dad, Will Orsino. My dad," I tell Will. "Bill Wilmot."

Will nods politely. "Nice to meet you, sir."

Dad grins, his eyes squinting behind his glasses as he smiles. "I always like a guy with the name William."

I groan at the joke. Dad's name, like Will's, is short for William. Will grins down at me.

"So," Mom says. "What are you two up to? How did you meet?"

I tell her that Will is a friend of Christopher's from college, how we met the morning after Christopher's party a few weeks ago, our agreed narrative since we hatched our plan; that Will's in the city on weekends doing work, and we decided to pay a visit to the conservatory. Straightforward and to the point.

"How nice," Mom says. She gives me a squinty look, like she's trying to sniff out the truths I've carefully omitted.

I just smile wide and bat my lashes. Who me? I have nothing to hide.

"Well, this is just too small a world," she finally says, turning to Will. "I'd love to hear all about you. Get caught up on your parents. Oh, I just have to give Isla a call. She'll be so thrilled you two met. Tell you what." She claps her hands together and smiles wide. "Why don't you come to family dinner?"

———

Will, of course, is too polite to say no. And he's *so* polite, he offers to drive my parents, who rode the train in, back to their house.

Which is how we end up flying down the highway, Dad in the front seat picking Will's brain about the mechanics of his electrical truck, a turn of events that Will, given his very enthusiastic, in-depth responses, seems all too pleased with.

I fend off my mother's periodic knee squeezes and meaningful glances up front.

Just friends, I mouth.

Mom winks and mouths back, very sarcastically, *Got it.*

I roll my eyes.

The drive is smooth, not too heavy on traffic, and soon we're walking into the house, Mom bustling into the kitchen, telling us to get comfortable and pour ourselves a drink.

Dad serves Will the water he asks for, since he'll be driving home soon, and me a glass of white, because I won't and I need something to fortify me while I navigate this surreal spin on the evening.

"So, Will," Dad says, swirling his whiskey in its glass as we stand in the family room, pictures covering the wall that I keep catching Will glancing at, a smile tugging at his mouth. "Talk to me about casks—the charring process, I'm fascinated by it. If you don't mind, that is," he adds.

The front door opens, and in walk Jamie and Bea.

"Did I hear someone asking about oak casks?" Jamie calls.

Bea's eyes widen as she clocks Will, then snap to me. I give her a deer in the headlights look that she reads perfectly, smoothing her expression and pasting on a smile.

Jamie immediately jumps into the conversation with Dad and Will. I drop back and whisper to Bea, "They found us at the conservatory, and before you know it, Mom's invited Will to dinner and he's driving us home."

Bea searches my eyes, looking for answers to fill in the missing pieces. But I don't have them, at least, none that I'm ready to share. "The conservatory, huh?"

She doesn't say it, but I know what she's thinking. *Awfully romantic.*

I flash what I hope is a convincing smile. "Turns out, we both like flowers!"

Relief rushes through me when she doesn't press me, doesn't call me out. She just clasps my hand in hers and says, "How about we go set the table?"

The door opens again as we cross the entranceway, Christopher holding the door for Kate. "Did I miss setting the table?" Kate asks hopefully.

"Nope!" Bea and I call.

Kate's shoulders droop. "Damn."

Christopher laughs as she shuts the door behind her. "Go help them, you menace."

She throws him a glare. "*You* help."

He grins, leans in, and kisses her cheek. "You and the gals do this. The guys and I will take dish duty after dinner, while you put your feet up and eat as much dessert as you want. How's that sound?"

She tries to hold her squinty glare, but it falls, and a dreamy smile replaces it. "Fine," she sighs.

Christopher steals one more kiss, this time on the lips—*ew*—and strolls off, joining the guys.

Kate gets one look at Will in the mix and immediately glances my way. "Um, what's he—"

"Come on," I tell her, taking her by the hand. "I'll fill you in while we set the table."

————

Somehow, dinner flows effortlessly. Will's more reserved than Jamie and Christopher, but that's to be expected. He's new to the dynamic, and we're a rowdy bunch. I remember when Jamie was that way, too, everything about him perfectly polished and tidy, sitting ramrod straight at the table, so painfully polite, when he and Bea were first together, and look at him now, elbows on the table, sleeves rolled up, hair mussed, cheeks flushed pink, as he laughs at something Dad says.

I catch Will's eye and wink. He winks back, or at least, I think he tries to, but it's more of a concerted, two-eyed blink.

I smile.

And then I feel the tiniest, painful pinch right in my heart. Because this evening feels so good, so right, I never want it to end.

But it will. And soon.

———

Arms across my chest, I walk out onto my parents' porch, Will behind me, answering my parents' calls good night and waving before he shuts the door behind him.

Facing me, Will blows out a breath. "Well. That was a curveball."

I snort, rubbing my hands against my shoulders. The temperature's dropped, and there's a chill in the air that's giving me goose bumps. "Ya think?"

"I'd say we managed that pretty well."

I smile up at him. "Yeah, I think so."

"Definitely not what I had in mind for a third date," he says, "but then again, real life is like that, right? Unexpected twists. It's good practice, figuring out how to roll with it."

The reminder—that this is practice, that all of this is, makes my smile slip, just for a moment, before I manage to tack it back up and meet Will's eyes.

He's watching me, his gaze intent. "I really like your parents."

"They're a lot," I tell him.

He shrugs. "So are mine. Well, my dad, not so much. He's generally pretty chill and quiet, but get a couple whiskeys in him"—he snaps his fingers—"he's the life of the party."

I laugh. "He sounds fun."

"He is," Will says. "You'd like him." He pauses, then says, "He'd like you, too."

"Yeah?"

"Mm-hmm." Will grins. Then he blows out a breath. "I don't think *your* dad hates me. Which is nice."

I bite my lip. Will doesn't have to care what my dad thinks of him, but he does. I find it impossibly sweet. "You kidding me? You took him on a deep dive through the history of whiskey distillation. You answered every question he had about your electrical truck. He *adores* you."

"We might have swapped numbers," Will admits.

My mouth drops open. "Seriously?"

Will grimaces. "He asked! I couldn't say no. Plus . . . I like the guy."

"Juliet!" Mom calls from inside, her footsteps sounding as she walks closer. "Don't let that beau of yours leave without taking some dessert!"

"You hear that?" Will wiggles his eyebrows. "I'm your beau."

I groan, mortified. "I swear I told her eight times we're just friends."

Mom pops her head out, holding a container of trifle filled with summer berries. Will takes it, then says, "Thank you very much, Mrs. Wilmot. I appreciate it."

Mom's cheeks turn pink. "Please, I told you to call me Maureen! And it's no trouble. Now, you drive home safe and give Isla and Grant a big hug for me, you hear?"

"Yes, ma'am."

Mom clutches her chest and sighs. "So polite."

"Get back inside, would you?" I gently nudge her in, pulling the door shut, before I turn back to Will. "You've got my mom wrapped around your finger, too."

Will smiles, and there it is, wide and rare, revealing his straight white teeth, setting the handsome crinkles in his eyes.

"What are you grinning about, huh?" I poke him in the chest, a smile breaking across my face, too.

Will clasps my fingers and holds them against his heart as he peers down at me, his smile fading to something soft, something that seems . . . almost tender. "I had a great time tonight."

"I did, too," I tell him.

Gently, he lets go of my hand and takes a step back, then another, before he turns and jogs down the steps.

"Text me when you're home safe?" I yell.

"Will do!" he calls over his shoulder.

"And make it flirty!" I hiss-whisper, loud enough that I hope he can hear.

When he glances back again, I know he has. He winks in that way of his—a double blink, eyes crinkled. "I'll give it a try."

· TWENTY ·

Will

"Sending a message to Juliet?" Mom asks.

I hit the button on my phone to turn the screen dark. I was about to, but now I sure as hell am not.

Pushing off the fence penning in our two milk cows, Daisy and Buttercup, I throw a stick that Hector sprints after across the grass. "Just checking the weather," I tell her.

Mom leans against the fence beside me, massaging her left hand's knuckles. "I still can't get over it. Of all the small-world connections."

I decided to get ahead of whatever story I knew was going to make its way to Mom, between Fee seeing us at the pub and Juliet's mom sounding so excited to share the news, by telling her and Dad first thing Monday morning over coffee about befriending Juliet, meeting her parents, making the connection between our families.

All week long, Mom keeps dropping by, asking questions, pressing me for details on our "relationship." I've told her the truth each time: Juliet and I are friends, and that's all we'll ever be.

I've tried not to dwell on the sadness that's come each time I've said it, knowing even our friendship will likely have to end when our paths diverge again, mine toward my life here, finding the woman I'll spend my life and run the business with, hers toward her life in the city and her hope of falling in love again. I'm able to move beyond the sadness not because I won't miss Juliet or because saying goodbye won't hurt, but because I know that every ounce of sadness I'll feel after leaving her behind, no longer having what we've shared, will have been worth it. Because it gave me the chance, even just this sliver of time, to know Juliet. And I'm a better man for it. I hope she'll feel her life is better for having known me, too. I'm trying so damn hard to be sure that's the case.

My mom's shoulder gently knocks mine. "Where'd that lovely mind of yours wander off to?"

I peer down at my mother and wrap an arm around her. "All over the place."

She grins, setting her head against my chest, quiet for a minute, before she says, "Are you happy, Will?"

I stare out at the land as the dying sun spills blood orange across the fields and the tops of the trees, gilding their green leaves as they sway in the wind. At Dad, who stands on the back porch, hands on his hips, head thrown back, as he laughs with Fest. At Miranda, perched on the swing hanging from the massive oak tree beside the house, sketchpad in her lap. At Hector loping my way, ears flopping, stick wedged in his mouth.

Breathing in deep, I nod. I am happy. I am happy *and*—happy *and* carrying this ache that's been with me since my weekends began with Juliet, sharper when I think about her and miss her, when there's so much I want to show her and share with her here but don't, because that would only make it harder when I have to stop, when I have to move on and face what can never be: my world and her world becoming *our* world. Because soon we'll have to say goodbye.

"Yeah, Ma." I squeeze her gently against me. "I am."

"Good," she says.

Hector drops the stick at Mom's feet, panting, his big pink

tongue lolling out of his mouth. She picks it up and chucks the stick as far as she can, which is pretty damn far for a sixty-three-year-old dealing with rheumatoid arthritis.

She arches an eyebrow. "Don't look so surprised. I used to be a dynamite softball pitcher."

"Like I could forget sitting on the first-row bleachers, watching you kick butt in the local league? That no-hitter you pitched against the Capulettis in the family tournament?"

"Those cankerblossoms," she mutters darkly. Ma's strictly against swearing; I've always loved what she uses in place of cuss words. "Buttercup got out *once*, barely tromped through their disease-ridden cabbage patch, and they try to say at the town hall that she's a 'threat to local agriculture.' Trying to take away *my* son's beloved cow because of a ridiculous hundred-year-old family feud that my child had nothing to do with? Your poor father and I had to shell out—do you know how much? I can't even stand to say it—to replace their 'prizewinning' cabbages. 'Prizewinning,' my backside!"

"Easy does it." That was a mistake, mentioning our neighbors, the Capulettis, who've had a gripe with Mom's family for generations, something Mom had hoped they'd get past when she moved here after having inherited the land from her aunt. Her hopes were swiftly, brutally dashed, and she's never forgiven them for it. Bringing up the Capulettis is guaranteed to get Ma fired up.

She shakes her fist to the east, toward the Capulettis' property, which begins a mile away, past a thick grove of trees very intentionally planted to block our view of them, and says, "Just try and mess with Isla Montag Orsino or anyone she loves, and see where it gets you!"

I give up trying to calm her down and figure I'll join in instead. Turning east beside her, I raise my bent arm, hand fisted, and slap my other hand down on my biceps, honestly my favorite way to say *fuck you*, which I learned from Dad's grandfather. My great-grandpa,

Pap, was already as old as God when I was born, but he hung in there long enough to teach me the art of skipping rocks and the proper use of every colorful Italian hand gesture he knew.

"William Campbell Montag Orsino!" She swats my arm down. "That lewd Italian gesture is not permitted on my property."

I shrug. "I'm a quarter Italian, and those 'cankerblossoms' have been mean to my mama. I can't help it."

"A quarter Italian," she mutters, rolling her eyes, but a smile sneaks out. "It's less than that, sweetheart."

"Not according to Pap."

"Your great-grandfather, God rest his soul, might have been Italian and brave enough, when he married a very fiery Scottish woman, to try his hand at producing her family's whiskey rather than his family's wine, but after that, not another Italian has joined the Orsino family, all the way down to your father—"

"Who met *you*," I say sweetly, "another fiery Scottish woman who'd inherited the land that ran right along his, and then he wooed you, and you lived happily ever after."

"Eventually," she says softly, as she leans back against the fence, staring out at the land. "We found our way to happily ever after, eventually." She turns and faces me. "The takeaway is, you are at most, eh, twelve percent Italian?"

"Still Italian enough to give our neighbors l'ombrello."

She rolls her eyes and pats my cheek. "I do love you, my stubborn one."

"Love you, too, Ma."

Wordlessly, she pushes off the fence, then starts to walk back toward the house.

I wait until she's far enough away that I'm not worried she'll be able to look back and see what I'm doing, then yank out my phone and open up my messages. Every evening, after work, I've been texting Juliet, and I don't want to miss a day, before I head back to her tomorrow morning.

I've been trying my best with the flirty texting, but I still feel awkward as hell. I've reverted to cheesy, silly pickup lines more often than not, but at least they always seem to get a laugh out of her. Starting yesterday, though, I threw out the idea of rapid-fire questions, just about the small personal stuff I'd want to know about someone I'm trying to learn well enough to figure out if I can build a life with them. The right or left side of the bed? Favorite kind of music? Early bird or night owl? We didn't get too far before we both crashed for the night, and I want to pick up where we left off.

I tell myself I want more practice, but I know the truth: I want more from *her*. I want to know Juliet, to learn more every time I talk to her.

> **WILL:** You up?

> **JULIET:** What romance! Nothing makes my heart race like a booty call pick-up line.

A laugh leaves me. Hector drops the stick Mom threw at my feet and barks when I don't throw it for him. I'm typing my response to Juliet instead.

> **WILL:** Fine, I'll send a better one.

> **WILL:** How's the evening treating you, beautiful?

> **JULIET:** Yeah, like that a lot. 10/10.

> **JULIET:** Evening's been pretty relaxing. Weather's gorgeous, so I've got the windows open and some candles lit. Wrapped up a couple writing projects,

and now I'm just unwinding. How about you, handsome?

My heart jumps. *Handsome.* She's never called me that. *She's practicing, you ass. Just like you.*

Except it doesn't feel like practicing, texting her, wanting to know how she is, how her day is ending, getting texts from her that feel like she wants that, too.

I drag a hand through my hair and tug, frustrated. It's getting harder to keep it separate inside myself—what's practice with Juliet and what's real. Over and over again, I've had to remind myself that fixating on that distinction is futile, because even if every second of it were real, she'd still be off-limits; nothing else can ever come of it beyond this month of practice that we've promised each other. Shaking my head, I push those thoughts away and type back.

> **WILL:** Good day of work. Getting ready to roll out this new whiskey, the one I've been giving samples of to clients in the city, so it's busy right now, but productive. Had dinner with my parents, and now I'm just throwing a stick for the dog because if I don't make sure he burns off this energy, he'll get the zoomies later on and wake me up tearing around downstairs.

I finally chuck the stick again for Hector, then snap a picture of him streaking across the grass, a splotchy blur of blue-gray and white. When he runs back and drops the stick at my feet, I crouch, then snap another photo, this one a close-up of his goofy dog face tilted sideways, ears flopped forward, pink tongue lolling out of his mouth.

WILL: Meet Hector

JULIET: OH. MY. GOD!!

I stare at her response, nervous. I've mentioned I have a dog but not his breed.

WILL: Is that a good "OH MY GOD" or a bad one?

JULIET: Will, I'm literally kicking my feet right now & making the most ridiculous noises! He's the sweetest boy! I want to kiss his squishy face! I need to scratch behind his velvety little triangle ears! OF COURSE IT'S A GOOD "OH MY GOD" I LOVE HIM!!

My heart's thudding in my ribs, a ridiculously wide smile lighting up my face.

WILL: I just wasn't sure. Not everyone likes pit bulls. A lot of people don't.

JULIET: Well, that's their problem. The bad rap pit bulls have is so unfair. Any dog, no matter their breed, that isn't socialized well, that's neglected or mistreated or bred in an environment specifically for aggression (looking at you, dogfighting), is potentially dangerous. That's not on the animals. That's on humans to do better.

WILL: I know we're talking about my dog, & this is probably going to sound very weird, but the fact that you feel that way & just went off about it is very hot.

JULIET: Is it? Going on a tirade isn't necessarily the definition of being flirty.

I smile down at my phone, then throw the stick for Hector and lean back against the fence.

WILL: Well, that tirade did it for me. 10/10.

WILL: I want to ask some more rapid-fire questions, if that's okay.

JULIET: I liked doing that yesterday ☺. Ready when you are!

WILL: Road trip or flight?

JULIET: Road trip!

I grin at her response. I love driving, enjoying not just my destination but the journey to get there. I'll fly places when it's the most practical way to get there, but otherwise, it's the open road, for me.

WILL: Same here.

JULIET: Favorite cheese?

I snort. This woman. My favorite *cheese*?

WILL: Gouda & if you hate it, don't tell me. I can't handle the pain.

JULIET: I LOVE GOUDA. It's smoky! It's creamy! Shit, now I want some.

WILL: It's the smokiness for me. Peat-smoked whiskey. Chargrilled veggies. Anything that makes me taste a bonfire in my mouth is a win.

JULIET: Yesss. When you're here this weekend, we've got to stop by Nanette's, my favorite pastry shop. They've been slow on rolling out gluten-free treats, BUT they recently added an ice cream booth & holy shit, their smoked chocolate caramel ribbon is TO DIE FOR.

WILL: Sold.

WILL: Next question's mine: What's the best thing that happened to you today?

She doesn't respond right away, and I'm about to poke her with a reminder that these are *rapid-fire*, when her text comes in.

JULIET: This bath.

And then a picture pops up. I nearly drop my phone.

A sea of bubbles. Candles flickering golden in the corners against the white subway tiles. Her knees breaking the water's surface, ten pink toenails peeking out farther down. It's a very tame photo, objectively speaking, but I'm just so fucking hungry for this woman, seeing a sliver of her legs, the suggestion of her naked body in warm, sudsy water, is turning me rock hard.

I know I'm breaking the rules, that I'm supposed to rapid-fire respond back, but I'm speechless, white knuckling my phone. Her next text comes through and startles me so badly, this time I do drop it. I scoop my phone up from the grass, brush dirt off the screen, and beg the blood that rushed south to come back to my brain, so it can process what my eyes are reading:

> JULIET: What about you? Best thing that happened
> to you today?

Well, that's easy to answer. I type my response back, then hit send.

> WILL: This photo. Obviously.

TWENTY-ONE

Juliet

I'm back in the tub again the next morning, soaking in piping-hot water, willing away the ache in my joints as steam curls from the tub into the morning light. I haven't heard from Will yet what the plan is for tonight, but whatever it is, I'd like not to feel like a corpse for it.

I've eaten breakfast and popped my hefty naproxen sodium. Now I just wait to see if it'll help. Waiting to figure out if my body's going to feel better. Waiting to hear from Will. Waiting to figure out how the hell I'm going to keep my body in check this weekend, when just the thought of him makes me ache right between my thighs. I'm too impatient a person to handle it—I'm not built for this much delayed gratification!

Like a divine universal blessing, my phone starts to buzz. As long as it's not a telemarketer, or that weird guy who keeps trying to order a pastrami sandwich when I've told him a dozen times he has the wrong number, I'll pick up. I need something to distract me from all this waiting around.

I dab my hand on the towel resting on the tub's edge.

My phone buzzes again. And again. And again. Too fast to be a phone call.

A text message thread to get sucked into! Even better.

Hands dry, I pick up my phone from its perch on the closed

toilet lid and lean my elbows on the tub's edge. The friend group chat is blowing up.

SULA: We've got a babysitter & Rowan's been sleeping through the night all week. I'm feeling well slept & SLUTTY. Let's go out tonight!!

MARGO: By "slutty," Sula means "slutty with her wife."

SULA: Babe, that's a given. We both know I only get nasty on the dance floor with you.

TONI: *& that dominatrix with the pink bouffant last year at the New Year's Eve party.

SULA: Antoni, let's not throw stones at glass houses—you were right there with me. Besides, things done when I've ingested absinthe don't count.

MARGO: L O L, that was the best night ever.

HAMZA: Toni was hungover for a week.

TONI: I regret bringing up that night. I'm getting nauseous just thinking about it. I can't even smell black licorice anymore without dry heaving.

BEEBEE: Dry heaving is the only appropriate response to smelling black licorice. Jamie's working today, but he doesn't have evening rounds at the shelters this week, so he's free & I can answer for us both—we're in!

KITKAT: I'm in too, but only if dominatrices are involved. I was traveling for work on NYE last year. I need to see what I missed!

SULA: Your wish just might be granted. It's a "hidden desires" theme night at the club. Margo's off, so she'll be on the fun side of the bar aka free to get nasty on the dance floor with me & all the other deviants.

MARGO: Dominatrices, here we come!

HAMZA: Have we started a drinking game? Take a shot of coffee every time someone uses "dominatrix/dominatrices"?

SULA: That's a dangerous game, Hamza. I think most of us are already chronically overcaffeinated.

CHRISTOPHER: I have never seen the word dominatrix/dominatrices so many times in one conversation. I should have known better than to pick up my phone during an investor meeting.

KITKAT: That's what you get for working on a Saturday! Leaving me all alone in bed this morning . . .

BEEBEE: GROUP CHAT VIOLATION STRIKE 1! Keep your smexy talk out of here.

TONI: Was that really smexy though? Like obviously they share a bed.

BEEBEE: Butt out of this Antoni.

TONI: 🙁

CHRISTOPHER: Kate, I just have this one call, that's it. I'm literally two rooms down from you in my home office.

KITKAT: Really?? Did I know that?

CHRISTOPHER: I told you last night I had a call but I wasn't going into town.

KITKAT: Wow. You must have told me when I was distracted.

CHRISTOPHER: You were definitely distracted 😈 🔥

BEEBEE: GROUP CHAT VIOLATION STRIKE 2! One more, & you're both out for 24 hrs.

CHRISTOPHER: Warning received. 🫡

SULA: Back to the subject at hand.

MARGO: (In other words, dominatrices).

CHRISTOPHER: Right. Kate & I will be there, with whips & chains.

KITKAT: Let's be clear about who'll be wielding the whips & chains in our duo, Petruchio 😏.

SULA: Dominatrix alert!

BEEBEE: STRIKE 3

MARGO: Oh, give them a pass.

BEEBEE: Fine.

BEEBEE: STRIKE 2.5

All caught up, I think over my response. Will and I presumably have plans. I could see if he wanted to come, too? Earplugs in tow? I debate texting the group, asking if we can add him to the list, when I realize our group chat image, a photo of all of us from last Friendsgiving, isn't at the top of my phone, no group chat name (normally, "FRANDS") at the top, either.

My heart's beating a little faster now, my face lifting with a smile as I tap on the many faces in the group chat at the top and scroll down.

There he is.

Will. Someone added him. Someone thought of him and included him, and shit, it makes my heart squeeze with happiness.

I wonder why he hasn't responded yet, then. Maybe he's waiting to ask me if I want to do this rather than whatever he had planned? But then why hasn't he texted *me*?

I check the time. Nine in the morning. Well, that explains it.

That poor guy. He's most likely driving, on his way here, and his phone has been going off nonstop this whole time. Should I add to that?

Maybe his phone hasn't been going off, though. Maybe he puts it in do-not-disturb mode while he drives. Or on silent.

Oh, even if he doesn't, I can't hold it in. I'm all fed up with waiting for one more thing. I send him a text to get the ball rolling:

JULIET: Hey, you. I imagine you're on the road, but just wanted to check in & see if you caught all those messages from the friend group & what your thoughts were. I don't know what you had planned for the day & if you'd want to fit it in. Let me know!

I'm setting my phone back on the toilet lid when it buzzes, the screen lighting up with Will's name. I am shameless. I pick it up on the first ring.

"Hey!"

"Hey, Jules." Will's voice echoes in my bathroom, and it does something funny to me, hearing his deep voice bounce around in here, while I'm lying naked in the tub.

I slap some water on my face. *Knock it off, Juliet!*

"Got your text," he says, "but as you figured, I'm on the road. Thought I'd call and we could talk this way, if you don't mind."

I bite my lip against a smile as I sink down into the water, leaning against my little inflated pillow suctioned to the back of the tub.

"I don't mind," I tell him, scooping up a handful of bubbles. "In fact, I'm honored. Gramps deigned to use his phone—not even for texting but for *calling*."

A soft laugh rumbles through the line. "Think you're funny, do you?"

"Sounds like you do, too."

"I'll have you know I actually *enjoy* phone calls, much more than texts. At least, with people I like. Telemarketers and nosy Great-Aunt Gertrude can take a hike, though."

"Gertrude is the most great-aunt name I've ever heard."

"She goes by Gert."

I laugh. "Oh, even better."

"So," he says. "I got all the group messages."

"Bet that was fun to experience while driving."

"It was pretty entertaining. I kept having Siri read them for me—hearing 'dominatrix' spoken in an Australian accent, something that wasn't on my bucket list, but now I see what I was missing."

A laugh jumps out of me. "Why Australian?"

"If I'm going to have entire conversations with my phone, might as well at least enjoy a good accent."

"You tell Siri please and thank you, don't you?"

"Robots," he says seriously, "are going to take over the world. And when they do, they will remember me as someone who treated them with dignity and respect. And then I will be spared, and all the fools who treated Siri like shit on the bottom of their shoe will see too late the error of their ways."

I'm laughing so hard my stomach hurts. "Is that what the big beard is about? Are you a doomsdayer? Do you have a bunker somewhere crammed full of dehydrated ice cream and fifty-gallon tubs of soup?"

"Don't need a bunker or postapocalyptic rations when you're on the robots' good side. As for the beard, it's the only thing keeping me from being an open book."

"What do you mean?"

"It makes my expressions harder to read—"

Something I know well and frequently find myself resenting.

"—and I'm shit at hiding what I'm thinking. Clean-shaven, I broadcast everything. Might as well have a transcript of my thoughts rolling across my face. The beard's my only protection."

"Well, I'm honestly just teasing," I tell him. "I like the beard. It's very . . . burly. It suits you."

"Nah, it's been unkempt for a while. I get so busy I don't even think about it, and before I know it my sisters are calling me Bigfoot and Yeti at family dinner. But maybe I shaped it up a little. You'll just have to wait and see."

I wiggle my toes against the edge of the tub. "When *will* I see?"

"Well, that's up to you. I did have plans for us this evening, but on the earlier side, at five. That was the only time they had a reservation. Depending on when this . . . event? with everyone kicks off, we can ditch my plan and do the event instead, or we can keep my plan and join them after."

"Given that the last event at the club started at eight, I think we'll be fine. And even if it starts earlier, I don't think we should change our plans."

Because I want time with you, just the two of us.

I don't tell Will that. I don't tell him that I've missed him all week, and I'd hate losing one of our nights together to a group outing, as fun as I know it will be.

"You sure?" he asks.

I blow out a slow, steadying breath and keep my voice light. "I'm sure. It would be very irresponsible to neglect our practice session."

"That's a good point," he says. "When I get into town, I'll let everyone know I'm coming."

"Perfect. I'll respond as soon as we hang up, so our RSVPs aren't too close together. Don't want to raise any suspicion."

There's a beat of silence that makes me uneasy. I'd give a million bucks—well, not a million; I don't have that kind of dough, between the limited income I'm earning from my freelance work, paying for insurance from the marketplace, and how expensive rent is for this apartment, now that I'm the only one living in it, but I'd fork over a hefty sum—to be able to see his face and read between the lines of his silence.

Did I offend him, when I mentioned not raising suspicion with the group? I know he's said he doesn't want to hide, but we've also agreed our practice plan is our private business.

Before the silence can stretch on any longer and send me into a panic, I ask him, "So what *are* our plans that start at five tonight?"

"It's a surprise," Will says.

Relief whooshes through me that he sounds fine, just like he did before.

"Can I guess?"

"You miss the part when I said it was a surprise?"

I smile, feeling playful. "Hmm. We're going to . . . the museum."

"Not doing this."

"Bowling?" I try.

"Oh, come on."

"What's wrong with bowling? I love bowling!"

"Me, too," he says. "You're just way off the mark."

I frown in thought. "We're . . . going back to the conservatory. Since you're bummed that we had to skip the carnivorous plant room last time because it was closed."

"Eh, you've seen one Venus flytrap, you've seen them all."

A laugh jumps out of me. "Jamie nearly got attacked by one, the first time he and Bea went together."

"Really?"

"Well, it depends on who tells you the story. According to Jamie, it just grazed his shoulder; he's very stoic about it. But how Bea tells it, you'd think he nearly lost an arm."

Will's deep laugh rumbles across the line.

I smile, shifting in the water. "You're really not going to tell me our plans?"

"I will, if you want," he says. "If it would stress you out not to know. I don't really like surprises myself, but I've heard that a surprise, done well at least, can be . . . you know . . . romantic. And that's what I'm making sure you get. Romance."

My heart spins so fast, I feel dizzy.

Practice romance, that sensible voice reminds me. *It's all practice, Juliet.*

Fine. It's just practice. But it's still giving me butterflies. And I intend to let them soar.

Smiling into the phone, I tell him, "Then surprise me."

"You got it," he says.

"When should I be ready?"

"Hmm, let's say four thirty? That work?"

I pull my phone away long enough to read the time and kick my legs miserably. Seven hours of waiting! I've got to find something to do with myself today, or I'm gonna lose it.

"Four thirty," I tell him. "I'll be ready."

"Excellent. And Juliet?"

"Yes, Will?"

"Wear something fancy, all right?"

Something fancy? Those butterflies whip round and round in my stomach. I bite my lip against a smile. "Okay."

The call ends. I sit there for a moment with an alarmingly goofy grin, the phone glued to my ear before I set it on the toilet seat's lid and plunge myself down into the water.

TWENTY-TWO

Will

I walk into Fee's studio apartment, dropping my bag just inside the door and walking the creaky floorboards, then open up my phone and the group chat to send my RSVP. A groan leaves me when I see Juliet's response.

JULIET: I'll be there! And I'm definitely dressing on theme 😏.

Dressing on theme? The theme, as I remember Australian Siri telling me, is dominatrices. I sigh heavily and thunk my head against the wall, trying to dislodge the image of Juliet dressed in tight black leather, smacking a whip against her palm.

It doesn't work.

Pushing off the wall, I pace the room some more, hoping reading the rest of these texts will do the trick.

SULA: HELL YESSS LET'S GO!!

MARGO: I'm taking bets on how many of us show up as a dominatrix.

HAMZA: *gulps coffee*

TONI: Well, now I've got a costume to put together, so if you'll excuse me, some of us have a job to do so we can close on time and hit the thrift store afterward.

SULA: I'm sitting five feet away from you, & the sum total of your work today has consisted of laughing at cat Reels on Instagram and painting your nails.

TONI: Excuse me, I have also been very diligently stamping bags with the Edgy Envelope logo.

SULA: While watching New Girl on your phone.

TONI: I can't help that it's been a quiet day at the shop!

MARGO: You two, take your bickering to a side chat. Everyone else, get your costumes together & let's meet outside at the club, 8pm sharp! Can't wait!

JAMIE: Just caught up on this over my tea break. I'm going to need 5 to 7 business days to process what I just read.

SULA: Too bad! You only have 7 hours! Good luck with those costumes!

JULIET: I went through a black leather phase in college & I've never been able to part with any of it, so I'll be shopping from the comfort of my closet. If anyone else dressing on theme wants to start somewhere that costs zero $, let me know!

Another groan leaves me, because there's the image again. Juliet. Black leather. All those curves. I'm nearly cross-eyed, I'm so turned on by the thought. Only by the grace of autocorrect does my response make a lick of sense:

> **WILL:** Late to this, but I'm in. Appreciate the invite!
>
> **SULA:** Yes, Will!!! We're at 100% attendance, folks (let the record show that I didn't invite Bianca & Nick but only because they already told us they're off doing cute coupley shit this weekend). SEE YOU THERE!
>
> **TONI:** Jules, what kind of black leather are we talking?
>
> **JULIET:** Photos incoming.

When the first image comes in, my phone clatters to the floor.

> **JULIET:** Oopsie! Meant that just for Ton. Please disregard.

The image vanishes with a pop as she unsends it, but I can't unsee it. A shiny black bustier. The thought of that wrapped around her waist, pushing up her—

"Dammit." I bend over the dresser and thunk my head even harder than I did on the wall.

Here I was, so relieved that Juliet and I would have something to do after this romantic dinner I have planned, that there'd be no loaded silences as I drove her home, no temptation to walk her upstairs and past her door and give in to this terrible, consuming want. But now that I know she's going to be dressed like this?

I brace my hands on the dresser and stare at my reflection in the mirror mounted to it. And then I tell my reflection the truth:

"You are absolutely fucked."

· TWENTY-THREE ·

Juliet

I've already buzzed him upstairs, and when Will's knock on my door echoes through the apartment, I'm ready to go, fancied up, just like he asked me to be. My hair falls around my shoulders in soft waves, ready to be twisted up later for my dominatrix outfit. I smooth my hands down my ivory dress as I step back from examining myself in my bedroom's full-length mirror, satisfied with what I see.

The dress's warm white hue makes my fair skin glow; the neckline is a flattering scoop that sits wide at the edge of my shoulders. My gold stud earrings, heirlooms from Grandma Viola, sparkle with tiny diamonds. I test the backs, make sure they're in tight, as I walk down the hall into the open concept living, dining, and kitchen space. Then I reach behind me, checking that the zipper that sits at the small of my back is all the way up. My comfy-footbed, low-heel nude pumps click softly on the wood floors.

"Come in!" I tell him.

After a second, I hear the door open and bang into the coat hooks on the wall, followed by a muttered curse, and smile to myself.

"Don't worry," I call. "I've been living in this apartment for years, and it still happens to me . . ." My voice dies off as I round the corner into the little entranceway. I freeze in my tracks.

Will stands in the foyer, wearing a deep gray suit, his jacket open, a crisp white shirt beneath it. He stares at me, mouth parted, eyes wide. A fierce blush creeps up his cheeks—cheeks that I can actually *see*.

The big, bushy beard has been shaved down to a thick, tidy scruff. Which means that, finally, I can see . . . all of him.

And he's breathtaking.

Sharp jaw, faint hollows at his cheeks, the tiniest cleft at his chin. I stare at his mouth, now that it isn't hidden beneath his beard. All I can think about is tasting that mouth, dragging his bottom lip slowly between my teeth, earning his groaning sighs.

"Your beard," I whisper hoarsely. "It's . . . not very beardy anymore."

Will brings a hand to his face, seeming self-conscious as he scrubs it along his scruffy jaw. His eyes are dancing over me. He looks . . . dazed. "Uh-huh."

"You look great, Will."

"Uh-huh," he says again. A thick swallow works down his throat.

I take a step toward him. "You okay, big guy?"

He shakes his head. "Nuh-uh."

A soft laugh jumps out of me. I smooth my hands down the lapels of his suit. "What's the matter?"

He's peering down at me, his gaze heated. His jaw tightens. He shoves his hands into his pockets, and I wonder why. Is he trying to keep them to himself? Good for him. I, however, am not strong enough to resist temptation.

"Jules," he says roughly, staring down at me still. "You look . . . perfect. Your hair. Your dress . . ." He drags his hands out of his pockets, rakes them through his hair, and blows out a breath. "Jesus."

My cheeks heat. I shrug, smiling wide. "Aw, this old thing?"

"I . . ." He huffs out a laugh. His hands fall to his sides. "I'm speechless. Which I know probably doesn't seem like it's saying much, but . . ."

I clasp his hand and squeeze. "Thank you," I whisper, smiling up at him. "Ready to bowl?"

A faint, rough laugh rumbles in his chest. He turns his hand in mine and gently squeezes back. "Ready when you are."

I should grab my stuff so we can go to wherever we're actually headed, but I can't seem to move my feet. My heart's flying as I stare up at him.

Will frowns. "What is it?"

"It's just . . . I can *see* you."

His eyes hold mine. "Is that . . . a good thing?"

"It's a fabulous thing." I reach for the off-white wrap I plan to bring in case I get chilly, hanging on the back of a dining chair, then my purse on the table beside it. "You're a fucking knockout."

His cheeks turn beet red. He ducks his head, staring down at his polished brown boots, and scrubs at the back of his neck. "Thank you," he says quietly.

When he peers up again, he offers me his arm. "Shall we?"

My heart spins. I take his arm and smile up at him. "We shall."

"Will," I hiss-whisper as we walk into the restaurant, my hand wrapped around his biceps. I've never been to this restaurant, but I know it's the epitome of luxurious fine dining and wildly expensive. "This is way too nice."

He steps behind me and tugs my wrap back up on my shoulders. "No, it isn't."

I don't have the chance to argue with him because he turns to the host, who stands with menus in hand, ready to guide us toward our table. We follow them, Will's hand on my back—my bare back—its rough warmth sending pleasure rolling down my spine. The host stops at a two-top tucked into a quiet corner of the restaurant, where candlelight dances across the dark linen tablecloth and a delicate crystal vase of peach-pink tea roses.

Will pulls out my chair, then slides it in after I sit.

I watch him unbutton his suit jacket with one hand, then drop into his seat across from me. Candlelight loves him. It sets his gorgeous hair aflame, glows in his striking gray-green eyes, washes warm across the planes of his face, and leaves sharp shadows that accentuate what I can see now is an unbelievably beautiful bone structure. My gaze travels down his face, the jut of his Adam's apple, the hollow of his throat revealed by the opening at his shirt collar. Down his broad shoulders and arms, to his hands. God, even his hands are beautiful—elegantly long yet rough-knuckled, his nails trimmed short and neat.

I cross my legs beneath the table against the ache building between my thighs. I picture those hands skating down my body, smoothing over my hips, gently parting my legs, teasing their way higher, higher—

Will's knees knock mine, wrenching me from my lusty trance. He scrunches his eyes shut. "Sorry."

I playfully knock my knee into his again. "Don't be. Footsie is classic flirting."

He meets my eyes, his expression tight. "I don't fit at tables like this."

"This table does not seem to be made with tall, long-legged guys in mind. Want to go sit at the bar instead?"

He shakes his head. "Nah. I'll be fine."

I pick up my menu and start to look at it. Gently, I clench his boot between my heels and squeeze affectionately, hoping it helps him relax and dispels the nerves that have settled between us.

When I glance over the menu, he's staring at me so intensely, I lower the menu a little, meeting his eyes. The faintest smile lifts the corner of his mouth, which I'm still pinching myself I can finally see so well. I drink in his face. I could stare at him for hours.

"Pinkie-promised honesty moment." He leans in slightly. "I'm nervous."

Butterflies swarm my stomach. I lean in, too. "So am I."

It's true. I am nervous. I know it's not an actual date, that this is all practice, but it still feels special, like the stakes are higher tonight.

"Remember." I squeeze his boot again between my feet. "We'll wobble together."

He swallows thickly. "Yeah."

After a beat, he sits back, and I do, too. I watch him clasp the carafe of ice water that's sitting at our table, and I reach for my glass, wanting to be helpful, to bring it toward him to fill. But my hand knocks over the glass, just as Will starts to pour. The glass clatters noisily against my silverware and rolls sideways. The water from the pitcher sloshes across my plate and onto the tablecloth.

"Shit!" I hiss. "I'm so sorry."

"God, sorry," he says at the same time, lunging for my water glass as it starts to roll toward the edge of the table. As he reaches for it, the audible *thunk* of his knee connecting with the table's leg echoes around us.

Will lets out a groan as he drops back into his chair with the glass and half-empty carafe in hand.

Mortification heats my cheeks. "Will, I'm so sorry. That was my fault."

Will shakes his head. His face is bright red. "Don't be sorry, Jules. It's okay." He reaches to set my glass back down, and his hand hits the end of my fork as he does, flipping it up into the air, then onto his plate with a clatter.

He drops his head and lets out a defeated sigh.

I reach for my fork carefully to take it from his plate, to put it back where it belongs, but in doing so, my knit wrap snags on *his* fork and drags it with me across the table.

Will peers up quickly at the sound of his fork falling from my wrap, clanging onto my bread plate. I know I should be even more embarrassed than I have been the past sixty seconds of nonstop disasters, but it hits me the way some moments do, when it's absurd how bad they are—I laugh. First, it's a squeak I try to hold in. I slap a hand over my mouth. A snort sneaks out next.

Will blinks rapidly, glancing from my face down to the fork that just fell from my wrap. His tongue pokes into his cheek. The corner of his mouth quirks up. His shoulders start to shake.

It feels like the end of Guess Who at game night, but even better. A blast of laughter jumps out of me, and I double forward. A deep, husky laugh rumbles from Will's chest. He covers his face with his hands as his shoulders shake harder.

"This is a *disaster*," he mutters.

"It really is," I croak.

After a moment, we finally manage to get ourselves together. Our eyes hold. Our amusement slowly fades.

Carefully, Will plucks the fork off my plate and sets it back in its rightful place. I watch him as he does it, so handsome in profile, his brow furrowed, his lips pursed in concentration. He peers up and registers me staring. A soft blush creeps across his cheeks.

I smile reflexively, because that's what looking at Will, being with Will, does to me. Gratitude washes through me, warm and sweet. I clasp his hand and cling to that comfort. I need that comfort. Because there's some kind of newness between us tonight that frightens me. I thought at first it was just the nerves, the butterflies from seeing each other fancied up, the palpable sexual tension and attraction that's undeniably there.

But I'm starting to worry it's something else, something beyond the comfort and familiarity of what we've built in the past few weeks.

Will turns his hand inside mine and rubs our palms together.

"Juliet—" he says.

Right as I say, "Will—"

I grit my teeth in frustration as our waiter appears, interrupting us. We pull apart, sitting back as they welcome us and efficiently swap out my watery plate, menu, and water goblet without a word about it. The wine menu is set in between us, and I'm told about all my gluten-free options. It's the entire menu, either as is or with gluten-free substitutes available.

My heart twists as I glance over at Will watching me intently, the tiniest curve up at one side of his mouth.

Our server leaves, and I knock his knee with mine. "How dare you?"

His eyes narrow a little as he leans in. "How dare I what?"

"Find a place where I can eat *everything* on the menu." I swallow against the lump in my throat. "I already forgot what that's like, what I used to take for granted—just looking at a menu and being able to pick whatever I wanted." A beat of silence passes as I try not to cry. "It means so much, Will. Thank you."

His gaze holds mine. "It was the least I could do, to make sure you could eat at the restaurant I brought you to."

I give him a playful glare. "Stop being too good to be true, Will Orsino."

"Trust me, I'm not."

"Lies," I tell him.

"Just you wait." He points to the menu. "You'll see."

"What do you mean?"

He leans in, voice lowered. "I have a very serious condition. Order-itis."

"Order-itis?"

"I can't order from a menu to save my life."

"What do you mean?"

He picks up the menu, tipping it my way. "That dish, the butternut squash paccheri?"

I nod.

"That's what I want." He grimaces. "But when our server comes back, order-itis will kick in, and I will either mangle the name, or I'll flat-out order another item that I don't even want."

"Why?"

"Anxiety, I guess? Who knows. I just get . . . flustered." He shrugs. "I've done it for as long as I can remember."

I bite my lip. "I hate to say it, because it can't be fun to deal with but . . . that's kinda cute?"

He arches an eyebrow as he leans in closer, skepticism etched in his features. A fiery lock of hair slips out from behind his ear and brushes his temple. "You'll be revising that statement when I order butter-squash nut-packs."

A laugh jumps out of me. I lean in and brush back that lock of hair, tucking it behind his ear, softly tracing the sharp plane of his cheekbone, before I even realize what I've done.

I start to pull my hand away, but Will catches it and clasps it gently. His eyes hold mine. Slowly I turn my hand inside his, then slide my fingers down until they're tangled with his, our hands resting on the table between us.

"You ordered a blueberry muffin and cold brew just fine," I counter softly, "that first day, at Boulangerie."

He nods, like he anticipated this. "I wanted a chocolate chip scone."

I bite my lip. "Oh."

"You can laugh," he says. "It's pretty ridiculous."

"Nope." I tangle our fingers tighter. "At Fee's, too? Did you not want the Reuben?"

"Oh I wanted the hell out of that Reuben. But Fee's like family. She's easy to talk to, so it was easier to keep my thoughts straight and tell her what I wanted."

With my free hand, I draw a menu between us, for us both to look at. "Well, I could always order for both of us?"

He sighs. "I thought about asking you to do that, honestly. But . . . I'd like to try, to see if I can break a thirty-four-year streak. Well, maybe thirty-one. That's the first time I remember doing it. At the farmer's market. I was three. I wanted a chocolate ice cream cone in the worst way."

I set a hand over my mouth. "I can't take it. Don't tell me how badly disappointed tiny Will was."

"I asked for a Firecracker Popsicle instead."

I groan. "Nooo."

"Or, as I said it back then, a fie-cwacka."

"Stop." I clutch my heart, in agonies. "I can't take it."

He laughs softly. "Like I said, maybe tonight will be different. I'm . . . willing to try, to take a chance on something I haven't for a long time."

I search his eyes, my heart racing. I know he's talking about ordering, but for a moment, I can't help but give in to a delusional hope that he's talking about something else, too. Something more.

Something that just might be us?

Don't hope, Juliet. Don't you dare do it.

I force myself to look away, to gently draw my hand back on the pretense of needing it to hold my menu.

"So, important question," I say to him, "even if you are ordering for yourself—are we sharing meals?"

Will looks offended that I even asked. "Obviously."

I throw him a teasing scowl. "How would I know if that worked for you?"

"Because it's romantic!"

I smile. "You get that tidbit from a certain romance novel I sent you home with last week?"

He peers down at his menu, dragging a hand along his jaw. "Not *just* the romance novel. Which I do like, by the way."

"Oh goodie! Have you gotten to the adorable grocery store meet-cute?"

He glances up, then leans in, voice quiet, "I might have just gotten to their first make-out."

I gasp. I know that romance novel very well—I've reread it twice, so I know exactly when that *very* sexy make-out happens and how far it is in the novel.

"You read that much already?"

"Audiobook," he says, eyes back down on the menu. "I've done a mix of reading the paperback in the evenings and listening to it when I had time during the day and on the drive down—at least, when Australian Siri wasn't telling me about this dominatrix party tonight."

I laugh. "I'm glad you like it so far."

He peers up again and smiles. "I do. Thanks for lending it to me."

"That one has a great dinner date. Did that inspire tonight?"

Will glances back down at the menu. "Not exactly." After a beat, he says, "*Lady and the Tramp* was my favorite movie, growing up."

Dear God. This man is going to kill me. "Are you kidding me?"

"It's my truth, Juliet. I won't deny it."

I sigh and shut my menu. "Well, now we *have* to get the pasta dish."

We step out of the restaurant, where the air outside is deliciously cool on my hot cheeks, which are flushed from wine and laughing and shameless flirtation. My hand drifts instinctively to its rightful place, wrapped around Will's biceps.

"So your sisters," I say to him. "Helena, Celia, Imogen, Miranda. Did I get the order right?"

He nods.

"You didn't say, where do you fall in birth order?"

"Oldest."

"No way!" I offer him a high five. "Me, too."

He meets it with a satisfying slap. "It's a tough job, bossing everyone around and always being right, but someone's gotta do it."

A laugh jumps out of me. "A cross to bear, but we bear it nobly."

Soft, husky laughter rolls out of him, too, and pleasure zips across my skin. I love earning his laugh.

Will stares down at me, drinking in my face. "What's that smile for?"

I squeeze his arm. "I just like you, Will Orsino. That's all."

His cheeks turn pink. His gray-green eyes glitter like starlight on frosty leaves. "I like you, too, Juliet Wilmot."

Will stops us at the valet desk outside, handing one of the valets his ticket and cash, while thanking them. Then he turns back and peers down at me, his gaze warm.

"When did you become a vegetarian?" I ask.

"On my twelfth birthday. When my mom gave me my first cow, Buttercup."

I smile. "Couldn't be any cuter."

"Who?" he asks. "Me or the cow?"

"Both."

He grins.

I tip my head toward the restaurant. "That was delightful."

"Especially," he says, "the butter-patch nut-squash."

"Especially that. And the golden beet salad that you accidentally ordered instead of the citrus salad. That was my favorite."

"It was pretty tasty," he admits, rocking back on his heels. "With the honey drizzle and goat cheese on top?"

"And the chopped pistachios." I hum with pleasure at the memory. "Delicious. Thank you again for dinner. For all of it. It was incredible."

He gives me one of those adorable double-blink winks. "You're welcome, Jules. I think it was pretty incredible, too."

A silence falls between us, and I brace myself for our usual post-practice-date debrief. Because I'm dreading it. I've been living in a dreamy little bubble for the past two hours, pushing away all thought of practice. I'm not ready for it to be burst, to crash back down to reality.

The wind picks up and Will turns to face me, nearly placing us chest to chest. Gently, he smooths back my hair, which the wind has whipped forward, tucking it behind my ears. His thumbs graze my cheeks, my jaw, whisper down the sensitive skin beneath my ears, down my neck, to my collarbones. I shiver, and it's got nothing to do with the cool evening air.

The valet rolls up to the curb beside us with Will's truck just as I'm leaning in, contemplating how reckless and wonderful it would be to kiss the hell out of him. Will takes a step back but still finds my hand with his and clasps it gently, drawing me with him and helping me into the truck.

As he pulls out, I hold my breath, braced for the practice debrief that hasn't yet happened, that *should* happen, because that's what keeps us in safe, familiar territory. But Will's focused on driving, apparently all thoughts of debriefing far from his mind. It's front and center in mine, and I should bring it up, keep us safe, I *know* I should. But dammit, I don't *want* to. I want tonight to feel fun and free of practicing for other people, planning for futures without each other. I want to stay in my dreamy little bubble just a little longer.

So, instead of doing what I should, I turn in my seat to face him, and ask, "What are you dressing as tonight?"

He frowns, his eyes pinned on the road. "I'm not telling you."

"Why not?" I ask indignantly.

"It's a *surprise*," he says. "Obviously. Tonight is the night of surprises."

"Rude." I slump back in my seat, arms folded across my chest. "You know my costume!"

"Not my fault you blabbed in the group chat."

I slug his thigh playfully.

"Hey, that's my driving leg, ma'am." He clasps my hand, but instead of moving it away, he threads his fingers through mine.

I melt at that, just a little—okay, a lot. This feels so good. Every moment has, since he picked me up. Even the awkward moments, the clumsy ones. It's all felt so damn good.

I can't think about it a second longer, can't let my mind wander down the path it wants to. The one paved with questions I shouldn't be asking:

Why does it feel *so* good?

Was that really practice tonight or was it . . . real?

Was that cryptic sentence really just about ordering food, or was it about . . . us?

Maybe tonight will be different. I'm . . . willing to try, to take a chance on something I haven't for a long time.

If it was about us, what does that mean?

And, the scariest question of all—have I romance-practiced my way with Will Orsino right into very real romantic feelings?

TWENTY-FOUR

Will

Juliet doesn't want me to give her a ride to the hidden desires party that starts in just under an hour. She promised she'd catch a ride with some of the friend group and wouldn't be taking the train to the event on her own, so I have peace of mind.

At least, for now. Until I see her dressed up like a dominatrix.

"Can't think about that," I mutter to myself, tugging off my suit jacket and tossing it onto the bed.

I tug down my suit pants next, remembering too late that my phone is in one of the front pockets. It clatters to the floor, and I scoop it up, relieved to see the message I've been waiting for.

> **FEST:** Made it into the city, but this traffic! Finally started moving at least. Be there in 10, so says Google Maps, but who the hell knows.

The message was sent fifteen minutes ago. I frown at the screen, not sure how I missed his text, when I had my phone connected to my truck. Then again, I drove back from Juliet's place to Fee's in a distracted daze.

Because I'm spiraling.

Our dinner date tonight didn't feel one bit like practice. I didn't talk about practice. Juliet didn't, either. And it felt so right, so good, even when it was awkward and clumsy at first, when my nerves got the best of me—but really, can I be blamed, when she looked like a goddess? I'm lucky I could form complete sentences.

Over shared meals, forks dipping from one plate to another, nudging each other, to try this bite *right* here, we talked so easily. Juliet asking about how I found Hector, my favorite music, about my parents, the distillery, the farm; wanting to know about my sisters, their birth order, their names, what they do for work; begging to see pictures of my niece and nephew; peppering me with questions about my agricultural studies in college, my trips to Scotland for work. My endless questions about her life growing up in the city, why she studied public relations and corporate communications in college, how her work has changed since she shifted to freelance business writing, her relationship with her sisters and parents, what romance novels are her favorite, where she wants to travel to, what flowers she'd grow if she had a garden all to herself.

Every moment of it . . . flowed.

That want for her that began weeks ago—hell, who am I kidding, it began when I saw her across a Scottish pub last December, and the work trip I'd taken in place of Mom, who was hurting too bad to travel, became infinitely more worth it—at first, it was simply lust. But ever since we started these practice dates, it's been snowballing, growing bigger, denser, packed with everything I've learned about her past, what she wants from her future, what I've figured out makes her smile and earns her laugh, what makes her feel safe and seen.

Unbuttoning my shirt, I stare down at the floor and try to calm my racing heart.

I told her, at dinner tonight, that I was going to be brave and order my meal, knowing there was still a very good chance I'd fuck it up—which I did—that I wanted to try anyway, to take a chance again and hope it might work out this time, when I haven't hoped that way for so long. And I realized, as I said it to her, that I wasn't just talking about swallowing my pride at the restaurant. I was talking about pushing myself, hoping for myself, in a much bigger arena—in my heart.

What *if* I held out hope for the kind of love with my future wife that Juliet believes in and wants for herself? What if I took a chance, trusted that I could give and receive what Juliet wants from a partner and that it wouldn't lead to hurt and rejection again? I still don't know if I believe that it's possible.

But . . . I think I *want* to.

And yet.

I know it's unfair to read into what Juliet did after I confessed that, the way she drew back her hand and breezily carried the conversation forward in that effortless way she has. Of course she couldn't read my mind, couldn't possibly know what I was really saying. I, of all people, as someone who struggles *mightily* to read between the lines of what others say and has experienced plenty of times how shitty it is to be resented for that, shouldn't expect it of her, shouldn't hold against her how she responded or endow it with some grander significance.

But my fear, my uncertainty, clings to what she did. And I can't help but feel in my gut that she pulled back because somehow she sensed what I really meant and it wasn't something she wanted from me.

Or worse, something she didn't think she *could* want from me, something she didn't think I could do any more than I could order a damn pasta dish off the menu without making an ass of myself.

"Yoo-hoo!"

Fest's voice from the other side of the apartment door makes me jump. I set a hand on my racing heart and breathe out slowly as I walk toward the door.

I open it a crack and hold out my hand. "Thanks, Fest. You can hand them over."

"Now, hold on," he says. The door smacks into my shoulder as he pushes against it. "Let me in."

I shove back. "Fest. Just hand over the clothes. I'm in my boxers."

"What do I care?" He shoves harder. Dammit, he's strong for a wiry man who's half a foot shorter than me.

"*I* care."

"Then put some pants on and let me in! This is how I'm repaid for being your errand boy? Sneaking around your parents' attic, stealing family heirlooms from right under their noses? Driving two hours on *my* Saturday night and suffering through godforsaken city traffic?"

Growling, I let the door fly open. Fest comes stumbling in, his hands full of garment bags holding the clothes I need for my costume.

I yank them from his arms. "Thank you very much," I tell him. "You can leave now."

He stares at me, blue eyes wide, wearing an obnoxiously large grin. He's got one of his usual loud ball caps on—this one is a neon rainbow watercolor print so bright, it hurts to look at it.

Tugging the ball cap off his head and revealing his mussed black hair threaded with silver, he fans his face. His eyes go straight to my barely there beard. "My goodness. Look at *you*."

I spin on the pretense of hanging up the clothing he brought, my back to him.

"I need to get ready now," I tell him, unzipping the first garment bag, "or I'm going to be late."

"Ready yourself, then," he says, his boots clomping across the floorboards. I hear the mattress creak and a contended sigh. "I'm in no rush."

"Fest," I snap, glancing over my shoulder. "Get the hell out of here."

He stretches his arms out wide, his face the portrait of martyrdom. "Can't an old man rest his weary bones for a few minutes?"

"You're five years older than me, not fifty. And you sat on your ass for two hours driving here," I tell him, turning back to the next garment bag, unzipping that, too. "What could you possibly need to rest for?"

"Your parents' attic," he tells me, "is so crammed full of shit, it was like spelunking, fighting my way to that storage chest. I barely made it out alive."

I roll my eyes. The dramatics with this man.

"Fine," I grumble. "But if I hear a word from you about—"

"About what?" he says, setting his hands behind his head. He kicks off his boots, then stretches his legs out onto the bed. "That you haven't shaved your face that close in over a decade? That getting dressed up tonight in this . . . attire is only something you'd do if there was someone who *very* much wanted to see you dressed up that way?"

I glare at him. "Yes. All of that."

"My, oh my," he says, clucking his tongue. "Willy's got himself a woman."

"Fest, I swear to God, shut your mouth, or I'll throw you out of this room."

He rolls his eyes. "You wouldn't lay a hand on me. I've been much more obnoxious before—"

"That's the damn truth," I mutter, pulling out the shirt, hanging it on one of the hooks mounted to the wall.

"—and you've never so much as laid a finger on me."

"Lovely to see you respecting my self-control, rather than exploiting it."

"Ah, c'mon," he says. "Talk to old Festy. Tell me all about her!

She has to be special if you finally let her wrap you around her finger. And that is the *only* thing I can assume has happened, given what I'm seeing here. The getup, the urgency to acquire said getup." He pauses meaningfully, and I know what's coming next. "The *shaving*."

I glance up at the ceiling, praying that portion over my bed will drop down and knock Fest out. I can't handle this.

"Fest," I mutter. "Ease up on me, okay? I'm . . . I'm trying to keep it together, and it's not going great."

I peer at my reflection in the mirror over the dresser, the battle I'm waging inside myself written all over my face.

I've shaved, when I've otherwise kept my big beard to hide because I didn't want to be seen by others but I've decided it's worth it to be seen by anyone, if only for the chance to be seen by her.

I've pulled this costume together, because, after noticing the books on her shelves, their spines creased and cracked, the ones she loves best, I knew seeing me in this outfit would make Juliet light up like she'd swallowed sunshine and earn that snorting belly laugh that I live for.

The Old Will would have done none of this. But the New Will has, and I don't regret a second of it. And that's how I know I'm in trouble. Because if I had my feelings for Juliet under control, I wouldn't have gone this far.

I'm wrenched from my thoughts when I hear the bed squeak, Fest's socked feet crossing the floor. Fest peers up at me, his expression somber, so rare for this man who's always happy, always joking and flippant. "Oh hell." He searches my eyes. "This is serious, isn't it?"

I glance between the costume I'm about to put on and my unfamiliar reflection. The Old Will wouldn't be caught dead with his beard shaved down to only a faint scruff or wearing an outfit like the one he's about to put on. But the Old Will hadn't met Juliet.

None of this would be, if it weren't for Juliet. This time with Juliet hasn't changed me, but it's challenged me, and rather than dig in and double down, like I would have in the past, I've reached and grown in ways I was so sure I would never want to, ways that are turning my preconceived notions, my sensible plans for my future, right on their head.

I turn back to the clothes hanging on their hooks and reach for the shirt.

"Yeah, Fest," I mutter. "It is."

TWENTY-FIVE

Juliet

My white dress is off, as are the nude bra and panties I wore beneath it. I could still wear them beneath my dominatrix outfit, but I don't want to. I want to embrace my character tonight as fully as possible. That calls for a slinky pair of black lace underwear and a matching demi-cup bra.

After I've got the bra on, I ease onto the edge of the bed and grab the panties resting there, then slide them up to my knees. I stand from the bed, and just as I've shimmied them over my butt, my left knee gives out. I fall with a plop back down to the bed.

Well. At least it wasn't the floor. Still, frustrated tears sting the backs of my eyes.

I've certainly made progress on finding a way to accept my body, rather than constantly resent it; to work with it, love it, even when it hurts. But sometimes, it still upsets me when my body reminds me of these new limitations.

After a deep breath, I stand slowly and take a step, testing my knee. This time, it stays steady, but I feel the wobble in the joint, the looseness I'm learning to pay attention to, warning that stability is not in the cards. Taking my time, I walk toward my closet and open the door. From the hook on the back, I lift the loop connected to the foldable black cane that I ordered online a few months ago, that I almost packed the day I first met Will at Bou-langerie, when I woke up feeling that threatening wobble in my knee. Sure enough, it gave out later on, and I fell into him.

But I don't want to fall into Will tonight. Not because he wouldn't be sweet about it, or because I'd be embarrassed when it happened—after having told him about my diagnosis, I've learned that he understands, from his experience with his mom, how to be supportive without smothering—but because I want to stand on my own two feet tonight. I want to feel like I can go and be wher-ever I am, and keep myself up on my own.

Tonight, if I wrap my hand around Will's arm, it will be be-cause I want to, not because I need to, because I want to enjoy touching him simply for enjoyment's sake.

I lift the cane off the hook and unfold it, popping the metal catches into each section until they slide into the holes and lock the cane's joints in place. Once it's assembled, I set the cane in my opposite hand from my wobbly knee and take a few steps back un-til I can see myself in my full-length body mirror. My gears start to turn with ideas about how the cane can work with my costume. The hair, the makeup, the daring outfit.

When I decided on this costume, I told myself, tonight I was going to channel my inner badass—a woman empowered in her desires and unafraid of embracing them.

I take a long look, examining myself, imagining my transfor-mation. I don't even have all of that costume on yet, just its slinky, sexy beginning. But as I stare at myself, I realize something—I don't *need* that costume to reclaim the woman who owns her de-sire for love, romance, intimate passion; the woman I've been reaching to become in these healing months isn't a far-off hope anymore.

She's already here, looking me right in the eye.

Margo and Sula, who picked me up in their cab, Toni and Hamza, and I are gathered outside the club, huddled together not because it's cold—it's a thick, muggy July night—but because we're jittery with excitement as we wait for the rest of the group to show up, giddy with the anticipation of letting loose and having fun.

I glance down the sidewalk, spinning my cane beneath my hand, hoping I'll spot Will, but I don't.

What I do see is a cab pull up, the door thrust open. Kate and Bea step out first and clock me immediately, then beeline my way. Kate lets out a loud whoop and claps her hands. Bea wolf whistles.

I pivot on my cane, doing a jaunty circle so they can get a three-sixty view of me—my hair swept severely back into a high bun that came to life after lots of hairspray and patience, my black cat eye and blood-red lips, my black suit with its plunging blazer, nothing but my bra beneath it, my tight black suit pants, the shiny patent leather boots with a sensible two-inch heel.

"You are a fucking smoke show!" Kate says.

Bea shakes her head admiringly. "*Damn*, JuJu."

I smile their way, proud and satisfied. "Why, thank you. So are you two!"

Kate bows in her ringmaster outfit, complete with a long leather whip tucked under her arm—a scarlet coat over a black bustier and matching tight black pants. She's wearing sky-high heels and a black top hat, so she towers over me. Her hair is down in long, soft brown curls sparkling auburn under the streetlights, falling nearly to her waist. Bea smiles from behind a black mask pluming with inky feathers, her eyes rimmed smoky and dark, making her irises pop vividly. She wears a long black coat but beneath it is a tight black leotard with a full, stiff matching tutu, black tights, and black ballet flats. A black swan.

"I love these outfits," I tell them. My gaze drifts past them to Christopher, who's in a lion's costume. I laugh.

Bea glances over her shoulder and sighs. "I'm still grossed out that we're going to have to see Kate play-whipping Christopher all night, but it's a pretty damn good couple's costume."

"And Jamie?" I ask, frowning as I glance around.

"The name's Holmes," his deep voice says behind me. "Sherlock Holmes."

I spin around, my mouth falling open. Jamie is dressed *perfectly* in a sharp three piece tweed suit and overcoat, a houndstooth-print deerstalker on his head, an old-fashioned pipe clutched tight in his teeth. "Wow," I tell him. "Step aside, Benedict Cumberbatch. There's a new Sherlock in town!"

Bea beams up at him. "While *we* don't match themes," she says, "we are embodying our hidden desires—mine, as the epitome of grace."

"And mine," Jamie adds, "being remotely capable of sleuthing cold-blooded murders from anywhere except in cozy murder mysteries from the safe confines of my couch."

"Sherlock Holmes!" Margo yells, drawing Jamie from our little circle toward the rest of the group. "I need to see that tweed up close and personal!"

Christopher's got his back to us, his phone out as he takes a picture of Toni and Hamza striking a seductive pose—Toni in a sexy floor-length black gown, holding a red pitchfork, and matching red horns on his head, Hamza, angelic in a tight white suit that fits him like a glove, a glittery halo headband on his head.

Kate asks, "And who are you, JuJu?"

I stand taller, drawing my shoulders back. "A persona of my own creation, Viola Cesario. By daytime, a heart-eyed writer of swoony historical romance. By night, a heartless dominatrix."

My sisters know I have a dream of one day writing and publishing romance. They know I've been trying to find my way toward re-claiming romance in my own life, too. They read between the lines of this hidden-desires persona. I feel them step closer, a small moment of sisters closeness.

"Viola Cesario," Kate says, "sounds like someone I'd like to meet."

Bea wiggles her eyebrows. "And I'd like to read her stuff. You know I love me a good spicy hist-rom."

"Maybe you will, one day," I tell them, before I break into a laugh. "Well, minus the dominatrix part."

———

Inside the club is absurdly loud, even from my seat at the round booth Margo reserved for our group, farthest from the dance floor and the DJ. If Will were here, I have zero doubts he'd have those earplugs in.

But he isn't here. I'm not worried yet. He's not late enough for me to worry about him—we only walked in ten minutes ago.

I'm worried about *me*. Because I miss him. Because I'm already having so much fun with everyone, and I still can't stop feeling like all of this would be even better if he were here.

And that does not bode well for just over a week from now, the end of our last practice weekend, when I'll have to say goodbye.

I try to push aside the missing as I sip my whiskey sour and watch my friends and sisters, dancing, laughing out on the floor. I don't feel like dancing just yet.

When I take another sip of my drink, I get only a burble of liquid through the straw. Somehow, I've already sucked down my cocktail. I don't feel the buzz yet, and I'd like that right about now, to quiet my racing thoughts.

Time for another.

Slowly, I stand, clutching my cane, and wend my way toward

the bar with a few swats of the cane at stubbornly obstructionist legs to part the way. Mobility aids are great for getting through a crowd.

Sidling up to the bar, I hook my cane on the ledge and safely wedge it between my chest and the bar top. I've just flagged down Margo's friend and coworker, Aila, who takes a look at my empty glass and winks to let me know they've got my refill underway, when a hand delicately wraps around my wrist.

"Basti?" a smoky voice says. "What are you doing here?"

I turn toward the voice and jolt. The woman holding my arm is gorgeous. Like, one of those people who is so beautiful, her features so perfect, it's almost freakish. Lush, rosy lips. Wide green eyes and thick dark lashes. Long, golden hair falling in waves, accented by thin braids bearing tiny blue and green flowers.

She's in what looks like a ren faire–type outfit—a flower crown of blue and green flowers that look honest-to-God real, a thin white shift falling off her shoulders, tight across the swell of her breasts, her waist cinched beneath a green corset that matches her eyes, and a sky-blue skirt beneath it.

For a second, I stare at her, wracking my brain. Something about her feels familiar. Where do I recognize her from?

"Oh." She drops my wrist as she gets a good look at my face, and her stunned expression dissolves to what I'm pretty sure is disappointment. "Oh God. I'm so sorry. I could have *sworn* you were someone else."

"That's okay." I smile politely, still trying to pinpoint where I know her from. I hate when this happens. "No harm done."

She smiles back, a little hesitant, and cocks her head to the side. "It's uncanny, though. Like I would have bet my entire wardrobe you were Basti. From behind, you could be her twin!"

"I'll take that as a compliment. As long as you tell me she has a great ass."

She throws back her head and laughs. "She definitely does."

"Then consider me flattered."

Her eyes hold mine for a beat.

I'm about to ask her if we've met before, when she says brightly, "Let me buy you a drink." She clasps my hand. "To make up for this?"

"Oh, no need!" I nod toward the bar, where Aila is, as we speak, making me another whiskey sour. "I'm all set."

"You sure?" she says.

I smile. "Totally."

"All right." She playfully rolls her eyes. "Well, I'm out of here, then. Have a great night!"

It must show in my expression, my confusion that she's leaving an event that literally started fifteen minutes ago.

She laughs a little sheepishly, then leans in. "I'm only here for a brand partnership. Get in, take pics, get out, ya know?"

My eyes widen. That's when I finally figure out how I know her. I'm talking to Olivia Tobias. A *huge* social media influencer. I don't follow many influencers, but I've always liked her posts because they're so damn beautiful—lots of shots of her in nature, flowers in her home, meals she's cooked, pretty dresses she's been gifted. I know it's all heavily curated and she's paid left and right to promote things, but it gives me a little serotonin hit, the same way reading historical romance does. Even though I know it's not remotely close to reality, I still just enjoy the beautiful escape.

"Olivia Tobias?"

"That's me!" she says.

"I follow your account!"

She sets a hand on her chest. "Stop it. You do?"

The feigned surprise is a bit much. She's got more than a million followers. It would be more surprising if I *didn't* follow her. But maybe she's just trying to be humble and kind.

I smile. "I do. You take gorgeous photos."

Her expression shifts to something softer. "Wow, thank you. Most people just say I'm really pretty or they love my clothes in my pictures, or they made that recipe I shared that I didn't even come up with, I just got paid to cook and post about." She sighs, her eyes holding mine. "It's like the only part of my social media that's actually me is invisible to people."

I frown in sympathy. "I'm sorry, that has to feel like shit."

"It really does! I'm a trained photographer. I love photography, and . . . nobody sees that."

"Well . . . what if you . . ." I bite my lip to shut myself up.

Who am I to give her advice? She didn't ask me for it. I have a bad habit of elbowing my way into people's business when I'm concerned for them that is part inheriting Maureen Wilmot's high-handed nurturer DNA, part growing up the protective oldest sister, part bad strategy for handling my anxiety that's triggered when I see people struggling.

"What if I what?" she asks, stepping closer. "Say what you wanted to say."

I hesitate. "What if you . . . posted about *that*? A lot of people don't understand how hard photography is. I only know because my sister is a photojournalist, and she's had a camera around her neck for as long as I can remember. But most people have no idea what all is involved, how much of an art it is. If you shared what photography means to you, what goes into these gorgeous images you create, if you opened up and showed that part of yourself to people, you might realize it's not that they're dismissing that part of you, it's just that they haven't known how to see it."

She smiles at me, but it seems tinged with sadness. "Basti said the same thing."

"Well, I'd say Basti and I are onto something."

Her smile fades a bit. She peers down and pulls out her phone.

"What's your handle?" She smiles up at me again. "I'd love to connect."

It wasn't that long ago that I had a killer social media presence for my PR consulting business. It's all been archived since last November, since I stopped consulting to take care of myself and get my life back together. If there were ever a moment to resurrect my business, it would be to tell Olivia Tobias my handle, reactivate my profiles, try to leverage a connection with her, even try to take her on as a client.

Nothing sounds less appealing.

Because I don't ever want to go back to working the way I did. I want this quiet, cozy life I've built for myself over the past almost year. I want to crank out enough articles to pay the bills and then spend every other minute of my time reading what I want, trying to write, cooking for fun and planting flowers and being with the people I love. I don't want the grueling long days I used to pull, the constant pressure I put on myself to lock in more clients, the nonstop events and networking and schmoozing. Sure, I'll always love helping people when I can; I'll always be an extrovert and love to throw parties, to bring new people together and enjoy seeing the connections they make.

But just because I *can* do it as my job doesn't mean I *should*.

"I actually don't have any public social media presence," I tell her. "Just a private account."

She freezes, phone in hand, her brow furrowed. "Seriously?"

"Yep."

"Of course." She pockets her phone and sighs.

"Let me guess," I venture, "Basti's the same way?"

Olivia throws up her hands. "You two really could be twins!"

I smile. "I've already got one of those, actually." Aila slides my drink onto the bar. I tell her thank you, pick it up, then lift my cane off the bar. "Nice to meet you, Olivia. Enjoy the rest of your night, and ... good luck, with Basti."

She blinks at me like I've surprised her. "What?"

"You just seemed so disappointed I wasn't her. I assumed it meant ..." I grimace. "I shouldn't have assumed, though. If I misread, I'm sorry."

"No ..." She sighs miserably. "You didn't misread."

"Friends first?" I ask gently.

She nods, looking glum. "She wanted more. And I didn't want to risk our friendship."

"Friends to lovers. It's not the low-stakes trope everyone makes it out to be."

A laugh jumps out of Olivia, but I catch her quickly dabbing the corner of her eye, like a tear snuck out that she doesn't want anyone to see. "I fucking love a friends-to-lovers romance."

"Me, too." I nudge her gently with my shoulder and give her an encouraging smile. "Good luck. I hope, however your and Basti's story ends, it's happy."

She squeezes my arm. "Thank you."

After a beat, I turn, starting back through the crowd, swatting more legs with my cane that come too close to bumping into me. I'm only focused on the two feet in front of me, making sure my path stays clear, so it's not until I'm right at the edge of the booth that I notice the only people there are mermaid Margo and Sula in her villainous octopus dress, thoroughly making out.

I take a step back before they can notice me and turn toward the dance floor, where everyone else is—

And then I run right into a hard chest swathed in a loose white shirt that looks straight out of a regency novel, a sweep of plaid tartan drawn down over one shoulder. My gaze drifts down that beautiful blue plaid of sky blue and grass green checked with charcoal gray, and my eyes go wide. I'm looking at a kilt held tight at his hips by a black belt, a matching black sporran slung across it. I take in two scuffed black boots that slouch at two very sexy knees—holy God, who knew knees could be sexy. The Highlander of my dreams stands before me.

"Sorry I'm late," Will says. "Turns out, kilts are a lot harder to put on than preliminary YouTube research led me to believe."

I peer up at him, dazed, delighted, smiling ear to ear.

TWENTY-SIX

Will

Juliet's smiling up at me like I'm the best damn thing she's ever seen. It makes me feel ten feet tall. I'd like to smile back, but I'm short-circuiting as I take her in, head to toe.

She's a vixen. Shiny black boots, tight black pants. A snug black blazer plunging low, revealing a torturously deep triangle of smooth white skin, the hint of a black lacy bra and the swell of her breasts.

I stand there, staring down at her, my hands turned to fists, no jean pockets where I can stow them to restrain myself. I want to touch her so badly it hurts. My heart kicks inside my chest, bangs and howls at how wrong it feels to look at her like this, to be this close and not be able to give in.

"Will!" she yells as the music ratchets up in volume.

Thank God she yells, because it's beyond loud in here, and I've got the earplugs in, somewhat muting the noise around us, but the thumping bass, the background sound of blaring music, voices shouting, would make hearing her impossible if she were any quieter.

"You're a *Highlander*!" she hollers, clutching my arm as she beams up at me.

I sigh as I peer down at her. "And you're going to be the death of me."

"What?" she leans in. "I couldn't hear you!"

I shake my head. "Nothing."

From the edge of my vision, I catch hands waving from the dance floor and glance up. Toni and Hamza, Kate and Christopher, Bea and Jamie, gesturing to join them.

Juliet grimaces and steps so close, we're nearly chest to chest. "It's so loud in here!"

She's not stating the obvious. She's acknowledging it for me, saying without saying it that she understands this might not be a great fit for me. Because she knows how draining I find these kinds of environments. In the past, when even an implication of my sensitivities and limitations would come up, prideful defensiveness would rear its ugly head. But not anymore. Not with her. With Juliet, I don't feel self-conscious—I feel seen.

And when her hand gently wraps around mine, squeezing tight, I'd swear she had my heart in her grip, because it squeezes, too. Not just because I feel a rush of comfort from her touch, but because we're standing here, where her sisters and friends can see us, and Juliet doesn't seem to care at all.

I hope it means she doesn't want to hide our closeness anymore, whether that closeness is practiced or real. Because the truth is, I don't want to hide it anymore. I don't know if *I* can hide it, either.

I clasp her hand and thread our fingers together. I watch her gaze drift down to my mouth, then back up. The music's beating around us, everyone from the group who's out on the dance floor hollering at us to join them.

I bend a little and say, close to her ear, "They're telling us to come dance." I hope, in the same way she showed me she knows this party could be hard but left me room to tell her what I can manage, that I'm showing her I see how this could be hard for her, too, that I'm putting the ball in her court, to tell me what she feels up for.

I've noticed the cane she's holding, and unless it's purely decorative for her costume, it probably means her knee's giving her problems. I hope she's not hurting. But if she is, I trust her to tell me the truth.

Juliet smiles up at me, and that sparkle in her eyes says she heard what I didn't say, that I made her feel not self-conscious but seen, too. "I could go dance for a bit . . . How about you?"

I nod. No, I'm not going to be able to take this chaos for long. But until I hit my limit, I'm going to dance my ass off with Juliet, drench myself in the pleasure of being close to her, watching her shine, happy and carefree with the people she loves.

She wraps her hand around my biceps and turns us toward the dance floor. "I know this is probably very inappropriate," she yells over the noise, "but I've got to ask: are you wearing anything under that kilt?"

I wiggle my eyebrows. "Wouldn't you like to know?"

———

The third time Juliet's knee gives out, she's got her hands around my neck, her cane hanging from the crook of my arm, and I'm glad, because I can tell she was about to go down hard.

I'm braced for the embarrassment she seemed to feel when it happened on our first practice date, but it never comes. She just clutches my neck tighter and says, "I've hit my wall here."

I nod. I have, too.

Over the past two hours, we've been out on the dance floor, then packed in with the group at the booth, gulping water, conversations stacked one over the other, then back out to the dance floor. My brain's buzzing from it. I've had the best time, but I've just about hit my limit.

She leans in a little and says, "Want to get out of here?"

I frown, confused. My gaze drifts to her sisters and all her friends, scattered on the dance floor. She's not worried they'll see us leave together?

"You sure?" I ask.

Her mouth quirks with a smile. "I'm sure. One sec!"

She plucks her cane from my elbow, then slips off toward her sisters, head bent as she talks to them. They both glance my way and smile. I have no idea what she's telling them, but I'm relieved that, whatever it is, they seem okay with it.

Juliet circles back to me and wraps her hand around my arm. "How do you feel," she yells over the music, "about getting a little surprise of your own?"

———

I don't usually like surprises, but I trust Juliet. She asks if I want to take her straight home—I do, not because I'm tired and ready to head back to my place, but because I want to take her back to her apartment and tear off her clothes and make her come until she begs me to stop, until she can't take one more ounce of pleasure.

Obviously, I can't tell her that, so I tell her *a* truth, if not the whole truth: that I'm not tired, that I'm up for something else, so long as it's not real loud.

And with that criterion, we set off, following not the instruction of my Australian Siri but of Juliet, who holds her phone close to her chest and tells me what turns to make and when, determined for me not to peek at the map on her screen.

I've been following her directions dutifully, and as I make our last turn, veering left, I still don't know what to expect of our destination, which is allegedly right around the corner. When I see what it is, I lurch on the brakes.

The parking lot drive-in sits right at the water's edge, a tall, wide screen to the left, the downtown skyline to the right, twinkling across the river.

A drive-in.

"What's the matter?" she says. Her hand settles on my thigh and squeezes gently. "Still too loud? We can do something else—"

"No." I shake my head, then glance her way, trying to force a smile even though I'm shit at it.

Juliet's reaction confirms this. "You look like you're in gastro-intestinal distress."

A snort jumps out of me. I think I'm in shock. Of all the places, the first time since we started our dates that she's the one who picks where we go, and this is what she chooses.

A drive-in.

A place that is all but sacred in my family, that has such a spe-cial meaning to it, one she has no way of knowing about.

Is this a sign? Or is the fact that I want it to be a sign, in and of itself?

"I'm okay," I tell her, squeezing her hand. "Promise. You just . . . surprised me real good. I would have bet the truck we were going bowling."

Her expression turns crestfallen. "Oh. We could totally do that, if you want. Especially since"—she points to the sign at the entrance—"it's rom-com night. Maybe you're not feeling that vibe—"

"Juliet." I squeeze her hand again. "I'm okay here. Pinkie promise."

That convinces her. Her smile returns as she sits back in her seat and claps her hands. "Eek! It's *How to Lose a Guy in 10 Days*. A fave. Have you ever seen it?"

I shake my head. "But I am obviously a convert to the genre."

She beams up at me. "You're gonna love it."

And she's right, I do. I laugh at all the antics, at Matthew Mc-Conaughey and Kate Hudson's absurd efforts to wear each other down that only end up making them fall in love. I tear up at the end. I love the heck out of it.

Fuck, the cloud I'm floating on when the movie ends is almost as good as endorphins after a hard workout. I think I'm about to do a deep dive into rom-coms.

"The love fern!" she says as we pull out of the parking lot. "Like, who thought of that? How can I crawl inside their brain? I feel like any time I try to write a funny moment, it's not nearly as funny as I want it to be."

"Are you writing a rom-com?" I ask, switching lanes.

She's quiet for a beat, then says, "I'm sort of chipping away at a historical romance, but a historical rom-com—at least, I'd like it to be."

I glance her way. "That's incredible, Jules. Can I read what you have so far?"

"God, no!" she yells, clapping her hands over her cheeks. "Are you kidding me? It's a dumpster fire of twenty thousand words that I constantly tweak and rewrite and never go any further than. It's the last thing I'd want to be your introduction to historical romance."

I smile as I accelerate. "Well, it wouldn't be. I've now read three historical romances, and I'm hooked."

"What?" She leans in across the console. "How? When?"

"Borrowed them from my mom—snuck them, actually. She would be an insufferable gloat if she knew I finally caved when she's been yelling at me to give them a try for nearly two decades."

Juliet sighs, then says, her voice shaky, "Tell me they haven't been Highlander romance."

"I could tell you that . . ." I throw her a quick smile before I set my eyes back on the road. "But I did pinkie promise to be honest with you."

TWENTY-SEVEN

Juliet

I will not jump his bones. I will not jump his bones. I will not jump his bones.

But, oh my *God*, he's read Highlander romances. Three of them! *Get it together, Juliet.*

I blow out a breath as Will drives his truck down my block, the apartment looming ahead. I can handle this. I can handle that my romance workout buddy, this sweet man who's become my friend, has read my favorite kind of romance. I can handle that he showed up dressed as a Highlander tonight, danced his ass off with me and my friends, and laughed and teared up at all the right parts of a rom-com that I adore. I can handle this and shove my desire for him back in the lusty closet from whence it came—

Except, that's the problem. My desire for Will isn't just physical anymore. It left the lusty closet, I'm not even sure when, only that it's been a while, and now that desire has filled a whole room—a room whose door has a name on it that I'm terrified to even *think*, let alone name.

But I know what it is. And not thinking or naming that word doesn't make it any less real or true—it just *is*, woven into the fabric of our time together.

The irony of it. I started this journey with Will, the man I decided was safe to walk with down the path of romantic love because he wasn't sure he was looking for that in his own life, or at least, he seemed sure he wasn't looking for it with me; whose place in Christopher's life made him safely, strictly off-limits. I was so confident Will was the perfect person to be my practice partner on that journey to feel safe again and trust myself while being romantic, because he was the last person I could fall for.

And it only led me to do exactly that.

Will stops the truck outside my apartment and hits his blinkers. There isn't a single space on the whole block, nowhere for him to park; he'll have to drop me off and go on his way. I'm inordinately disappointed. If this is a sign from the universe, to keep my feelings to myself, I deeply resent it, even if I know it would be the sensible thing, the *safe* thing to do.

Maybe I don't want to be safe anymore.

Torn, tortured by how much I want to act on everything I'm feeling, I turn in my seat as far as I can and face Will, searching his eyes, wishing I saw in them some answer to my questions—*Do you want me the way I want you? Do you think you could ever want what I want? Could you want it with me?*

But, for all his talk of how he wears his thoughts on his face without that big beard to hide them, I can't find a single damn clue.

So I focus on what I do know—how wonderful every part of tonight was with him, how wonderful *he* was. "Thank you, Will. For all of this. Dinner. Coming to the party with everyone. The drive-in. It was . . . really, really lovely."

He nods, his hands tight on the steering wheel. "Yeah, it really was," he says quietly. "Thank *you*, Jules."

This is when he's going to open his car door, walk briskly around his truck, and help me down. This is when I'll hug him good night without rubbing myself on him like a cat in heat, then walk myself upstairs to my apartment.

But not yet, a quiet voice whispers inside me.

I pause for a beat, that voice echoing in my head, a tug in my gut telling me it's right.

"Will."

"Hmm?"

Desire races through me as his gaze darts to my mouth, as mine darts to his. Every edge and corner of my body is warm with longing.

"Why did you *really* slam on the brakes," I ask carefully, "when you realized I'd chosen the drive-in?"

Will's quiet, his gaze searching mine. A long, slow sigh leaves him.

"Pinkie promise," I say quietly. "Remember?"

Slowly, he reaches for my hand and clasps it in his. He hesitates for a beat, then says, "It probably sounds . . . odd, but in my family, there's a tradition. When you take someone to the drive-in . . . it's the place you take the person you love."

My heart takes off, flying in my chest. "What?"

He stares down at his hand clasping mine. "Started with my great-grandfather. When he was young, Illyria wasn't as built up as it is now, not much to do. When the town got a drive-in, it was a *big* deal, and the drive-in became what you did as teens, where you went to flirt and get frisky, standard stuff. He was a good-looking, charming guy, had a lot of ladies interested in him, and he took them on dates—to the lake, where they'd go fishing, for an ice cream, for a walk around town. But never the drive-in, because that was something he was saving for the woman he was serious about. The first day he met my grandma, he asked her if she wanted to go to the drive-in."

Good grief, could that be any more romantic? My eyes well with tears. "Because he knew?"

"Because he knew," Will says. "'Like a lightning strike,' was how he always told it. 'When I saw her,' he'd say, 'it was like a lightning strike, straight to the heart—I knew I loved her, and I always would.'"

His hand squeezes mine gently.

"And so it became a tradition," he tells me. "My grandpa did the same thing with my grandma. Then my dad with my mom. Never once took a lady to the drive-in, until they knew she was the one." He smiles to himself. "My parents still go to the drive-in, every anniversary."

"Oh," I breathe out, setting a hand on my heart.

"I never thought I'd do that," he says quietly. "Because . . . based on . . . you know, how it went for me, when I tried dating . . . I sort of gave up hoping I'd ever get there."

My heart aches. It's taken everything in me during our time together not to challenge Will's notions about what I think he should hope in, about the kind of love a deserving someone could give him and how much they'd love what he'd give them in return. It's nearly painful now, keeping myself quiet, but I do. Even if, since the moment we started, I've sworn to myself I would do as much as I could to *show* Will that the person worthy of him would love him romantically and feel just as loved by him. As much as I want him to see the possibilities that I see, to hope for himself the way I hope, I can't do that for him. I've done what I could, as we've practiced, and that's as far as I can build the bridge toward his belief in what's possible—the other half has to come from him.

Will peers up at me, and his eyes hold mine. "So when you . . ." His throat works with a swallow. "When, out of all the places you could have chosen for us to go, you picked the drive-in, it . . . it messed with me. It got me thinking, and it's not the first time my mind had gone there, Juliet, but it sure as hell felt like the closest it came to wondering if—" His voice breaks off. He clenches his jaw tight. "I'm gonna say something, and if it's not something you want to hear, I need you to promise you'll tell me that, all right?"

My heart crashes against my ribs. "Promise," I whisper.

He holds my gaze as he says, "I've spent a long time believing, telling myself, that this wasn't something worth hoping I could have with someone, that it wasn't worth trying for again, after being . . . hurt, so many times, when I did."

I nod, because I know that. He's trusted me with that truth.

"But . . . when I'm with you, Juliet . . ." He stares down at our hands, his thumb sweeping gently across my skin. "I doubt that belief. When I'm with you . . . I want to try, to hope. With . . . you."

My heart's flying, hope soaring through me.

"Thing is . . ." He clears his throat roughly. "Thing is, I don't know, if that old belief goes out for good, what would take its place. I don't know if it will be everything you've told me your heart wants, or if we'll still end up where I've ended up before— you feeling like, despite my best effort, I've only offered you a shadow of that."

I can't take another moment of him doubting himself like this, not when he's shown me just how capable he is of demonstrating love—familial, platonic, romantic—when he's shown me love in so many ways, even if it was under the guise of practice. "Will, I would *never* feel that—"

"Please," he says roughly. "Hear me out."

I bite my tongue, because it's the only way I can keep myself quiet, and nod.

"If I were a stronger man," he says, "I'd wait until I knew. Until I could tell you crystal clear that I'm sure, when I offered you everything you deserve and desire, Juliet, that you'd feel it, that you'd never doubt its power or purpose . . ."

His eyes search mine. "But I'm not. I'm not strong enough. I can't stand to spend another second in your presence without you knowing that I might not be sure yet, if my heart's love will be enough for you—" He brings my hand, clasped inside his, against his chest. "But every corner of that heart, in all its imperfection, *is* yours, if you want it. And if you don't . . . well, I'll more than understand."

I stare at him, my heart glowing, tears pricking my eyes. Joy bursts through me, like water from a dam, held-back hope rushing out and spilling through me. Then, fast behind it, threatening to swallow it up: fear.

I *am* afraid. I am as afraid as I knew I would be, when it came to this moment, to realizing I had fallen for someone again. Because, while the Old Juliet used to run after romance, arms wide for wild love, believing that would always be enough, the Old Juliet didn't know heartbreak. She didn't know the debilitating doubt, the panic-inducing pain, that could come when it fell apart.

This time, faced with the possibility of having what I've hoped for, what my heart has finally healed enough to ache for again, I *know* what it will be like, if I give myself to this, and it ends.

It will be devastating.

But.

I will survive it. Because I am strong—stronger than I gave myself credit for at first, when my life fell apart last year. If I have learned anything in these almost nine months, it is that I can survive so much more than I knew, that even when pain knocks me down, I can get back up.

So, yes, I am afraid, at the thought of finally giving in to all I feel for Will, at hearing his humble honesty that he worries I might see him as having fallen short, feeling that anxiety inside myself that he might see me as having fallen short for him, too.

But when I started this journey with Will, I made a promise to him—that we'd both be brave, that we'd both get on that bike and wobble together. I promised myself that there'd be no more hiding from the joys of life, the thrill of love, out of fear of the pain that losing them might bring.

Quiet at first, I press my hand, still tucked inside his, hard over his heart. And then I tell him, my voice steady, my heart brave, "I want this. I want *you*."

His eyes dart between mine. His hand wraps tight around my fingers, where beneath them I feel his heart beating fast against his chest. "You do?"

I nod, my fingers sinking into his shirt, tugging him toward me. "So much. And I need you to hear me, Will. You *are* a strong man. It takes strength, courage, to open up your heart, when you're afraid it could get hurt. It wouldn't be strength that held you silent about how you feel until you were sure you could trust I'd see everything in your heart that you want me to—it would be fear." I press my hand against his heart. "You're brave, Will. And you make me feel safe to be brave, even when I'm afraid, too. Because I *am* afraid. I'm afraid of how much you mean to me, how much I want this, not because I don't trust you or believe in you, Will, but because of how much I *do*."

"Jules," he whispers brokenly.

I cup his face, my thumb sweeping tenderly along his cheek. "Will."

The moment his name leaves my mouth, an SUV two spots down pulls out, leaving an opening for his truck.

We glance to the open space, then back to each other, and smile.

Thank you, universe.

———

The door to my apartment bangs open as we tumble inside, hands frantically scouring each other's bodies. Our kisses are deep, open-mouthed, tongues stroking, groans and sighs. Finally, *finally* I'm kissing him again. I could cry, I'm so relieved.

Will paws around, feeling for the door until he connects with it. He sends it flying shut with an echoing *boom*.

"Wait, baby," he mutters, tearing his face away from our kisses just long enough to see what he's doing as he bolts the door and turns the handle's lock, too.

"No more waiting," I whine against his neck as I kick off my boots, then press up on bare tiptoes, licking into the hollow of his throat.

"Fuck," he groans.

Will steps clumsily out of his boots as I kiss my way down to his chest, then he starts to walk me back down the hall, stopping halfway, pressing me against the wall. He slows our kisses, his hand at my jaw, holding me there, his tongue stroking mine, slow, silken. Heat coils in my belly.

"You taste so good," he mutters against my mouth.

I sigh into our kiss. "So do you."

He grunts as I drag my hand up his thigh, deliciously close to the hard, thick weight of him pressing into my stomach. Gently, he takes my hand and draws it away, linking our fingers together, pressing them against his chest. Right over his heart.

Will stares down at me, jaw tight, eyes on fire. "You sure you want this?"

"I have never been surer of anything," I tell him. "And if you ask me again, the dominatrix is going to come out."

He groans a laugh into my mouth as I kiss him, as I lose myself to the pleasure of his hips rocking against me, the heat of his body tight against mine. Aching need thrums between my thighs, at the tips of my breasts. My skin beads with sweat.

"Touch me," I beg.

He smiles against my neck as he wraps his hands around my back and tucks me close. Breathless pants leave me as he kisses his way down to my collarbone, then nips it softly. "I am touching you."

I grab his hand and set it between my thighs, rubbing right where I need it.

He swears into my neck. And then he grabs me by the butt and lifts me up. I wrap my legs around his waist, lock my arms around his neck.

My fingers dive into his hair as I kiss him, as I work myself against the hard, thick weight of him right at my pelvis. "I really hate clothes right now," I pant.

"They're the worst."

"Says the guy in a skirt. I'm practically sewn into these pants."

Will laughs as he walks us through the living space, down the hall, straight to my bedroom. "I wish this kilt were as uncomplicated as a skirt. It better not take as long to get it off as it did to get it on."

"I've read a couple hundred Highlander romances, Will." I nip his bottom lip gently with my teeth, earning a grunt of pleasure. "I'm prepared for this, and I promise you, that kilt will be off in no time."

"I'm going to hold you to that." Gently, he lowers me down until I'm standing. Nothing about what comes next is measured or controlled, no slow, savoring striptease. I frantically shove away the tartan plaid draped over his shoulder and drag his shirt over his head. Will fumbles with my blazer's buttons and all but rips it off of me. I yank at his belt buckle, letting it fall with the sporran to the ground, then tug the plaid wrapped around his body just enough to loosen it at his hips.

"How did you do that?" he asks breathlessly, shoving down his kilt. "I had to roll myself up like a goddamn burrito, and you just get it right off."

"Told you I would." When the fabric drops to his feet, I let out the most pathetically needy sound. My question from earlier is answered—he *did* wear underwear—but it's still a glorious sight, the gray boxer briefs low at his hips, bulging with his erection. I palm him and stroke hard.

"Jules," he begs, gently nudging my hand away, sinking to his knees, quickly unfastening my pants' button, dragging down the zipper. I hold on to his shoulders as he peels my pants down my legs, then helps me step out of them.

Will stands and reaches for my hair, which I've started tugging at, the pins and hair tie stubbornly resisting my stiff fingers' efforts. "Let me?" he asks.

I peer up at him, our frantic desperation gone, tenderness filling the space between us. Nodding, I set my hands on his waist. Will leans in and deftly plucks out the pins, kissing my temple, my forehead, my cheek, as he draws out each one. He kisses my mouth, slow and soft, as he unwinds my hair, then drags out the hairband. I grip his waist hard and press up on tiptoes, eager for more.

My hair falls to my shoulders, and he sinks his hands into it, then tips my head back, fucking my mouth with his tongue, just how I want him to take me. Slow and hard, dragging back, making me chase him until he plunges back in.

I'm so keyed up, it's going to kill me. I'm going to die of waiting.

Slowly, torturously slow, he drags his knuckles across the hem of my panties. Back and forth. Back and forth. I try to rock my hips, chasing touch where I'm so desperate for it, I could cry.

My breath is ragged and fast. I'm aching so badly. I feel like one touch from him where I need it, and I'm going to go off like a firework.

"Please," I beg, rocking my hips toward him.

He kisses my neck, my jaw, right behind my ear. "Be patient, Juliet."

"I can't. I can't wait."

He huffs a rough, husky laugh against my hair, then sighs. "I love how much you want it."

"I want *you*," I tell him, on the verge of tears, my voice thick with need. "I want you so much."

"I want you, too, baby," he mutters into my hair. "Easy, Jules. I've got you." His teasing fingertips finally dip lower, grazing my curls, my pelvis—

I gasp as he *finally* strokes down where I'm soaked, where a pulse pounds between my legs. "Will," I gasp again.

"You're drenched," he whispers, swirling around my clit, watching me shamelessly riding his hand. His touch is so light, so teasing.

"Well. I did just watch Matthew McConaughey for two hours," I tell him unsteadily, my eyes falling shut. "Can you blame me?"

He laughs into our kiss. "That's who this is for?"

"You know it's not." A shiver waves through me, the first promise of my release already building inside me. "It's all for you."

Will groans as I say it and reaches behind me, with a few efficient movements of his fingers undoing my bra. It falls down my arms, and Will drags it off, then tosses it aside. "Look at you," he whispers. "Juliet, you're absolutely perfect."

"I'm not perfect," I mutter.

"To me, you are." He bends and kisses right over my heart, above the swell of my breast. His nose dips and grazes my nipple.

"Will, please," I beg. "*Please.*"

"Demanding woman. I'm trying to savor you."

"Savor me later." I drag my hands down his chest, over his erection. "Just make me come first."

Laughing, he hoists me up again and walks me over to the bed. I flop back onto the mattress, arms falling listlessly over my head, and smile up at him.

Will drops to his knees, grips me by the hips, and yanks me to the edge of the bed. "This okay?" he asks.

I nod frantically. "Very okay."

Gripping my panties, he drags them down my legs, then tosses them aside, too. His hands splay up my thighs as he stares at me, gaze intense, jaw tight. "Fuck, you're pretty."

I blush, throwing an arm over my face. "Will."

Gently, my arm is drawn back. Will's looming over me, his hand gliding up my ribs, cupping my breast, thumbing my nipple. I bite my lip as he softly tugs my nipple, barely keeping my eyes from rolling back. He stares down at me. "I need you to watch, Jules. I need your eyes on me when I make you come."

He reaches for a pillow and lifts my head, propping it behind me, so I'll have no choice but to see him going down on me. He kisses me, his tongue licking into my mouth, his hands wandering me, teasing over every exquisitely sensitive square inch of my skin. His palm grazes up my thigh and draws it toward him, opening me wider, and then he circles my clit, taps it lightly. I arch up under his touch, whimpering into our kiss.

When he kneels back down at the edge of the bed, he cups my butt in each hand, like a man preparing to feast. His flattened tongue drags right up my center, then flicks my clit. I cry out, my hands flying to his head, sinking into his hair.

He eases a finger inside me, and I bite my lip, moan in satisfaction. My thighs tighten against his shoulders.

"So good." I nod feverishly. "Please, don't stop."

He hums against my clit and eases in a second finger. White-hot pleasure incinerates me, a raging fire burning through my veins.

The next stroke of his tongue, he circles my clit, a hot, wet swirl that makes my eyes flutter shut. I tighten my grip in his hair. "That," I whisper. "I *love* that."

He does it again, and again, a slow stroke up, then wet, rhythmic circles. He presses his free hand, splayed wide, up my stomach, my ribs, and cups my breast, plucking at my nipple.

I pant, frantic for release. Every time I'm sure this is as far as I can go, Will shows me there's even more. "Faster," I beg. "It's so perfect, just faster."

He curves his fingers and starts fucking into me in earnest, his tongue still circling, wet and hot, faster, too. I'm gasping, yanking at his hair, the poor man, but I'm so close, right on the edge. When he crooks his fingers farther inside me, my legs jerk up, my knees bending reflexively. I can barely breathe, it's so intense, so unbelievably good—his tongue wet and warm on my clit, his fingers thick and crooked inside me, his soft hair brushing against my thighs, his big, rough hand cupping my breasts, caressing tenderly across my stomach.

"Come for me, Jules." He pulls away from my clit just long enough to kiss the inside of my right thigh, then my left. "And watch me when you do."

I force myself to look down at him as I feel my body tightening, my nipples peaked and tender, aching under his touch. He looks up at me, too, his face feverish, eyes bright, cheeks flushed, and licks his way up to my clit once, twice, then circles it—

I cry out his name as I clench around his fingers, pulse against his hand, my hips arching up with each lightning bolt of pleasure that strikes through me, electric and blinding.

My orgasm lasts forever, shock after glorious shock waving through me, as he licks me slowly, kisses my thighs, tenderly eases his fingers out, then over my clit, where I'm so sensitive, I can barely take it.

Gasping, I open my arms. "Will," I croak. "Come here."

Without a second's hesitation, he gets up, bends over me, and hoists me back onto the bed. Then he drops onto the mattress beside me, curling me into his arms.

I drift my hand over his heart, up his chest to his hair, still panting for air as I peer up at him. I cup his face and guide him close, kissing him long and slow. "That," I tell him breathlessly, "was the best orgasm of my life. I'm going to sleep for a month."

Will laughs, husky and low. "Not yet, Juliet."

My brow furrows. "You can't seriously expect to get another one out of me?"

"One?" He shakes his head, brushing away the hair from my face. "Nah. I was thinking we'd go for low double digits tonight."

A laugh wheezes out of me.

Will presses me back onto the mattress, looming over me. "You doubt I can do it?"

I shake my head, still laughing. "I doubt I can *survive* it."

"I know you can," he says softly, planting a kiss between my breasts, at the hollow of my throat, behind my ear. "I'm going to give that to you, Juliet, I promise you. Because that's what you deserve. Because I have been fantasizing for weeks about all the ways I could touch and learn you, tease and please you, make you come again and again."

I shiver as, somehow, a fresh wave of desire crests through me.

Will feels it and smiles against my hair, nuzzling my temple. "That's my girl."

A sigh leaves me as his hand slides between my legs.

"Will," I whisper.

"Hmm?" He kisses me softly, his nose nuzzling mine.

"I really think—ah!" I bite my lip as he circles my clit.

"You think what?" he mutters against my neck. He kisses behind my ear.

My body's warm and loose from my orgasm, from this new thread of pleasure weaving through me at his touch, but I'm also stiff and sore from hours of dancing, from the aches I've been battling since I woke up. "I think that," I say quietly, "as much as I want you to give me that many orgasms in one night . . . I also don't know if I actually can survive it."

Will's touch slows, his eyes searching mine. I'm worried he's going to pull away, that he's going to hear me discouraging him.

But he doesn't. He just dips his head and kisses me gently. "All I want is for you to feel good, Juliet. Whatever that looks like. You tell me what you need, and I'll listen."

I swallow against the lump in my throat and kiss him back. I curl my arm around his neck and draw him close, nudging my hips toward him, pressing my pelvis against his hand, showing him I still want this. "One more," I whisper.

He grins against my mouth. "Happily."

· TWENTY-EIGHT ·

Will

I wake up, blinking slowly, squinting against bright morning light filling Juliet's room. It takes my eyes a moment to focus, but then I see her, sitting on the bed beside me, her hair wild and frizzy, haloed around her head. My shirt from last night drapes over her body, slipping off her shoulder.

She smiles. "Hey, you."

I peer up at her and smile. "Hi, beautiful."

My limbs are heavy, still groggy from sleep, but I need to touch her. My hand slides across the sheets, cool, crinkled cotton, up to the satin smoothness of her thigh. I wrap my hand around it, my thumb sweeping over her skin. "How'd you sleep?" I ask.

"I fell asleep mid-kissing you," she says, eyebrows raised, "and didn't move until I woke up ten minutes ago. So I'd say I slept pretty darn well, though I did *not* mean to fall asleep when I did. Apparently, all it takes is two orgasms from you, and I go comatose."

I grin, remembering how beautiful she was when she came, head thrown back, lush mouth parted, dark hair spilled across the pillow, crying out my name. A happy sigh leaves me. "Glad to hear it."

She rolls her eyes, but she's smiling. "How'd *you* sleep?"

"Like a rock."

Her smile fades a little, as her eyes search mine, and I know, dread settling in my chest, what's coming. "Just before I fell asleep, I tried to touch you. You did the same thing that you'd done, right when we came into the apartment last night. You took my hand and held it instead. You . . . stopped me. All you did was give last night, Will. And I never got to give back."

I swallow roughly, anxiety humming through me. "What can I say? Giving is my love language."

Love. The word lands like a bomb in the room.

"It's gifts," she says quietly.

I frown. "What do you mean?"

"Gifts," she says, "are the love language."

Juliet links her fingers with mine and draws my hand onto her lap, staring down at it, tracing the veins across its back, up my wrist, to my arm. "I think maybe you're thinking of another love language—acts of service."

Slowly, I sit up and lean against the headboard. I battle nerves, unsure where this is going. "You saying I served you well last night, Juliet?"

She gives me a pointed look. "You know you did." With her other hand, she starts to massage my hand, the hand that touched her last night, that learned her and pleased her and made her come undone. A groan leaks out of me as she rubs beneath the base of my thumb.

"And now," she says softly, her eyes holding mine. "I want to serve *you*. But, Will, you have to let me."

"I know," I tell her, a rough swallow working down my throat. "I just . . . panicked. You were worn out, and I was . . . really keyed up. I didn't want to ask you for more than you felt you had to give or hurt you when you were already hurting."

She nods. "That makes sense." A faint smile lifts her mouth. "But you wouldn't have hurt me. And I would have told you if I couldn't handle something you wanted. Do you think, next time, you can trust me that way, and ask for what you want, even if you're not sure what I'll say?"

Our eyes hold. Our fingers dance against each other. "Yeah," I whisper. "I do." A beat of silence hangs between us as we stare at each other. "Come here?" I nod my way.

Juliet crawls toward me, settling in, tucked against my side. I wrap an arm around her and curl her even closer, her head on my chest, then grab her thigh and drag it over mine. Her head heavy on my chest, her chest pressed into mine, her thighs weighing down on my own, send soothing calm washing through me.

Squeezing her hip, pressing a kiss to her forehead, I try to tell her, as words escape me, that I want to say more, that I want to explain. It's just . . . hard.

"I . . ." My words catch when I try to begin. "I . . . historically have not . . . enjoyed receiving what I gave you last night. Well, no, that's not exactly true. I *do* enjoy it, but it's often been hard to enjoy when it comes with touch that I don't like, when I've worried that asking for what I want will make my partner feel . . . inconvenienced." I peer down at her, trying to lighten up what I've just confessed. "Plus, getting you off just really does it for me."

"What if," she whispers, her hand cupping my face, her thumb tracing my lips, "I told you that getting *you* off really does it for *me*?"

Air rushes from my lungs as her thigh nudges higher up my leg.

"What if"—she presses a kiss to my neck, my jaw—"I told you that the thought of you telling me everything you like, of me doing that and giving you everything you need to make you come, makes me so obscenely wet."

My hand slides from its place curled around her shoulder, down her hips. I squeeze her ass. "Jules," I breathe.

"What if," she mutters against my collarbone, nipping tenderly with her teeth; her hand drifts down my arm and finds my hand, too. "I said that I'd love it if you showed me, if you taught me everything you like, so I can make you feel as good as you deserve to?"

"Juliet," I plead. I don't even know what I'm pleading for, just that I'm overcome—by how safe she makes me feel, how deeply I want her, how brave she makes me want to be.

"Will," she says softly, peering up at me.

I bend my head and kiss her, tugging her against me. She smiles into our kiss, her hand cradling my jaw. "Show me?" she whispers.

I nod, swallowing thickly. With her hand in mine, I set it over my heart and press. "Pressure," I whisper. "That's what feels good."

She smiles. "Okay. So, no light, teasing touches."

I shake my head.

"What else?" she asks quietly.

Slowly, I guide her hand down my chest, then my stomach. My hips jump as our hands graze the tip of my cock. I'm hard, almost painfully so, from how good it feels to touch her like this, from the memories of making her come last night.

Her hand rests at my hip, and I pull my touch away. "Touch me," I tell her.

She smiles wide, her eyes bright as blue flames, biting her lip as her soft, warm hand splays across my stomach like I showed her, across my hips. I rock them toward her touch. Lower, lower, until she's clutching the sheet, drawing it back, exposing every hot, aching inch of me to the cool morning air.

Juliet reaches back, opens her nightstand drawer, then turns back toward me, a small bottle of oil in hand. "Thumbs up? Thumbs down?"

"Scented?" I ask. So many strong scents give me headaches.

"Nope. Just almond and jojoba oil. Here." She snaps open the lid and wafts it my way, not coming too close. "Take a whiff."

I sniff it and get nothing. Falling back against the headboard, I tell her, "That'll be good."

"Good," she says, her voice perky, as she sets some oil in her palm. Her smile is wide as she settles back against me, wedging her thigh once again high over mine.

My mouth falls open as I watch her grip me at the base and stroke up, firm, squeezing at the tip. My head falls back as she glides back down. "Shit," I mutter, nudging my hips into her touch.

"You poor man." She *tsk*s softly, stroking up my length again. "Look at the state you're in."

I sigh, eyes still shut, my hand falling to her hair and sinking into those wild bedhead waves. "I had a lot of fun getting myself into that state. Pretty sure I slept with an erection, I was so turned on from it."

I feel her smile against my skin as she kisses my neck, my collarbone. "So glad that I'm here to take care of you, then—that I *get* to take care of you," she adds, her voice softer.

A groan leaves me as she tries something different, swirling her hand around the head of my cock, her thumb gently circling the tip. "How's that?" she asks.

I nod quickly, dragging open my eyes, finding hers. I rake my fingers through her hair as I stare down at her. "Fucking perfect."

She smiles, so sexy and gorgeous—her hair mussed from writhing against the pillows last night, her lips still swollen from our kisses.

My balls draw up tight as she strokes down again. I'm about to come already. It's hardly surprising, given how I denied myself last night, the weeks I've spent desperate for her. But still, I don't want it to end already.

"Breathe," she whispers against my mouth, her kiss slow and sweet. "Breathe, Will."

I draw in a deep tug of air as she eases off, then cups my balls, gently massaging them. My cock bobs, aching from the absence of her touch. I'm panting, my hand fisting around the sheets.

"God, Will," she whispers. "You are fucking magnificent."

I swallow thickly, my hips rocking up, my body chasing the pleasure of her touch. "You make me *feel* fucking magnificent."

She grips my cock again, a bit harder this time, and, holy hell, it's so good, my jaw tightens, my molars clacking together.

I swear under my breath. Breathless, heart pounding, I watch her slick hand wrapped around me, working me up and down.

"Fuck," I moan, drawing her close, crushing her to me. I kiss her hard, cup her breast, rolling her nipple with my thumb. "I have to touch you. Let me touch you."

"You can touch me," she breathes, as she strokes me, slow and hard, "but not to make me come. Let me just give you this." Her tongue dances with mine, sending me higher, higher, so dangerously close to release.

She squeezes up my length, then backs off and swirls her hand around the tip, making me bite back a curse. "How's that?"

"Don't stop," I beg. "Don't stop, please—"

"I won't," she says against my neck, kissing my jaw, the base of my throat, an impossibly sensitive spot beneath my ear.

Heat rockets through me, making me arch my hips into her hand, pumping myself in her grip.

"Faster?" she asks.

I nod feverishly. She tightens her grip, quickens her pace. Lightning strikes my body, bolts down my spine and soars deep inside me.

"I'm gonna come," I pant. I kiss her messily, desperately, and she meets me right where I am, her thigh slipping higher over mine, her pelvis grinding against it.

She gasps when I press my thigh harder between her legs. "Well, turns out I am, too," she pants.

It undoes me, hearing her say those words, knowing that just touching me like this has gotten her there. She rubs her thumb against the tip of my cock and whispers, "Give it up, Will. Come on. Come for me."

I clutch her tight against my chest as my orgasm tears through me, a tidal wave of pleasure so intense it knocks the air out of my lungs, makes my hips lurch wildly as I spill against her hand, across my stomach. Juliet's mouth falls open and she arches into me, her body tremoring, her leg's grip tightening around mine.

The heady realization that she came stretches out my orgasm, sends a fresh wave of release pouring out of me. I thrust into her hand, working myself as I kiss her, as I breathe in the jagged, panting cries that leave her lips.

Gradually, our movement slows. Juliet's body relaxes as mine does, too. Our kisses turn deep and languid. Finally, she drops her head to my chest, her face flushed, a wide, satisfied smile lighting up her face. My head thunks against the headboard as I peer down at her, breathing heavily. "That was . . ."

"Fucking incredible," she says hoarsely.

A husky laugh jumps out of me as I pluck a few tissues from the nightstand on my side of the bed and quickly wipe clean her hand, then my stomach. "Took the words right out of my mouth."

"Speaking of mouths," Juliet says, her gaze dipping down to my cock. "I can't wait to blow your mind with mine."

My jaw clenches at the deeply arousing thought of it. "Juliet, have mercy on me. I've got a refractory period to deal with."

She laughs and draws me down for a kiss, tumbling over top of her. "I can think of a very pleasurable way to pass the time until you're on the other side of it."

Just as I'm settling in between her thighs, my phone goes off, loud enough that I hear it from inside the sporran. I groan into her neck. "Nooo."

Juliet glances toward the floor, where my sporran vibrates with the muffled sound of my phone's alarm. "What's wrong?"

"What time is it?" I groan.

Juliet reaches for her nightstand, turning the clock toward us. "Eleven thirty."

"Shit." I flop back on the bed, scrubbing my face with my bare hands.

Propping herself up on one elbow, she peers down at me. Her hand settles on my chest. "What's wrong? Do you have to be somewhere?"

"Uh-huh." I rake my hands through my hair. "Damn client schmoozing. I'm canceling."

"Why would you cancel?"

"Because I'd much rather be here in bed with you."

"I know." She smooths my hair off my face. "But this can wait. You said you needed time, after all."

I give her a flat look. "My refractory period isn't *that* long."

A laugh jumps out of her. "Well, then cancel it, if you want. But *I* don't mind if you keep that appointment." She leans in and kisses me. "As long as you take me with you."

· TWENTY-NINE ·

Juliet

Will shuts the truck's door behind me and clasps my hand. "Thanks for wanting to come."

"You kidding?" I squeeze his hand and smile. "Thanks for letting me tag along."

"You are hardly tagging along, Juliet." His expression turns serious, his thumb gently stroking the back of my hand. "I'm real happy you wanted to come."

Staring up at him, I feel those butterflies soar through me, wild and free. We were only apart for an hour, while I freshened up and threw on a dress, and Will dashed home to change into clothes that weren't an eighteenth-century Highlander's, but I missed him, and now I'm a giddy jumble of joy to have him back until I have to see him off tonight.

I press up on tiptoe and kiss him. "I'm excited. I get to see you in action, all intense Mr. Business, talking whiskey."

He grimaces, gently pulling his hand from mine. Setting it low on my back, he guides me toward the pub a couple of buildings down the block. "Please keep your expectations low. It's a simple conversation, an obligatory whiskey at the bar, nothing interesting."

"Maybe to you." I peer up at him. "But to me, this is new and *very* interesting. You've spent time with my parents, my sisters, my friends—you've seen my life, but I've seen so little of yours, and now I get to. I can't wait."

His cheeks turn a lovely shade of pink as he shifts the small box of Orsino whiskey he brought with him, tucked under his arm. A soft smile lifts the corner of his mouth. "You can't be sweet like this in the pub. I'll turn bright red." He points to one pink cheek. "*Again.*"

I bite my lip against a smile. "But I *love* when you blush."

"Easy for you to say. Your face doesn't turn bright red at the drop of a hat."

"Okay, point taken. I'll behave myself."

Will's smile widens, and he wraps his arm around my shoulders, drawing me close, as we walk toward the door. "Well. Don't be *too* well behaved. We want to have some fun, don't we?"

"So," I whisper as we step inside the pub. "How do you want to play this?"

He snorts. "It's a business call, Jules, not a bank heist."

"Aw, come on. You said you wanted to have some fun. We could do a little role-playing. You're the silent, serious, gorgeous ginger sitting at the bar sipping a whiskey. I'm the bubbly brunette who sidles up to you and asks you to tell me *all* about it."

His eyebrows jump up. "Role-playing, huh?"

My cheeks heat as I smile up at him. "If you're into that kind of thing."

"Can't say I have been," he says, his gaze dancing over my face. "But, not for the first time when it comes to you, I'm inclined to reconsider my stance."

"What's that mean?"

Will brushes his knuckles gently down my cheek. "It means you have a knack for inspiring this gramps to get off his rocker—out of his rocker? You know what I mean." He frowns. "Hopefully."

I beam up at him. "I think I do."

Gently, Will nudges me forward. "Come on, let's get this over with."

We settle in at the short end of the bar, away from the crowded string of people filling the long portion of the bar that stretches the depth of the building. Will rests the box of whiskey on the bar, then tugs my barstool close. I pat his thigh, smiling encouragingly. I can see his nerves setting in as he clocks the bartender down at the other end.

"What is it?" I ask.

Will scrubs at the back of his neck. "It's easier, when I know them, but this is the first time I've met this owner—Mari's her name." He nods his chin toward the woman at the far end of the bar and clears his throat. "I just get nervous, when making introductions, trying to get an initial read on clients."

I squeeze his leg gently, searching his eyes. "So it's getting started that's hard."

He nods. "Harder. It's generally hard, or maybe not hard, but . . . draining, the socializing. It's just less so, once they're familiar and we have . . . rapport, I guess."

"So, when we met, when you first talked about what you were looking for in your future . . ."

"Wife," Will says, holding my eyes.

My heart rate doubles as he stares at me, heat in his eyes. "This is the kind of scenario where she'd team up with you? This first part is where she'd maybe . . . help."

Will nods, his hand settling over mine where it rests on his thigh. "Yeah, it is."

Marriage used to be my dream. So much so, I ran headlong toward it with my ex when he proposed after only a few whirlwind months together. Now I think about it differently. I think about it as a place where I might one day find myself on the path of a loving journey, not the destination I'm desperate to rush toward.

Still, the word *wife* coming from Will's deep, quiet voice makes something stir inside me, an excitement, a quiet, curious *maybe someday* whisper through my thoughts.

I turn my hand so our palms touch, curl my fingers around his big, callused hand. "Will . . ."

"Yes, Jules." He peers down at me, his gaze warm and intense.

"Maybe today, I could do that? If . . . you wanted?"

His cheeks heat. "Be my wife?"

I narrow my eyes at him playfully. "Be your *teammate*."

"You did throw out the possibility of role-playing," he says.

"I did." I search his eyes. "But not that one. I don't want to play a part with you anymore, at least, not a romantic one."

Will nods. "I don't want that, either. I think I made it pretty clear last night, but if not . . . no more practice? Now it can just be . . . us?"

I smile so wide it makes my cheeks ache. The joy that spills through me feels too big to contain. "Just us."

His thumb sweeps across the back of my hand as he stares at me. He's quiet for a moment, before he says, "Do you . . . do you think one day, you'll want to be . . . married?"

My stomach knots, and my heart clangs against my ribs. "Someday, I think so. If it's right, if the person I love"—that word's weight ripples through the space between us, shimmering with promise—"if they wanted it, too."

Will nods, a faint smile lifting his mouth. "Good to know."

The owner Will nodded toward when we came in, Mari, who's been down at the far end of the bar, seems to have appeared out of nowhere, flicking coasters onto the bar and clunking down two waters. We pull apart just enough to turn and face her.

"Hi," she says flatly. Her short, dark hair is mussed, her tattooed skin shiny with sweat. She looks fried and stressed.

I've lived in the city and spent enough time in bars to recognize a frazzled, worn-out bartender. I flash her a warm smile. "Hi."

"How are ya?" Will says politely.

"Oh, I'm shit," she says.

Will falters. "Uh." He clears his throat. "Sorry to . . . hear it."

Mari grunts in response.

"Long day?" I ask.

She gives me a quick, weary glance, dragging a couple of empties off the bar top nearby and dunking them into the soapy water on her side of the bar. "And it's going to get even longer. My musicians canceled. Got food poisoning, the assholes."

I grimace sympathetically. "That's unfortunate."

"Unfortunate," Mari says, "is an understatement. These weren't just any run-of-the-mill performers that I can try to get last-minute replacements for—they sing and play Scottish folk songs, and I have a whole goddamn horde of the Scottish Society members about to show up here, expecting a whole afternoon of traditional music that I promised them. *And* I just ran out of their preferred whiskey. Fucking shipping notification said it would be here three days ago." She wipes the sweat off her forehead, glaring down at the soapy bubbles. "I'm screwed."

"What kind of Scottish folk songs are we talking about?" I ask.

Will gives me a *What are you up to?* look.

I squeeze his hand.

Mari unearths her phone, taps it a few times, then spins it on the bar top, so I can see an email with a lineup of songs. My gaze drifts down the list.

And an idea comes to me. I squeeze Will's hand again. *Trust me, okay?*

"You happen to have a guitar lying around?" I ask her.

Mari glances up, her gaze narrowed. "Yes. Why?"

I smile brightly. "Because I might be able to help you out. I can do that set."

She blinks. "*You* know all those songs? And you can play them on the guitar?"

"You pick up a lot when you spend a month in Scotland," I tell her. "And while I'm not as great a guitarist as I used to be, I can still probably manage to strum simple chords and accompany myself."

Will squeezes my hand again. I can feel his concern radiating off him in waves.

"You're shitting me." Mari folds her arms across her chest. "Seriously?"

I softly sing the first few lines of "The Skye Boat Song." When I'm done I flash a little jazz hands and smile. "You tell me."

Mari's arms drop to her sides, her expression stunned. "You're hired."

My smile widens. "Glad to be able to help. I think we might be able to help you with your other problem, too. The . . . whiskey shortage?"

I glance to Will, raising my eyebrows. He glances from me to the bartender, then to the box of whiskey he set on the stool beside him.

Mari frowns as he lifts the box and rests it on the bar. Then Will offers his hand across the bar and says, "Will Orsino. Great to finally meet you."

Mari takes his hand, shakes it firmly, then folds her arms across her chest. "Orsino Distillery." She nods. "Sells well. But it's not the Scottish Society's favorite."

Will flips open the box lid and unearths a beautiful glass whiskey bottle that glows butterscotch in the light. A dark blue label, intricate gold lettering that spells out Orsino Distillery's name, and below it, *Aged 30 Years*.

"Trust me," Will says, uncorking the bottle, reaching for a glass that sits, inverted, at the bar's edge. He flips it over, deftly pours a taste, and slides it Mari's way. "Soon, it's going to be."

———

Will's been watching me as I sit in a quiet corner on the other side of the pub with Mari's guitar in my lap, willing my fingers to do what I want them to. But they really aren't. I can strum, very barebones, but even that makes my wrists ache.

"Shit," I mutter, shaking out my hand.

I glance over my shoulder and catch Will glancing my way again, torn from focusing on his conversation with Mari, which seems to be going fine, now that he got over the initial nerves of meeting her and introducing himself.

I nod toward her, indicating he should focus on Mari, then mouth, *I'm okay!*

He gives me an intense look and lifts his pinkie. A reminder that I'd be honest.

I grimace and revise: *I'm so-so.*

Will turns back to Mari, seems to politely excuse himself, then walks right toward me.

"Hey, big guy." I bat my eyelashes, trying for a wide, breezy, *no problems here* smile. "Things seem to be going well with Mari."

"It hurts," he says without preamble, pointing at my hands clutching the guitar.

I sigh. "Yeah, it hurts. I think I might just have to sing and wing it without the guitar. Which I really don't mind. Ya girl's done her fair share of karaoke, and those machines crap out more often than you think. I'm a seasoned veteran of singing unaccompanied, at this point."

Will drags a chair from the nearby table and sits, then gestures for the guitar. "I'll take that, if you don't mind."

I frown. "Why?"

"Because," Will says, starting to pluck at the strings, bending his head to listen for its pitch. He's tuning it. "You won't be singing unaccompanied." He peers up and gives me one of those adorable, delightful double-blink winks. "You'll have me."

———

Dusk hangs heavy in the sky, lilac streaks against the deep orange dying light. I stand on tiptoe on the sidewalk outside my apartment, my arms wrapped around Will as we kiss. "I had the *best* time."

Will sighs against my mouth. "Me, too. You have such a beautiful voice, Jules."

"Ah." I wrinkle my nose. "It's fine."

"It's *beautiful*," he says softly. "You had the whole place wrapped around your finger."

"The Scottish Society did seem pretty happy," I admit.

"As did Mari," he says. "Jules, between her and the Scottish Society, we sold so much damn whiskey." A laugh rumbles in his chest. "Fest is going to go cross-eyed when he sees those orders."

I rest my hands on his chest. "You did that, Will."

"Nah." He shakes his head. "*We* did." He smiles down at me, cupping my face. "Maybe we make a good team, you and me."

I smile up at him, my hand resting over his heart. "Maybe we do."

He bends for a kiss, but I stop him right before he can. Will frowns. "Why won't you let me kiss you?"

"Because you need to know I am furious with you!" I kiss him hard, to ease his disappointment, to reassure him I'm only being playful. "You were holding out on me. The incredible guitar skills, all that fancy talk about whiskey when you were charming the Scottish Society! What other secrets does Will Orsino hold?"

He grins and steals a swift, soft kiss. "Suppose you'll just have to wait and see, won't you, lass?"

It's like a thunderbolt rattling through me, the impact of his words. Because he didn't just say them; he said them with a soft, burring Scottish accent.

My mouth drops open. "You were dressed like a Highlander last night and you didn't talk to me like that? Not *once*?!"

His smile deepens, and he nuzzles my nose with his. "Had to make sure you liked me for my charming personality, first, Juliet. Couldn't risk you falling only for my dashing Highlander persona."

A laugh jumps out of me. "Though your capacity to fulfill the Highlander fantasy is definitely a perk, I've fallen for every part of you."

Will stares down at me, his gaze intense and heated. "I've fallen for every part of you, too, Jules."

Those butterflies race through me, and my heart skips. It feels so wonderful, so good, and for a moment, fear whips through me, a vicious wind scattering those happy butterflies.

What if all of this is *too* good to be true?

Trust it, that quiet voice inside me whispers. *Be brave, Juliet.*

"It's late," Will says quietly. "I should get on the road."

I nod, pushing away the fear, reaching for my courage. "You should."

Will's hands drift, low on my back, then lower, curving affectionately over my ass. He tucks me close, kisses me hard again, then pulls away, dropping his forehead to mine. "I'm gonna miss you so much."

My eyes slip shut, my fingers scraping softly through his hair. "I'm going to miss you, too."

Will leans back enough to stare down at me, his eyes searching mine. He tucks my hair behind my ear, his thumb softly sweeping my bottom lip. "I'll figure out a way to come down on Friday. I know it'll only be a day earlier, but it's better than nothing. I don't think I can last five days without you."

I draw his thumb into my mouth and suck. He groans, scowling playfully down at me. "Juliet, behave yourself."

"You said I shouldn't behave *too* much," I whisper, holding his eyes as I flick the tip of his thumb with my tongue.

His eyes darken. "Don't look at me like that."

I let his thumb go with a pop. "Like what?" I ask innocently.

He shakes his head. "You know exactly what I'm talking about."

"Fine," I whisper, peeling myself away from him, but then giving up and throwing my arms around his waist, hugging him hard. "Just come back, okay?"

He hugs me tenderly, his arms curled around my shoulders, his mouth pressed to my hair. "I will, Jules. I promise."

I let him go, somehow, my arms clutched around me against the cool evening breeze as I watch his truck pull away. His arm darts out from his window.

I throw my arm up into the air and wave, pressed on tiptoe. I wave and wave until his truck turns the corner.

Just as he's out of sight, the wind shifts and turns warmer, like a blanket wrapped around me.

Love, it seems to whisper, as it rustles the leaves above me. *Love.*

I stand on the sidewalk, rooted to the pavement. And for the first time since it started drifting through me, I let it stay—the knowledge, the truth that snuck up on me, like a slow drip into a bucket that's now filled to overflowing, spilling out no matter how hard I try to keep it in. I *love* Will.

I don't know if Will is ready to say that yet, if he feels that way. But *I* know my heart, and for me, for now, that's enough.

Slowly, I let myself into the building, take my time up the stairs, humming the first song I sang while Will plucked deftly at the guitar beside me. I feel warm to the bone, remembering that, remembering last night. Everything that happened in such a small, sweet window of time. Everything that came before it, slower, softer, leading us to this.

Back inside my apartment, I shut the door behind me, then traipse across my apartment, down the hallway to my room.

For the first time since I met Will, I'm excited for the inevitable that will come, once I fall asleep. Because I know the kinds of dreams I'm going to have, the dreams I've been having for him.

And this time, when I wake up in the morning, I'll enjoy the memory of those dreams, knowing Will's out there, wanting me, waiting as eagerly for me as I am for him—for the next time those dreams can all come true.

THIRTY

Will

This week has absolutely kicked my ass. But I anticipated that, knowing the influx of business and tourism we're expecting this weekend, for the eclipse. What I didn't anticipate was how damn grumpy it was going to make me—I've barely had time to text Juliet during the day, and our calls at night have been late and short because she crashes early and my days are stretching too long into the night. At least, tomorrow morning, I finally get to go back to her.

Mom's corralled us all at the house for a late Friday evening meal, a hasty casserole dinner scarfed down by all the family who've pitched in to prepare us for more tours of the distillery, more tastings, more hay rides and pony rides and barn animal petting sessions. Every garden is weeded to perfection, every corner of the tasting rooms polished to a shine.

I'm near delirious with exhaustion.

But I have a conversation that I've been putting off that can't wait any longer.

Dad's out on the back porch, in his rocker, plucking at his banjo, a habit he picked up for unwinding at the end of the day, when he thankfully gave up smoking his pipe.

"Hey, Dad. Got a minute?"

His voice is low and a little scratchy, like always. "Will." He nods to the guitar resting between his rocker and the cushioned wicker chair Mom always sits in. "Join me."

I sit on Mom's chair and help myself to the guitar, picking quietly in harmony with the tune he's playing. I've heard that tune my whole life, and I learned guitar by ear, first picking up the melody he was playing, then learning how to riff and harmonize with it.

"How's it going, Pops?"

He chuckles. "Besides the fact that this house is currently overrun with hot-tempered, stressed-out Orsino women, going fine." He ends the song and starts a new tune. "They worry too much. This weekend will be fine."

"It's just how they cope with caring. They want it all to be perfect."

"Nothing's perfect," Dad says. "But you're right. It's because they care." He glances my way, his gray-green eyes like mine holding my gaze. "And how are *you*, son?"

I peer down at the guitar, on the pretense of listening to his melody, figuring out how I want to join in. Like I don't know this song as well as I know my own name.

Dad lets my silence hang for a while, then says, "You and I . . . I know we aren't real big talkers, but, so you know, if you ever *do* need to talk, I'm here, son. I love you. You can tell me anything."

I peer up at him, my heart picking up its pace, searching for the words, how to begin.

He clears his throat. "Just . . . wanted to say that. In case you had any doubt."

"Thanks, Dad." I swallow roughly. "That . . . means a lot. And . . . I love you, too."

There's a shriek inside the house—Eleanor's for sure, followed by banging doors. She and Miranda are probably playing tag hide-

and-go-seek, because Eleanor's like Hector—if she doesn't get her zoomies out, she'll never fall asleep.

Quiet settles again in the air, crickets chirping in the grass. I pluck at the guitar because it helps to give me something to do, as I try to formulate my thoughts, as I work up the courage to ask what I've been wanting to since I came home Sunday night. After everything changed with Juliet.

"Dad," I say quietly.

He doesn't look at me, just keeps on plucking at the banjo. "Yes, son."

"When . . . you met Mom, when you first got married, you two weren't in love, right?"

He hesitates. "Well, I wouldn't say that."

"But that's how you tell the story."

"That's how your *mother* tells the story," he says. "Took her a while to realize she was madly in love with me—don't know why." He winks the way I do, the only way we can—a double blink, eyes crinkled tight at the corners.

I frown at him, stunned. I've grown up being told my parents married at first because it was the least expensive, most efficient way to combine their adjacent properties, to allow them to begin a shared vision for their land and business that they believed in. And then, gradually, they fell in love.

"So it was Mom who wasn't sure at first?" I ask.

He tips his head from side to side. "Think she knew. She was just too scared to admit it."

"Why?"

"'Cause it happened so fast," he says, picking at the banjo, his gaze far off. The wind rustles his silver hair. A small smile lifts the corner of his mouth, and he scratches at the side of his beard. "She just . . . needed time, to settle into it."

"But for you?"

"For me . . ." He shrugs. "It was love at first sight, but I'll admit I only understand that now in hindsight. I didn't know I loved her at first, either."

My hands slip on the strings, sending a twanging, out-of-tune note ringing through the air My heart starts pounding inside my chest. "What do you mean?"

He's quiet for so long that anyone else might be uncomfortable with our stretched-out silence. But I know him. I'm *like* him in this way. I just sit there quietly and wait.

"The first time I met your mother," he finally says, "it was like, all my life, the way I saw my world was as a house, with a known set of rooms, each for a place in my life—work, friends, family, hobbies, interests. I was so sure those were all the rooms there were for me. But when I met your mother, it was like . . . another door appeared in my world, and I knew there wasn't just another room on the other side of that door but a whole universe."

My heart's flying, my breathing tight, as I listen to him.

He peers down at the banjo, picking softly. "I don't know if you believe in soulmates, Will, but I think that's who your soulmate is—someone whose existence blows your world wide open, someone who makes you want to be brave and curious. When I saw your mother, I felt a sense of possibility like I'd never felt with anyone else. I didn't know her, but I wanted to. I didn't think I loved her yet, but there was nothing I wanted more than to open that door she'd made appear and walk, hand in hand with her, into all that possibility. Soon enough, I figured out what that wanting was." He glances my way and shrugs. "Love."

"When?" I ask. "How?"

He blows out a breath. "I wish I could tell you. It just . . . crept up on me. It wasn't like I suddenly woke up one day, sat across from her at the table, sipping my coffee, and sensed a damn lick of difference in how I felt about her. It wasn't the feeling that had changed or grown. I just . . . finally had a name for it."

I sigh heavily, eyes down on the guitar as I pluck slowly at its strings, my mind turning. Could it be that simple? Have I loved Juliet since she blew my world wide open, I just haven't recognized it for what it is?

"This about that lady you've been driving down to court every weekend?" he asks. "A certain Juliet?"

My hand slips on the guitar again, another off-key twang ringing in the air. "How'd you know?"

Dad grins. "Your mother, Will, has been on the phone—good Lord, has she been on that phone—talking with your young lady's mother. I remember them getting along well enough, through Fee, but now? Those two are as thick as thieves."

I blink. Stunned. "We told Juliet's parents we were just friends."

He laughs, hoarse and husky. "And your mother heard that from her, I'm sure, but she also knows all too well what can come of two people being 'friends.'" He pauses for a minute, then says, "It's all right to be scared, Will. It's natural, the first time you recognize those feelings in yourself—if that is what you're feeling."

"It is?"

"Sure," Dad says. "The most important people in our lives—because of how deeply they matter to us, how much of ourselves we entrust to them—it means they hold our heart in their clutches. That is terrifying. And some days the fear of how . . . exposed that makes us feel, all the unknowns it introduces, well, that fear is *loud*. But the love, the joy it brings you, the hope it gives you, can be even louder, the more you turn toward it, the more you give yourself over to it, the more you choose it. That's how love gets the last word."

I sit there, the guitar quiet in my hands. "Thanks, Dad," I tell him quietly.

He nods, then reaches over and grips my arm, squeezing hard.

He doesn't say another word as I sit beside him on the porch, and I don't, either. I watch the sun fade, already begging it to be tomorrow, for the sun to come up.

So I can finally step into this whole universe I've found in how I feel for Juliet. A world I hope she'll want to step into with me, hand in hand.

· THIRTY-ONE ·

Juliet

Will never came into town like he said he would yesterday. Never called. I waited up until my eyelids couldn't stay open another second, hoping I'd hear from him.

I woke up to a phone whose screen had no new messages. No missed calls.

I'm freaking out. I'm trying not to, but I'm freaking out. At first, I told myself maybe he got a late start in the day. But then the hours rolled by. That's when the hurt settled in. Had he forgotten? Had he decided to blow me off? I couldn't believe that. Next came the worry. But I told myself, if something had happened to him, Christopher would have heard, would have told us.

I finally caved at 9 p.m. and texted him.

JULIET: I missed you today. What happened?

I waited and I waited. Until I couldn't wait anymore, and I slept.

Now it's morning, and I'm awake; the sun is shining, and while there's no explanation for what's going on with Will, I'm determined to compartmentalize and carry on.

Because today is a big day, the biggest day of the year besides

Valentine's Day for the Edgy Envelope—Sula's stationery and paper shop—the big annual sale, and today, I'm helping out.

Examining myself in my reflection, I smooth my hands down my red skirt and force a smile as I say, "Hi! Welcome to the Edgy Envelope."

I frown. "Too peppy. Warm and welcoming without being overbearing." I blow out a breath, rolling back my shoulders, dusting off a piece of lint on my fuzzy pink sweater tank as I try again. "Hi. Welcome to the Edgy Envelope."

Smiling, I nod once at my reflection, satisfied. "That's better."

"JuJu!" The door to the apartment swings open. Bea catches it before it bangs into the coat hooks, judging by the quiet that follows, only the soft click of the latch as she shuts it. It makes me miss Will, how he'd bang the door into the coat hooks every time he came in.

"JuJu?" my sister calls.

"Back here!" I yell.

Bea bounds down the hall, then stops at the threshold. A snort jumps out of her. "Oh boy. We did it again."

I take in what she's wearing and feel a laugh jump out of me. Bea's wearing my outfit, but inverted. Her blouse is scarlet like my skirt. Her skirt is the same pale pink as my sweater. "Well, we ran a pretty high risk," I tell her, "considering we were ordered by Sula to dress for the occasion."

"That woman's lucky I love her," Bea mutters, sidling up to me in front of the mirror so she can inspect her reflection. "Giving me a dress code. These are *not* my normal colors."

I smile at the rhinestone pink headband holding back Bea's sideswept bangs, which she's started growing out. "You in pink, BeeBee. Never thought I'd see the day."

"The things I do for Sula," she grumbles, adjusting her headband. Turning to me, she looks me over. "You look real pretty,

JuJu. But . . ." She tips her head when her gaze lands on my face. "You okay?"

I swallow back the immediate threat of tears and force a wide smile. "I'm fine. Come on." I grab my foldable cane off the closet door hook, just in case I need it, and take her hand in mine, dragging her out of the room. "We're going to be late!"

———

"Welcome," Sula says, marching across the lineup of employees like a general about to lead us into battle, "to the Edgy Envelope's busiest retail day."

Bea bites her lip.

I can't look at her or I'll break out in a grin, and this does not seem like a grinning moment.

"What you're about to face," Sula says, the gravity of her delivery somewhat undercut by the pink hearts bouncing like antennae from her red headband, "is people at their most desperate. They want to stock up on the perfect cards, snag the ideal necklace, the best box of chocolates, the prettiest flowers"—she gestures toward the stand of bouquets my mom started assembling from her greenhouse and selling to Sula last year—"because we're going to charge them only sixty percent of what we normally do, and sales turn people into jungle animals. In short, they need your help both finding everything they want and remembering their higher angels. We cannot fail them."

"No pressure," Bea mutters.

I bite my cheek so I won't laugh.

"Are you ready?" Sula asks.

"Aye, aye, Cap'n," Bea says, saluting her. "But, quick question— where's Toni?"

"Bathroom," Sula says. "He'll be out any minute, I'm sure— holy *shit*." Sula stares past us, her expression stricken.

Bea and I turn around and see exactly why Sula looks so upset. Toni stands just outside the bathroom. He looks terrible. He's clutching his stomach, his complexion paper white. Actually, it's a little green, too.

"I think . . ." he croaks, "that I'm sick."

We all take an immediate step back.

Sula sighs. "You just spent twenty minutes in the bathroom and came out looking like a corpse, of course you're sick."

"I'm sorry," he whispers miserably.

"Honey," Sula says, "you have nothing to apologize for. You're sick. It happens."

"I sent out an SOS to all the strapping guys I know," he says, "so hopefully someone can come in and help you with moving inventory as you run out."

We all give him a look.

"What?" he says defensively, standing taller. "I'm strapping."

"I weigh two of you," Sula says flatly.

"So I'm a wiry strapping," Toni says. "I'm still the muscles of this operation."

Sula rolls her eyes. "Of course you are, hon. Thank you for putting out an SOS. Now go home and get some rest."

Toni looks like he's going to cry. He opens his arms and walks toward Sula.

"I love you, Antoni," Sula says, taking another step back, "but for the love of God, keep your pestilence to yourself. Off you go."

Toni smiles faintly. "Okay, I will. I'm just gonna grab my bag—" His hand flies to his mouth. "Never mind, I'll be in the bathroom."

"Oof," Bea mutters, turning toward me. "Poor Toni. Poor us. This is going to be rough."

She's right. For the next two hours, it is pretty rough. We're slammed with patrons, Sula working the floor, Bea and I running the registers, Bea dropping off her register when we start to run low on cards, jewelry, and chocolate, then quickly restocking them.

When it seems like we might have a lull for the first time since we opened, I make my way to the storage closet. It's dark and cozy in there, cool and quiet. I just need a minute to myself.

Suddenly, there's a knock on the door of the storage closet. "Yes?" I ask.

Bea eases open the door, and Kate steps in behind her. "Hey, JuJu," Bea says.

Kate shuts the door and smiles.

I glance between them. "What's up? Why are you here?"

Bea's presence makes sense, but not Kate's. Kate's not even working the sale today. She had a photography shoot booked this morning with a nonprofit devoted to preventing food insecurity, her photos slated to be used in a feature article. She couldn't back out of that, even though we definitely could have used the help.

"Just wrapped up my shoot," Kate says, "and a little birdie told me another little birdie was on the struggle bus."

I frown at Bea. Bea doesn't look sheepish or sorry at all. "I've known you since we were zygotes," she says. "I can tell when you're not okay, even if you say you are."

"You didn't *know* me when we were zygotes," I grumble, leaning back against the wall and propping my feet up on a box. "We weren't conscious beings at that point."

"My point still stands." Bea plops down on the floor beside me and clasps my hand. "You don't have to tell us, but if you want to, we're here." She glances toward our sister as Kate eases onto a box labeled *4" x 6" matte card stock* and smiles encouragingly.

Kate then digs around in her cross-body bag and pulls out a small pastry box. "Or you can just sit here and eat your feelings."

I hesitate for a second, then slowly reach for the box. "Maybe . . . I can do a little bit of both?"

Kate grins, whipping open the box. "That's the spirit."

————

Bea's mouth hangs open with her dark chocolate cupcake, her expression shocked. Kate's got cream cheese frosting on her nose from startling so badly at my news, right when she was about to bite into her pumpkin cupcake.

"Wait." Bea chews twice, then swallows what was clearly still an uncomfortably large bite. "So you and Will have been romantic for weeks?"

"Practicing romance," I emphasize.

"I'm gonna need a little more than that," Kate says weakly.

I tell my sisters about Will's and my plan, hatched in Christopher's backyard, the practice dates, the flirty texts, the idea I had to incorporate him into our friend group to avoid raising suspicion.

"But then . . . practicing," I say quietly, staring down at my hands, "it . . . stopped feeling like practice. It felt . . ."

"Real," Bea says gently.

I glance up, meeting her eyes, searching them. "Yeah."

Bea smiles and pats my hand. "I have some experience with how the lines between rehearsing and reality can blur when you're pretending with someone."

"You do?"

Bea squints an eye and tips her head from side to side. "Yeah," she says sheepishly, glancing between Kate and me. "Jamie and I, when we were first"—she makes air quotes—"'dating,' we weren't really. We were faking it."

My mouth falls open. "You *what*?"

Kate kicks her feet in the air, squealing delightedly. "What a *turn*! I did *not* see that coming!"

"Well," Bea says, meeting my eyes, "I mean, you and the douche waffle and the friend group were all up in our business, trying to pair us up when we did *not* want to be paired up, so we decided we'd fake date and get you all super invested in us, then break up in epic fashion and crush your hopes, teach you a lesson about meddling."

"Jesus, BeeBee." I blink, stunned. "I . . . Wow. I *never* picked up on it being fake. I didn't even catch a whiff of a performance."

"That's because," she says, a smile lifting her mouth, "it really wasn't, at least, not for long. Of course, at first it was, but we quickly figured out we were going to be garbage at passing as a couple unless we spent some time together and got to know each other well enough to pass as a believable couple. So we started hanging out, talking, trying to understand each other, and . . . we ended up falling for each other."

A disbelieving smile breaks across my face. "You fell in love while *pretending* to love each other."

She nods. "Yeah, we did. I mean, we hit a bit of a bump in the road, of course—"

"Because of him." I refuse to even say my ex's name. We all know whom I'm talking about. Guilt sits heavy in my stomach. "That's why you broke up, wasn't it?"

"Took a *break*," Bea corrects. "It was just a *break*!"

"But you did it for me, you jerk!" I grab her shoulders. "How could you do that? Because you thought I'd have a fit when I saw you with Jamie? You didn't think I'd be able to be happy for you and compartmentalize the fact that my shitty ex had been Jamie's friend? I mean, Bea, Jamie loathed him, kicked him out of his life for good, after what he did. Sure, I would have probably needed some time, but that was mine to take, not yours to force on us."

"We're getting sidetracked," Bea says briskly, smoothing her hands down her skirt. "I realize it probably wasn't a super-well-thought-out response, and I apologized to Jamie and he forgave me, and we made it through, because here we are, planning to get married. The point is," she says, holding my eyes, "I think I understand what happened with Will. What I don't understand is why you're sad."

I stare into my twin's eyes, seeing all her love, her empathy. Tears blur my vision.

"Ooh, no, no," Bea whispers, swiftly wiping under my eyes. "Applying makeup is a Herculean effort for you these days. Let's not have to do a repeat. We both know you hate how I do your makeup when I try."

I laugh tearily, falling into her shoulder.

Kate stretches out her legs, her face drawn as she watches me. She pins my feet between her boots and squeezes affectionately.

I glance between my sisters. "We finally turned the corner, last weekend, from friends to . . ."

"Lovers?" Kate asks gently.

I nod. "And he was really busy all week, which I got. They're gearing up for this big festival and a huge tourism influx for the eclipse tomorrow, and I didn't mind, but then he was supposed to come into town yesterday, because . . . because he couldn't wait another day, and he didn't."

"Did he have an explanation?" Kate asks.

I shake my head. "I never even heard from him."

Bea frowns. "That doesn't seem like sweet Will."

"No," I mutter miserably, my head slumped on her shoulder.

"Christopher would have heard," Kate says, "if he ran into some kind of trouble."

"That's what I've been telling myself, too."

"Then what's going on?" Bea asks, her brow furrowing even more. "It doesn't add up."

"It doesn't," I agree. "And that's the thing—whatever caused him not to show up yesterday, whatever's kept him from reaching out to me and explaining himself, that's not what I'm freaking out about, not primarily."

Kate peers down at me. "You're freaking out that you care so much."

I nod. "And not just that I care, that I'm assuming the best of him. And this is . . . exactly what I was afraid of happening!"

"What do you mean, JuJu?" Bea asks softly, her hand going to my hair, combing its stray pieces back from my face. I had the silly idea to pin it up and make it look fancy, but in the hours I worked my tail off, it's just fallen out of those pins.

"Look at what I've done." I lift my thumb. "I've told myself I wouldn't get mixed up with one of Christopher's friends again, and what do I do? I get myself all turned around for one of his dearest, oldest friends." I lift my pointer. "I told myself I'd be more level-headed, that I wouldn't always assume the best in someone, when I had feelings for them—here I am, even after he's ghosted me for twenty-four hours, spinning up excuses for why he must not be at fault." I lift my middle finger, which feels appropriate. "We've been hanging out for barely a month, not even half those days spent in person, and I've gone and fallen in lo—" I clear my throat. "And I've fallen for him, so quickly. I've fallen quickly before, and look how that toxic terrible mess turned out the last time I fell fast and hard—toxic and terrible!"

"Hey." Bea pats my shoulder. "Take a deep breath." She glances over at Kate. "And listen to us. You know I've had a bad breakup before, that I understand wanting to protect your heart after someone's bruised it. But just because something was bad with one person doesn't mean it will be bad with another. Jules, you have such a big, open heart, doesn't it make sense that when your heart recognized someone wonderful like Will, it fell head over heels? The fart-face was the bad number in your equation last time, not you."

I laugh. "Fartface." My laugh becomes thick as I dab my eyes. "But I'm the common denominator!"

"Exactly," Kate says, leaning in, clutching my shin. She holds my eyes intently. "You were the only good thing about your relationship with your ex. And now, you've got something that's night and day from that. It's got all your goodness and all his goodness, too."

Bea nods in agreement.

I wipe my nose, sniffling. "I'm so scared of this. How much I feel, how much I . . ." A heavy sigh leaves me. "I'm just . . . scared."

Kate nods, gently squeezing my ankle as she sits up again. "If I have learned anything since I came home last year, since Christopher and I finally figured out what we mean to each other, it's this: you can't outrun your feelings, especially your fear. You can deny them, suppress them, numb yourself to them. And sure, it makes you feel safer for a while, better even. But it doesn't last. The feelings, they're still there. And you either continue to hide them from others, hide *yourself* from others, too—which is so damn lonely. Trust me," she adds. "Or . . . you can face those feelings and share them with the people who matter, so they can see you and support you, so you can feel so much less alone."

I nod. "Thanks," I tell both my sisters, glancing between them, blinking away tears, "for cornering me in a closet and making me feel my feelings."

Bea kisses my temple. "You bet."

"And for the cupcakes," I add, nodding to the box.

Kate salutes. "What sisters are for."

I smile between them, my heart lighter, unburdened. No, I'm not at peace. I'm anxious about Will still, and my heart feels fragile. But I am okay. I can make it through this.

Groaning, I ease onto all fours, then stand upright. "Well," I tell Bea, "we should probably get back, make sure we haven't left

Sula high and dry. But first, I need to go fix my hair in the bathroom real quick." I feel around at it, half out. "It's a mess."

Bea stands up, too, dusting off her skirt. "I'll head back and help. You take your time in the bathroom."

Kate's phone buzzes in her pocket. She pulls it out and frowns as she reads it. Then her expression blanks. She pockets her phone. "Actually"—she clears her throat—"maybe not the bathroom."

She glances toward Bea. Bea frowns, her eyes darting between Kate's. She checks her phone, which has started buzzing, too. Her eyes widen.

"Am I missing something?" I ask. I left my phone behind the desk. "Please tell me Toni isn't sharing his puke live updates still."

Bea pockets her phone. "Speaking of that . . . Toni, well, let's just say what he did to that bathroom is not something you want to see, JuJu. Sula gave it a good scrub and air freshener spray, but . . ." She shakes her head.

I shrug, starting toward the closet door. "Eh, I'll hold my nose. I really need a mirror to fix my hair—"

Kate darts in front of the door, splayed against it. "I wouldn't do that if I were you, Jules. Sometimes the scars of gastrointestinal violence are no match even for industrial-strength cleansers."

Bea gags behind me. "Too far," she mutters.

I'm annoyed now. I don't know what they're up to, but I'm losing my patience and the pins in my hair are really starting to pull. "Okay, then. Where *should* I go fix my hair?"

Kate smiles as she steps aside. "I'd suggest heading to the delivery bay."

"Fine," I mutter, tugging open the door and turning left toward where our delivery trucks back in for us to unload inventory.

Bea calls out, "Sula's got a great piece of scrap metal back there! Works like a charm, if you don't mind looking like you're half as tall and four times as wide."

I roll my eyes, turning the corner into the bay, and come to a dead stop.

There's Will, standing just inside the doorway, hair wild and windblown, wrinkled gray T-shirt, ripped old jeans, boots whose laces aren't even tied. My gaze dances over his high cheekbones, that long nose with the bump at the bridge, those wide silver-sage cat eyes with their gilded russet lashes. The faint freckles scattered across his skin.

Our eyes meet and those butterflies take off.

"I forgot," he says quietly, his eyes holding mine. "In all the chaos of the week, I completely forgot I told you I'd come down yesterday. I got so wrapped up with all that we're doing, I totally forgot to tell you there was just no way I could get to you before today. When I remembered, I was going to call you, but then I realized I didn't have my phone. And *that* is because Eleanor—"

"Your niece," I say softly.

He pauses, like I've caught him off guard. "My niece, yes, she told me she might have accidentally dropped my phone in the toilet. As in, she *did* drop my phone in the toilet. She tends to sneak my phone when she's at my parents' and she's gotta do a number two, because it takes her a while and she likes to watch *Bluey* episodes while she waits. Her moms don't let her have *their* phones for that purpose, given the risk of it ending up . . . exactly where mine did."

My hand comes to my mouth. I'm smiling like a goofball, but the relief, the joy of seeing him, the flat-out hilarity of this anecdote, it's too much—I can't help it.

"I didn't have your number memorized—I have *nobody*'s number memorized," he goes on, "and even though I know I could have asked my mom to call your mom and get your number, I was afraid to do that, because we hadn't talked about what you were comfortable with, who you wanted to know, and I know it's been important to you to keep this private. I didn't want to dismiss that just because I was worried you'd be pissed at me, which would be understandable, obviously—"

I bite my lip. I have never heard this man talk so much. And he's still on a roll.

"Then I debated driving straight to you last night, but, Juliet, I was so tired I couldn't even see straight, and I knew, if I got behind the wheel that tired and got myself in an accident on my way to see you—"

"I'd have throttled you," I tell him, stepping closer, clasping his hand. "Because your safety is precious to me. *You* are precious to me."

His eyes search mine. "I am? Even after I—"

I throw my arms around his neck and press my mouth to his, a long, firm kiss. His body relaxes; his arms wrap around my back, drawing me against him. "Even after," I tell him. "And I hope . . . when I make my mistakes, you'll feel the same way about me."

He laughs softly, tucking his chin over my head. "Baby, I couldn't feel any other way if I tried."

I set my head against his chest, listening to his beating heart, and smile. "I know the feeling."

THIRTY-TWO

Will

Sula shuts the door to the Edgy Envelope, flips the sign from **OPEN** to **CLOSED**, and slumps against the glass, hands raised over her head. "We did it!"

Juliet smiles tiredly from her perch on a stool at the register desk. I stare at her, worried she's worn herself out, and she must read the concern on my face, because she mouths, *I'm okay.*

"Bea, Jules, Kate," Sula says, drawing each of them into gentle side hugs, one after the other, "you were incredible, thank you. William"—she turns toward me, arms open wide—"gimme a hug, you inventory-restocking rock star."

Sula's always been nice to me since we met, but definitely not demonstrably affectionate, like the others. I throw Jules a quick surprised glance as Sula tackles me into a hug.

Juliet lifts her eyebrows, smiling wide.

"Thank you," Sula says, slapping my back. "So much. We could not have done it without you."

"Happy to help," I tell her as we step apart. "I'm glad Toni texted me."

Kate slumps onto the desk. "I'm so hungry. And I only helped half the day. You guys have to be dying."

"Yep," Jules tells her. "My stomach is eating itself."

"Dinner's two minutes away," Sula says, eyeing her phone.

Bea lifts her hands in praise. "Thank God. I'm going to eat the shit out of that guacamole."

The doorbell rings, and I jog toward it, accepting the giant bag of food and handing the delivery person a cash tip.

We tear open our Mexican and all settle in around the front desk, Juliet and Bea on stools, Sula, Kate, and I standing.

"So," Kate says, crunching on a chip. "Jules was saying your family's farm is expecting a big tourism boom this weekend?"

"Already ticked up pretty heavily toward the end of the week." My sisters all reassured me they could handle today without me home, promising to keep me updated via text. It's mostly been Miranda relaying updates from the others, but it's helped to hear things have gone well. "Last I heard, they were slammed today, but that's good for business, so no complaints."

Sula asks, "So is your farm, where it is upstate, in the path of totality?"

Jules and Bea roll their eyes.

"Not this again," Kate groans.

"If I had a nickel," Jules says, "for every time Sula said 'the path of totality,' I could retire right now."

"If I took a shot," Bea tells her, "every time Sula said 'the path of totality,' I'd—"

"Have alcohol poisoning," Sula grumbles, chucking a chip at Bea's head. "Yeah, yeah, so sue me, I'm in awe of this rare, incredible natural phenomenon that's happening in our backyard. I'm *so* sorry."

Bea dips the chip Sula tossed at her in guacamole and hands it to Sula, a peace offering. "We're just teasing, Sul."

Sula crunches on the chip. Peace offering accepted.

"So, is it?" Jules asks. "Is your land in the you-know-what?"

I grin. "The path of totality?"

Bea, Jules, and Kate throw up their arms, yelling in offense.

Sula smiles up at me. "I love this guy."

"Yes, it is," I tell Juliet, eyes down on my food to avoid her gaze.

My plan begins with inviting her up to my home tomorrow, to see the eclipse, get a tour of the place, stay the night. She can meet my parents and sisters and niece and nephew, who'll be busy enough that they won't have endless time to grill her and overwhelm her. A solid first introduction.

"I wish I could see it," Sula says. "But hotels have been booked up for like a year. And you know traffic is going to suck if we were to drive up for the day and try to drive back after."

Kate nods. "Yeah, that's true."

"Wait!" Bea says, dropping her chip, dusting off her hands. She pulls out her phone from her skirt pocket. "Jamie's house, the one his aunt gave him, it's in your town, too, Will! Illyria, right?"

I nod. "That's right."

"There's plenty of room," Bea says. "We could all fit. At least, I think we all could. But, I mean, there are couches, air mattresses; we'll make it work."

Sula stares at Bea. She looks like she might cry. "Are you suggesting what I think you're suggesting?"

Bea nods excitedly. Sula sets her hands on both sides of her face.

Kate throws back her head and yells, "Road trip!"

The sun is the faintest nectarine sliver, curved on the edge of the horizon. Juliet and I hold hands as we sit on what I have been reassured are the now repaired and reinforced swings of the play set straddling her backyard and Petruchio's, swaying slowly, sipping our to-go coffees. She smiles at me over her coffee cup. I smile back. She drags her tongue against its edge, and I narrow my eyes at her. "Don't look at me like that, not right now."

She shrugs happily. "Just remembering last night fondly."

I groan. We were both so exhausted after all day at the Edgy Envelope that we collapsed into her bed and barely managed to make out before we fell asleep. The last thing I remember is Juliet's bite of my bottom lip, her tongue dragging over it, before I crashed.

I woke up desperate for her, but there was no time—we have a full day ahead of us, and we have to hit the road as soon as possible so we don't get stuck in the worst of the traffic caused by folks driving to see the eclipse.

I shake my head. "You're cruel."

She grins. "I like cuddling and making out with you. Get over it."

My phone buzzes in my pocket, and I pull it out, reading the message.

"Christopher's up?" she asks.

I nod, pocketing my phone. Juliet stands from the swing, leans in, and kisses me softly. "Good luck."

I watch her walk across the yard, just like I did that first day, up the steps, until she's inside her parents' house. And then I get up, too, and walk the length of Petruchio's house, turning the corner for his porch. Sinking onto his front steps, I text him back, Out front.

For a few minutes, I sit there, elbows on my knees, hands laced together, eyes on the horizon. When I hear the creak of his front door opening, I glance over my shoulder.

Petruchio stands on his threshold in sweatpants and a T-shirt, frowning, looking a bit worried. I texted him an hour ago that I needed to talk, but I didn't tell him why. I feel bad for making him uneasy, but I couldn't tell him what I wanted to talk about over text. This is an in-person conversation.

He shuts the door behind him, scrubbing at his hair, which is sticking up every which way, a coffee cup in his other hand. "Want to come in?"

I shrug as I pick up my coffee from the step beside me. "We can talk here. There. Up to you."

He crosses the porch and lowers onto the steps beside me. "What's going on?"

I turn my to-go cup in my hands. "I need to talk to you."

His eyes dance between mine, his frown deepening. "I'm listening."

"Sorry for the early text, if I woke you up," I tell him. I sip my coffee and try to steady my racing heart.

"I wasn't asleep," he grumbles.

My cheeks heat. "Oh. Uh . . . sorry for interrupting . . . that."

He gives me an arched eyebrow, a hidden smile behind his cup as he sips his coffee. "That's all right. So . . . what's going on?"

I set my coffee beside me on the porch and clasp my hands together, steadying myself. "It's Juliet."

He freezes, coffee cup halfway to his mouth. "What about her?"

I peer up at him, holding his eyes, searching them. "I . . ." My jaw works. I blow out another long breath. And then I tell him everything. How Juliet and I met in Scotland, and again in his backyard, and didn't exactly become friends so much as romance workout buddies. How, when I wasn't making the rounds with clients in the city or hanging out with the friend group, these past weekends, Juliet and I were going on practice dates. And then I get to the part that matters most.

"It changed," I tell him. "Grew. We . . . It's not practice anymore. For either of us."

He stares down at his coffee for a beat, then sips it. "I see."

My brow furrows. I watch him closely as he sips his coffee again and peers over at me. Is he . . . smiling?

That's a good sign, I hope.

"I'm telling you this," I say to him, "because I know she's like a sister to you, because you love her like family and you're protective of her, and she's told me she had her heart crushed by someone she met through you, and it made things messy for a while. Given all that, I'd understand if you were wary of me . . . wanting to be with her."

"Hmm." He tips his head, his smile still there. "I think . . . if it were any other person, Orsino, I would be."

"Yeah?"

His mouth lifts in a faint, knowing smile. "I've had a hunch for a while that there might be more going on. And while it might not have taken you long to fall for her, I know you haven't entered into that feeling lightly, because I know you, friend. I trust you. And I trust Juliet to know her own mind and heart, too." He brings his coffee to his lips and drains his cup. "You don't need my stamp of approval, not that I'm even sure you came here for it."

"I didn't," I tell him truthfully. Even if he didn't understand, the choice to be together or not would be mine and Juliet's alone. "But it would mean a lot to have it."

He nods, his eyes holding mine. "Then consider it given. And now," he says, pushing off the step and standing, "you'll excuse me. I've got a big day ahead of me, an eclipse to see, a rental van to brave with Sula rambling about 'the path of totality,' *and*, most importantly, a very demanding woman hoping I'll come back upstairs. It's not in my best interest to keep her waiting."

· THIRTY-THREE ·

Juliet

"Oh, birdie," Mom says, her eyes shiny with tears threatening to spill over. "I'm so happy for you."

I smile down at my coffee from my perch on the kitchen stool, then glance back up at her and Dad, still in their pajamas, Mom in her flower nightgown and knit sweater, Dad in his lopsided robe, his hair all over the place.

"He seems like a good, kind man," Dad says, reaching for my hand and gently patting it. "That's what you deserve."

"Thanks, Daddy."

"And you're all traveling up to the eclipse, then?" Mom says.

I nod. "Big road trip. I'm excited to meet his family."

"You'll *love* Isla," Mom says. "And Isla will love you."

"I hope so," I say quietly.

Dad winks. "There's not a soul in this world who couldn't love you, Juliet."

My heart clutches at his words. "You're sweet to say it, but . . . there are certainly people who don't love me, and I'm okay with that." I shrug. "I only need love from the people I love, too."

Mom nods.

"There was . . . one more thing," I say, peering down at my coffee, "that I wanted to talk to you about."

They both ease onto the stools on the other side of the island, maybe sensing that this is something to settle in for.

"I know the past nine months, I've worried you. My bad breakup, my health issues, quitting my job . . ." I blow out a breath, then meet their eyes. "You have been so supportive of me, in so many ways, and I can't thank you enough for that. The meals when I needed them, time at home when I wanted somewhere comforting to be, all the time and conversation and love you've lavished on me."

My mom bites her lip. "But . . . ?"

I hold her eyes and say, "But at some point, it started to feel like you saw me as breakable, when I'd just been bruised, fragile when I'd only been feeling some legitimately tough emotions as I figured out my life. Yes, I hurt some days, and no, my body doesn't do everything it used to, but I am strong, even when I'm struggling. I'm okay. I won't pretend to know how hard it is to watch your child struggle. And I know you want to support me—*I* want your support, too. I just . . . need you to follow my lead, on how I talk about my illness, how I deal with it. I need you to trust me to take care of myself and trust that when I need help, when I'm hurting and I need you, I'll tell you."

Mom sighs heavily and reaches across the table, knowing this conversation is for her more than Dad. "I'm sorry, birdie. I'll do better, promise."

Dad reaches for my other hand and clasps it, firm and warm. "We're always here for you, Juliet. Just say the word."

"Thank you, both of you." Slowly, I stand from my stool, smiling between them. "I'd stay for breakfast, but I've got to get going."

"Bring Will around again, soon?" Mom calls as I start out of the kitchen.

I turn in the doorway and grin. "You kidding? I couldn't keep him away from your cooking if I tried."

Will's home is the stuff of dreams. I feel like I've stepped back in time, a lady in one of my historical romances, in her long gown, walking the gardens, her fingertips brushing the delicate blooms, her gaze drinking in field after field.

The illusion would be easy to hold on to, except that Will and all my friends and sisters, his family, and a horde of tourists sit on the grass, our goofy paper eclipse glasses perched on our noses.

"It's stunning," Sula whispers thickly. She's got her hand wrapped around Margo's, their daughter, Rowan, perched in her lap.

Margo nods and brings Sula's hand to her mouth, her eyes not on the eclipse but her wife. "Yeah, hon. It is."

Bea sits inside Jamie's bent legs, her hands clasping his knees, his chin resting on her head. Kate and Christopher lie side by side on a blanket, arms behind their bent heads, saying something to each other and smiling.

Toni and Hamza sit side by side, Toni resting his head on Hamza's shoulder.

My cousin Bianca peers up at the sky from her piggyback perch on Nick, her boyfriend.

And all of Will's family is scattered around us, too. His beautiful sisters with their fiery hair, his adorable niece and baby nephew, his mother standing beside his father, hands clasped as the world grows eerily dark.

Will's arm curls around me, his hand softly rubbing along my shoulder. "Where'd you go?" he says quietly.

I smile up at him. "Nowhere. I'm right here, in my happy place."

He smiles, too, his eyes dancing between mine. "It makes me real happy, knowing you're happy here."

I nod. "The happiest."

As I settle in his arms, I let my gaze wander again, up to the eclipse, getting closer and closer to totality, to the crowd of people gathered around.

A tall woman with long blond hair stands up from where she was sitting on the ground, holding out a hand for another woman, who stands, too, shorter, her hair dark and shoulder length, a heart-shaped face. Something about the first woman feels oddly familiar.

I watch the familiar woman walk hand in hand with the shorter, dark-haired one as they move away from the crowd, presumably so as not to be in the way, until they stop just a dozen feet from us, to the side of our group, for a selfie. That's when I realize why the blond one looks familiar.

Will notices my interest in them and glances down at me. "What is it?"

"That," I tell him, "is Olivia Tobias. Huge social media influencer. You should try to connect with her, give her some Orsino Distillery merch, ask if she wants to take photos of the farm and the experiences you guys offer. It would probably give you a great boost."

Will makes a noncommittal hum in the back of his throat.

I peer up at him. "What's that sound supposed to mean?"

Maybe I was being pushy, telling him how to advertise his businesses, what opportunities to pursue.

He smiles down at me. "You just seem to have a good head for business. Might have to keep you around, put you on the payroll."

My heart jumps as I think about what he said he was looking for when all this started, what he confirmed when I asked him about it at the pub last weekend, what he needed from the woman who would be his business partner.

His wife.

And it's . . . everything I'm good at. Networking, wining and dining, connecting people, being my extroverted, engaging self. A scary, beautiful dream flits through my mind as I stare up at him. I wonder if Will can see it in my eyes, all that I'm already hoping for, all that terrifies me and thrills me in equal measure. The life we could share here, the incredible team we would make.

The joy we'd bring each other.

I bite my lip as I peer up at him. "I'd certainly be interested to hear what you have in mind."

Will tucks my hair behind my ear and kisses me softly, discreetly, a quick, gentle press of his lips to mine. "I don't want to lay my offer out on the table *here*," he says meaningfully, nodding to all the people surrounding us. "I'll just say I think you'll be pleased with my terms."

Those butterflies take off in my stomach, a glorious, fluttering swoop. "Looking forward to it," I tell him, settling back against his chest.

I glance around again and notice Olivia's still close by, standing chest to chest with the same woman, who smiles up at her. They lean in and kiss, slow and sweet. I look away, giving them privacy, smiling to myself. I hope that's her Basti, the woman she mistook me for at the club—she certainly looks like me from behind— short, curvy, dark hair to her shoulders, a heart-shaped face that in profile looks a little like mine. I hope Olivia's gotten her happy ending, too.

"Still think we should try to get Olivia Tobias on board," I tell him.

He laughs softly.

I poke his stomach. "What's so funny?"

"That woman"—he nods toward Olivia—"she's one of those influencer ladies whose profile Ma sent me."

I sit up. "What, as in someone you should try to pursue?"

He nods.

"Never mind. Social media influencers with over a million followers are a dime a dozen." I wave a hand. "We can find another one. I don't need that kind of competition hanging around."

"You goof," he says, dragging me back inside his arm, tucked tight to his chest. "Like I could ever want anyone but you."

THIRTY-FOUR

Will

"Who's a good pup?" Juliet croons to Hector, crouched in front of him as he licks at her jaw.

He's a puddle for her, butt wiggling in excitement, tail thumping against the pavers outside my house. Juliet squeals as he licks her ear and wraps her arms around him. "You're the sweetest pupper, aren't you?" She's full-on baby-puppy-talking to him now, smile wide, nose wrinkled, eyes scrunched shut as he licks her face. "The sweetest, sweetest pupper."

I stare down at them, my heart so damn full.

Juliet peers up at me, beaming. "I love him."

I crouch, joining them, my hand drifting steadily down Hector's back. "He loves you, too."

Juliet smiles softly, her eyes holding mine. "Think so?"

I nod, my gaze fixed on her. "Know so. He never stood a chance." Glancing back at a panting, happy Hector, I pat his flank, then stand. "Love at first sight."

Offering Juliet my hand, I draw her up to stand, because I know crouching for long hurts her knees.

"Love at first sight," she says quietly, her fingers lacing through mine. "I thought that was the stuff of fairy tales."

"Me, too," I tell her. "It seems . . . improbable. But Dad, he said something that made me think there's some truth to those fairy tales, after all."

"Oh?" Juliet smiles as I draw her inside my arms. Her hands settle on my chest. "And what was that?"

"He said . . ." My gaze dances over her face. "He said it's not so much that you know you love someone at first sight, it's just that . . . you feel its possibility, like you never have before." I draw her closer. "Like you never will again. And one day, when that possibility's blossomed into love, you'll look back and understand that seed for what it was, even though it looked so different when that first sight planted it, when it began as something unrecognizable from what it is now."

Juliet's expression softens. Her hand circles over my heart. "That . . . is beautiful."

I nod. "It is."

Slowly, Juliet presses up on tiptoe toward me, desire and longing bright in her eyes. I know, if I kiss her, exactly how this will go. I'll scoop her up and drag her upstairs to my bed.

And I want that, so much.

But not yet.

I duck her kiss, my lips landing gently at her neck, where I whisper, "Juliet."

"Hmm?" she says faintly as I kiss behind her ear, along her jaw.

"Do me a favor?"

"Sure," she breathes.

I pull back, holding her eyes. "Go upstairs? There's a balcony. Just go there, and . . . wait for me." Drifting my hand along her back, I tell her, "I won't keep you waiting long."

Juliet peers up at me, curiosity in her expression. She lifts her pinkie. "Promise?"

I hook my pinkie with hers and smile. "Promise."

THIRTY-FIVE

Juliet

Standing on the balcony of Will's home, I stare up at the stars, sparkling like diamonds in the pitch-black velvet sky. Because this is where I was told to be, and if I've learned anything in the past month, it's that Will Orsino can plan the heck out of a romantic date—if he tells me to go stand on a balcony, I'm not going to say no.

The air is warm, a breeze lifting my hair, wrapping me in the scent of roses and wisteria curving up the trellis at the end of the pavers leading to his front door. I shut my eyes and drink in the beauty of this moment, the joy filling my heart.

But then I hear the soft strum of a guitar, and my eyes snap open. I peer down over the balcony and gasp.

Will. Standing below me, a guitar strap around his shoulder, his hands plucking softly at the strings. And then he starts to sing.

I clutch the railing.

He has a *beautiful* voice. Deep and rich, yet soft.

The words weave through the air, wrapping around my heart, like vines that burst into bloom with each lovely line that he serenades into the night.

> *You were a lightning strike, lighting up my heart.*
> *I was once smitten, twice shy,*
> *But you still gave me a chance, let me play a part,*

Let me learn to love you, believed in me when I
    Didn't.
And when the curtain came down, roses at your feet,
All I could do was look at you and think,
That if you let me love you for as long as I live,
My life would be complete.

Tears spill down my face as he strums softly, then stills his hands over the strings, staring up at me.

"William Orsino," I call over the balcony, my voice thick, my heart bursting with love. "Get up here this instant."

Will grins. "Yes, ma'am."

I rush inside, through his bedroom, its deep green walls like a forest, dark and magical, glowing with candles, past his big bed with its cloud-white sheets and comforter that I'm going to throw him down onto, very, very soon, if I have my way.

Clutching the railing, I race down the stairs as fast as I can, but he's already there, running toward me, wrapping his arm around me, lifting me up.

I clasp his face in my hands, and I kiss him, long and sweet, my heart flying. "I love you," I whisper. "I love you so much."

He stops with me at the top of the stairs, my legs wrapped around his waist, his hands splayed across my back, and holds my eyes. "I love you, Juliet. With all my heart. I'm sorry I ever doubted that was possible." He shakes his head, starting to walk me slowly toward the bed. "You saw and believed it when I couldn't, what was true all along, from the moment I met you."

I wrap my arms around his neck, searching his eyes. "And what was that?"

He kisses me tenderly, reverently. "That not only could my heart be loved and love you . . . it was *made* to love you."

Tears fill my eyes. "Will."

"Juliet."

"You love me," I whisper.

He nods. "Endlessly."

I kiss him, my hands in his hair, drawing him so close, as close as I can get him. "Take me to bed."

Silently, he walks me to the bed's edge and lowers me to the ground. Our eyes hold each other as we peel away each other's clothes, slow, savoring—nothing rushed this time.

"I've been tested," he says faintly as I kiss his throat, the hard, round curve of his pectoral muscle. "Negative for everything."

I nod as I kiss my way over to his heart. "Me, too."

"I've got condoms, though—*shit*." He drops his head to the crook of my neck as I stroke him in my hand, enjoying every inch of him, velvet hot and hard.

"I'm on the pill," I tell him. "So I don't need them, if you don't."

"Uh-uh," he says dazedly as I stroke him. His hands wander over my breasts, cupping them as they fill his hands, plucking at my nipples.

I try to draw him back with me onto the bed, but he pins me against him, his hands wandering low along my back, curving over my ass. "Will," I whine. "Hurry."

I moan faintly as he kisses the corner of my mouth and throw my arms around his neck again, rubbing myself shamelessly against him, because now I can, as much as I want, after so much waiting. I've got a lot of time to make up for.

"Hurry?" he whispers into our kiss. "Why, you got somewhere else you need to be soon?"

"I just might. I'm a very busy lady," I tell him faintly as he kisses his way down my neck.

"Well, damn. Think you've got some time for little old me first?"

I smile, my eyes falling shut. I reach for his length between us and give him a nice, firm stroke. "I think I could squeeze you in."

"Jules," he groans, clearly exasperated by my juvenile innuendo.

A snort sneaks out of me. "Come on, that was good. And I'm also going to assume it's pretty accurate, given what I've got in my hand—"

"Juliet," he sighs. Still, his voice is warm with affection, his touch tender and sensual. "I'm trying to be romantic, here."

"Oh, well, in that case," I whisper against his jaw, breathing him in, the heat of his skin, the whisper of herby soap, which was clearly designed with the express purpose of making me a horny mess. "Romance away."

"Thank you," he mutters, lifting me and tossing me onto the bed.

I squeak in surprise, delighted and beaming as he crawls over me. I cup his face, take his mouth with mine, our tongues stroking, sucking, harsh panting breaths, as Will kisses me fiercely.

I sink my hands into his hair, drawing him down over me. Will shifts until he's stretched out over me, his weight settled between my thighs. I sigh in pleasure, raking my hands up his back.

Our mouths meet again, in deep, slow kisses, sharp tugs of air drawn against each other's mouths. His tongue strokes mine, wet, hot, making my hips roll beneath his, begging for that same sensual rhythm. I'm aching, but not in pain—in glorious pleasure, warm and wanting, in the pulse between my legs and deep inside me, in my nipples as they rub against his chest, the sensitive stretch of skin at the nape of my neck where his breath fans hot and fast, making goose bumps bloom in its wake.

"Juliet," he pants against our kiss.

I sigh his name, pleasure spilling through me as he rocks his hips into mine. "Will."

"You're so beautiful," he whispers.

Will cups my breast, my panting breaths morphing to cries of pleasure when he plucks rhythmically at my nipple. He kisses me, swallowing the sound. I wrap my legs around him, pulling him close, so close, until he can't get any closer.

Will breaks our kiss to shift his weight, to settle over me on his elbows. He doesn't kiss me again, only stares down at me, his gaze roaming my face.

I ask breathlessly, "Everything okay?"

Gently, he brushes back the hair that has stuck to my temples. "Yes. Am I crushing you?"

"Not at all." I reach for him, try to pull him down for another kiss, but he holds steady, his eyes holding mine.

His eyes search mine. "I'm only going to say this once, because . . . I know that's important to you, not always having it brought up, how much your body can hurt . . ."

I nod.

"I know I can't take away your pain, as damn hard as I wish I could. I just need to know, before we do this, that I won't ever be adding to it. That you'll tell me if I'm hurting you," he says. "If I'm too heavy, if anything is uncomfortable, okay?"

I smile up at him, this man I love so very much, and lift my pinkie. "Promise."

He smiles down at me as he hooks his pinkie with mine, then lets go, bracing himself over me again.

His eyes hold mine. My breath stutters in my chest. And then he lowers his mouth to mine.

I let him torture me in that wonderful way he has, rocking against me, working me up. My feet scramble against the bedsheets. My hands rake down his back. When I can't take another second, I pull away from our kiss and gently press on his shoulders. Will searches my eyes.

"Lie down," I tell him.

He flops onto his back. And now it's my turn to crawl over him. Will's eyes grow hazy as I straddle his waist. I bend down and kiss him, tongue and teeth. His hand dives into my hair. He grunts as I shimmy down, rubbing myself against his erection.

He reaches for me, but I gently duck his hand, crawling lower, planting kiss after kiss on each freckle of his skin.

"Jules," he sighs, his voice tight with need.

"Let me enjoy myself, impatient man." I grin, kissing a freckle at his hip, lower, on his thigh, then the other, until I'm at the edge of the bed, bent over him. I grip his length and stroke it, the way I've learned he likes. He groans as I pump him firmly. And then he swears when I take him in my mouth. Time for Will to endure a little delicious torture of his own.

He grips the bedspread with one hand and finds my cheek with the other, cupping it tenderly. I moan around him, loving how hard he is, his taste, the feel of him as I take him deeper.

He gasps. "Jules."

"Hmmm?"

He reaches for my arm, panting for air. "Come here. Please."

"Just a minute," I tell him, returning to the very pleasurable task at hand. For a few minutes, I tease him, light sucks, cupping his balls, flicking the tip of his length. His hips start to rock in earnest beneath me. His hand shakes as it cups my cheek.

"Juliet, I need to be inside you."

I release him with a pop and scramble up him.

He grins up at me as I lean down for a kiss. "Those were the magic words, huh?"

"So magical," I pant into his mouth. "I need you. I need you now." Pausing, I glance toward the headboard, then back to him. "Can we . . . Can we sit up? I want to see you. I want to be close that way, face-to-face."

Will sits up, bringing me with him, then reaches behind him, propping the pillows against his headboard. He scooches back against them. "Like this?"

I crawl his way in answer, then press him back so he's reclined a little against the pillows. Efficiently, I straddle his waist. It puts us at the perfect height, our faces lined up, just how I wanted. I lean in and kiss him tenderly. "This okay for you?" I ask.

"Juliet, you're about to let me be inside you—you could ask me to stand on my head and I'd find it beyond okay."

A laugh falls out of me as I kiss him again. "I love you," I whisper.

And I love that I don't even know exactly when it happened, not like it seems to in my favorite stories, when it's some grand epiphanic moment. Falling in love with Will has been like slowly wading into water since the moment I saw him, and now I'm saturated, neck-deep in it, its power and beauty, our trust, and tenderness, and safety surrounding me.

Slowly, I lift up on my knees. I rub gently at my entrance, spreading my wetness, holding his eyes. Will sets his hands at my waist as I reach for him, as I guide him inside me. We both gasp as I sink down on him, as he fills me, so full, so exquisitely perfect.

"Jules," he whispers, his voice breaking. He draws me closer by the hips until we're touching, chest to chest, hearts pounding against each other. I kiss him tenderly as I roll my hips forward.

"I can't do the up and down," I admit quietly. "It hurts my hips. But I can do it like this." I show him what I mean, rocking forward, then back. The flicker of an orgasm begins to warm in my belly, as my clit brushes his pelvic bone, as he pulls me even tighter against him.

He sighs against our kiss, wrapping his arms around my back, lower, over my ass. "I feel you," he whispers brokenly. "I feel all of you. You're so warm and tight, baby, so wet."

"No Matthew McConaughey rom-com needed here," I pant.

A hoarse laugh jumps out of him. "All right, all right, all right."

I laugh, too, throwing my arms around his neck, kissing him deep and hard. Our laughs dissolve to groans.

With Will guiding my hips, I rock faster. My orgasm's building furiously, stoked by his feathering kisses along my neck, his hand wandering to my breast, kneading it and plucking at my nipple. "Close," I whisper.

"I want it, Jules." He squeezes my ass, moving me against him. "I want every needy little sound, every second of your pleasure. I want to feel you come all over my cock."

I gasp at his words, at the orgasm spurred on by them as it knocks into me, making me do just what he asked, scream in pleasure as I tighten my legs around his hips, as I ride him hard and hasty, soaking up every wave of euphoria that I can.

Will groans as I move faster. His hips start to buck underneath me. His legs start to shake. "Baby," he pants. "I'm gonna . . . Oh God—"

"I know," I tell him, swallowing his moans, his rough, panting breaths, with a hard, bruising kiss. His tongue dances with mine. I drink in his harsh exhales against my mouth, feeling him swell even more inside me, feeling him stroke even deeper into my body.

He pulls away just enough to hold my eyes as his expression morphs from the edge of torturous pleasure to breathless bliss. I cup his neck, never breaking his gaze, as he grips my hip hard and thrusts up, frantic, until he stills, deep inside, and spills into me.

His eyes fall shut as he buries his face in my neck, his arms clutching me so tight, I feel his heart slamming in his chest, hammering against mine. He rolls his hips softly, erratic but easing, as if, like me, he's greedy for every single moment of this, to make it last as long as possible.

Finally, he falls back onto the pillows, pulling me with him. We tip sideways, until we're facing each other, a tangle of legs and arms, winded laughter as we sink back and slide in under the sheets.

Will stares at me as he draws me close. I set my hand over his racing heart and smile, sated, sleepy, so impossibly happy. "That was," I whisper, pausing for a much-needed breath of air.

"Perfect," he whispers. His hand comes to rest over mine, where it sits over his racing heart. He searches my eyes.

I shake my head, smiling.

"What is it?" he asks breathlessly.

I lean in and give him a loving, lasting kiss. "To think, we're just getting started."

He smiles against my kiss. And with that kiss, with his tender hands drawing me close, seeking me beneath the sheets, he tells me he's right there with me—wide-eyed, wonderstruck by the road ahead of us, a road we'll walk together, stretched out to the horizon.

Full of possibility.

THIRTY-SIX

Will

Walking through a field of wildflowers with Juliet Wilmot on my arm, I smile, my heart so impossibly full, it feels like it could burst.

Juliet smiles up at me, too. Afternoon sunlight kisses her skin, warms her cheeks, sparkles in her eyes. "I love your family," she says.

My smile deepens. I'm still basking in the afterglow of lunch with all my family, Juliet at the table with us. How easily she fell into their rhythm, the rowdy conversation, the jokes and laughter, how, already, she's won over Eleanor, who was sitting on her lap by the time we finished eating. "They love you. I told you they would."

Summer's lush beauty glows around us—golden sun, tall lime-green grass, a sea of magenta, violet, and buttercup-yellow blossoms. Any other day, I'd be stopped in my tracks, soaking in the glorious view, the vast beauty all around me. But not today. Because Juliet is here. And her beauty is the only beauty I see.

"I'm glad you were confident," Juliet says, playfully glaring up at me. "I, however, had some very natural nerves about my first Orsino family meal."

"That's all right," I tell her. "I was there to smooth things over until you felt comfortable. That's what partners do, after all."

Juliet smiles. "Yeah, it is." She tips her head. "What's your astrological sign?"

I frown. "Leo, I think? Why?"

Her eyes widen. "Wait, when is your birthday?" Her eyes widen even more. "I don't know your birthday!"

A laugh jumps out of me.

"Will, I'm freaking out—I told you I loved you and let you do very deliciously filthy things to me last night and I didn't know your birthday!"

"Ah." I curl an arm around her and draw her close. "I didn't know your birthday, either. Doesn't mean we love each other any less. Just means . . . there's lots left to learn." I peer down at her, happy to see concern dissolving from her expression. "When *is* your birthday?"

"June 20," she tells me. "I'm a Gemini."

"August 15," I tell her.

"Definitely a Leo," she says. Her smile returns. She's beaming up at me.

"What is it?" I ask.

Juliet clasps my hand in hers again. "Two things. First, I get to celebrate your birthday with you—it's right around the corner! And second, we're an *excellent* astrological match."

I grin. "I'll put together my birthday list for you ASAP, but I can give you a hint: all gifts will be received in the bedroom."

"Spoken like a true Leo." She bites her lip, heat in her eyes, then draws me down for a kiss.

"Astrology, the zodiac . . . You believe in that stuff?"

"I find it compelling." She peers up at me, love in her eyes. "Do you?"

"Hadn't up to this point, but . . ." I squeeze her hand. "I imagine I could be persuaded, if it's got something good to say about you and me being together."

A soft noise of contentment leaves her. Glancing out across the land, she sighs happily and squeezes my hand again. "I love it here," she says.

Peering down at her, I feel my heart start to race. Because that's something I want us to talk about, soon. If she thinks she could build a life up here with me.

If she'd want to.

I squeeze her hand back. "I'm glad."

"So," she says, as we start walking again, passing near the barn. "Google told me that cows live a maximum of twenty years. Which means Buttercup the cow who converted you to vegetarianism is either ancient or I actually met Buttercup 2.0."

I smile. "Do you believe in reincarnation, Juliet?"

She laughs softly. "I don't know. Do you?"

"I do," I tell her. "And to me, the spirit of Buttercup reunited with and lives on in Buttercup 2.0. That or I'm just too devastated that she passed and I'm desperate for anything to help me avoid my grief."

"You are such a sweetly sensitive soul."

"With tree trunks for biceps," I remind her, making a feigned serious expression.

She laughs.

I slip her hand from my arm and turn to face her fully. I step close, until I can see the blue-green flecks of her irises, their stormy gray edges. "What's so funny?"

She tips her head. Her hand settles over my heart. A soft smile lifts her mouth. "I just love you, my strong and silent, gentle giant."

"Gentle giant, huh?"

"Mm-hmm," she murmurs, pressing up on tiptoe.

I take her mouth with a fierce, loving kiss. Then I bend, throw her over my shoulder, and swat her ass.

Juliet squawks, scaring a flock of birds from the trees.

"Will Orsino! What are you doing?"

"Just living up to my description!"

She laughs against my back and swats my butt, too. "Then carry on, gentle giant!"

"Where to?" I ask.

She presses up, and I shift her, lowering Juliet so that her legs can wrap around my waist, her dress rucked high at her hips. She kisses me soft and sweet and tells me, "Home."

I stare at her, my heart pounding as I reach within myself for the courage she deserves. "Do you think ... one day, you could call this home? Do you think you might want to live a life here, with me?"

She stares down at me, love shining in her eyes, her hand settled over my heart. "I think that sounds like a dream come true."

Will

One year later

I can count on one hand how many times in my life I've cried, and even then, it only got as far as my throat getting thick, my eyes growing wet. That was all I ever allowed myself, even though there was this tug inside me, an ache to give in. But each time, I blinked and stopped myself, swallowed roughly, cleared my throat, pushed past it. Each time, I denied myself.

Today makes up for all of them.

I stand on my family's land, where this wedding is taking place on a picture-perfect summer evening, and watch Juliet walk down the aisle, her gaze holding mine, her smile wide. She's got it together—poised and gorgeous, her dark waves artfully braided with butter-yellow tea roses and sky-blue delphinium, her hips swaying as the breeze whips her blue dress, making it dance around her lush body like water.

I stare at her as I stand at the end of the aisle, and twin tears streak down my cheeks, following the path of the ones that came before them. I'm a fucking mess.

"I hate to be the bearer of bad news," Petruchio says quietly out of the side of his mouth, his head barely turned so he can speak over his shoulder, "but if you're this wrecked when she's a *brides-maid*, you're going to be fu—"

"Yes, I *know*," I grumble, still staring at Juliet. "Now kindly shut up."

He snorts softly, turning his head back toward the aisle, and then the air whooshes out of him as Kate starts walking our way next. A suspiciously wet throat clear follows.

A grin tugs at the corner of my mouth. "Enjoying a taste of your own medicine?" I ask.

"Shut up," he mutters, wiping at the corner of his eyes.

As Juliet reaches the end of the aisle, she throws me a wink. My knees wobble a little.

I watch her step away and then turn to the bridal side, her gaze on the end of the aisle, where Bea will show up any moment on Bill's and Maureen's arms.

But I don't glance toward the end of the aisle. Not yet. Because Juliet is all I can look at, as light glances off her cheekbones, her full, soft lips. A dark tendril of hair sweeps across her face, and she tucks it behind her ear, then readjusts her grip on the delicate bouquet in her hands. My heart clutched when I overheard Bea talking to her last year about what size bouquet would be comfortable, because she didn't want Juliet to hold something that would be hard on her wrists and fingers. I love the way Juliet's sisters love her, in the big and small ways, that they cherish her the way I try to every day.

As Kate finishes her stroll down the aisle, she joins Juliet, shoulder to shoulder. She grins at Christopher and leans past Juliet, pointing to her cheek, mouthing, *You've got something right there.*

"Woman," Petruchio mutters roughly. In my peripheral vision I catch him wiping away another tear from his face.

The sound of quiet acoustic guitar, its plucked-strings melody echoing in the air, grows richer, as the other guitarist joins in, loud and lively. My gaze finally follows Juliet's, landing where her sister Bea stands in her long lace dress at the end of the aisle, arms locked with her parents', a flower crown of yellow and blue blossoms woven around her dark hair, a matching bouquet clutched tight in her hand. Bea beams straight down the aisle at Jamie as she and her parents take their first steps.

A soft sound leaves Jamie, and I glance his way, where he stands in his deep-blue suit, eyes fixed on Bea's, hand over his heart, fingers curled into the fabric, like it's too much, he can't contain it, *everything* he feels as he watches her walk toward him.

I know that feeling. I feel it every day I wake up to the sight of Juliet in my bed, snoring softly, mouth parted, her hair a wild, dark mess spilled across her pillow. I just lie there, watching sunrise warm her skin through the curtains, the rise and fall of her chest with each steady breath, and it feels like a miracle. That she loves me, that she's made her life here, that it's not a wild, far-off hope that one day she won't just agree to make her life here for now but for always.

I've had a ring in my pocket for ten months. I bought it the morning of the day that Juliet moved in, because I already knew what I'll know for the rest of my life—that I love her with all my heart, that I want every day she'll give me, that I want to build a life with her and do my damn best to make her endlessly happy.

So many times I've almost done it, dropped to one knee, scrounged around within myself for words that could possibly do justice to how much I love her, how deeply I want our happily ever after. But it's a bit intimidating, proposing to someone who's read eight hundred (and counting) romance novels, who cries her way through every swoony, extravagant rom-com love declaration; someone who has such a beautiful way of expressing loving sentiment.

I'm not a man of extravagant words, much as I try. I've read my fair share of romance novels the past year, too, and every rom-com movie night, I sit on the couch with Juliet in my arms, trying to soak up every detail from those books and films, to figure out the perfect way, the perfect time, to ask her to be my wife. It's never felt like what I planned would be enough, would sweep her off her feet the way I want to. I could kick myself for exhausting the most romantic gesture I've still been able to think of to date—serenading her on the guitar while she stood above me on my balcony.

I watch Juliet as she takes Bea's bouquet and hands it to Kate, who smoothly adds it to her own. When Juliet turns back, as her eyes meet mine, it hits me square in the chest, the knowledge, the understanding:

There's no such thing as the "perfect" moment or words. Or maybe it's just that perfection is much simpler than I thought. Maybe perfection isn't the *how* or *when* but the *what*—the truth, that I love Juliet and I want to spend the rest of my life with her. Maybe that's enough.

As if she knows what's brightening inside me like a flame bursting to life with the rushing air of realization, Juliet smiles wide. I smile back.

Just over a year ago, Juliet and I pinkie-promised each other honesty always, never to hold back or hide our truth.

I can't wait one more day to keep my word.

———

"Will!" Sula and Margo's daughter, Rowan, yells my name at the same moment she connects with my legs, her arms wrapping tight around me. "Let's dance!"

"I just escaped Eleanor," I whine to myself, but I still scoop up Rowan, because I'm a sucker.

Over the past year, I've become another honorary uncle to Rowan, my go-to Guess Who partner for game nights in the city, and fellow lover of dogs. I adore her, and if I weren't the closest I've been to *finally* catching Juliet's parents to ask for their blessing after trying like hell the past three hours, I'd agree to dance in a heartbeat.

Maureen and Bill are *right* there, talking closely with my parents. It would be perfect.

"Willllll!" Rowan pleads. "Dance!"

"Come on!" Eleanor yells from the dance floor, doing the moonwalk. "You just danced with me! What's stopping ya?"

I sigh and look up to the sky, begging for a way out of this that won't crush little Rowan's heart.

When I glance back down, my gaze instantly finds Juliet across the dance floor, where she's standing with Toni, Hamza, Kate, and Petruchio, her head thrown back in laughter. As if she's sensed me staring at her, she turns; her gaze meets mine. A smile warms her face as she glances down at Rowan in my arms, Eleanor shimmying toward me.

"I really am such a sucker," I grumble, spinning with Rowan toward Eleanor.

"Wheeee!" Rowan squeals.

We dance our way through the song with Eleanor—a snappy number I don't recognize but that seems to hold a special nostalgia for Jamie and Bea, who are dancing their asses off on the dance floor, smiling wide. When the music finishes, I'm saved from a feisty preschooler's demand for an encore when her mothers swoop in and scoop her up.

"Let's give Will a chance to charm someone else," Margo says.

Sula winks at me, then gestures behind her shoulder, to where Juliet's parents are now sitting at their table on the edge of the dance floor, no one else around them. "Go get 'em," she says.

"How did you . . ." I frown as she pats my shoulder.

"If your eyes had laser beams, you'd have burned right through them," Sula tells me. "Plus, I watched you watching Jules walk down the aisle." She winks. "I can put two and two together."

Bianca, Juliet's cousin, pops her head in, Nick right beside her. "Oh, are you going to do it? I can't wait! When's it going to be? Tonight? Tomorrow?"

"Do what?" Rowan asks.

Eleanor pops her head into our little circle, too. "I feel like we're telling secrets."

"Uh." Bianca grimaces, realizing we're in dangerous territory. Little kids cannot keep secrets. "We're . . . planning to . . . play . . . Sorry!" she says to Rowan and Eleanor.

"Sorry!" Rowan yells, clapping her hands. "I want to play now!"

Eleanor's already yanking Bianca toward the long table scattered with board games, glowing under the lights strung up between the trees overhead.

Nick gives me an encouraging nod and a wide smile as he walks backward, following Bianca and Eleanor. "You've got this, Will."

"Good luck!" Margo says, a wide smile on her face.

"On what?" Rowan yells.

Sula tickles Rowan. "Come on, you. Let's go grab some cake and play Sorry!"

As soon as they head off toward the game table, I take a deep breath and start toward Bill and Maureen.

"Will!"

I freeze, then slowly turn, my plan once again held at bay by the only person who could stop me now.

Juliet smiles as she walks toward me, then sets her hands on my chest, palms drifting up my dress shirt. "Hi."

I swallow roughly, tight with nerves, as I wrap my arms around her waist. "Hi."

She tips her head, her gaze searching mine. "Everything okay?"

I stare down at her, and all the stress and anxiety about finding her parents, asking them, taking this last step before I can ask her to marry me, melts away.

"Everything's great," I tell her honestly, "now that you're here."

She beams. "And you used to think you couldn't flirt to save your life."

"I couldn't, and we both know it."

A sigh leaves her as she wraps her arms around my neck. "Guess you're a fast learner, then. You've been an excellent flirt for as long as I can remember."

"I had an excellent teacher," I remind her.

"I was your romance workout buddy." She gives me a playful glare. "I wasn't your *teacher*. What you figured out with me, you could have figured out with anyone—you just had to believe in that possibility, Will."

"No," I tell her quietly, tucking her closer. "I wouldn't have figured it out with *anyone*; I wouldn't have wanted to with anyone else. Just you."

Her eyes grow wet. She shakes her head. "I love you so much, Will Orsino."

"I love you, Juliet Wilmot." I kiss her tenderly. "With all my heart."

Juliet leans in, her voice soft and low. "Will." I know that voice, what it means, what she wants, when she says my name like that. My body hums with desire. "I kinda want to get out of here."

"There you are, Will!" Bill's voice shatters the moment, making Juliet jump in my arms.

"Dad!" Juliet smiles tightly as she takes a step back, her cheeks pink. "You were looking for Will?"

"I was." He grins at her, then turns my way, lifting his eyebrows. "Have a minute?"

I nod, my heart suddenly sprinting in my chest. "Yes, sir."

Juliet threads her arm through mine, but Bill leans in and rests his hand over hers. "*Just* Will, birdie."

Juliet frowns as she glances between us, withdrawing her hand from my arm. "Oh . . . sure."

Bill winks her way. "Your mother and I want to pick his brain some more about that, uh . . . property down the road that we were looking at."

Her eyes widen. "You're looking at houses *here*?"

Bill tugs at his collar. This man is as bad at lying as I am. "*Looking*, yes. You know, in a casual . . . looking . . . way."

"Jules!" Kate calls, waving Juliet toward her, Bea, and the photographer with their camera clasped in hand across the dance floor. "Sister picture!"

Juliet's smile returns. "Coming!" She turns and presses a quick, gentle kiss to my cheek. "Come find me when you're done."

I nod, cupping her face, my thumb grazing her cheek. Her smile deepens. "I will. Promise."

Her father and I watch Juliet start toward her sisters. Bill sighs with relief. "That was close."

I turn toward him. "I would ask how you knew I wanted to talk to you, but apparently I've got intent broadcasted on my face." I scrub at my jaw, missing the thick beard that I often still keep, to hide my expressions so well. I shaved it short, to nearly scruff, for the wedding. And for the look it put on Juliet's face that led to very pleasurable activities that made us nearly late for the rehearsal last night.

"Call it a hunch," Bill says. He claps an arm around my shoulders and grins. "Now, let's go see you turn Maureen into a puddle of joy."

Juliet

I'm sore everywhere. And it's for the best reasons. Dancing for hours, jumping up and down as we closed the night with "Shout!," getting way too physically demonstrative as we played Pictionary turned charades in pajamas with our friends and siblings who hung around at Will's place after Jamie and Bea drove off the Orsino property in their vintage car, headed for Jamie's upstate home just fifteen minutes away.

And, of course, being thoroughly, deliciously ravished by Will last night, starting the second he shut the door behind the last straggler and pinned me against it.

I sigh happily as I roll in bed onto my back. I open my eyes and blink against the bright sunlight, knowing what I'll see—Will in bed beside me, propped up on one elbow, peering down at me, a soft smile tugging at the corner of his mouth.

But today, there's no smile. Just an arresting, beautiful stare. Those wide, pale gray-green cat eyes, morning light warming his skin.

Gently, I poke at the small cleft in his chin. "What are you looking at?"

"The most beautiful woman in the world," he says quietly.

A wide smile breaks across my face as I shake my head and trail my finger lightly down his throat, playing connect the dots with each cinnamon freckle leading to his chest. "Nonsense."

He gently combs his fingers through my hair, smoothing it off my face. "The truth."

I clasp his wrist and stare up at him. My heart is so full, so happy, glowing like the sun outside. Every morning, I wake up, even on the sorest, stiffest days, the days my chest is tight with anxiety and fears sneak through the cracks of my confidence, so impossibly happy that he's here, that Will sees it all, that he loves me for it.

I'm one big ball of love and hope and joy.

And it's not the wedding last night talking, though I *am* a sucker for weddings—I'm a hopeless romantic, after all. It isn't just that I'm soaring from the thrill of seeing my twin happily married and sharing that incredible joy with Will. It's not because I witnessed heartfelt vows and danced and laughed and played the night away with my favorite people, as beautiful as that was.

I'm just dizzyingly desperate to marry him. I have been for so long, I can't even remember when I didn't feel this way, so ready to tell him I want him not just for now but for always.

I have never known love like this, and I know that I never will again. The way Will and I love each other is like those beautiful flowers creeping up the trellis outside our home—growing, bending, weaving together, nurtured with care and nourished richly, so they can thrive and blossom, changing with the seasons yet always entwined even in the harshest months, on the coldest days. The woman I am when I love Will is my best self, and that's not *because* I'm always at my best, but because Will loves all of me and I'm safe to love him just as much, as we share our flaws and fears and frailty, knowing our love isn't burdened by those truths but strengthened for having weathered them, and nothing could be better than that.

"Will," I whisper, my hand settling over his heart.

His eyes search mine as he sets his hand over mine and tenderly rubs at my knuckles. "Juliet."

"Will . . . will . . ." A soft laugh leaves me. It's not the first time I've encountered the linguistic challenge of having a partner named Will whom you want to ask "will you" questions. Between the two of us, I'm the one with words always at the ready, but right now,

I'm tongue-tied, searching for how I could possibly articulate how much I love him, how much I want to marry him.

"William Campbell Montag Orsino . . ." I clear my throat, smiling up at him, feeling tears start to prick at the corners of my eyes. "Will you—*mmph!*"

I'm cut off by the warm, firm press of his mouth on mine, his big, heavy body gently pressing me into the mattress. I gasp against his kiss as he cups my breast and thumbs my bare nipple.

"Let me," he whispers against my neck. His lips graze my jaw, my throat.

My heart skips. Did he sense what I was about to ask him? Does he mean what I think he means? I want to press him for an answer. I don't want to wait a second longer, but Will Orsino is a connoisseur of my body, and as he settles his weight between my legs, every word on the tip of my tongue dissolves.

"I love you," he rasps as he reaches between us and feels me, wet and hot, my hips lifting toward his touch.

"I love you, too," I tell him, my voice breaking to a whimper as he tenderly strokes and teases me. His hard length presses into my hip as he curls a finger inside me, then another. I moan, loud and hoarse as he grinds his palm against my clit.

"Please," I whisper. "Please don't make me wait."

He holds my eyes as he gently draws away his hand and grips himself at the base. "I won't." He fills me with each hard, hot inch of him, his gaze never breaking from mine, and I know he knows, that while at first it was such a frustration for him, now he reads between the lines of my words better than anyone. "I won't make you wait," he says roughly, stroking deep inside me, drawing back, then rocking in again. "Promise, Juliet."

I'm too sore and soft-limbed to bring much to the table physically, and Will knows. It's not the first time I've wanted sex but needed him to do the heavy lifting. He hoists me up at the hips effortlessly and shoves a thick pillow beneath my backside. Then he curls his arms around me and holds me close, and fills me again and again, so all I have to do is all that I can—be held, be loved, be given everything he wants to give me.

Wrapping my arms around his neck, I press my lips to his, our breaths jagged, our kisses slow and deep. Heat licks through me, tight, coiled pleasure in my breasts as they rub against the coarse, springy cinnamon hairs on his chest, deep inside me where he strokes and fills me so perfectly, in the aching, sweet pulse between my thighs that he rubs with each grind of his hips.

Our skin is slick, the sheets stuck and twisted around us. We're how I always want us to be—enraptured and entwined, as close as we can be. Hearts pounding, we move. My hips canting frantically, helplessly into his, Will's grip on my ass wide and possessive, moving me with him.

Deep, ragged groans leave him as I gasp his name over and over.

"Jules," he whispers against my kiss, "easy, baby. Let me," he says again, "let me give you what you need."

I bite at his lip. "You said you wouldn't make me wait."

"Woman." A hoarse laugh leaves him. "I'm going as fast as I can."

A laugh leaves me, too, but it morphs into a cry of pleasure as he drifts down just far enough to take my nipple in his mouth, biting lightly, then biting the other, sending glorious sensation bolting through me. I clutch his hair, rake my fingers down his back. He lifts his head, kissing at the exquisitely tender spot on my neck beneath my ear, and drives into me, then seats himself, not pulling back, only grinding his hips to mine in tiny, terrifyingly perfect circles. My eyes roll back, then fall shut. Pleasure strikes me like lightning, flying through my body, arching it up into his.

I scream his name because all of this—the bliss, the shock of its intensity, the pure, thrilling euphoria of release—can't possibly stay inside me.

Will jolts as he feels me come around him, each tight, hard spasm that wracks me and makes me gasp. "Jules," he says, rough and low, pulling back to meet my eyes. His face tightens, his jaw locks, his chest heaving. "Love you. I love you—"

I watch him, the pleasure breaking across his expression, his mouth falling open, the tremor that shivers through him as he spills into me. And then I draw him down, his weight over mine, and kiss him as he rocks into me, riding out every last wave of his release.

"I love you," I whisper against his lips.

He shivers again as he falls over me, then brings me with him as he rolls onto his side. "We . . ." he pants, "are so twisted up in these sheets."

I smile up at him, sleepy and sated, cupping his face. "I know. But I don't mind one bit."

He sighs heavily and draws me tight in his arms. My eyes start to drift shut. I feel his lips press, warm and soft, to my forehead. "Sleep, baby," he whispers. "And, Juliet?"

"Hmm," I mutter drowsily.

"When you wake up and get dressed, can I ask a favor?"

"Sure," I tell him, barely managing the words, I'm so dazed and deliciously tired. "What is it?"

"Wear the purple dress." He presses a tender kiss to my hair. "You know the one."

———

This time, when I wake up, my eyes aren't even open, but I already know what's different. Will isn't here. His words, broken and whispered, however, still are, like the lingering light filling our bedroom, warm and sparkling with promise.

Let me.

I bite my lip against my smile as I wriggle happily, nervously, in the now-smooth sheets.

I throw them off wildly and ease out of bed. I splash off my face, brush my bedhead waves. I slip on the purple dress that I wore to our first date, clumsy and clinging to the doorway as I step into the flower sneakers I wore, too.

My reflection greets me in the bathroom mirror as I brush my teeth. Glittering eyes, flushed cheeks. Hope beats through me in tempo with my heart.

And then I make my way down the stairs, clutching the banister, not as fast as I want but as fast as I can manage. I throw open the door and stop in my tracks.

There's Will, in that same pumpkin-orange shirt he wore on our first date, standing beneath the wisteria and rose trellis.

I grip the doorway, steeling myself to stay steady.

But it's so damn hard. Will smiles at me, that soft, sweet smile only for me. Hector sits at his feet, tongue lolling as he pants. His tail thumps hard on the slate pavers as he looks at me, and I know how hard it is for him to obey the command Will's given him to stay, to wait.

For me.

Slowly, I push off the doorway and draw the door shut behind me. I take one step toward Will, then another, my heartbeat pounding in my ears.

Hector whines, glancing between us.

"Stay," Will tells him again, his eyes fixed on me.

"He can come," I tell him gently. Hector whines up at Will again. I'm a softie for Hector, and all three of us know it.

"He can wait," Will says, those stunning eyes fixed on me as I draw closer. "I had to wait thirty-four years for you, Juliet. He can wait thirty-four seconds."

I laugh softly, but it's tinged with the threat of tears thickening my throat.

Finally, I'm a step away from Will, under the canopy of blossoms, drenched in their lush, lovely fragrance.

I don't tear my gaze away from Will as I glide my hand across Hector's head, then feel his rough sandpaper tongue, warm and wet along my palm.

"Juliet," Will says quietly. "Hi."

My heart clutches. The same words he said on that first date, on our do-over when I walked across the café and he watched me, every step of the way.

I play my part, my smile wobbling as I try not to cry. "Hi, Will."

"I'm not going to offer you a handshake," he says, quoting himself.

My vision blurs with tears.

"Because, this time," he says, "I'm exactly sure what I should offer you." Slowly, his gaze never leaving mine, he sinks to one knee.

Tears spill down my cheeks. I lift my hands to my face, heart racing, my fingertips wet as more tears slip from my eyes.

"Viola Juliet Wilmot," Will says quietly, "just over a year ago, I hatched a harebrained scheme with you based on the belief that the love you wanted was the last thing I would ever have. I've learned a lot since then: that you are the most generous heart and you have a beautiful gift for loving people in a way that makes them feel loved so damn well, that I am imperfect and so are you, but we fit perfectly, in a way I never knew was possible.

"I know we started off determined that romantic love would be the last thing we'd ever share, and as terrible as it is now, the thought of ever being in your presence and doing anything but loving you with everything I am, I will never regret how we began. Because if we hadn't, I would have never been brave enough, never tried, never had the chance to learn that I could love you and that you could love me, and that would have been a tragedy."

I step closer, my dress drifting over his bent knee, and I clasp his dear, handsome face. I've given up trying not to cry. I just stand over him, loving him, listening to him, letting my tears run free. Hector's doggy tail wags in the air as he sniffs at Will's shoulder, then nuzzles my hip, his happy dog pants the only sound in the silence that holds between us like a bated breath.

The wind dances through the air, ruffling Will's sun-kissed copper hair, swaying my dress as I stare down at him. I don't rush this moment; I don't speak a word or fill his quiet. I stroke his cheek and wait.

Will swallows thickly as tears fill his eyes, too, and when he speaks, his voice is rough, jagged with emotion. "I don't often have the right words, let alone the perfect ones that you deserve. But I do have this—a heart for loving that's all yours, for always, if you'll have me. If you'll . . ." He sighs heavily, his hand clasping mine, pressed hard to his cheek. Then he reaches into his pocket and pulls out a carved wood box. Carefully, he eases it open, revealing a sunshine-gold band, a dazzling, starry diamond. "Juliet, will you marry me?"

I nod, smiling so wide, my tearstained cheeks ache. "Nothing would make me happier. Yes, Will." I laugh through tears, bending toward him as he slips it on my finger. I watch him tug at a clasp that widens the band, making it slip easily over my often swollen knuckle. Then he folds the clasp back until it clicks and the ring rests snug at the base of my finger. I stare down at my beautiful ring, beautiful to not just my eyes but my heart, then at Will, laughing, crying, doubled over with joy. "I get to marry you!"

He bolts upright, sweeps me fiercely into his arms, and whoops so loudly, his chickens beside the house startle with a noisy *squawk* and rustling feathers as they dash away. Hector barks and takes off in a run of tight, happy circles around us as I throw my arms around Will's neck and kiss him with every ounce of love I have.

"I've been wanting to do that for ten months," he mutters as he peers down at me.

My eyes widen as he gently eases me back to the ground. "Ten months?"

His eyes glow in the sun as he nods, his gaze holding mine as he says simply, "Yes. I haven't been waiting to know when I wanted to marry you. I've been waiting to ask. I wanted it to be the perfect moment. The perfect words . . ."

I stroke my hand softly up his arm, shaking my head.

"It was perfect," I tell him. "This moment, those words." With my other arm still wrapped around his neck, I draw him down for a long, loving kiss and whisper, "Because this moment is ours, and those words were yours, straight from your heart. Nothing could be more perfect."

He smiles softly, then leans in, kissing me again. "You said yes."

"Of course I did, you goofball. Have you seen yourself? You're a tangerine vision of tall, towering virility. How could I say no?"

He glares playfully down at me. "Oh, real funny."

"I love that you wore it," I whisper, holding his eyes. "I love everything about this. I love how happy I am with you, Will. I know we won't always be happy, that hard seasons and hurts will come, but . . . I'm so glad I'll face them with you. And when life softens and warms and blooms again, we'll have made it through, right where we belong. Together."

He presses his forehead to mine and holds me, and for a moment it's nothing but warm summer wind rushing through the grass and the sweet perfume of a canopy of flowers, the thud of Hector's pounding feet in the dirt, and our soft, steady breaths.

But then a roar of applause, hoots, and whistles erupts behind Will, startling us.

We both turn and glance over Will's shoulder. A laugh leaves me like a burst of champagne, at long last fizzy and free.

All across his parents' back porch stand Will's siblings, his niece and nephew and Rowan leaning on the railing, hands like binoculars around their eyes. My parents stand shoulder to shoulder with his, our mothers clutching each other and clearly crying. There's Kate and Christopher, Sula and Margo, Toni and Hamza, Nick and Bianca, and for some inexplicable reason, Jamie and Bea.

I gape at them all. After the wedding last night, only my parents were staying at Will's parents' for the night. Everyone else got rooms at the bed-and-breakfast in town that Will's sister Imogen and her husband opened up earlier this year. "What on earth are they all doing there?" I ask. "Did you tell them?"

"No. But I have been standing out here for two hours, throwing sticks with Hector while you slept, so they were bound to notice and figure it out." Will sighs. "The perils of small-town living. Word travels *fast*."

I smile, resting my head against his chest as I wave at them all. They all wave back, my sisters jumping up and down, Jamie whistling with two fingers set at his mouth, Christopher applauding over his head so loud it sounds like thunder clapping across the field.

"I love it." I peer up at him. "I love you."

Our eyes hold each other's. Will smiles and tenderly cups my face. "I'm real glad, baby. I love you. So damn much."

"We're going to get *married*," I tell him.

He grins down at me. "Yeah we are." He steals one more kiss, then says, "Not that they haven't already figured it out, but what do you say we go tell them anyway?"

I beam a smile up at him so bright, it puts the sun to shame. And then I slip my arm inside his. "I'd say that sounds perfect."

· ACKNOWLEDGMENTS ·

My book acknowledgments tend to be lengthy, but these will be (relatively) brief, not because I love this story any less or because it was easier to write than its predecessors (frankly, the opposite is true, on both counts), but because I'm simply lost for words to explain how grateful I am to be here, at the closing chapter of this series as well as season of my writing life that has been so pivotal to my career and so dear to my heart.

It's no coincidence that I wrapped up the Wilmot Sisters series with two characters whose experiences so closely connect to my own—in Juliet, a romantic knocked back by heartbreak and living with chronic illness; in Will, a neurodivergent man who guards his heart closely yet fiercely loves the few who have it. That the Wilmot Sisters unfolded the past few years as I healed as a person and grew as a writer like never before, and culminated in this journey of two characters who are most closely reckoning with what I did as I built the story world that led us to them, seems only fitting. I've gotten to the place where I could dig so deep, write so close to the heart of myself, and I hope, speak to those on that hurting and healing path that I have been on, in part because of the many people who have loved me so well along the way, who've cheered me on both personally and professionally, and reminded me I was never alone. I write stories that I hope make every reader in some way feel a little less lonely, a little more seen and loved. I'm grateful that in my life, that affirmation isn't just the stuff of fiction—it's a fact of my existence, thanks to them.

Thank you, every one of you, my dear friends—you know who you are—for sticking with me in this hard, beautiful season, for growing with me and inspiring me and making me feel so safe to dream and reach and hope and be brave.

Thank you, Sam, my rock-star agent, for always being there with words of wisdom and insight, calm, and confidence. I am so thankful for you and so excited for what's to come!

Thank you to everyone at Berkley who has worked so hard and touched these stories, from their design to their marketing, their editing and their production. They are beautiful books that I am so deeply proud of, and I'm incredibly grateful for the part you've played in making them so.

Thank you, my dearest Dr. B, for loving me even when I'm damn near unlovable (aka, extremely stressed and on deadline), for reminding me, in how you love me, why I write what I write: because I believe the only love that's worth our hearts is love that loves *all* of us, love that grows as we grow and makes us want to be our best selves because we're loved even when we're at our worst. And thank you for not getting *too* grumpy about me writing ("another!") ginger love interest; I promise, even though you're definitely not a redhead, you'll always be my favorite hero.

Thank you, my two sweet peas, my wonderful, wise, goofy, smart, loving, one-of-a-kind kids, for inspiring me to keep going even when I'm tired, even when it's hard, even when I don't know how I can. You're truly the best I will ever give this world, and you still make me want to be better—as a person, a writer, a mother, a friend. I'm so lucky to be your mom, and I'm so grateful for all the ways you show me that you love me and that you're proud of me, and for all the ways you let me love you and show you how proud I am of you, too. Love you always, to the moon and back.

Thank you to every reader, bookseller, librarian, for giving your time and energy and creativity to uplift my stories, for supporting them and making this dream job of mine a reality. I will always be grateful for you, forever pinching myself that I get to write stories you want to read.

Finally, to every tender heart out there, every sensitive soul that's been hurt and is trying to heal, I hope you hold tight to *your* hope and the belief that you deserve, and can, and will be loved, in the many beautiful ways we can be loved, by people who love *all* of you—your weirdness, fears, needs, and dreams. If those people are slow in showing themselves in your life, I'm sorry; please know you're not alone, that lots of us have done the work to heal and grow and have waited for good people and good seasons; sometimes they just take time to make the scene. Take care of yourself while you wait and never settle for less while you do. If you need some loving company, a reminder of what's possible and what you deserve, know my stories are here for you, an affirmation and hope of what's to come.

Once Smitten, Twice Shy

CHLOE LIESE

READERS GUIDE

1. If you're familiar with Shakespeare's *Twelfth Night*, what are some similarities and departures that you noticed between the play and this modern reimagining, in plot, themes, character names, and relationships? What do you think of those? And, if you're not familiar with *Twelfth Night*, do you now find yourself curious to read the play, see it performed live, or watch a film adaptation?

2. Speaking of film adaptations, the early-2000's rom-com starring Amanda Bynes and Channing Tatum, *She's the Man*, is a modern reimagining of *Twelfth Night*. If you're familiar with the film, what did you think of it? Did you spot any parallels or nods to the film in *Once Smitten, Twice Shy*?

3. *Once Smitten, Twice Shy* features a heroine who has mixed connective tissue disease as well as celiac disease, and a neurodivergent hero (autism). What was it like for you to see the world through their eyes? For those who aren't neurodivergent or don't have these or other chronic illnesses, do you think reading from their perspective impacted how you might perceive and engage people who identify as such? Are there some ways you relate to Juliet's and Will's experiences and perspectives?

4. Shakespeare's *Twelfth Night* is a comedy that both pokes fun at and also celebrates romantic love. At the outset, Duke Orsino

thinks he's in love with Olivia and asks Cesario (who is Viola disguised as a man for her safety after being shipwrecked and stranded in Illyria) to woo Olivia on his behalf, then when Cesario tries to woo Olivia for Orsino, Olivia promptly falls in love with *Cesario*. While Viola (as Cesario) spends time with Orsino in his confidence, trying to help him win Olivia, Viola finds herself falling in love with *Orsino*. And when Viola's true identity is revealed as she is reunited with her twin, Sebastian, from whom she was separated in the shipwreck, Olivia promptly falls in love with *Sebastian*, and Orsino realizes he loves *Viola*, even though he's only known her as his friend Cesario. It's a playful story of mistaken identities and comedic confusion, but it also has an undercurrent of depth, as it ends with an unexpected discovery of clarity beneath all this surface-level confusion. At first glance, *Twelfth Night* could seem like it's portraying love as a flippant joke—something people fall in and out of on a whim, flimsy and inconstant. But looking deeper, particularly at the dynamic between the two principal roles of Orsino and Viola/Cesario and how the story ends, the play portrays—and I would argue, *champions*—another kind of love built from friendship, which grows quietly and steadily, surprising in its depth and intensity when finally recognized. Do you see this portrayal of love in the evolution of Orsino and Viola/Cesario's relationship echoed in Will's and Juliet's journeys? In what way?

5. If you've read the previous two Wilmot Sisters books, *Two Wrongs Make a Right* (a reimagining of *Much Ado About Nothing*) and *Better Hate than Never* (a reimagining of *The Taming of the Shrew*), how do you feel this story wrapped up the series? Did you notice references to the past two stories, and if so, did you enjoy how they were incorporated into *Once Smitten, Twice Shy*? If you haven't read

one or either of the previous books in the series, do you want to now? Which one would you start with?

6. This story revolves around two people who've been hurt in the realm of romantic love and learned to guard their hearts closely but who also want to heal and be brave enough to open their hearts to romantic love again. Given that, do you feel like Will's and Juliet's journeys made sense to begin with friendship while practicing romance, even though they were initially attracted to each other before they embraced their genuine romantic connection? Was that a satisfying journey to experience? In what way?

7. You might have noticed some references to another Shakespeare play in this story—*Romeo and Juliet*. We have our heroine, Viola *Juliet*, who goes by Juliet. And we have our hero, Will, who wants to learn how to feel like more of a "Romeo," confident in flirting and being romantic. Beyond those two nods to the play's titular characters, what other references to *Romeo and Juliet* did you find? For those who met Juliet in the first Wilmot Sisters book, *Two Wrongs Make a Right*, were you expecting her story to be reimagining of Shakespeare's tragedy?

8. At the start of the story, Will and Jules are determined to only be friends. Their decision to keep their relationship within those safe parameters comes from a place of wanting to protect themselves from further hurt and because they're both limited by preconceived notions of possibility for themselves and for a relationship with each other. Have you ever had a relationship with someone, romantic or otherwise, that grew to be more open and vulnerable over time? Did you discover a deeper connection and intimacy as that unfolded? If so, how did that impact your relationship?

9. At the end of *Once Smitten, Twice Shy*, we see Juliet and Will deeply in love, newly engaged, a happily ever after in Illyria ahead of them. What did you think of how their story ended? If you could read another moment in their happily ever after, down the road, what moment would that be, and why?

Keep reading for a preview of

Only When It's Us

the first romance in Chloe Liese's Bergman
Brothers series, available now!

· ONE ·

Willa

Playlist: "Hurricane," Bridgit Mendler

I've been told I have a temper.

I prefer to be called *tempestuous*. Big word for a soccer jock, I know, but work in a bookstore as many summers as I have, and you can't help but broaden your vocabulary.

tempestuous: typified by strong, turbulent, or conflicting emotion
For better or for worse, that's me, Willa Rose Sutter, to a T.

Is my fuse a little short? Sure. Are my responses occasionally disproportionate? Sometimes. I could learn to simmer down here and there, but I refuse to subdue the storm inside me.

Because inextricably knotted with my tempestuousness is the force of nature that is my drive. I'm competitive. And *that* is an advantageous personality trait. I'm an aspiring professional athlete, set on becoming the world's best in my sport. To be the best, you need raw skill, but even more so, you have to be hungry. You have to want it more than anybody else. That's how far-off dreams become reality.

So, yes. Sometimes I'm a little feisty. I'm scrappy and hardworking, and I like to win. I don't settle. I won't give up. *Nothing* gets in my way.

Which is why I seriously need to get my shit together, because something *is* about to get in my way. My eligibility for next week's match against our biggest rival hangs by a thread, thanks to the Business Mathematics course and the professor from hell.

I'm late to class, trying not to limp because of how much my muscles ache after a brutal practice. As I scurry down the ramp in the massive lecture hall, it takes everything in me not to say *ouch-ouch-ouch-ouch* with every single step I take.

The room's packed, only a few stray seats remaining in the very first row.

A groan leaves me. Great. I get to show up late and make that super obvious by sitting front and center. As quietly as I can manage with muscles that are screaming for ibuprofen and a hot bath, I slip into an empty spot and silently extract my notebook.

Professor MacCormack continues scribbling equations on the board. Maybe my late entrance went undetected.

"Miss Sutter." He drops the chalk and spins, dusting off his hands. "Good of you to join us." Dammit.

"Sorry, Professor."

"Get caught up from Ryder." Completely sidestepping my apology, MacCormack spins back to the board and throws a thumb over his shoulder to the right of me. "He has my notes."

My jaw drops. I've asked Mac for notes three times so far this semester, when I had to miss due to traveling games. He'd shrugged, then said I needed to "problem solve and figure out my priorities." This Ryder guy just *gets* them?

That temper of mine turns my cheeks red. The tips of my ears grow hot, and if flames could burst out of my head, they would.

Finally, I turn to where Mac gestured, sickly curious to see this guy that my professor favors with lecture notes while I'm left scrambling to catch up with no help whatsoever. And I really need that help. I'm barely holding a C minus that's about to become a D, unless God looks with favor on his lowly maiden Willa Rose Sutter and does her a solid on our upcoming midterm.

Rage is a whole-body experience for me. My breathing accelerates. From the neck up, I turn into a hot tamale. My heart beats so thunderously, my pulse points bang like drums. I am *livid*.

And it's with that full-body anger coursing through my veins that I lay my eyes on the favored one. Ryder, Keeper of Notes.

He wears a ball cap tugged low over shaggy dark blond hair. A mangy beard that's not terribly long still obscures his face enough that I don't really know what he looks like, not that I care. His eyes are down on the lecture notes, tracking left to right, so I can't see what they look like. He has a long nose that's annoyingly perfect and that sniffs absently, as if he's completely clueless that I'm both watching him and that he's supposed to be sharing those lecture notes. The notes that I could have used to avoid failing the last two pop quizzes and our first writing assignment.

My eyes flick back up to MacCormack, who has the audacity to smirk at me over his shoulder. I shut my eyes, summoning calm that I don't have. It's that or tackle my professor in a blind rage.

Eyes on the prize, Willa.

I need to pass this class to stay eligible to play. I need to stay eligible to play because I need to play every game, both to maximize my team's chances for success and because Murphy's Law states that scouts come to games you miss. Well, really it just states that if something can go wrong when it's real inconvenient, it will. The scout scenario is my version of it.

The point is I need the damn notes, and in order to get them, I'm going to have to swallow my pride and explicitly petition this jerk who's ignoring me. I clear my throat. *Loudly.* Ryder sniffs again and flips the page of the printout in front of him, his eyes glancing up to the equations on the board, then back down. Does he turn? Acknowledge me? Say, *Hi, how can I help you?*

Of course not.

MacCormack prattles on, his notes both on the chalkboard

and the projector screen, where his words unfurl as captioned text in a large, clear font. The next slide pops up before I got it all written down, and I grow angrier by the minute. It's like Mac *wants* me to fail.

Taking a steadying breath, I whisper to Ryder, "Excuse me?"

Ryder blinks. His brow furrows. I have the faintest hope he's heard me and is about to turn my way, but instead, he flicks to a previous page of the printout and scribbles a note.

I sit dumbfounded for minutes before I slowly face the board, fury shaking my limbs. My fingers curl around my pen. My hand whips open my notebook so violently, I almost rip off the cover. I want to scream with frustration, but the fact is that all I have control over is the here and now. So I bite my tongue and start writing madly.

After twenty minutes, MacCormack drops his chalk, then turns and addresses the class. In the haze of my wrath, I vaguely hear him lob questions. Students raise their hands and answer, because they've actually followed this lecture, because, unlike me, most of them probably don't have two lives pulling them apart. Athlete and student, woman and daughter.

Because they have leeway, wiggle room, which I don't. I *have* to be excellent, and the problem is that this pressure is instead turning me into an absolute failure. Well, except for soccer. Over my dead body will I fail at that. Everything else, though, is going to shit. I'm a scattered friend, an absent daughter, a lackluster student. And if this professor would just cut me a damn break, I'd have a chance of at least scratching one of those failures off my list.

MacCormack must feel my eyes burning holes into him, because after he accepts the last answer, he turns, looks at me again, and smirks.

"Professor MacCormack," I say between clenched teeth.

"Why, yes, Miss Sutter?"

"Is this some kind of joke?"

"I'm sorry, no, that is not the correct formula for calculating compound interest." Turning back to everyone, he offers them a smile I have yet to be the recipient of. "Class dismissed!"

I sit, stupefied that I've been swept aside by my professor yet again. It's the cherry on top when Ryder rises from his seat, slides those precious notes into a worn leather crossbody bag, and throws it over his shoulder. As he secures the flap on his bag, his eyes dart up, then finally meet mine. They widen, then take me in with a quick trail over my body.

Ryder's eyes are deep green, and damn him, that's my favorite color, the precise shade of a pristine soccer field. That's all I have time to notice before my resentment blocks me from appreciating any more of his features. When his gaze returns from my sneakers-and-sweatpants ensemble, our eyes meet, his narrowing as he processes whatever terrifying expression I wear. I am enraged. I'm sure I look murderous.

Now he acknowledges my existence, after so thoroughly ignoring me?

Rolling his shoulders back, he straightens fully. All I can think is, *Wow, that's not just an asshole. That's a tall asshole.*

I shoot out of my seat, sweeping my notebook off the desk. Jamming my pen into the giant messy bun on top of my head, I give him a death glare. Ryder's gaze widens as I take a step closer and meet those nauseatingly perfect green eyes.

A long, intense stare-down ensues. Ryder's eyes narrow. Mine do, too. They water, begging me to blink. I refuse to.

Slowly, the corner of his mouth tugs up. He's smirking at me, the asshole.

And just like that, my eyes drag down to his mouth, which is hidden under all that gnarly facial hair. I blink.

Shit. I hate losing. I *hate* losing.

I'm about to open my mouth and ask just what's so damn funny when Ryder backs away and pivots smoothly, then jogs up the ramp of the lecture hall. I stand, shaking with rage, pissed at this jerk and his odd, dismissive behavior, until the room is virtually empty.

"Cheer up, Miss Sutter." MacCormack switches off the lights, bathing the lecture hall in gray shadows and the faint morning sunlight that streams through the windows.

"I don't really know how to be cheery when I'm about to fail your class and I can't afford to do that, Professor."

For a moment, his mask of detached amusement slips, but it's back before I can even be sure it ever left. "You'll figure out what to do. Have a nice day."

When the door falls shut and I'm left alone, I sink into my seat once again, the whisper of failure echoing in the room.

———

"He really just walked off?" Rooney—my teammate and roommate—stares at me in disbelief.

"Yup." I'd say more, but I'm too angry and winded. We're doing technical drills, and while I'm in the best shape of my life, ladders always kick my butt.

"Wow." Rooney, on the other hand, isn't winded one bit. I've decided she's a mutant, because I have never heard that woman short of breath, and it's not for lack of trying. Our coach is a clinically verified sadist. "What a dick."

Rooney looks like a life-size Barbie. Classic SoCal girl—legs for miles, glowing skin and faint freckles, a sheet of platinum-blond hair that's forever in a long, smooth ponytail. She stands and drinks her water, looking like a beach model as the sun lowers in the sky. I, on the other hand, look like Dolores Umbridge after the centaurs got her. My wiry hair puffs madly from my ponytail, my cheeks are dark pink with exertion, and my muscular soccer quads are shaking from effort. Rooney and I could not be more opposite, not just when it comes to looks, but also personality, and that's perhaps what makes us such good friends.

"No doubt, he's a dick," I confirm. "But he's the dick who has what I need: past lecture notes and the ones I'll miss when I'm gone for two more classes during away games."

We both jog toward the next section of the field to start one-touch drills. I run backward first, Rooney flicking the ball into the air before she lofts it my way. I head it back, she volleys it to me, and I head it back. We'll do this until we switch directions; then it's her turn.

Rooney serves me the ball, and I head it down to her feet. "So if that guy won't give you the notes, what are you going to do?"

"I don't *know* what to do. That's my problem. I see no solution for a guy who downright ignores me. I know I can be a little prickly, but I was polite. Whereas he was just . . . rude. I don't get why. And I really need those notes."

Switching directions, I scoop the ball onto my foot and softly kick it into the air, right to Rooney's forehead.

"Honestly," Rooney says as she returns my pass with a header, "I'd say the issue is with your professor. He's obligated by our student contract to accommodate your schedule, and this behavior is overtly hostile to your efforts as a student athlete. If I were you, I'd print out our agreement, head to office hours, and remind that jerk that he's ethically and legally bound to support your learning while you earn his college more publicity and money than his pathetic academic papers have *ever* contributed."

Yeah. Rooney looks like Barbie, but she's got stuff between her ears. She'll make a great lawyer one day.

"Maybe. But this guy's a hard-ass, Roo. I think he'll just make my life even more miserable if I do that."

Rooney frowns, heading the ball back again. "Okay, so show him the contract, but do it nicely. Kill him with kindness. Do whatever it takes to be sure you're eligible to play next week. We need you, and honestly, Willa, I think if you don't play, you'll internally combust."

As we finish our drill, the ball drops to my feet, and I stare down at its familiar shape. It's a view I've seen a thousand times—that black-and-white ball set against bright green grass, my cleats on either side of it. Soccer is the one constant in my life; everything else has been unpredictable. I live and breathe this sport, not only because I want to be the best, but because it's the only thing that's kept me going sometimes.

Rooney's right. I can't miss; I can't be ineligible. I'm going to have to suck it up and do whatever it takes to pass this class.

"Come on," she says, throwing an arm over my shoulder. "My turn to cook tonight."

I fake a dry heave, earning her rough shove that sends me stumbling sideways. "Great. I needed a good cleanse anyway."

Photo courtesy of the author

Chloe Liese writes romances reflecting her belief that everyone deserves a love story. Her stories pack a punch of heat, heart, and humor and often feature characters who are neurodivergent, like herself. When not dreaming up her next book, Chloe spends her time wandering in nature, playing soccer, and most happily at home with her family and mischievous cats.

To sign up for Chloe's latest news, new releases, and special offers, please visit her website and subscribe.

VISIT THE AUTHOR ONLINE

ChloeLiese.com
Chloe_Liese
Chloe_Liese
Chloe_Liese
ChloeLiese

Ready to find
your next great read?

Let us help.

Visit prh.com/nextread